SILENCED AT THE BOOK SHOW

KIM GRISWELL

Storm

Ebook ISBN: 978-1-83700-076-0
Paperback ISBN: 978-1-83700-077-7

Cover design: Dawn Adams
Cover images: Dawn Adams

Published by Storm Publishing.
For further information, visit:
www.stormpublishing.co

ALSO BY KIM GRISWELL

A Pacific Northwest Cozy Mystery Series

Murder at Last Chance Cove

Death in the Haunted Wood

For my mystery-loving mom who taught me to read before I could tie my shoelaces and was at my side when I first stood on a Pacific Northwest shore, gaping in wonder.

A hushed chill crept along the Necanicum River as it slid soundlessly through the slumbering town on its way to the Pacific. Its mirrorlike surface reflected row after row of puffy pink clouds in a sky a breath away from morning. The frost-tipped grass along the riverbanks blazed like pink sparklers in the hands of wide-eyed children. The sun stretched and yawned, throwing beams of light over the Coast Range and across the sleeping town. One sunbeam illuminated the yellow-and-white-striped canopy of a four-wheeled Surrey cycle. Canted sideways, the pedal-powered four-wheeler blocked the Broadway Bridge. A horn shattered the silence. A delivery driver, rushing through his morning rounds, abandoned his truck, stormed toward the cycle, and peered inside. Morning held its breath.

ONE

Saffi Graywood pulled the manuscript box from the bottom of her closet, determined to free up space for her latest pair of sloggers. She scooted the light blue waterproof shoes with fat yellow bees far enough to the right to slip the yellow rainboots speckled with pecking chickens beside them. Once she'd made room, she opened the boot box resting on her bed and parted the tissue paper to admire her latest purchase from Last Chance Mercantile.

The quaint general store smelled of chocolate, eucalyptus, and leather. It sold everything from hoodies to hand warmers, retro candies to canning jar candles, herringbone caps to embroidered hankies. Over the past few months, it had become Saffi's favorite downtown store. When she'd spotted the cherry-red boots with cawing ravens and quill pens, she had plunked them down on the counter and said, "Sold!" With the arrival of the winter rains in Last Chance Cove, a second pair of waterproof boots seemed both prudent and necessary.

Did three pairs make a collection? Saffi wasn't sure, but if nothing else, three pairs of waterproof shoes showed a commitment to her chosen lifestyle. Since the sudden death of her husband Levi three and a half years ago, traveling, living, and writing in a twenty-eight-foot Rambler Trek recreational vehicle in the Pacific Northwest had become as comfortable as the worn sweatshirt she'd thrown over a pair of winter leggings before this morning's bike ride. The Lake Monsters logo had long since cracked in the dryer, but it was one of the few items she had held onto from Levi's long tenure teaching literature at Vermont College. She would wear it to rags before letting it go.

Fortunately, her current home at the edge of the ever-churning Pacific was not a "dress up to go out" kind of place. Last Chance Cove RV Park was a "bundle up or be drenched" kind of place, where winter storms rolled off the Pacific to steamroll the town. Saffi loved the cove, downpours and all. She could not have found a better place to cozy up and write if she'd tried. Actually, she had tried, but this place had something she had failed to find in three years of traveling: friends worth keeping.

Of course, there was one fish spine that couldn't stop poking at her: Bill Kidd, the grizzled park manager with the yellow-toothed pirate's grin. Since the day she arrived, the misogynistic manager had made it his mission to take the best-selling writer of *Aunt Saffi's Bedside Reader* down a pegleg or two. Until... he had handed her a manuscript ten years in the making and begged her to read it, the very same manuscript she had just set on the closed toilet seat to make way for her new sloggers.

Now that she'd excavated the tome from her closet, she had to face the fact that she'd promised to read it. Bill had kept his end of the bargain—he had let her back into the park when she returned from a weeklong sleuthing trip. That adventure had included enough murder, theft, arson, and Halloween horrors to make her rethink her urge to unravel mysteries. Despite her admission that she had not "quite" finished reading his book, Bill had checked her into her favorite space by the estuary. Space 32 felt so much like home she had paid upfront for the three-month maximum stay.

Saffi lifted the manuscript box from the toilet lid. It weighed at least two pounds. Two pounds of a misogynist's musings about his life, from time served in Iraq to time served in Last Chance Cove RV Park. What had she been thinking?

Exactly at that moment, her cellphone rang. She'd chosen the sonar sound for Poppy Morales, her Manhattan editor whose calls were not to be ignored.

"Poppy?" A call from Poppy was as rare as a tsunami, and—if she owed her editor pages or revisions—almost as terrifying. "What's wrong?"

"Wrong?" Poppy's laughter pealed across the miles. "How could anything be wrong when I'm about to board a plane for green and gorgeous Oregon! I'm taking the red-eye so I can watch the country light up with fireworks."

Saffi sucked in a breath. "Wait. What?"

The silence lasted so long Saffi feared a stroke or something worse had stopped her editor's breathing.

"The North Coast Booksellers Trade Show?" Poppy's voice rose from raspy alto to knife-sharp soprano as she spoke.

Saffi moved the phone far enough away from her ear to prevent a brain aneurism. "Isn't that *next* weekend?" Her own voice squeaked like a pinkie mouse.

The sound of a pen tap-tap-tapping came through the phone, a habit of Poppy's when she had become too irritated for words. "It's the first weekend of the new year, as always. You *know* that."

Of course she knew that! She had been counting down to the Trade Show with blog posts for weeks, hoping to generate excitement among readers and booksellers who might be attending. *Travels with Aunt Saffi* was her favorite way to get involved with fans of her best-selling *Bedside Reader* series. Her posts featured excerpts from next year's book: lighthouse ghosts, gold-filled shipwrecks, a medical examiner's tips on separating accidental drownings from murder. Her teasers aimed to whet readers' appetites for the intriguing, odd, mysterious, unbelievable—but true—articles she had packed into the latest volume of *Aunt Saffi's Bedside Reader*.

Unfortunately, her least favorite follower and real-world stalker, who went by the online identity Jay GoodVender, had been counting down as well. While her posts were punchy, Good-

Vender punched back, questioning her research, mocking her sources, and offering contradictory quotes from his own "experts." His last comment had sent chills down her spine: *The best part of the Pacific Northwest Booksellers Trade Show? Getting a signed copy of Aunt Saffi's FINAL Bedside Reader.*

When she'd shared the comment with Troy—fishing tour guide, photographer, sometimes sleuthing partner, and the best snuggler on the cove—he had advised her to take a break from the stress over the Christmas holiday. She had been more than happy to oblige. Fireside cuddles in his cottage on a hillside overlooking the cove had brought smiles to her face and a warm glow to the rest of her body. Last week, they'd come up for air to celebrate Christmas Eve with Saffi's cove besties, Delilah—the barista who knew everybody's business—and Glenn—the baker whose mouth-watering cookies were to die for.

Wait! A week ago? Saffi opened her laptop to check today's date. *Oh, no!* She was about to miss her first New Year's Eve in Last Chance Cove.

"Poppy! I have to go. I'll call you in the morning, I promise."

"Don't you dare!" Poppy gasped. "The opening banquet is tomorrow night, Saffi. All the booksellers that matter will be there. I promised them Aunt Saffi, so you *will* attend!"

Saffi tossed her cellphone onto the bed and started yanking off layers: worn sweatshirt, T-shirt, yesterday's sports bra, which she'd picked up off the floor this morning. Thank Raven she didn't have to decide what to wear tonight. She'd bought an emerald-green cowl-necked cashmere tunic with an asymmetrical hemline that brought out the lioness in her honey-brown eyes. The swinging sweater made her ample hips look super sexy, instead of super-sized. It paired perfectly with the black leggings she'd pulled on this morning—fresh from the drawer instead of from the pile by her bed. She really needed to do laundry, but she had put it off until the latest rainstorm rolled through.

How had she lost a whole week? It was the RV lifestyle, Saffi decided. Laid-back and lovely... until she really needed to be at a particular place on a definite day at a certain time. *Arrgh!* She stared at her unruly silver-streaked black curls in the bathroom mirror. No amount of sprucing up would tame her hair, but a shimmer of rose blush and a few sweeps of maroon mascara gave her the glow-up she needed for a beachside fireworks show. Saffi grimaced at herself to check her teeth, huffed into her cupped hand, grimaced again, then reached for her toothbrush. *Floss, brush, rinse.* There! She was done, and just in the nick of time.

Saffi dug around in the storage area beneath her sleeper sofa and pulled out two bottles of champagne. The cold that crept through the uninsulated walls of the slide-out in which the sofa sat had chilled them to perfection. *Good!* She grabbed her new boots from the closet and stuffed her feet inside before heading into the night.

Outside, constellations sparkled above the Pacific as if the fireworks had already begun. Across the park, on the berm that protected the front row of RVs from winter's worst waves, the bonfire was already in full bloom. Flames shot up the driftwood pyramid and sent sparks toward the stars. Saffi loped around the graveled park loop, trying not to turn an ankle in one of the ginormous rain-filled potholes.

"Saffi!" a familiar voice hooted, and Delilah waved from a beach chair near the bonfire.

Saffi huffed her way up the sandy path to join her friends. Glenn, her friend with the floppy pop-star fringe, saluted with a roasting stick then went back to impaling a bratwurst. Walter and Martin—the historical museum docents who reminded her of curmudgeonly Muppets—lifted their champagne flutes and wiggled them at Saffi.

"You're late!" Martin grumbled.

"You remembered the bubbly!" Walter's pudgy cheeks dimpled in a smile.

Saffi rounded the fire and rewarded him with one of the two chilled bottles with a wink. He handed the bottle off to Mellie, Last Chance Cove's Frida Kahlo lookalike and raven-mad artist. She popped the cork and filled Walter's flute, and her own, before reaching across to fill Martin's.

"Sit!" Delilah patted the empty beach chair beside her. The curly-haired redhead had pasted so many crystals on her pearlescent white fingernails her hands shot off sparks.

New Year's Eve in Last Chance Cove! Saffi maneuvered herself into the low-slung seat beside the barista. She had been looking forward to this night for weeks. Friends around the fire. Fireworks exploding overhead. And all of the above on an unseasonably warm clear-sky night. What could be better?

She should have been bubbling with excitement. Instead, she clutched the second champagne bottle between her thighs as Poppy's voice echoed in her head. "I promised them Aunt Saffi, so you will attend!" She would. *She had to.* But... how?

"Saffi." Delilah tapped on the aluminum arm of her chair. "You're wrestling that bottle like you've got Dwayne Johnson in a leg lock. Not that I'd mind doing that myself." She wiggled her eyebrows. "But if you don't relax, you're gonna pop the cork right out of that thing."

Saffi threw up her hands and wailed. "Delilah! I have to be in Seaside this time tomorrow!"

Delilah's mascaraed eyes widened. "Seaside? For the booksellers show you told me about?"

"Yes!" Saffi tried to relax her hold on the bottle. The last thing she needed was champagne spew drenching her leggings. "What am I going to do?"

Delilah patted Saffi's thigh. "It's New Year's Eve. You're gonna roast wienies, eat greasy potato chips, and wash it all down with a champagne chaser. And if you're lucky"—she leaned closer to Saffi —"you're gonna smooch the mouth right off that gorgeous man standing behind you."

Saffi twirled around so fast she would have dumped herself out of the stumpy chair if the man with the Montana-sapphire eyes hadn't knelt in the sand to stop her tumble.

"My hero!" Saffi rewarded Troy with the kiss he'd earned.

"Ugh! Get a room, would you?"

Bill. Saffi glanced up. Perfect timing, as always.

As Bill staked out a spot near the bonfire, his German shepherd, Smudge, darted around the circle of chairs. When the shepherd suddenly reversed direction, he sprayed sand on everyone and everything nearby. Glenn jumped away, trying to avoid the sandbath. The brat on his roasting stick fell at his feet. Quick as lightning, Smudge snagged the sausage and gulped it down, sand and all.

"Cut the crap, Smudgie." The evil eye Bill gave his best friend made the dog's tail wag and his tongue loll between his canines, dripping saliva. Smudge's best impression of a smile, Saffi supposed.

As the friends—along with the piratical park manager Saffi still considered an interloper—toasted marshmallows, roasted brats, ate, and sipped champagne, ideas for how Saffi could get to Seaside by noon the next day flew around the bonfire like sparks.

"You can... drive it in a day... if you push it," Bill mumbled over the fire-roasted corncob he gnawed between words.

Saffi blinked, trying to ignore the yellow bits between his nicotine-stained teeth. "In case you haven't noticed, I don't have a car. And the RV's way too slow to get me to Seaside by tomorrow afternoon."

"You could take a bus." Walter took a sip of bubbly.

Glenn passed a bag of buttery wedding cookies around the circle. Saffi snagged the last two and got a glower from Delilah for her troubles. "What?" she mumbled, spewing powdered sugar on her chest. Glenn had inherited his uncle Kevin's cookie-baking business and Saffi was addicted. When Delilah stuck out her hand, she reluctantly relinquished the second cookie. "Fine. So, how long does the bus take?"

"Eleven hours." Delilah licked powdered sugar from her fingers. "It's purgatory on wheels. Especially when the toilet backs up. Which happens more often than not. Whoo-ee!" She waved a hand in front of her face.

The buttery bite of cookie in Saffi's mouth suddenly lost its taste.

"Fly," Troy said between bites of the chocolate-chunk cookie he'd snatched as a second Kevin's Kookies bag made the rounds. "A buddy of mine has an air taxi."

Fly! Saffi did a fist pump. Leave it to Troy to find a solution. She ran a thumb along the corner of his full lips then turned it over to stare at the melted chocolate. Would it be gross if she stuck it in her mouth? Or sexy? A sudden silence made her glance up. Everyone around the bonfire seemed to be waiting to see what she would do. Saffi tucked the offending thumb under her thigh as if she had no idea why they were all staring.

By the time fireworks burst from the barge in the middle of the cove, Saffi had a plan. Troy's pilot friend was in town, available, and eager for the fare. His price almost caused a hot flash, but if she wanted her books to remain bestsellers, she needed to stay on the right side of *book*sellers. The flight would leave at ten in the morning and arrive in plenty of time for Saffi to check in to her hotel room, have a confab with Poppy, and dress for the banquet.

What could possibly go wrong?

TWO

At the ungodly hour of 6 a.m., Saffi dragged herself out of bed, wishing she had skipped that third glass of champagne. She threw on her bathrobe, stuffed her feet into sloggers and stumbled outside, half asleep, to tug her suitcase out of her RV's front basement compartment. Back inside, she opened the suitcase to let it air out, then put the electric kettle on for tea. While she waited for the water to boil, she stacked the clothes she'd planned for her weekend trip on the bed. Leggings, jewel-toned tunics, thigh-length sweater dresses—fitted at the top, flowing around the hips—and a windbreaker that folded into a handy pouch. Undies, of course. Warm socks. Finally, she fished out a sexy peignoir set that had been wadded up in the back of the bedroom cabinet since Levi's death.

The Hollywood-style lounge set was emerald green, perfect for showing off the honey in her brown eyes. She had saved the slinky garments "just in case," though she had feared she would never again find a reason to wear them. She gave the silk robe and lacy gown a sniff. The slight hint of mustiness from hanging out in an RV by the sea could be vanquished by a tumble in the dryer with a lavender sachet. The dryer would take care of the wrinkles as well.

Saffi's excuse to pack the emerald peignoir had been unexpected. Troy's pilot friend, Scott, had invited him along for the flight. During the weekend convention, Saffi would schmooze and sign books. The two buds would hang out doing... whatever it was men did when they hung out together. Probably something to do with fishing or whiskey or both. Scott would spend nights with his sister who lived in Seaside. Troy would share the riverside suite Poppy's assistant had booked for Lowry & Lowenstein's bestselling author. They would fly back to Last Chance Cove when the convention ended after Sunday's brunch. Anticipation bubbled the oxygen in Saffi's blood.

Booksellers' shows she'd done and done again. A weekend in a fancy-pants hotel suite with Troy? That she had *not* done.

A chuckle in the back of her mind interrupted her drooling. *Don't fall too fast, my girl. You might not see the potholes coming until it's too late to avoid them.* Saffi bit her lip. Levi. He'd left her a cache of wit and wisdom. She didn't always heed it—even when she needed it—but she cherished it all the same.

An hour later, Saffi bumped her suitcase down the RV's two steps. Blue skies greeted her with wide-open arms. So did the man leaning against the metallic blue truck with the white-wave logo on the door.

"You look—" Troy stopped, face twitching in amusement.

Saffi stared down at the outfit she'd chosen. The airplane cabin would be heated, he'd told her, but she might feel the chill at 12,000 feet. She had paired her thickest leggings with a school-bus-yellow travel sweater. It had a red wiener dog's head and front legs across the chest with the red dog's tail and back legs wagging just below her waist.

Troy tapped the wiener dog's nose. "At least you'll be easy to spot if the plane goes down."

Saffi pursed her lips. "There will be no talking about planes going anywhere but up."

"So... no landing?" he teased.

Saffi ruffled his short, tight, silver-gray curls. "Yes, landing. Landing is good. As long as it's a nice slow glide."

The six-seater parked outside Scott's airport hangar looked like toy planes Saffi had played with as a kid... the kind you pulled back so they would zip across the floor when you let go. Her belly might have had fewer moths flitting about if Scott had not hoisted himself onto the wing and slid through the window to get to the captain's chair.

Once he'd buckled in and adjusted a headphone with attached mic, Troy's buddy looked more like a pilot than some random guy in sunglasses with a cap that said, "Just Wing It!" As he went through a checklist involving screens, knobs, levers, and gauges, Saffi settled into one of the small plane's unexpectedly cushy gray leather seats.

Shoulder harnesses. *Check!* Cup holders for the coffees they'd picked up along the way. *Check!* Fold-down executive writing desk near Troy's knee. *Wow!* "Shouldn't I be over there?" She pointed at the laptop-size desk.

Troy buckled his shoulder harness, then took a sip of coffee. "Ask me again once we're airborne."

Up front, Scott was having a running conversation with the tower as he prepared for the flight.

"Ready to fly, folks?" he called over his shoulder.

At exactly that moment, Saffi's cellphone pinged. She scrambled it out of her sling bag and glanced at the caller ID. *Poppy.* She held up the phone, hoping Scott could see it.

"I need to answer this." She poked the screen to take the call. "Poppy?"

Scott, oblivious to her hand-waving, turned the key and the engine sputtered to life. The plane shuddered a bit, followed by loud clicks and a whir as the prop started to twirl. As the blades whirled faster and faster the sound grew to the volume of the RV park's commercial lawnmower.

Saffi pressed her ear to the phone. Poppy's voice sounded frantic, but she could only make out a few words. Something about a fiasco? A vendor?

"Poppy!" she tried to interrupt. "We're taking off. I'll call when we land." After which Poppy shouted something that Saffi heard all too well: *Or I will murder someone!*

Troy's eyebrows shot up but Saffi waved away his worry.

"With Poppy, every problem is larger than life. My guess? The organizers put her in the wrong booth. Definitely a murderable offense."

Feeling only slightly guilty, Saffi put her phone into "airplane mode" and stuffed it back into her bag. Whatever frantic message her editor had been trying to relay could be delivered in person in a few short hours.

When they reached their cruising altitude of 10,000 feet, Saffi forgot all about phone calls and editors. Other than the occasional open-mouthed "wow" turned Troy's way, she could not take her eyes off the jagged edge of the North American continent. Rivers writhed and coiled, winding their way to the sea. Some widened into estuaries. Others bulged out to become bays. Mountain ranges rolled one into another like green paper crumpled in an angry god's fist.

Saffi was aware of occasional conversation taking place between cabin and cockpit, but she didn't pay attention to a word until the plane's airspeed began to slow.

"Haystack Rock!" Scott announced.

Saffi spotted the iconic haystack-shaped rock just offshore. They had reached Cannon Beach. Seaside was mere miles away. Seconds later, Scott gave a craggy ridge a buzz cut before the plane sank toward a long shallow lake off to the right of the town. Saffi grabbed Troy's hand and sucked in a breath. For a few tense moments, she thought the plane would come down in the water but when the tires touched down, they squeaked on asphalt. The bumpety-bump of landing felt a bit like hitting potholes in the RV park's gravel drive.

"We're here!" Troy squeezed her hand. "You can either kiss the ground or me."

It was the easiest choice Saffi had made all morning.

. . .

Scott's sister, Amanda, dropped Saffi off in front of the Necanicum Inn with her suitcase. She gulped the fresh air flowing down the river from the sea, grateful to be out of the van. Either Amanda had several children at home or one very messy toddler. Oatie O's, beach toys, juice bottles with spill-proof tops that had spilled anyway, superhero action figures with missing limbs... the vehicle smelled like six kids and a dog put away wet and left to molder.

"I'll take the guys to my place and give you time to settle in." Amanda waved. "Toodle-oo!"

Much as Saffi would have preferred to keep Troy at her side, this was a business trip. She needed to check in to her suite and connect with Poppy. She leaned down to give Troy an apologetic smile. "I'll let the desk clerk know you'll be joining me later."

Trapped in the backseat of Amanda's mom van, all he could do was blow her a kiss and shrug. Saffi returned the air-kiss as the van pulled away, then grasped the handle of her suitcase and marched toward the four-story inn overlooking what must be the river after which it was named.

The clerk behind the front desk looked up and offered Saffi a welcoming smile. "Checking in?"

Saffi nodded. "Saffronia Graywood. I'm booked into a river-view queen suite?" She hated the way her voice tilted what should have been a statement into a question. But in her long history of trade show attendance—both as a best-selling author and an unknown—not a single check-in had ever gone smoothly.

"Ah, yes. You're the keynote speaker at the booksellers' show." The desk clerk's intelligent brown eyes sparkled behind two-toned frames, tortoiseshell on top, creamy green on the bottom. A slightly gap-toothed smile made the clerk look mischievous. Saffi glanced at her nametag: *Phyllis.*

"License and credit card, please." Phyllis held out her hand.

"Uhm. My publisher was supposed to have paid for the room upfront."

Phyllis withdrew her hand and glanced down at the computer screen. "Yes. Yes. Of course. The room has been taken care of. The credit card is for incidentals and the driver's license is part of standard hotel security procedures. Wouldn't want to take any chances with our guests' safety, now would we?"

Safety sounded good, but Saffi had once been "incidentally" charged $150 for an organic cotton spa robe someone had nicked from her room after she checked out. But when Phyllis's hand snaked out again, she handed over a platinum card.

"I have a guest staying with me."

Phyllis winked. "I know."

The statement jolted Saffi to attention. How could the desk clerk know? She hadn't even shared the "Troy factor" with Poppy. Her editor had a short list of reasons why mixing business with pleasure at a trade show was a bad idea. She had the list because Saffi had *written* the darned thing for her third *Bedside Reader*. Poppy had enlarged the page and posted it behind her desk for her underlings and authors to read.

1. Your pleasure partner will distract you from the job at hand and tank your career.
2. Your pleasure partner will eat all of the truffles from the trade show gift basket.
3. Your pleasure partner will wash them down with the entire contents of the hotel minibar.
4. Your pleasure partner will show up at your booth, drunk as a skunk.
5. What happens at a trade show does *not* stay at the trade show. It gets posted on social media.

Saffi brushed aside Phyllis's wink. The Necanicum Inn was the official convention hotel. The desk clerk must have her confused with another of the hundreds of guests arriving this morning.

"I'll have him stop by with his driver's license when he arrives," she told the clerk. "Please put his incidentals on my card."

"Already taken care of," Phyllis assured her.

"I'm sorry?"

Phyllis winked again. "I hope you enjoy the little surprise upstairs."

Saffi liked surprises, but not the kind billed to her credit card. She snatched her credit card and room key card off the desk and clutched the handle of her roller bag. As she walked away, she could almost feel the desk clerk's eyes on her. What did the woman think she knew? *Seriously*.

"Ma'am?" the desk clerk called out.

When Saffi looked over her shoulder, Phyllis made a little brushing motion with her hand. "You have a bit of—" She pointed at Saffi's rear.

When Saffi brushed at the back of her down coat, her hand came away coated with what she could only pray was peanut butter. Could this check-in get any worse?

THREE

Room 402. Saffi read the number written in Sharpie on her key card. When the elevator opened, she tugged her suitcase inside, then pushed the button for the top floor. At the fourth floor, the elevator dinged, the doors opened, and she stepped into a long straight hallway. Saffi turned left to follow the arrow toward her room and got ready for a slog. When she reached the corner room, she slipped the key card into the card reader. The light flashed green and she opened the door to the scent of fresh flowers.

"Sweet!" She spotted a glass vase filled with yellow carnations on the tiny kitchen's granite counter. Had Troy set this up ahead of time? So far, she'd found him to be practical, capable, and thoughtful. But romantic? If it *was* Troy, this was a first.

Saffi pulled her sling bag off her shoulder, shrugged out of her coat, and rolled her suitcase along a petal-strewn path into the bedroom. Not just romantic. *Over-the-top* romantic. The queen bed's pristine white duvet was *covered* in flower petals. Saffi felt her throat close against the sweet floral scent gone feral. She stepped closer, then froze. The yellow petals on the bed had blood-red tips.

This was no romantic gesture. Someone had ripped apart yellow carnations and then, what? Dipped the petals in actual blood? Trying not to shudder, Saffi leaned down to sniff, then recoiled. She recognized that acrid smell, and it wasn't blood. The petals had been inked with red Sharpie.

"What the heck?"

Saffi glanced around the room, hoping a clue would catch her eye. She spotted a small white envelope addressed to Aunt Saffi propped against the lamp on the bedside table. Heart thudding against her ribcage, she drew out the card and read the inscription: *No one deserves these more than you.* The note looked to have been written with the same red Sharpie. The whole display seemed to have one goal: to instill instant fear in Saffi Graywood. Who would do such a thing? And why?

The choice of yellow carnations made her brain itch, and not in a good way. These days, most people saw flowers as a way to say, "I love you!" or "Get well soon!" but in the Victorian era, flowers were used to deliver all kinds of messages. Want to say, "I miss you"? Send zinnias. Think someone is full of himself? Go with narcissus. Saffi had included a flower symbolism chart in *Bedside Reader, #16.* For the life of her she couldn't remember the meaning of yellow carnations. It probably didn't matter. These days, only the most nerdy of trivia nerds would send a message with flowers. The nerdiest nerd at the trade show, as far as Saffi knew, was her.

Unless... Saffi had last seen the trivia fan she believed to be her stalker on Halloween night dressed as a killer clown. He had spritzed something from a fake flower into her face that smelled so much like chloroform, she had coughed it right back into his face. By morning, the clown's silver-and-black Mini-Winnie had disappeared from the park where they'd both been camping.

Saffi hadn't seen him since, and she didn't want to, especially not at a booksellers' show where she was due to keynote. Was it possible? Had her stalker tracked her to Seaside as he'd tracked her to Last Chance Cove and the Haunted Wood RV Park? If so, the desk clerk downstairs had made a huge mistake. Phyllis had not let Saffi's beau into her room to leave a romantic surprise. She had allowed an enemy into a space that should have been a sanctuary. A space that now smelled sinister instead of sweet.

A sudden wave of nausea swept over Saffi and she rushed to the sliding glass doors that led onto the balcony. Once outside, she gulped deep breaths of ocean-washed air to settle her stomach. For a second, she wished Troy had been with her when she discovered the bloody petals. He would have wrapped his strong arms around her and assured her that everything would be OK.

Comforting though the thought might be, she shook it away. She did not need a man to rescue her. She had survived the death of her husband and two murder investigations on her own. She was Aunt Saffi—best-selling author and keynote speaker! And she would not let a nutcase with a red Sharpie spoil a trade show she had been looking forward to for months.

With her vow to the universe accomplished, Saffi relaxed enough to take in her surroundings. Four stories below her balcony, the river was a mirror, still and clear enough to reflect the wooden boardwalks along its edge and what looked like the convention center across the way at the far end of the block. If she looked between the buildings crowding either side of the street to her left —Broadway, if she remembered correctly—and squinted a bit, she had a postage-stamp-sized view of waves rolling toward the shore. In the distance, Tillamook Head loomed above the town, mist tickling its toes. A perfect convention location. *Thank you, Willow!*

Poppy went through editorial assistants so fast Saffi seldom had time to learn their names, but Willow stood out. Not only had she outlasted her predecessors, she seemed to understand the rigors of writers on the road. She made a point of doing whatever she could to make Saffi's life easier with whatever chintzy budget Poppy gave her.

Vehicles poking across the Broadway Bridge caught Saffi's attention. Broadway seemed to be the main artery to the town's touristy center, but pedal-powered Surrey cycles with fringed tops clogged the inbound lane. Cyclists weren't the only ones navigating their way into town. Pedestrians surged seaward, crossing the bridge on raised walkways on either side of the traffic lanes. As they reached the other side of the bridge, at least half the walkers took a right onto the boardwalk. Most had bookbags slung over at least one shoulder. Some had bags hanging from both hands. Booksellers, Saffi decided, striding with purpose toward the convention center. Tonight's banquet would officially open the trade show, but booths would open to buyers, sellers, writers, and publishing pros at noon. It was long past time to let her editor know she had arrived.

Saffi dug her cellphone out of her sling bag and thumbed it out of airplane mode. She watched in horror as the screen lit up with messages, one after another, all from Poppy.

"Oh no!" She poked open the first message. *Call me.* Then the second: *Right away.* Then the third: *Has your plane crashed? Or are you ignoring your EDITOR!!* Saffi's hand trembled as she put through a call. By now, Poppy would be mad enough to rip a thesaurus apart with her bare hands.

"Saffi. Are you OK? Are you safe?"

She had never heard Poppy sound so shaken. Did she already know about the suite invasion? If she didn't, this was not the time to mention bloody flower petals strewn across her bed. "I'm fine. I just checked in and the view is amazing."

"View? You're looking at the view at a time like this!" Poppy's voice went from shaken to shrill. "Your whole career is on the line. Meet me in the kombucha bar. Now!"

"Wait? What kombucha bar?"

"On the mezzanine above the lobby."

Before leaving the room, Saffi called the front desk. She wanted to grill Phyllis about the flowers until she melted like cheddar on toast, but with Poppy's "Now!" still ringing in her ears, she didn't dare. Instead, she demanded an immediate cleanup of the mess the intruder had made. She let the desk clerk know in no uncertain terms what would happen if the pink petal-shaped stains on the white duvet were charged to her credit card, and she assured the clerk that she had every intention of finding out who was responsible for the floral carnage.

After thunking the hotel phone into its cradle, Saffi took the stairs, which were much closer to her room than the elevator. Clomping down them at top speed without twisting an ankle was much more difficult than she had anticipated. Halfway to the bottom, she deeply regretted the decision. She stopped for a second to huff in as much air as her struggling lungs would allow, then renewed her thumping rush. Once she reached the ground floor, she pushed through the door and frantically scanned the lobby. *Kombucha bar. Kombucha bar*. What did such a thing even look like?

Then she remembered: the mezzanine. She glanced up and immediately spotted a familiar stylish figure perched on a barstool. *Poppy*. Her editor had that pinched well-preserved look of an aging New Yorker. Saffi wasn't sure whether the look came from a lifetime of looking down one's nose at the rest of the world or from reacting to the gag-inducing smells blowing up from the grates along the city's sidewalks.

Poppy looked as carefully put together as usual, which boded well. If someone had died, say, or the publishing company had decided to close, surely she would have dressed in something less chic than a loose-cut gray pinstriped suit with a classic white button-up shirt. She had even popped up the back of her collar to frame her olive-toned heart-shaped face. Not a single silver-white hair in her short spiky pixie was out of place.

As if sensing someone's gaze, Poppy turned with a look of brooding impatience. Saffi grasped the stair rail and rushed up the curving staircase to the mezz. After the obligatory close-but-no-skin-contact cheek kiss, Poppy patted the stool beside her. "Sit!" she commanded.

The small nook was empty except for the bartender polishing pint glasses behind the bar. Instead of beer logos, the four taps had Brew Dr. Kombucha on tap.

Poppy nodded at the taps. "Drink. You're gonna need it."

Once Poppy started talking, Saffi wished her editor had chosen a place that served beer... or wine... or eighty-proof single malt whiskey.

"Some delusional nobody," Poppy fumed, "has knocked off your *Bedside Readers*. And these – these backwater bozos let him rent a booth, *knowing* you were keynoting the convention. I snatched a few of them bald, let me tell you."

Saffi almost choked on the slug of kombucha she had just downed. Poppy patted her on the back as if burping a baby, which, embarrassingly, made Saffi belch. "Sorry." Heat rose up her cheeks. "What do you mean by 'knocked off'?"

Poppy looked at her like she was being purposefully obtuse. "I *mean*, he's copied the look, the content categories, everything!"

Dazed, Saffi shook her head. "Isn't that a copyright violation?"

"Saffi! This isn't about copyright. You're a brand! We trade-marked the *Bedside Reader* formula years ago. This guy is in direct violation. I've tried to reach our lawyers but they're not picking up." *Just like you*, her red-tinged hazel eyes accused.

Saffi took a deep breath before daring to say what came to mind. "It's New Year's weekend. They're probably enjoying family time."

Poppy glared. "With the retainer we pay them, they don't *get* family time!"

Saffi was pretty sure they did. She was also pretty sure she wasn't going to argue this or any other point with her irate editor. "Is there anything we can do?"

Poppy took a sip of kombucha and thunked the pint glass on the counter as aggressively as a drunk being refused another shot. "Believe me, I *have* been doing things! Not only did I give the trade show organizers a piece of my mind, I threatened to pull you from the program if they don't do something about him. *And if they don't get rid of this guy ASAP*, the North Coast Book-sellers Association will be named in the lawsuit we'll be filing." She rapped her knuckles on the copper bar. "As soon as those lawyers stop guzzling champagne and return my bloody phone call!"

Saffi had to bite her tongue to keep from reminding her editor that booksellers were the lifeblood of every author. They literally held her success—or failure—in their hands. If Lowry & Lowenstein sued the booksellers association, she could kiss her Pacific Northwest sales goodbye.

Once Poppy polished off her rose-colored kombucha, she pulled a book from her *Bedside Reader* branded tote. The tote featured the cover of Saffi's upcoming *Reader*, not due out until spring. Lowry & Lowenstein would be giving totes to the first fifty convention-goers to visit Booth #22 in its prime position midway down the middle row. When the show opened, booksellers, buyers, and autograph seekers would spill through the door and be swept right to Aunt Saffi's table, Poppy had promised.

"Take a look," Poppy handed the book to Saffi. "I snagged it while he wasn't looking."

Before Saffi had seen the offending knockoff, her heart had felt pinched. Once she held it in her hands, not so much. The cover was an amateurish attempt to copy the *Bedside Reader* look, probably produced by a low-bidding freelance designer who had little to no book experience. The interior *did* include material somewhat similar to what Saffi sought out for her readers, but the writer clearly did not understand Aunt Saffi's winning formula. The book read like a decade's worth of professional journals, pop culture magazines, and newspapers chopped up and then clumsily pasted together in a lurching Frankensteinian version of her popular readers.

"Poppy. Not only is this a knockoff, it's so far off the mark nobody's going to take it seriously. I'm sure the trade show organizers will do right by us. By the time we get to the convention center, this guy will probably be packing his boxes."

"He'd better be. And you, Aunt Saffi, had better be ready to do whatever it takes to hold onto your spot at the top of this year's trivia list."

"Whatever it takes," Saffi promised, thinking Poppy meant wining, dining, and signing.

When Saffi flipped the knockoff reader to examine the back cover and get a look at the person trying to steal her formula, she recoiled. The face staring out of the author photo looked as malicious as it had when she'd seen it at the Haunted Wood RV Park. Geek-chic black glasses, pompadour of matte-black hair, pale skin with rouge-red cheeks: the knockoff author was *Bedside Reader* fan turned stalker—Jay GoodVender.

"Saffi?" Poppy put a hand on her arm. "What is it?"

"It's him," she whispered.

Poppy's brow furrowed. "Him, who?"

"The-the *stalker*." Saffi looked away from the photo to meet her editor's eyes. Then she told her about GoodVender's blog post comment about her "final" *Bedside Reader* and the "bloody" petals left on her bed.

"Oh, crap. This is even worse than I thought." Poppy grabbed the book from Saffi's limp hand and stuffed it into her tote. "Let's get going. It's time to rid ourselves of the competition."

Saffi slipped off her barstool, ready to march into bookish battle. Poppy gathered her things, eager to join the fray, then she looked down at Saffi's wiener dog sweater and sniffed. "Please tell me you're not going to the exhibit hall dressed like a kindergarten teacher."

Saffi chuckled. "With you looking like that?" She waved a hand at Poppy's chic outfit. "Not on your life."

As they crossed the lobby to the elevator, the doors shooshed open. "Perfect timing!" Poppy crowed, but Saffi wasn't crowing. She was watching a woman dressed in the inn's housekeeping uniform stumble out of the doors. Saffi stepped forward, arms open, and the woman slumped into them. "Help..." The word whispered between her lips and the familiar sickly-sweet scent of chloroform came with it.

Saffi tried to hold the unconscious woman upright, but she couldn't. The woman's weight took them both to their knees. As

Saffi eased the housekeeper's body toward the carpeted floor, she spotted something that made her heart thud like a raven flapping its wings against her ribcage. The woman's fingertips looked like they had been dipped in blood.

FOUR

The minute an ambulance wailed into the parking lot, Poppy instructed Saffi to go upstairs, change clothes, and make her way out of the inn as quickly as possible.

"Do *not* let yourself get sucked into this, Saffi. You are not a sleuth. You're an author. *My* author. I need you at the convention center before the exhibit hall opens, not over here involving yourself in a criminal investigation." Poppy hoisted her *Bedside Reader* tote onto her shoulder and made for the elevator before Saffi—or anyone wearing a uniform—could stop her. "I'll meet you at the side door in fifteen," she called over her shoulder. Then she pointed to the door leading into the parking lot, the one that did not have emergency personnel streaming through it.

Poppy Morales... practical, as always. Focused on the job at hand. A bit cold? Sure, but Poppy had a whole publishing company's health to think about, not just one unfortunate woman's.

Saffi, however, had the housekeeper's red-tipped fingers on her mind. Those stains told her two things: one, this case already involved her, and two, she now knew exactly who had tossed those petals across her duvet. Not her stalker—at least not in person. The housekeeper. She did not want to leave for the convention center with fear hanging over her like the sharpened blade of a guillotine.

She paced the lobby, waiting for the emergency techs to finish checking the woman's vitals and bring her round. If she could get close enough to ask her a quick question before the police arrived, she might learn who was really behind the floral menace. After all, the housekeeper would have no reason to frighten a hotel guest. To the housekeeper, Saffi was simply a stranger staying in the inn's luxury suite, perhaps one with a seriously kinky manfriend. *It happened.*

Activity around the EMTs did not calm down as Saffi had expected. It ramped up as one of the techs detected an irregular pulse and another unbuttoned the top of the housekeeper's uniform to stick electrical leads on her chest.

The solvent smell of chloroform had convinced Saffi the housekeeper had been knocked out but would be fine. Chloroform didn't kill, did it? As the EMTs readied the stretcher to roll out of the lobby, Saffi tried to push closer. "Excuse me? Can I just?"

When the inn's security officer stepped forward with suspicion in his eyes, Saffi ducked her head and veered away. She needed to know why the housekeeper had left those bloodied petals, but, clearly, now was not the time. Since talking to the housekeeper would have to wait, she would do the next best thing: confront Phyllis, the desk clerk who had teased her about a surprise in her room.

She spotted the clerk pressing her palms on the counter and standing on tiptoes, frantic for a better view of what was happening. When Saffi reached the desk, Phyllis scrambled backward.

"Sorry. I need to find the manager," she apologized. "I'll be... I'll be right back."

Sure you will. Saffi plastered haughty across her face, hoping to intimidate the clerk into answering without thinking. "Of course. It's better that I speak to management about the man you let into my suite."

Phyllis froze, then her lips hardened. The brown eyes behind her two-toned frames went glassy. "Don't be absurd! Our guest safety policy would *never* allow such a thing."

Saffi wiggled her fingers. "Didn't you tell me I would find a little 'surprise' in my room?"

Phyllis tugged at the white collar of her blouse, pushed her tortoiseshell and cream-green glasses up her nose, then nodded. "OK. Yes, I did. A man called the desk earlier. He asked if he could put flowers in your room to surprise you."

Saffi stiffened. "And you just... let him?"

Phyllis's eyes widened. "Of course not! I told him to bring the flowers to the front desk, and I would make sure house-keeping placed them in your room before your scheduled arrival."

Saffi pursed her lips. "And did he ask you to have your house-keeper strew petals across the duvet?"

A red glow suffused the desk clerk's cheeks. "He did." She leaned forward. "We do our best to accommodate romantic impulses, Ms. Graywood. Most women *like* them."

"It might have been romantic, if the petals had not been made to look like they've been dipped in *blood*."

The desk clerk reeled so hard she had to grab the desk to steady herself. "This is a stunt, right? I mean, you write about things like this in your *Bedside Readers*."

"Does that look like a stunt to you?" Saffi turned to point toward the EMTs loading the housekeeper into the ambulance. "I assume that's the housekeeper you sent to my room. I noticed red stains on her fingertips. And now, she's been attacked."

"Attacked?" Phyllis sucked in a breath. "What makes you think that?"

"The chloroform on her breath."

"This can't be happening. Marisol will be OK, won't she?" Phyllis covered her mouth and started trying to back away again.

Saffi let the question hang in the air, unanswered. "Phyllis." She gentled her voice to sound as calm and reasonable as possible, though inside, she was seething. She quirked a finger to draw the clerk back to the counter. "Can you describe the man who brought the flowers?"

"I can do better than that. I can tell you his name." The desk clerk's nod was professional, as if she'd made up her mind to stop prevaricating and be of assistance.

"His name?" Wow. If her stalker had done this, he was getting more brazen by the minute.

"Nick. He's the delivery driver for Ocean Blossoms, the flower shop down the street." She pointed toward North Holladay.

The air went out of Saffi's inflated dream of nailing her stalker once and for all. "How about the man who called? Anything you remember about him? Word choices? Accent?"

"What really stuck out," Phyllis said, "was his voice."

Saffi cocked her head. "How so?"

"Adenoidal. Like he had a stuffy nose or something."

Though the malicious sound of her stalker's blog post comments echoed in her head, Saffi had never heard his voice.

"I'm so sorry this happened, Ms. Graywood. And... poor Marisol." Phyllis teared up and her face tightened with remorse. "I'm going to lose my job, aren't I?"

For the first time, Saffi realized what she really saw in the woman's eyes: abject fear.

"Phyllis," Saffi leaned closer and whispered, "there's someone I want you to keep a lookout for." She described Jay GoodVender, from his black pompadour and glasses to his rouged cheeks. "If you see him, call me." She gave Phyllis her cell number. "And share the description with the rest of the staff if you can. He may be behind what happened to Marisol."

Saffi reached out and squeezed the desk clerk's hand. When Phyllis nodded, Saffi let go. "I'll do my best to make sure none of this jeopardizes your job." She had no idea what, if anything, she could do to help Phyllis, but she had to promise her something. She needed eyes in this inn.

Phyllis's lips trembled. "You will?"

Saffi nodded, then gave her a sideways smile. "Unless that duvet with the petal stains shows up on my bill."

Just as Saffi strode away from the front desk, Poppy stepped off the elevator. Her eyes narrowed when she saw that Saffi had not yet changed out of the bright yellow wiener dog sweater.

"I'll have complimentary wine and chocolates sent to your room, Ms. Graywood," Phyllis called after her. "Yours, too, Ms. Morales."

Poppy lifted a manicured brow. "What was that all about?"

Saffi filled her editor in on what she knew about the housekeeper's condition and the information she had wrung out of Phyllis as they made their way across the Broadway Bridge. By the time they turned onto the boardwalk, steam was coming from Poppy's nostrils. She was more determined than ever to bring Jay GoodVender to his knees, just as the weight of Marisol's body had brought Saffi to hers.

The second they stepped into the convention center lobby, things went from grave to ghoulish. The larger-than-life mounted poster announcing Saffi's keynote must have looked wonderful when the convention organizers placed it on the easel just inside the double front doors.

KEYNOTE SPEAKER
Saffronia Graywood
The One and Only Aunt Saffi of Bedside Reader *Fame*
"The Key to Being Trivia's Number One!"
Date: Friday, January 2. Time: 9:00 a.m.
Place: Necanicum Room

The organizers had chosen Saffi's favorite author photo from an outdoor shoot. The photographer had somehow coaxed her into looking highly intelligent yet approachable: enigmatic smile, honey-brown eyes clever yet mischievous, silver-streaked black curls carefully tousled rather than frantic. The look would have been a tribute to the photographer's skill, except for one thing: someone had drawn a giant red circle with a slash across it, dead center of her face. They'd reddened her eyes, added fat red veins down her cheeks, and drawn devil horns on her head. *Childish much?* Saffi didn't have to guess to know who.

"I swear to everything holy I am going to *murder* that guy!" Poppy fumed.

The gaggle of convention-goers milling about in the foyer turned as one toward Poppy. She gave them a flippant wave and smile that said, "Not really." But those close enough to see the deadly glint in Poppy's hazel eyes hurried away with furtive glances over their shoulders.

Saffi, who had learned a lot about suspicious behavior from two murder investigations, leaned closer. "Let's keep the threats between ourselves." She put a hand on her editor's arm and gave it a meaningful squeeze.

The Pacific Room—where booksellers, publishers, and authors were putting finishing touches to their booths—was not yet open, but the exhibitor badges dangling from red lanyards around their necks got them past the security guard with a nod.

"This way!" Poppy waved for Saffi to follow as she hurried past aisle after aisle before turning into the one farthest from the entrance doors. Saffi knew from previous trade shows that her editor's short-heeled black leather boots had been fitted with orthotic insoles for hours of standing in or—in this case—dashing through convention centers. Instead of trying to keep up with Poppy, Saffi slowed, feeling, for the first time today, the excitement of a convention where she could meet new authors and discover new books.

The back aisle seemed to be self-publisher's row, simple booths divided by hip-high blue curtains strung between metal posts, backed by matching floor-length curtains. Some booths had one folding table with a single title stacked on top. Others had several titles and a banner with a company name and logo hanging from the back curtain. All along the row authors were breaking down boxes and looking for spots to stow them out of the view of browsers.

Saffi ran her fingers over the glossy cover of a memoir, *Mermaids at Midnight: Tales of a Fisherman's Daughter*. A leather-faced woman with sea-kinked red hair fading toward white and a fearless grin straightened from the box she'd been emptying. She tugged the tail of her loose crew-neck sweater over the waistband of her flouncy tapestry skirt.

"I'll be signing as soon as the doors open," the woman said. Her eyes shone with a feeling Saffi remembered all too clearly: fear mixed with hope and sprinkled with a dash of reckless certainty. Saffi felt nostalgic for the naïve beginner she had once been. After all, her *Bedside Reader* had started as a self-published title. She had introduced it at a New England booksellers' convention much like this one almost twenty years ago. Her current publisher had picked the series up after sales figures made it clear that *Aunt Saffi's Bedside Reader* was much more than a one-hit wonder.

As she stood there reminiscing, the memoir author smacked herself on the forehead. "You're the keynote speaker! Aunt Saffi!" She put a hand to her chest. "I'll be in the front row, writing down every word you say."

"Oh, my." Saffi could feel a blush rising. "I'll have to say something useful, then. How's this: cut out the boring parts."

The woman snorted. "You're just like your books. Snarky and smart. Don't take any guff off that wannabe down the aisle. He's not the first man to take credit for a woman's idea and he won't be the—"

"Saffi!" a familiar voice demanded. "Here!" Poppy stood at the end of the aisle, waving impatiently.

"Better go!" Saffi gave a little wave to the fisherman's daughter. "And your book looks amazing. Good luck!"

Saffi double-stepped toward Poppy, who turned toward a booth and spread her arms wide. The minute she saw the signage, Saffi's mouth fell open in shock.

Jay GoodVender's Original *Bedside Reader*, a foamboard sign hanging from the curtain at the back of the booth proclaimed. *If you've been reading inferior imitations, it's time to discover the real thing!*

"*Inferior* imitations?" Saffi ground her teeth together. "That scheming, stalking, slimy, no-good clown!" Rage washed through her, and she knew exactly how Poppy had felt when she'd said she wanted to murder him.

The clown was missing in action, his booth set up and ready to go. *Out chloroforming housekeepers, perchance?* Stacks of knockoff *Reader*s like the one Poppy had pilfered earlier lined a blue-skirted exhibit table. GoodVender had produced an author poster so similar to the one announcing Saffi's keynote she wanted to yank it off the stand and rip off his smarmy head. The poster announced his participation in Saturday afternoon's "Why Self-Publishing Matters" panel where he would "reveal the truth" about the origins of the *Bedside Reader*.

Saffi unzipped her sling bag and yanked out her cellphone as if it had personally plagiarized her books. "First, photos. Lots and lots of photos. Document everything! Second—get those lawyers on the phone. New Year's is over!"

FIVE

Saffi stalked back to the lobby breathing fire. After taking a few snaps of the defaced keynote poster, she yanked it off its stand in the lobby and marched to the North Coast Booksellers Association booth with evidence in hand. "This is unacceptable."

"Saffi Graywood!" The two women and one man handling the booth stood up at once, smiles plastered across their faces, eyes bright with alarm. These three had clearly already faced Poppy's ire.

"We're so honored to have you here," the man gushed, stretching out his hand for a shake.

Saffi ignored his hand, preferring to waggle the poster at the trio. "Thank you for inviting me. It's an honor, but if something isn't done about this"—she slapped a hand against her defaced face—"I won't be staying."

At that point, the trio's fight-or-flight response kicked in. The youngest of the three—a woman with wide eyes, fawn-brown skin, and long box braids decorated with filigreed silver cuffs—shrank against the booth's back curtain. She groped at the cloth behind her as if searching for an opening that would allow her to flee the increasingly uncomfortable situation. The man pulled his hand back and started fiddling with his name badge. *George*, Saffi read.

She took in his man bun, jeans, and casual gray blazer over bone-white crew-neck sweater and thought, *Seattle bookstore assistant manager*, content to let someone else face off with the scary author.

The third member—a trim middle-aged sophisticate who reminded Saffi of a younger Poppy—went straight for fight. She put a hand on the table and leaned forward. "Ms. Graywood, we have a contract!" The white ribbon attached to her convention badge identified her as the North Coast Booksellers Association's executive director. The red ribbon beneath it made both Saffi and her certitude sway. The woman, Eileen Esterhaven, worked for the biggest family-owned bookstore chain in the Pacific Northwest. As indies went, she represented the one that could take a great white shark-sized bite out of Saffi's sales.

Saffi gulped. "I'm sor—" She felt a presence at her back and turned just as Poppy pressed forward, cutting off the apology before Saffi could finish blurting it out.

"Your contract with Lowry and Lowenstein includes a cancellation clause. It allows us to pull our author if there is any threat to her security."

The woman pulled back. "Have you been threatened, Ms. Graywood?"

Saffi waggled both the poster and her eyebrows. She wasn't yet ready to share her suspicion that GoodVender had threatened her with a bedful of bloody petals and chloroformed a housekeeper at the Necanicum Inn.

Apparently, a defaced poster wasn't enough for Eileen. She crossed her arms and shrugged. "Someone's not a fan. It happens. We bring spares, just in case. Fia, put up a fresh keynote poster, would you?" The young woman stopped trying to escape and stepped forward with a question in her dark eyes. "In the storage room beside the loading dock." Fia scurried out of the booth. The silver cuffs in her long braids clinked like chattering teeth as she glanced back to make sure neither Saffi nor Poppy was nipping at her heels.

"Look, Eileen?" Poppy glanced at the woman's badge as if she didn't already know all too well with whom she was dealing. "We both know who defaced this poster. The man who knocked off our author's best-selling series. The same man your association allowed to have a booth in this trade show. That very man, Ms. Esterhaven, has been *stalking* our author for more than a year, both online and in person. Therefore, you will either resolve the situation, or we will invoke the cancellation clause and pull our author. Am I clear?"

Saffi stood on the boardwalk outside the convention center, watching a young family paddle duckboats down the river. Each two-seater held a parent and a child. The competitive kids were pedaling as fast as their knobby knees would go. The parents were too busy taking photos to do much pedaling. They were making much better memories than Saffi would have when she flew home to Last Chance Cove.

The altercation with Eileen Esterhaven et al doused Saffi's fire like a sudden cloudburst. She'd gone from furious to more fearful than she wanted to admit, even to herself. At any second, she might come face to face with Jay GoodVender. His mention of her "final" *Bedside Reader* in his blog post comment could refer to ending her career. But if he'd been behind the bloody petals or the attack on the housekeeper? His stalking behaviors were escalating into far more dangerous territory.

Saffi sighed. She needed to talk out her fears with someone who would offer support and sympathy. She thought of phoning Delilah but chose Troy. If her fears turned out to be founded rather than fanciful, he was nearby, rather than hundreds of miles away.

When Troy picked up her call, she heard an ear-splitting whistle followed by a shout. "Wow! Would you look at the size of that one!"

"Troy? Where are you?" she asked after her ear stopped throbbing.

"Crabbing. Over on the 12th Avenue Bridge."

Saffi looked upriver toward a distant bridge lined with men, women, and kids. They were too far away to see in any detail, but their movements told her they were dropping crab pots over the side and then hauling them back up. "Scott didn't want to spend more time with his sister?"

"Are you kidding?" Saffi had never heard Troy sound quite so frightened. "She has five kids!"

Saffi chuckled. "I guess that explains the van."

"Yeah. Did you get that, uhm, gunk off the back of your coat?"

"You saw that?" Saffi squeaked. "And you didn't warn me?"

"Sorry. Amanda sped off like the hounds of hell were chasing her. If I'd known they were waiting for her at home, I'd have jumped ship with you. I don't know how she keeps up with that mob."

After discussing the size of the crab Scott had pulled out of the river on his first throw, Saffi told Troy about her morning.

"This GoodVender. You're sure he's the stalker?" Troy's voice sounded skeptical and worried at the same time. "Wasn't he painted up like a clown at the Halloween Spooktacular?"

"I saw him without makeup earlier that day," Saffi reminded him.

"OK, but, other than gut instinct, do you have any evidence that he's the stalker?"

What was it with men? "Other than my gut? Troy, gut instinct isn't some woo-woo thing. It's your brain crunching a lot of data and cluing you in on what your unconscious already knows. In case you haven't noticed, listening to my gut is the way I live my life." She hated the way her voice became huskier as she talked, but tearing up did that to her.

"Sorry. What?" Troy had the spaced-out sound of someone who was only half listening. "This kid just pulled in the white whale of crabs. You should see this thing!" Cheering erupted in the background and Troy muffled it, probably by covering the phone with his hand.

Saffi had called Troy for a bit of support, not to have her

instincts discounted or to hear about the size of anyone's crabs. "Sounds like you're busy," she said. "Guess I'll catch you later."

Troy chuckled. "Catch you later. Good one."

Saffi stabbed the red button to end the call so hard she almost dropped her phone. Three years from losing the love of her life. Three years of letting her heart heal. And then... Troy. The first time she'd seen him, her body had reminded her that she was a woman in her prime. She'd known it was time to stop waiting, to open up. She wasn't sorry she'd taken that step. But this wasn't some made-for-TV movie. Broken hearts leave scars. Scars are much tougher than the tender tissue they replace, but they stretch and pull and pinch. Saffi was feeling that pinch, and it came from playing second fiddle to a giant crab. *A crab! Really?*

Note to self: Next time, call Delilah.

Saffi stuffed her phone into her bag and joined the crowd jostling to get into the building. She'd wasted too much time fretting and the doors to the exhibit hall were about to open. She had one tool that might get her to the door ahead of the mob. She touched the two women in front of her on the shoulders and lifted her author badge with its jaunty yellow Keynote Speaker ribbon. "Could I just...?" She made a parting motion with her hands and— miracle of miracles—the sea of convention-goers parted before her. "Bless you." Saffi beamed. These were her people. Instead of making her feel lower than a common crab, they made her feel like Moses raising his staff of power to wave the Red Sea out of the way.

Then the doors opened, and the sea rushed in to engulf her. Saffi gulped and did what everyone else was doing—rode the tide inside. As Poppy had planned, the wave swept straight to the Lowry & Lowenstein booth, then stopped. When she held out a frantic hand, Poppy plucked her from the crowd and ensconced her behind a table piled high with Advanced Reader Copies of her next *Bedside Reader*.

Poppy put an Elsa Peretti red lacquer ballpoint pen in Saffi's hand and Willow plunked a to-go cup down by her elbow. One whiff told Saffi that Poppy's assistant had made the coffee run. Though her editor knew Saffi's preference for steam and whipped cream, she usually found the closest imitation of a coffee drink to supply Saffi with caffeine during signings. Not Willow. Like most New York City publishing interns and assistants, Willow came from money and graduated from one of the prestigious Ivies. Smith College, if Saffi remembered correctly. Despite her elite upbringing—or perhaps because of it—Willow always remembered Saffi's go-to coffee drink: a Mexi-mocha with whipped cream. Saffi took a slow happy sip, gave Willow a thumbs-up, then went to work.

The ARCs Saffi signed were not the final proofed version of the book and they weren't for resale. They were provided to booksellers to encourage them to make store orders and to reviewers to get as much media attention as possible, in print and online.

Willow quickly settled the wave of autograph seekers into some semblance of a line. She went down the line, writing each person's name on a yellow sticky note. Poppy sat beside Saffi, ready to paste each sticky on the title page of an ARC. All Saffi had to do was read, sign, and glance up to greet the person with a friendly smile or a bit of chitchat. Most were booksellers excited for their first look at her new annual. Some were fans hoping to snag a copy for their collection. A few were locals, including a slightly pudgy man wearing a striped button-down shirt beneath a blue jacket who introduced himself as head of Seaside's chamber of commerce. He thrust a brochure featuring local businesses into Saffi's hand. She thanked him with a smile and put it in her tote to look at later. If she had downtime during the convention, she definitely wanted to explore the town.

Instead of leaving, the man stepped back a few paces and took a few shots on his cellphone. "For the chamber's website, if that's OK."

"Free publicity? More than OK." Saffi looked up from signing a book to strike an authorial pose, but just as he snapped a picture, her hand cramped around the pen, and she grimaced. *Perfect!* She put down the pen, flexed her fingers, rubbed her hands together, and went back to work. One by one, the stacks of ARCs shrank. By the end of Saffi's first signing, only a single ARC remained on the table. She was rubbing her wrist and rolling her shoulders when Willow placed the last book in front of her.

"For Jay," Saffi read the name aloud, signed *Aunt Saffi* with a flourish, glanced up, then froze.

"Aunt Saffi. Stealer of intellectual property. We meet at last." Shoeshine-black hair, geek glasses, cheeks so pink they looked rouged, eyes blacker than malice. The stalker she knew as Jay GoodVender cocked his head sideways. "You're older than your photo. Quite a bit rounder, too."

The stalker's hyper-nasal voice bypassed his mouth and came straight through his pointed nose, exactly the adenoidal voice Phyllis had described. Any doubts Saffi had that this was the man who had called the inn, sent flowers, and chloroformed Marisol disappeared.

Saffi tightened her grip on the poppy-red pen as she considered the many things her research had taught her one could do with a ballpoint. *Give a choking victim a tracheotomy. Tighten a tourniquet. Conceal a secret message. Poke an eye out, and, of course, stab an assailant—or someone threatening to destroy your career—in the jugular.* She was a bit appalled at how quickly she had gone from feeling nothing but good will toward everyone in line to imagining murder methods. Only one thing stopped her—the knowledge that Poppy had entrusted her with her favorite pen, purchased from Tiffany & Co. of New York. Engraved, of course.

There had to be a less murdery way to get rid of Jay—preferably before he wrecked her reputation at Saturday's panel. That's when it hit her. *The poster!* She would show the picture she'd snapped of Jay's author poster to Marisol. If the housekeeper could identify him, her stalker would end up exactly where he belonged: in jail.

"Author photos. They do make us look our best, don't they?" Saffi tapped her photo on the back of the ARC she'd just signed.

"Too bad *your* poster will have to come down, now that you're leaving the show."

GoodVender leaned so close Saffi could smell grilled-onion burger on his breath. "You think getting me kicked out of the convention will keep the truth from coming out? It won't! I have *proof* that you stole my idea."

Proof! What kind of ridiculous crap was he spouting? Saffi cringed away and Poppy stepped forward, cellphone in hand, punching numbers. She moved out of view to complete the call, and Saffi prayed her editor had security on speed dial.

"I've signed my series with a publisher." GoodVender thumped the book Saffi had signed for him on the table. "My *Original Bedside Reader* is going to knock yours off the shelves! Your career is dead, and there's not a thing you can do to stop me."

Poppy caught Saffi's eyes above the cellphone. *Oh, really?* In earlier encounters, Saffi's instinct had been to hide from her stalker, or flee. Now? GoodVender thought he could take credit for *her* series? Steal *her* hard-won success? Sign with a publisher willing to trade on the *Bedside Reader* name to publish a knockoff! She clutched the red lacquer pen so hard it hurt and half rose from her seat. Now? Aunt Saffi was ready to fight.

She was never certain whether what happened next was an accident or more of the bad karma that rolled over her stalker on a regular basis. But before she could put a pen through his eyeball or, at the very least, think of a pithy putdown, GoodVender had been plowed over by a rolling convention tote on wheels.

"Oh, my gosh. I am so sorry. I did *not* see you standing there!" The tote driver reached out a hand toughened by what Saffi imagined were years of sorting fish by her father's side. "Here, let me help you up."

It took some doing, but Saffi managed to suppress the genuine smile that threatened to spread across her face.

"Get away from me, you termagant!" GoodVender glared.

The woman withdrew her hand, then used it to brush back her sea-kinked reddish-white hair. "That's a mighty big word for someone sitting on his can in the middle of an exhibit hall." The memoir writer Saffi had met earlier turned toward the table with a wink. "Aunt Saffi, I was hoping to get a book signed, but it looks like this noodlehead took the last one."

Willow hurried forward to pick up the book Saffi had just signed from the opposite side of the aisle where it had flown when GoodVender went sprawling. As the leggy editorial assistant straightened, she tossed back her perfectly highlighted shoulder-length blond hair and swept her bangs from her forehead. She came back to the table, blue eyes on fire, and reached for the pen Saffi held in a choke hold.

"Erasable ink." Willow smiled. She pulled off the pen's hidden cap and went to work with the white eraser. After blowing away the eraser crumbs, she took a yellow sticky off the cube and stuck it on the newly cleaned page. "Who would you like Aunt Saffi to sign this to?"

Saffi had appreciated Willow before. Now? She would beg, plead, cajole... even put it into her contract... to make sure the young woman landed a permanent position at Lowry & Lowenstein.

"Jemma Weathers." The memoir writer looked at Willow with grudging admiration.

"Here." Saffi picked up a fine-tipped red Sharpie the man from the chamber of commerce pushed across the table. The look on his face told her exactly what he thought of the altercation: bad for business, bad for his town.

As Saffi signed Jemma's ARC, she asked questions about the memoir writer's day. It had gone well. Jemma had sold some books and taken orders from bookstores from Cannon Beach to Astoria.

"I even had a Powell's buyer stop by." Jemma beamed.

Saffi was impressed. Portland's most iconic bookstore would be a coup for anyone. She could still remember the excitement she'd felt the first time she spotted a stack of *Bedside Readers* on the first floor of the world's largest indie bookstore.

Both the fear and the hope Saffi had noticed on Jemma's face earlier had faded. Only excitement remained. As they chatted, a security guard with broad shoulders and the belly of someone forced to eat too much concession-stand food strode down the aisle. He nodded to Poppy. She slid her cellphone into her right blazer pocket as the guard hooked a hand through Jay GoodVender's arm.

Thank you, Saffi mouthed, and Poppy quirked a wry smile. *It's what I do*, her eyes replied.

"Up you go, buddy." The guard hoisted GoodVender to his feet.

"I'm not your buddy," GoodVender spluttered, adjusting his glasses and brushing off his slacks. "But now that you're here, this – this *person* assaulted me." He jammed a thumb toward Jemma. "She rammed that *ridiculous* tote right into me."

The guard glanced at Jemma, Saffi, and Willow. They continued their conversation as if ignoring Jay GoodVender was the best way to make him go away.

"Come with me to the office," the guard said. "You'll need to fill out some paperwork. Liability insurance, and whatnot."

"You are not getting away with this!" GoodVender shook a finger at Saffi. "Any of it. I will *end* Aunt Saffi, if it's the last thing I do."

"Hmm." Saffi winked. "If one of us has to go, I'm pretty sure it will be you."

If she'd known what was to come, she would have zipped her lips and let GoodVender have the last word.

SIX

Saffi returned to the Necanicum Inn with one thing on her mind—checking in with Phyllis. She was sure the photo on her phone would prove Jay GoodVender's guilt. All she had to do was get it in front of Marisol. Surely Phyllis would know if the housekeeper had regained consciousness. She spotted her behind the desk, frantically checking in a long line of arrivals.

Saffi's attempt to slip stealthily along the front desk to catch the clerk's eye left her feeling more like Mr. Bean than James Bond. She knocked over a plastic holder filled with "Welcome to Seaside" brochures. As she scrambled to gather them from the carpet, someone tripped over her hand. She stood without looking to apologize and her shoulder sent a to-go cup of coffee flying.

"Please!" The woman who'd lost her coffee waved Saffi toward the desk. "Get it over with before someone gets hurt."

The heat in Saffi's cheeks felt like flames, but taking Jay down before he did more harm was worth the embarrassment. She stepped up to Phyllis, glanced over her shoulder to make sure no one could hear, then whispered her request. "I need to show this to Marisol." She held up her cell so Phyllis could see Jay's author poster.

Phyllis glanced at the photo. "Looks like the guy you told me to watch out for."

Saffi nodded. "I think he's the one who attacked Marisol."

The desk clerk ran her tongue across the gap in her teeth. "The police aren't letting anyone in to see her. Except her girls."

Marisol had kids? Of course she did. Working mamas went the extra mile for hotel guests. Tips mattered. Had Jay tipped her to spread those red-tipped petals then attacked her to cover his tracks?

"If I share this with you, can you make sure Marisol sees it?"

"I'll do my best." The desk clerk pointed at the line behind Saffi. "But not until after the rush."

It only took a few seconds to AirDrop the photo to Phyllis's cellphone and hightail it to the elevator. As the doors whooshed open and she stepped inside, the lobby erupted in applause. Saffi hung her head, grateful that no one actually knew who she was. Then the convention badge dangling against her chest came into focus. *Saffi Graywood. Keynote Speaker.* Wonderful!

Once inside the shelter of her corner suite, Saffi breathed a sigh of relief. It was short-lived.

"Saffi!" A familiar voice called from the balcony. "What has been going on over here?"

"Troy!" She pressed her lips together. She still felt a bit miffed that he had rhapsodized about crabs instead of listening when she'd needed him. If he had, he'd already know what was going on. She tossed her tote on the sofa and joined him, getting comfortable in one of the two white plastic deck chairs before she shared her day. She included the gory detail about the floral "surprise" she'd found on the queen bed, the attack on the housekeeper, and Jay's in-person threat to destroy her career.

By the time Saffi finished, Troy was wringing the balcony rail as tightly as she had clutched Poppy's red pen. "He'd better hope I don't get my hands on him."

Saffi quirked a brow. "Sorry. You'll have to stand in line. Behind me, Poppy, Willow, and Jemma."

Troy raised his brows. "Jemma? Tell me more." His voice rumbled encouragement.

Leaning against the balcony rail with a chill ocean breeze ruffling his clipped slate-gray curls, Troy made Saffi's heart skip a beat. Literally. For a second, she wondered if she was low on Vitamin D, but... *no*. The man made her body pulse like she'd knocked back a four-shot latte. She could barely remember why she had been so irritated with him earlier. Something about crabs?

Get a grip, girl!

Saffi licked her lips then painted a word picture of Jemma Weathers, the self-published author who had taken GoodVender out with a rolling book tote. The story got the reaction she'd hoped for earlier. Troy stepped away from the rail and reached for Saffi's hands. He pulled her to her feet and into his chest.

"Saffi Graywood." He breathed against her hair. "I'll stand behind you and your Amazons anytime."

He smelled of man sweat and, to be honest, slightly fishy. But they both planned to shower before tonight's banquet, so who cared?

"I'm sorry I let that crab grab my attention," he whispered. "I should have been listening. And I definitely should have trusted your gut. It let me into your life, after all." His chuckle held the kind of caring she'd been longing for earlier.

"And my very luxurious hotel suite," Saffi teased as she guided him back inside and slid the glass door closed.

"Yes, well, before we can enjoy it properly"— Troy headed straight to the vase on the kitchenette counter—"these have to go!"

He didn't just throw the yellow carnations into the kitchen trash. He took them downstairs to chuck them into the dumpster near the parking lot. By the time he returned to the room, his cheeks had reddened as if he'd taken the stairs three at a time to get back to her as fast as possible. But he still had more than enough oxygen to make her forget everything except the way his body felt against hers.

It felt like safe harbor. Like home.

. . .

Streetlamps flickered to life and reflected like tiny suns in the river's sunset-infused water as the *Bedside Reader* crew—plus Troy—took the Broadway Bridge across the river. They turned onto the boardwalk that led to the convention center, chatting about innocuous things like which authors had new books out and which editors had switched companies since the last booksellers' convention. They avoided discussing Saffi's stalker and the attack on Marisol, determined to enter the banquet in an upbeat mood.

When they arrived at the convention center, they found Eileen Esterhaven, executive director of the North Coast Booksellers Association, stationed just inside the double front doors. She pounced on their group the minute they entered.

"I cannot apologize enough for what happened earlier. Just after the doors opened to the hall, we informed Mr. GoodVender that he would have to vacate his booth and leave the premises. He seemed to take it in stride. Unfortunately, so I've been told, the minute we left he joined the line at your booth."

Poppy ground the heels of her beige and black pumps into the convention center's blue carpet tiles and Saffi steeled herself for a stand-off.

"Tell me, Eileen. How do you intend to safeguard our author during tonight's banquet?" Poppy tilted her head back to look down her nose at Eileen. "And during tomorrow's keynote? Maybe you haven't heard, but Jay GoodVender attacked a member of the housekeeping staff at the inn where we're staying this morning."

"Attacked?" Eileen's voice went shrill. "Do you have proof?"

Poppy narrowed her eyes and pursed her mouth with the certitude Manhattan editors earned after years in the publishing trenches. "We are still awaiting confirmation. But until the police step in, we need your assurance that Saffi will be safe."

Eileen adjusted the nautical-themed Hermès scarf draped over her blue satin blouse—a calculated pause after the gauntlet had been thrown down. "Mr. GoodVender's photo has been messaged to every security guard's phone. There will be at least one guard in every room for the duration of the convention. Two in the banquet hall tonight and one patrolling the corridor."

Saffi had never known anyone who could sniff the way Poppy did. It was equal parts acceptance, disdain, and dismissal. Sniff delivered, Poppy lowered her chin and nodded. She took off her camel-colored wool coat and held it out as if expecting a cloakroom attendant to scuttle forward. Troy took the coat and draped it over one arm, then hooked Poppy's hand over his other arm and led her away. Willow followed, hands linked behind her prep-school-straight back.

Being a step behind, Saffi got a good look at the evil eye Eileen Esterhaven gave Poppy. Then the association's executive director noticed her standing there, raised both hands in a shrug and offered a polite—though far from contrite—smile. "You're lucky to have Ms. Morales in your corner," she said.

Saffi gave Ms. Esterhaven a pondering look. "I hope I have *you* there as well."

Eileen took a step forward, hands outstretched. "Of course. Of course you do! Fia, George, and I will do whatever we can to make this trade show a success. You, Aunt Saffi, are the star of the show. Our attendance numbers jumped by ten percent when we announced that you would be here."

Ten percent sounded big, but for a convention of this size, it probably represented about forty attendees. Still, it lifted Saffi's spirits tremendously to count booksellers among her fans. She'd learned years ago that having booksellers hand-sell your titles increased sales significantly. And if they loved your book enough to feature it in an Indie Next List of bookseller favorites, an author could take that to the bank. At least... the piggy bank.

Saffi offered Ms. Esterhaven a genuine smile. "It's an honor to be here. Really. Poppy says a nonfiction writer has better odds of winning the lottery than being asked to keynote."

"True. You were Fia's idea," Eileen admitted. She started down the corridor and motioned for Saffi to follow.

Great. The skittish fawn had been responsible for inviting her. With Jay GoodVender rocking the boats on Eileen's Hermès scarf, she must be regretting the decision. But when Eileen turned toward Saffi with her own smile, it reached her eyes.

"Fia lobbied for you for months. George had his eye on a thriller writer from Seattle. I wanted the young adult novelist who won this year's Oregon Book Awards. But I checked your sales numbers at my stores. They beat the others by a mile. Plus, Fia assured me that you have a cult-like following in the 'nerdy northwest.'" She set the words off in finger quotes. "So, I voted with Fia. George pouted but the attendance jump won him over."

Eileen's kind words meant the world to Saffi. She'd felt off-kilter since Poppy told her about the *Bedside Reader* knockoffs. Discovering that her stalker was behind them had made it so much worse. Saffi cleared the thickness from her throat before daring to speak. None of those things were Eileen's fault. "I can't tell you how much I appreciate your vote of confidence. And—honestly—I feel awful about the way I freaked out when we first met."

"Oh, no!" Eileen waved her worries away. "I completely understand."

"I just—" Saffi pressed her eyelids and shook her head, nearly overcome by the sudden desire to weep. She hadn't had a full-on weepfest since she arrived in Last Chance Cove last June. But before that, the smallest thing could trigger the feelings of deep loss and loneliness she had experienced since Levi's death. The bloody petals on her bed and watching EMTs attaching leads to Marisol's chest... those were far from small things. "I'm sorry." She sniffed and tugged the corners of her eyes. "Good-Vender has been stalking me for a year. He came here for a showdown and he's not going to give up until he gets one. He's going to crash the banquet. Or tomorrow's keynote. I feel it in my bones."

Eileen's eyes hardened. She put a hand on Saffi's shoulder and gave it a squeeze. "Stalkers make my blood boil. My team will do *whatever* it takes to make sure he doesn't get anywhere near you.

Here we are." She motioned Saffi through open double doors into a room that teemed with people.

The convention center's setup crew had taken down the wall between the East and West Necanicum rooms to make a space big enough for the banquet. Round tables covered in blue cloths filled the room, their tops set for ten. Tall tables had been placed strategically along the walls to facilitate conversation as attendees sipped glasses of wine and munched appetizers. Despite the room's size, it could not absorb the cacophony of booksellers, authors, and publishers meeting and greeting after a year of nothing but the occasional phone call or email.

The minute Saffi entered the hall, Poppy rushed toward her and Eileen took her leave. Saffi watched the executive director thread her way across the room to two figures staring out the floor-to-ceiling windows facing the river. Fia's box braids and George's man bun made them easy to recognize. When Eileen reached them, the three convention staff members went into a huddle. Seconds later, Fia and George both glanced over their shoulders at Saffi. She felt terrible about how she'd come down on them earlier —especially Fia, who had championed her keynote. She smiled and gave a little wave, hoping the friendly gesture would help them relax and enjoy the evening, but their brows furrowed even deeper. Saffi sighed.

"Earth to Saffi!" Poppy snapped her fingers. "Here's how we're going to play this. You and I will work the room. Touch base with as many booksellers as possible before the meal service begins." She quirked her finger toward Willow. "Locate our table and find out who our dinner companions will be. Take this list." She pulled the top sheet off a long narrow pad and handed it to Willow. Saffi took a peek. Poppy had listed her top ten booksellers, the ones she wanted to keep happy or those who represented markets she'd yet to crack. "If you don't see any of these names at our table, find Fia. She's the program assistant and will be much easier to persuade than Eileen or George. Two or three from the list would make my evening."

Before Poppy finished talking, Willow had already started scouting tables in search of the one reserved for their group.

"Troy." Poppy turned to Troy as if he was another soldier in her regiment. "I think you—"

Troy held up a hand. "I'm a fish out of water in this crowd, Poppy. How about I attend to Saffi's every whim and keep an eye out for Jay GoodVender? In case he makes it past those two."

He pointed toward two scruffy young men wearing dark sunglasses as if they'd walked off the set of *Mission Impossible*. Shoulders back, thumbs tucked into the waistbands of their black jeans, they strolled the room, heads turning right-left-right. Every few seconds, one of them lifted a handheld radio and mumbled into it. The convention center guards she'd seen earlier wore neat gray uniforms. These two had the word "SECURITY" stamped in yellow on the backs of zippered black hoodies. Either hoodies were standard issue for extra security guards on the kickback Oregon coast or these two were posers looking for a free meal.

"Thanks!" Saffi lifted onto the toes of her Italian leather boots to brush a kiss on Troy's cheek. "I suspect their radio communications have more to do with locating the hottest young women in the room than watching out for GoodVender. But if *you* find him, no punching."

Troy put a hand on her shoulder and leaned toward her ear. "I'm a dunker, not a puncher."

Poppy arched her eyebrows. "Behave, you two. We're here to sell books." But when a group of fans entering the room schooled around Saffi like fish, Poppy gave Troy a second look. She tapped a finger on her lips, then nodded. "A few poses for the social media mavens won't hurt Aunt Saffi's sales one bit."

At conventions, Poppy carried a *Bedside Reader* in her cherry-red Marc Jacobs tote at all times. She pressed one into Saffi's hands then turned Troy toward the audience and smooshed the two of them together.

"Smiles," she hissed from behind them.

"I don't know—" Troy began but before he finished, cellphones started snapping.

Saffi could imagine what the posts would look like. The open "o" of the word "know" would make the handsome, weathered man in the gray cable-knit fisherman's sweater look surprised, as if he'd been snatched out of the crowd to pose beside Aunt Saffi. Her honey-brown eyes, crinkled with worry, would make her look older. *Thank you, Jay GoodVender!* She had enough self-doubt without letting his insults live rent-free in her head.

As if sensing her discomfort, Troy leaned down to kiss her upturned forehead. Then he rested a finger on the top of the book as if they were showing it off together. When he set his mouth in the mischievous quirk that had first drawn her to him, Saffi's heart went butter soft.

"How'd you know what to do?" she whispered through her smile.

He bent toward her ear. "Photographer, remember?"

She remembered. They'd met in front of a wall of his photos at the Last Chance Café. He'd asked if she saw something she liked. Totally flustered, she'd mumbled something about how amazing his work was, but the quirk in his grin told her he knew exactly what she'd been checking out, and it wasn't the artistry of his photos.

A commotion in the corridor drew her out of her memories. Seconds later, the men in black hoodies bolted between banquet tables and raced through the door. The cellphones moved as one toward the banquet hall's entry door but once the guards hit the corridor there was nothing to snap.

<h1 style="text-align:center">SEVEN</h1>

Troy's first instinct was to barrel after them, but Poppy persuaded him to stay at Saffi's side. "If that lunatic"—she bared her teeth—"makes it in here, someone needs to guard her."

Willow guided them to their seats at one of the tables closest to the river view. Streetlamps reflected in the river and cast a haunting glow on the boardwalk. Figures strolled along the walk or leaned against the wooden railing and stared into the depths. Except for one figure. Dressed all in black, he stood directly beneath a lamp as if he wanted to be seen.

"Is that...?" Saffi squinted.

Just as the man lifted his hand to wave, two figures raced down the boardwalk. One tackled him to the ground. The other yanked his arms behind him, zip-tied his wrists, then lifted him to his feet and perp-walked him toward the bridge.

Eileen Esterhaven burst to her feet like a plover startled from its sandy nest. "What are those idiots doing?" She slammed her wineglass down on the table and stalked out of the room. Fia and George exchanged glances, then stood and followed in her wake.

Saffi's first thought was that the guards were just doing their job. Her second? The realization that GoodVender had not been on convention center grounds. Someone, perhaps the booksellers association, was about to get sued. *Poor Eileen.*

Rumors swept through the room like wildfire in a windstorm. Everything from, "He had a gun," to "He was just waving to someone." A few minutes later, sirens broke through the melee and blue and red lights pulsed from the other side of the river.

"Well!" Poppy folded her napkin into a triangle and placed it in her lap. "That's one way to get rid of the competition." She beamed at the booksellers and fans around the table. A few laughed nervously but others widened their eyes and glanced at their neighbors.

Saffi caught her editor's eye and lifted her brows. *Careful, Poppy.*

"Saffi," Poppy broke the uncomfortable silence. "I'm sure you must have some chilling tales about writers who have been stalked."

Saffi had even more stories about "arrests gone wrong," but this probably wasn't the time to share those.

"Ah, yes." Drawing on her, admittedly shallow, reservoir of "learned" extraversion, Saffi smiled at the attentive faces around the table. Booksellers who faithfully promoted her, booksellers considering adding *Bedside Reader* to their shelves, a million-follower book reviewer, the head of Oregon's public library system, a buyer for a major bookstore chain who just happened to be in the area for the weekend—that coup belonged to the incomparable Willow—and Jemma Weathers, who'd earned her spot at the keynote table with a well-aimed rolling book tote.

Saffi regaled her listeners with her favorite stalker story. "During a US tour in 1947, Charles Dickens said he couldn't drink a glass of water without a hundred people staring down his throat." She purposefully took a drink from her water glass, then glanced up. Since all eyes were on her, the gulp got the chuckle she'd hoped for. She went on to describe what happened when Dickens returned to the states twenty years later. "A wealthy Baltimore socialite not only stalked him from city to city, she beat up a female fan who brought flowers to Dickens's room." The flowers reminded Saffi so much of what Jay had done, she stopped abruptly. "Well. Enough of that!"

Several table guests used the opening to ask Saffi to sign copies of previous editions of her *Bedside Reader*. Poppy dug through her bag for the pen Saffi had used earlier and turned an accusing glare on Willow when she couldn't find it.

Willow held up her hand. "I gave it back. I swear."

"Saffi?" Poppy's eyes narrowed.

Saffi laughed off the accusation. "I *love* that pen," she told her audience. "If it didn't have Poppy's name engraved on it, I would definitely abscond with it."

Willow unearthed a cheap gel pen from her convention bag. Once Saffi finished signing books, attention turned to the bane of all banquets: the food.

"If they serve chicken instead of seafood, I'm out of here." Jemma thumped a meaty fist on the table.

Troy leaned forward. "If you get desperate, I have a couple of boiled crabs on ice back at our room."

Saffi widened her eyes. "Crabs? In our room?"

By the time everyone finished sharing rude jokes, Saffi had covered her face with both hands. She'd forgotten how rowdy book people could be after a few passes with the wine bottle, but she was sure they all rose in Troy's estimation somewhere between the piñon-crusted cod and the triple-chocolate mousse parfaits. Dessert finished, their table mates wandered away one by one, some to talk to friends they'd spotted, others to the restrooms.

Desperate to escape air and conversation grown stale, Saffi persuaded Poppy to join those making a hasty exit out the front door. Once outside, she discovered them hurrying toward a line of Surrey cycles. The two- and four-person cycles had been outlined with fairy lights and hung with jingle bells. Saffi was instantly enchanted.

A pudgy man wearing a Santa suit walked along the line of cycles handing out brochures and saltwater taffy. "Welcome to

Seaside!" He plopped a wrapped pink taffy into Saffi's hand and beamed, his round cheeks glowing in the cold.

"What's this?" Saffi stopped beside Fia, who was helping tipsy banquet-goers climb into the foot-powered rigs.

For once, Fia didn't skitter away. Instead, she urged Saffi toward one of the Surreys. "It's the Jingle Tour! Courtesy of the Seaside chamber of commerce. The town keeps its holiday lights on until the end of January. Didn't you see it in the convention brochure?"

Saffi shook her head. Other than checking the times for her signings and keynote, she hadn't bothered. For her, this trip was work—not play.

"Don't worry. I reserved this four-seater for your party." Fia waved a hand as if expecting Saffi, Poppy, Troy, and Willow to duck inside.

At any other time, pedaling through the nighttime streets of Seaside in the glow of holiday lights would have set her heart on fire. Right now, as winter's chill pinched her cheeks and sent frozen fingers down the collar of her flouncy jacket, Saffi hesitated.

"Sorry!" Willow bowed out first. "After that meal, I need to walk."

"Ah." Fia nodded, then pointed westward. "There's a mile-long promenade along the beach."

"Perfect." Willow turned beachward to walk off the extra calories her innate politeness had required her to consume.

When Poppy pleaded the lingering effects of jet lag, Troy put an arm around Saffi's shoulders. "What about you? Too pooped to pedal?"

Before Saffi could plead exhaustion, a voice called out and Fia turned. She waved, then hurried toward a Surrey cycle parked in the shadows. The man behind the wheel wore a black hoodie so much like the one Jay GoodVender had been wearing earlier that an electric jolt of fear stiffened Saffi's back. When Fia ducked down to climb in, she stopped herself just before shouting out a warning.

Nothing overruled exhaustion like an overly suspicious nature. She tugged Troy toward the four-seater and ducked inside. "Follow that cycle!"

When she explained her worry to Troy, he reminded her that they'd seen her stalker carted off to jail. "It can't be him."

Troy was right. Of course he was. Jay had not been the only one hanging around the convention center wearing a black hoodie. The young security guards wore them too. Capturing GoodVender could have given one of the scruffy guards enough juice to coax Fia into joining him for the tour.

"Let's just make sure, shall we?"

Troy grasped the steering wheel with both hands. "The chase is on!"

It took both of them pumping full bore to catch up to Fia and the man in the black hoodie as they trundled across the 12th Avenue Bridge. Glancing to her right, Saffi could see the tour leader upriver, crossing the Broadway Bridge. Car horns, shrieks, laughter, more horns, and the sound of voices raised in song rang out across the town. The song was picked up by one Surrey cycle after another, but Saffi struggled to make out the lyrics.

"Are they singing about Granny being run over by a reindeer?" she asked.

Troy snorted. "With this crew, they're probably *doing* the running over. Not *being* run over."

Saffi chuckled. She hummed along with the countrified Christmas song until raised voices in the cycle in front of them broke through. Saffi strained to hear what seemed to be an argument, but with all the singing and jingling and horn blaring, she could not make out a single word.

The turn onto Broadway took them beneath twinkling sea stars, strung between poles on either side of the street. Streetlamps wrapped with red lights marched from the bridge to the sea. Though night had dropped like a shade and the temperature continued to plummet, the holiday lights warmed Saffi's spirit. Her feet slowed on the pedals and the tension in her shoulders began to relax. But as their cycle passed the Necanicum Inn, a raspy caw split the night.

A black shadow launched itself from one of the hotel's corner balconies. Was that the fourth floor? The shadow winged toward them—black on black until it reached the glow of the streetlamp at the edge of the bridge. *Raven!* Saffi gripped the edge of her seat. The last time her totem animal showed up in the night, a woman had been murdered.

The raven swooped across the bridge and landed on a concrete post with a bas relief sculpture Saffi couldn't make out in the darkness. The black bird fidgeted, dancing foot to foot as it settled. Then it folded its wings, tucked its head into its shimmery black breast, and went still. Waiting.

Troy, who knew of Saffi's relationship to Raven, glanced her way. "Should we be worried?"

Saffi chewed her lip. "I don't know." Her attachment to Raven began while researching myths for *Bedside Reader, #2.* Civilizations as distant in time and place as the Norse and Native American tribes believed Raven to be a messenger, either between the realms of life and death, or between the gods and humankind. Unfortunately for Saffi, she was neither priest nor shaman. When Raven called, she knew to listen, but as far as what the message meant...? Unless she tripped over a body, she seldom had a clue.

The cycles ahead of them stopped in front of the Carousel Mall. To Saffi's surprise, Fia climbed out of the Surrey cycle in front of them. She hurried toward the mall's front doors, glancing back as if to make sure she wasn't being followed before pushing her way inside. When the cycles started forward again, the one Fia had abandoned turned onto a side road.

"Should we follow?" Troy slowed as they reached the turn.

With Fia clearly out of harm's way, the frantic energy Saffi had felt earlier drained away. "No. Jay GoodVender destroyed my day, but I don't need to let him wreck our night." She lifted her chin toward the sea. "Let's go."

When they reached the turnaround where the road met the

ocean, Seaside's white sand beach glowed like polished pearls beneath the moon. Something inside Saffi shifted, loosened. She inhaled... a long, slow, salt-filled breath that expanded her lungs and drove away the darkness Jay's deeds had left behind. Troy put his arm around her shoulders and drew her into his comforting warmth.

Then Saffi noticed something—not a sound, but the absence of one. The Pacific had gone quiet, its waves hushed as if the sea held its breath. Waiting. As Raven had waited on the bridge.

EIGHT

Saffi awakened at first light to a cacophony of horns. She blinked, stretched, and—forgetting her night's companion—bopped Troy in the jaw hard enough to make him groan.

"Sorry!" Saffi sat up, pulling the duvet to her chin as her brain struggled to figure out how she had ended up in a room with a giant TV on the wall and a view of Tillamook Head beyond the room's sliding glass doors.

Seaside! She had a keynote this morning, but the pink-tinged clouds stretching fingers toward the ocean told her she still had plenty of time to snuggle.

A raven's shrill alert followed by the flutter of wings on the balcony begged to differ. Saffi scooted to the edge of the bed and pulled the silky emerald robe she'd tossed over a chair last night toward her. She slipped her arms into its cool folds and reached her toes into the hotel-provided slippers. Standing shoved her feet the rest of the way in, and she shuffled toward the sliding glass door. Whatever was happening outside, Raven was not going to let her sleep through it.

"Come back." Troy's voice sounded groggy with sleep. "It's too cold without you."

Usually, Troy ran hot and she ran cold, making her a perfect heat sink for his over-revved metabolism. Saffi found the fireplace remote control and clicked on its gas-fired flames.

"Be right back." *I hope.*

Once she slid the door open, the raven shuffled its position on the rail to point its beak toward the bridge. Saffi sidled up beside the black bird and immediately spotted the reason for the bedlam. A four-wheeled Surrey cycle with a yellow-and-white-striped canopy sat crosswise on the bridge, blocking traffic. A man— perhaps the driver of the bread delivery truck closest to the cycle— was leaning under the canopy to look inside. Had it been aban-doned? Left behind by a woozy librarian from the Jingle Tour? The thought made Saffi chuckle and her breath formed a small cloud in the early-morning chill.

But then... the man jerked back as if pulled by a string, ran to the side of the bridge, and vomited over the concrete railing into the river. Saffi's gag response kicked in and her cheeks bulged in sympathy. She turned away and rushed into the room.

"Troy!" She grabbed his hand to pull him toward her side of the bed. An impossible task. The man was harder to budge than a bag of concrete. "Troy!" she repeated. "Something's happening. Down on the bridge."

As she talked, she threw off the robe and fumbled in the suit-case she'd been too distracted to unpack for something warm to wear. She tugged out a pair of fleece leggings and a swingy thigh-length Merino wool tunic. She pulled the tunic over her head and was halfway out the bedroom door when Troy mumbled something about going commando. Horrified, Saffi looked down to see pale bare legs. As she wriggled into silk undies and tugged the fleece up her legs and over her dimpled bottom, the hubbub outside grew to include the whoops of a police car. When sirens converged from every direction, Troy bolted out of bed.

"What's going on?"

Saffi pointed to the sliding glass door, then put up a finger to stop him as he had stopped her. "Robe!"

He yanked one of the plush hotel-provided robes from the closet and stuffed his feet into the boots he'd left by the bed.

Now that would make a good post! Sorely tempted as she was to take a pic and up her click count, Saffi refrained. Whatever was happening outside took place on the bridge where Raven had waited last night. It was bad. Her instincts told her the booksellers' trade show with its lovely side dish of Troy was about to take a far less appetizing turn.

Three hours later, Saffi stood behind the podium in front of a standing-room-only crowd. She tugged the back of her swingy fox-print sweater dress away from the red-and-black plaid leggings she'd worn to keep the seaside chill at bay. In her rush to dress after the morning's commotion, she had forgotten that a room filled with people would create its own heat. She loosened the red scarf she'd looped around her neck, hoping the increased airflow would cool the excess heat her body had decided to generate, today of all days.

The room buzzed as if the walls had been invaded by a swarm of bees, but the room did not smell of honey. It had overtones of books, canvas totes, and coffee. Lots and lots of coffee. The mocha Saffi had gulped down earlier pulsed in her veins. She hoped it would give her the boost she needed to get through a talk irrevocably altered by this morning's tragedy.

Fia's introduction had been meant to settle the crowd. She had delivered a brief bio of Saffronia Graywood, AKA Aunt Saffi. She had shared the North Coast Booksellers Association's excitement about the keynote. As promised, Fia had said, the best-selling author of *Aunt Saffi's Bedside Reader* would divulge the secret to creating books that sold millions of copies.

Saffi gripped the podium, nerves jangling as if she clutched a live wire. Fia's introduction sounded like this would be just another keynote speech. *Impossible.* A man had been found dead just a boardwalk away from the Necanicum Room where the audience now sat, waiting expectantly for Saffi to say something—anything—

to allay their fears. They wanted to be reassured that the death on the bridge had no connection to the convention. They wanted to feel safe as they listened to speakers and browsed books. Most of all, they wanted to hear that the death had been a tragic accident.

Saffi glanced at Poppy and Willow, sitting in the front row, either to show their support or catch her if she crumpled to the floor. She supposed they thought their stiff smiles looked encouraging. They did not. They looked grim. She glanced at the notes on her iPad, pasted a smile on her face that probably looked just as funereal. Then she scanned the room, capturing eyes as she connected with her listeners.

"I don't know about the rest of you, but by about sixth grade, I was convinced that nonfiction was a snoozefest. All those dry-as-dust textbooks, right?"

She saw nods and smiles, but also confusion. Was the keynote speaker going to leave them in the dark? Ignore the Surrey-cycle-sized elephant in the room?

"Then I discovered *Ripley's Believe It or Not*. It was filled with nonfiction trivia, a sideshow I couldn't look away from. I started digging around to see if the things I was reading could possibly be true. They were, and I was hooked. Ripley's taught me the key to best-selling trivia books. Share true stories that will instantly capture a reader's attention."

Audience members shifted uncomfortably in their seats. It was time.

"Many of you are aware that a tragedy happened on the bridge overnight. An event that began with a jingly jaunt around town ended—for one person—in death." The murmur rose as if the bees had begun to swarm. Saffi moved her lips close to the microphone and spoke slowly. "It's hard to look away, isn't it? Almost impossible to concentrate on anything else, to listen to someone speak."

Saffi swiped her iPad to the page of notes she had typed out just after she and Troy returned from the bridge.

"I promised you keys for creating a number one trivia book. Maybe you think I should stop right now. Pause for a moment of silence." She paused, but only for a second. "The key to my *Bedside Reader* is simple: I pay attention to what captures *your* attention. Newspapers are known for choosing front-page stories using the formula, if it bleeds, it leads. When disaster happens, we can't look away. It's perverse, isn't it? The way we creep past the scene of an accident. Play and replay those 'fail' videos. Watch the towers fall on nine-eleven, again and again and again."

She had achieved her moment of silence. Not a single person whispered or squirmed or stood to leave.

"Would you like to know what people in our nation's capital did when Union and Confederate troops clashed for the first time in the American Civil War? Senators, representatives, reporters, and ordinary people trekked to the battlefield to gawk. They brought opera glasses and picnic baskets. They watched and nibbled sandwiches until—horror of horrors—panicked soldiers fleeing the field overran their position. That's how the First Battle of Bull Run got the nickname 'the picnic battle.'

"Like me," Saffi continued, "some of you may have raced toward the bridge in the early-morning chill, anxious to discover what had happened. Was it just a Surrey cycle left behind on the bridge causing a traffic backup, or had someone been hurt? If one of your friends or colleagues hadn't shown up for breakfast, fear might have coursed through your body. Was that person safe?"

Heads drooped. Hands folded. People glanced at those seated beside them, looked over shoulders to spot colleagues in the crowd as if to reassure themselves.

"Science credits—or blames—the amygdala for making us slow down and take in the details of an accident, a disaster. Or, in this case..." Saffi paused. "A murder." She watched for reactions as a wave of understanding washed across the room. Saffi's brain had already absorbed the shock of what she'd seen on that bridge. Now, it wanted data. Who paled? Who squirmed? Who half stood as if ready to flee?

Poppy stiffened, then uncrossed and recrossed her legs. Willow paled even more than she had earlier when Saffi shared the news.

She had walked toward the promenade alone after the banquet. What had she seen, or done? Jemma Weathers, seated front and center, crossed her arms and set her lips in a scowl.

The biggest reaction came from Fia. She slipped from her seat just behind Saffi and skirted along the wall toward where George and Eileen sat at the back of the packed room. Was she thinking of last night? Of abandoning a man in a black hoodie to rush inside the Carousel Mall?

"The amygdala," Saffi went on, "triggers our survival instincts. We pay close attention because we need to know how, or whether, the danger we perceive will affect us. Will that little skirmish in Manassas, Virginia settle the Civil War, or will the death toll surpass all other wars combined? Should we duck and cover? Raise our fists to fight? Should we run for the exits?" Saffi waved toward the exit doors.

Almost as if on command, convention security officers pushed the double doors open. Fia whirled, eyes wide as blue-clad police officers marched inside, some going to the left side of the room, some to the right, and one up the center aisle. Some audience members gasped, some laughed nervously, a few clapped as if the men in blue were part of Saffi's presentation. But when the tall officer who strode up the center aisle turned to face the room, his ruddy face grim with determination, the hall went silent again.

The officer took off his hat, ran a hand across his buzz-cut ginger hair, wiped sweat on his pants leg, and tucked the cap beneath his arm. "Ladies and gentlemen, my name is Eric Boyd. I'm police chief here in Seaside. I apologize for any inconvenience, but due to a possible threat to public safety, this keynote is canceled."

Saffi's heart lurched as she watched another ripple of shock sweep across the room. People turned in their seats, some started to stand, to look around, to reach for bookbags and purses. The chief made a sit-down motion with both hands. "We will get you out of here as soon as possible, but first we'll need to check IDs and ask a few basic questions."

Eileen Esterhaven leapt from her seat in the back corner. "What kind of questions?" she demanded.

"Basic," the chief repeated. "Where are you staying? Where were you last night between midnight and two a.m.? Can anyone vouch for you?"

As the entire audience realized they were being asked for alibis, the room erupted. The chief ignored the uproar. Instead, he walked to the end of the first row. When he stopped in front of Poppy and Willow, Saffi's heart stuttered.

"You, you." He pointed at Poppy and Willow, then turned back toward the podium and pointed at Saffi. "And you. Please follow my officer upstairs." He waved forward a young policewoman.

Saffi was not surprised that Chief Boyd had singled them out. She had known this moment would come since she angled past looky-loos and police officers on the Broadway Bridge this morning. She had pushed forward for a glimpse of what the bread truck driver had seen inside the Surrey cycle but instantly regretted the impulse. Inside the Surrey sat a man wearing a black hoodie, head cocked back, tongue swollen past his lips, eyes wide with shock. The string of holiday lights wrapped tightly around his neck had purpled his skin to the color of a rotten plum.

Jay GoodVender.

She had wanted him gone. Out of the convention. Out of her life. She had briefly considered jabbing a ballpoint into his jugular, but that had been hyperbole. This? This was murder.

NINE

Saffi shifted her bottom on the uncomfortable plastic chair, waiting her turn outside the command post set up in the convention center's Sunrise Room. When the door opened, she half stood, then froze as a pudgy man wearing a blue jacket over a striped button-down shirt rushed out of the room. His gray comb-over looked like it had been plastered to his head by sweat. His cheeks were the color of boiled lobster. As he strode past, the gray legs of his slacks scrubbed against each other and Saffi realized she had seen those round cheeks somewhere. The ones on his face, of course. Not his backside.

Really, Saffi? Jokes? At a time like this? She ignored the jab. If her inner voice didn't understand the value of sophomoric humor in stressful situations, it could just clam up.

"Ms. Graywood?" Chief Boyd called from inside the room. "Come in, please."

Saffi took a deep breath. Imagining herself in tai chi's mountain pose, feet grounded in Earth, she breathed in confidence and credibility. She breathed out timidity and tension. Then she strode into the Sunrise Room, headed for the brown laminate table, pulled out a hard blue plastic chair across from Chief Boyd, and took a seat.

The spectacular view of Tillamook Head just past the chief's shoulder should have captured her attention, but she could not take her eyes off the intensity and intelligence in his pale blue eyes. She clasped her clammy hands in her lap to prevent nervous fidgeting, which she knew from her own sleuthing made even the innocent look guilty.

A green folder sat on the table in front of him. A half-filled coffee mug sat within reach. He offered Saffi the same—convention center drip—but she politely declined. When he opened the folder, Saffi was surprised to see quite a few sheets of paper. One of them was a photocopy of the front of the ARC Lowry & Lowenstein had handed out at the booth. Another was a photocopy of the cover of Jay GoodVender's bogus *Original Bedside Reader*. The chief flipped through several other pages, slowly, as if he wanted Saffi to see them. To her surprise, one sheet was a flyer from an event so far in the past it was a miracle anyone remembered it. Saffi remembered. It was from the East Coast Booksellers Association Convention where she had debuted her self-published *Bedside Reader*.

When the chief turned it over to reveal the next page, he tapped the pale pink forefinger of a natural redhead on a yellowed newspaper clipping: *Local Polymath Hosts Nonfiction Panel*. The photo showed a panel of four authors plus the host, a much younger—but instantly recognizable—Jay GoodVender. Two of the panel members were familiar faces—authors she still ran into at conventions, one face she no longer recognized. The fourth? She saw the fourth panel member in the mirror every morning.

"Where did you get that?" Saffi leaned forward, struggling to read the upside-down copy.

The chief grasped the corner of the article as if she might snatch it and tear it to bits. "You knew the victim, Jason Verkaufen." It was a statement, not a question.

"Who?" She shook her head in bewilderment.

"Perhaps you knew him by his pen name, Jay GoodVender."

Jason, not Jay. Verkaufen, not GoodVender. *Really?*

"No! Yes, I mean, I know the name GoodVender." Saffi pursed her lips. *Loose lips sink more than ships, Saffi.* She tried to stop herself but the anger she'd held in for so long tumbled from her mouth like projectile vomit. "He's been stalking me on my blog for more than a year, and, more recently, in person. Yesterday, the delusional, bloviated egotist showed up at my book signing to taunt me in person!" Saffi clenched her hands in her lap and let her eyes tell the chief what she didn't dare put into words.

Oh, boy.

"Bloviated. *Hmm...* Never thought I'd need a dictionary to solve a murder." Chief Boyd opened a laptop, then looked at Saffi. "Can you please state your full name?"

Saffi would not be distracted. "The housekeeper at the Necanicum Inn? Marisol? I'm pretty sure GoodVender attacked her. He was *not* good people."

The chief lifted his eyes from the keyboard. "Thank you, Ms. Graywood! I was hoping an amateur sleuth would come along and solve that case for me."

What did a heart attack feel like? Pressure on your chest? Bulging eyeballs? Being unable to catch your breath or utter a single word? If so... Saffi was definitely having one.

"GoodVender told me you fancied yourself a sleuth."

"What else did he tell you?" Saffi could not keep her voice from rising. "That I pay attention to details? Did you even notice the red stains on the housekeeper's fingertips? She was *chloroformed* shortly after spreading petals that looked like they'd been dipped in blood across the bed in my suite. GoodVender was behind the whole thing. I'm sure of it!"

Chief Boyd didn't even blink. Instead, he looked back down at his laptop. "Solving crimes is difficult, Ms. Graywood, and it is dangerous, especially for amateurs. That said, I will be happy to take your statement about the attack on the housekeeper once we finish *this* statement. Shall we continue?"

Here we go again! This wasn't Saffi's first time on the wrong side of a police officer's desk during a murder investigation. The last time, her lack of motive had kept her out of jail. This time? Saffi licked her lips and gave Chief Boyd what he'd asked for: her name. "Saffronia Graywood."

"Middle name?"

Saffi shook her head. She didn't have one, but it might as well have been "Motive."

Over the course of the interview, Saffi learned that upon his arrest, Jay GoodVender had produced a folder of information that he claimed would prove her theft of his intellectual property. During that long-ago panel, he'd told the chief, he had shared his outline for *Jason Verkaufen's Book of Fascinating Facts* which he'd been working on for more than a decade. Saffi had used his outline to morph her own "amateurish" trivia book into *Aunt Saffi's Bedside Reader*. GoodVender swore that Saffi would do anything to remain on the *Bedside Reader* throne, including pushing to have him unjustly arrested.

"Would you, Ms. Graywood?" The chief scratched the line etched into his forehead from years of wearing a hat with a band too tight for his head.

"Would I what?" Saffi took the obtuse route.

"Do anything?"

Instead of answering, she pointed at the green folder. "Jay GoodVender just *happened* to have that folder on his person last night when the security guards arrested him?"

"He did."

The little slimeball. He had stood there on the boardwalk in full view of the guards. He had taunted them. Dared them to come for him. Then he had waited at the rail, making sure Saffi—and everyone else at the banquet—watched his arrest. Handing over the folder to the police had been his plan all along. Then he'd told the police what must have seemed like a plausible story about *her* stealing *his* series idea.

Ridiculous! The *Bedside Reader* concept had been hers since the first self-published edition. She didn't need to kill GoodVender to protect her career, although... if someone had not beaten her to it, right now she would be sorely tempted.

"So what?" she demanded. "GoodVender showed you that folder, which is clear proof that the man has been stalking me, and instead of locking him up, you let him *go*?" Saffi put as much censure into her honey-brown glare as she could muster.

Chief Boyd closed the folder. "The security guards were outside their jurisdiction. They handcuffed a man for standing on a public boardwalk. We had no reason to hold him."

"That's unfortunate, since someone out there wanted him *dead*."

The chief's mouth fell open in disbelief, but Saffi had reached her limit. She scraped back her chair and stood. "Now that I've answered your questions, I'll be on my way."

The chief stood as well. "I have no reason to detain you at this time. But I have a folder full of reasons to require you to remain in town until further notice."

"Not to worry, Chief. I have a convention to finish. Now, if you could tell me where you're keeping my editor?"

The chief's pale ginger brows furrowed. "Your editor?"

"Poppy Morales."

"Ah." The chief tapped the folder on the table. "Of course. We are holding her at the station on suspicion of murder in the first degree."

Saffi wobbled out of the Sunrise Room, head spinning so hard she had to clutch the person standing just outside.

"Saffi? What's wrong? Are you OK?"

Saffi blinked and took slow deep breaths to stave off the vertigo before glancing up at her savior. "Willow?"

The young woman put an arm around Saffi's shoulders and guided her to a nearby seat. Then she pulled an unopened bottle of water from her *Bedside Reader* tote and unscrewed the cap. "Here. Drink this. You look like you've seen a ghost or something."

Saffi sucked down the water like it had come straight from the Fountain of Youth. Her brain kicked in to tell her that folks who drank from the legendary fountain in St. Augustine, Florida did not grow younger. They either grimaced and gulped or spit out the nasty sulfur-scented stuff. The *Bedside Reader* factoid stopped her head from spinning. After screwing the cap onto the nearly empty bottle, she told Willow what the chief had shared.

"Poppy? Arrested?" Willow whisked the curtain of blond bangs out of her eyes with a finger. "I should call New York." She stood suddenly, blue eyes filled with concern, but before she could march away the door to the Sunrise Room opened. Chief Boyd stepped outside.

"Willow Durst?"

The young assistant's spine stiffened. "Yes?"

"If you please." The chief held the door open.

Willow's blue eyes held the first hint of desperation Saffi had ever seen in them. "Your signing! We left the booth trashed yesterday."

She patted the assistant's arm. "Don't worry. I'm on it."

"Tell Reese I'll be there as soon as I'm done."

Reese was Poppy's current intern. According to Willow, his flight to Portland yesterday had been delayed. He had made it to Seaside late last night but missed the entire first day. "And call New York!" Willow's voice rose to a very unladylike level as the door to the Sunrise Room began to close behind her.

The minute the door shut, Saffi pulled out her cellphone. She called the Manhattan office of Lowry & Lowenstein, gave the receptionist her name and demanded to be put through to the publisher. The twenty-something on the other end of the line sounded skeptical. "Hold, please." Saffi listened to about five seconds of smooth jazz, then the young woman was back on the line. She apologized profusely for putting Saffi on hold and transferred the call. It didn't take long to explain the situation.

Bob Lowry hadn't made it to the top of a publishing company letterhead by hesitating to do whatever needed doing. "Don't worry, Saffi. We'll have her out of there this afternoon. In the meantime, if there's anything I can do for *you*—anything at all—don't hesitate to call."

Beyond getting Poppy out of jail, Saffi could not think of a single thing her publisher could do. But there was something *she* could do. Something she absolutely had to do! Catch GoodVender's *real* killer. And she knew exactly where to start.

TEN

To find the culprit, you must know and understand the victim. The quote from an FBI profiler's tell-all book repeated in an endless loop as Saffi thumped down the stairs to the first floor. She had about a half hour to get into the exhibit hall and examine Jay Good-Vender's booth before her noon book signing. If she was lucky, the local cops would not have realized they needed to tape it off. She stopped at the bottom of the stairs to catch her breath and assess the scene.

If the exhibit hall had looked as secure when Saffi arrived at the trade show as it did now, she would not have wasted a second worrying about Jay GoodVender. Uniformed police officers stood at parade rest at every door. Security officers in gray uniforms or black hoodies checked every convention badge at the exhibit hall entrance, comparing the name on the badge to the person's government-issued ID. The rules had apparently changed. No ID. No entry. Badge or no badge.

The scrutiny the guard in the black security hoodie gave Saffi at the door to the hall reminded her of TSA officers the time she'd flown out of LAX after a bomb scare. She returned the scrutiny. The scruffy-haired guard looked familiar. She pictured him in dark sunglasses, then nodded.

"You're one of the guards who arrested that guy outside the banquet."

His neck and cheeks reddened as if he'd mainlined cherry Kool-Aid. Before he could say anything, Saffi gripped his hand like it was a fishing pole with a tuna on the line. She squinted to read his name tag. "Zach? I hope you don't mind if I call you Zach." She didn't wait for a yes or no. "I just have to thank you." She shook his hand and released it. "The cops told me you screwed up, but you didn't. That man was dangerous. He'd been stalking me for a year. If not for you..." Saffi met his startled eyes with her warmest honey-brown gaze, hoping to gain his confidence and fish for information. "I don't know what he would have done."

The young guard's blush deepened. "I, uh. You're welcome." He flexed his hand to release the fingers she had cramped.

"Small-town cops, huh?" Saffi shook her head.

The guard shuffled his feet. "Naw. They're cool. My uncle Eric said we acted rashly, but I kinda think he was proud." He offered a lopsided grin.

"Why do you think that?"

The guard shrugged. "He said he admired our initiative. Then he said if I ever wanted a badge like his I'd better cut the crap."

"Uncle Eric, huh? He's a police officer?"

Zach's chest puffed out. "The chief."

The chief! Jackpot! "Zach." Saffi stepped close enough to invade his personal space. "Have you heard about the woman they arrested? You know, for killing that guy?"

Zach literally twitched as his good sense warred with his desire to impress her with his insider knowledge. "I might have heard a thing or two."

Saffi understood the power of the pause. She waited.

Zach spilled. "Some hoity-toity New Yorker."

"Really? Your uncle must be Super Cop. I don't think I've ever seen such a quick arrest."

"Don't have to be super anything to catch a killer who tells a buncha people she's gonna murder a guy who ends up dead."

Saffi's chest tightened. A corridor filled with people *had* witnessed Poppy's threat to murder GoodVender. "People make threats they don't mean all the time."

"True that." Zach rolled his shoulders and stepped away as if growing impatient with the conversation, anxious to scrutinize more badges, or afraid she'd grab his hand again. She asked her last question before he could squirm away.

"So why the rush to judgment?"

"Miss Hoity-Toity didn't have sense enough to take her engraved pen with her after she'd done the deed."

Oh, Poppy! You didn't.

The minute the thought crossed her mind Saffi smashed it under a metaphorical boot heel. A black widow of a thought. A betrayal of the worst kind. The only thing Poppy had ever killed was a foul sentence or a bad article that even Saffi had to admit deserved to die. Poppy was her rock. Her champion. The person who had put the weight of a publishing company behind the *Bedside Reader* series and kept it there, doing the heavy lifting of promotion and bookselling so Saffi could roam the country in her RV and write. Poppy would do anything for Saffi.

Anything, Saffi prayed, short of murdering the competition.

A wisp of memory tickled Saffi's brain. Something about Poppy's pen. But when Zach waved her into the exhibit hall, the tickle wriggled away like a minnow.

Saffi hurried to the back aisle, nodded to Jemma who glanced up from signing a book for a buyer, and made her way to Jay Good-Vender's booth. She was too late. Yellow police tape wound around the booth in such a haphazard fashion Saffi wondered if Zach and his buddy from last night had done the honors. GoodVender's author poster had been crisscrossed with yellow tape, something he fully deserved for what he'd done to her poster in the lobby. Strangling him was a bridge too far, but... the man had made his own karma. As Saffi stood there considering playing Twister to wiggle her way inside, footfalls in the aisle made her turn.

Jemma had stopped just behind her, green eyes as hard as glass, hands on both hips. "Guess you don't have to worry about that chum ball anymore."

"I wish." Saffi shook her head. "He seems to be trying to bring me down from beyond the veil."

Jemma's brows twitched upward in question.

"They arrested my editor. Without her, I don't know what will happen to my books."

Saffi quickly realized how callous that sounded and cringed. "Not that it's about me. It's about her. She didn't do it, and I'm going to prove it."

Jemma studied her for a moment, then nodded. "I have a feeling you could do just that, if you put that fine mind of yours to it."

Warmth spread through Saffi's chest. "Thanks, Jemma. For everything. Including yesterday." She linked her arm through Jemma's and walked her back to her booth. A half-stack of *Mermaids at Midnight* waited for buyers that might or might not show up with the convention in such disarray. "I'm glad you still have a copy." She picked up a book and opened it to the title page. "Would you sign it?"

Jemma grinned. "Nothing would make me happier. Who shall I sign it to?"

"Aunt Saffi, of course!" Saffi rustled in her sling bag for a twenty and a five. Jemma grinned her gratitude.

Watching Jemma inscribe the book triggered the minnow of memory Saffi had been unable to grasp earlier. When she had signed books for her banquet table companions last night, Poppy had been unable to find her engraved pen. She had been frustrated with Willow, wondering if her assistant had taken it. Willow swore she didn't have it.

Perhaps, Saffi mused, someone had walked away with it during the signing that afternoon. Someone who ended up in GoodVender's Surrey cycle. Who had the opportunity? Fans had been swarming the table. The guy from the chamber had been snapping photos. GoodVender had been at the booth. It would be just like him to steal Poppy's pen out of pure spite. Then there was Jemma.

Saffi glanced at the weathered fisherman's daughter. The kerfuffle between the memoir author and GoodVender had provided quite a distraction. Anyone—Jemma included—could have taken the pen then, either accidentally or on purpose. Maybe one of the people standing around the booth wanted to frame Poppy for a murder they had already planned to commit.

Rein it in, Saffi. You were the one clutching the pen like a weapon.

Too true, and she had signed every ARC with it. Except... as Jemma thumped the fine-tipped red Sharpie she'd used to sign her memoir against the table, Saffi realized that wasn't true. Willow had taken Poppy's pen when she erased Saffi's note to Jay on the title page. Saffi had re-signed the final ARC to Jemma with a red Sharpie someone had handed her. For the life of her, she couldn't remember who.

After Jemma handed over the signed memoir, she grasped Saffi's free hand and squeezed. "Don't let that sleaze burger's death get you down, Aunt Saffi. Some men just need killing."

ELEVEN

Saffi did her best to school her face and tamp down the shudder Jemma's words caused. As she took her leave, she could almost feel the memoir burning her hand. *Some men just need killing.* Those were gut-level words, grounded in experience. Had the fisherman's daughter just become the number one suspect in Jay's death? Saffi didn't know, but she had a feeling the book she grasped might hold clues.

With the clock ticking down to book-signing time, Saffi headed for Lowry & Lowenstein's center aisle booth. A young man hunched listlessly in a chair in the back corner, thumbs scrolling double time on his phone. The intern, Reese, Saffi supposed. Was he *job hunting*? Or simply killing time? He hadn't even bothered to pick up the sticky notes and stray papers that lay scattered across the floor. If Poppy had not been behind bars, Reese would be on the next flight home.

When Saffi cleared her throat, he jumped to his feet as if she'd fired a starting pistol.

"Aunt Saffi! You're here." His gaze darted left, then right. "I, uh…" A flush rose up his neck.

"Hi, Reese." His eyebrows rose as if he couldn't believe she knew his name. "How's it going?"

"Dead." The word escaped before he could stop it. He clapped a hand across his mouth as if to stop whatever had tried to follow.

Though convention-goers packed the hall, they hurried past the L & L booth like it was a crime scene. Jay GoodVender had done Saffi more harm by getting himself murdered than he had ever done while alive. It was all she could do to stop herself from screaming in frustration.

"I need to look for something Poppy might have left here yesterday." Saffi found it hard to believe Poppy's pen had been discovered in the Surrey cycle. Maybe it was a different pen. A different person Named *P. Morales*.

"Sure. Of course. Of course." Reese shuffled his feet as if unsure what to do next.

Saffi pawed through the bags and boxes Poppy and Willow had left behind yesterday, hoping to find the red lacquer pen among the bits and bobs. After a few minutes, she had to accept that Poppy's pen had not been left in the booth. The one found in the cycle had to be hers.

They had anticipated a crowd after Saffi's keynote. Attendees usually rushed to beat one another to the front of the keynote speaker's signing line. Talk of textbooks, amygdala, and authors strangled in Surrey cycles had certainly been a buzz kill.

Saffi put her hands on her hips and scanned the booth. What would Willow have been doing if she wasn't being grilled by the police chief? Besides boxes of ARCs and last year's annual reader, Poppy had brought plenty of Aunt Saffi swag. Rolled posters, postcards, bookmarks—all branded with the Lowry & Lowenstein logo and featuring the soon-to-be-released spring *Bedside Reader*.

Saffi pulled a rubber-banded stack of bookmarks out of a box and rubbed the embossed logo with her thumb. The whimsical book-reading L & L lion had always made Saffi smile. She fanned the bookmarks out on the table, then turned to Reese. He nervously adjusted the expensive-looking designer glasses perched on his slightly bulbous nose, pursed his lips, and blinked.

"Willow will be back soon," Saffi said. "You might want to—"

She waved a hand at the disorganized booth. "I'm signing at noon." She glanced at her watch, then lifted her wrist so Reese could see the numbers.

"Eleven fifty!" Reese startled like a squirrel. He darted toward the table, then froze as if he'd spotted a car barreling toward him. Saffi followed his gaze to the exhibit hall entrance where Willow had just reached the door. Zach glanced at the assistant's badge and reached for the ID she held out.

Reese zipped back and forth across the booth grabbing bits of trash from the floor and stuffing them into an empty box beneath the table. Next, he pulled a box cutter out of his back pocket and sliced through the tape on an unopened box of books. By the time Willow reached the booth, he had loaded the table with freebies, ARCs, and copies of the previous year's *Bedside Reader*.

Willow flicked her cascading bangs off her forehead. Her gaze swept across the booth, then landed on Reese. "I see you took Poppy's advice to stay off your cell while you're in the booth. Great job cleaning and restocking." She gave him a brisk nod, but her lips quirked up in a somewhat affectionate smile. Perhaps she saw him as *her* protégé rather than Poppy's.

Reese eased out of Willow's view then pressed his hands together and mouthed, "Thank you!" at Saffi, who compressed her lips to hold back a grin.

As Willow stowed her tote and arranged two chairs behind the table for herself and Saffi, Reese pulled the "author signing" poster from behind the chair he'd been loafing in earlier and set it up on a tabletop stand beside the books. To kill time and try not to think about just how quickly her career might croak without Poppy, Saffi turned to Willow. "How'd it go with Chief Boyd?"

Willow wrenched her hair around so it fell over one shoulder, crossed her long perfect legs and laced her fingers together to grasp her knee. "He let me know that the solo walk I took after the banquet means I don't have an alibi."

Saffi had thought the same thing. She looked down, but Willow must have seen suspicion in her eyes.

The assistant's cheeks reddened and she pounded her fists on her thighs. "Going after us is absurd! Arresting Poppy? They're not even looking for the real killer, are they?"

Saffi lifted her hands. "If they're still interviewing people, they must be collecting clues. And clues"—Saffi twirled her pointer finger in the air—"can lead *away* from a suspect as well as *to* one."

For example, to you... or to me, for that matter. Saffi kept the thought to herself.

"Saffi." Willow leaned over her knee to get closer and lowered her voice. "You can fix this, right? I mean, you've already solved two murders far more complicated than this one."

OK. Maybe Willow wasn't guilty. Guilty people seldom wanted sleuths on the case.

Saffi shook her head. "Honestly, I stumbled over the truth both times."

Willow straightened. "I do not believe that for a second. You're Aunt Saffi. Tracking down the truth is what you do."

Saffi licked her lips. "There is something I've been trying to figure out," she admitted. She couldn't think of a single reason for Willow to strangle Jay or frame her boss for his murder. But if she was going to keep Poppy out of jail, she needed to track down who had left the editor's red pen in the Surrey cycle at a dead man's feet.

"I knew it! You're already on the case!" Willow's blue eyes sparkled.

Arrgh! How could she trace Poppy's pen without betraying Willow's trust? She couldn't. Saffi took a deep breath. "A source told me that Poppy was arrested because they found her pen in the Surrey cycle." Saffi waited a minute for that to sink in, then she tapped the young assistant's knee. "The engraved pen Poppy was looking for at the banquet? The one you borrowed from me to erase the inscription I wrote to Jay."

"Me?" Willow squeaked. "You can't possibly think I—"

Before Saffi could answer, a book plopped down on the table. "Would you please sign this to 'my favorite fan.'"

The familiar rugged voice warmed the chill now coming off of Willow, and Saffi smiled up at Troy. "I'm sure I can come up with something more, uhm, personal." Heat rose in her cheeks as she thought of possible options.

Troy bent closer to her level, a North Coast Booksellers Association staff badge dangling from his neck. "Yes, please."

Saffi tugged the badge as she half stood to give him a peck on the cheek. "Change of career?"

"Eileen gave it to me. Apparently, the guards won't let anyone in without one. Especially if they're with the *Bedside Reader* party. Bunch of criminals, or so I hear."

Willow bolted from her chair. "We most certainly are not!" When she glanced at Saffi, her blue eyes held betrayal instead of trust.

Way to go, Saffi! The worst part of sleuthing was pushing people she liked as hard as those who set her teeth on edge.

Troy's quirky smile morphed into a frown. "Everything OK?"

Saffi itched to reassure Willow. She also craved the assistant's answer to her question about Poppy's pen. Both would have to wait. As soon as she signed Troy's book, a line appeared behind him, as if by magic. Willow snatched a pad of sticky notes and a red fine-tip Sharpie from the table. She marched from person to person with a stiff back and a shaky-faky Ivy League smile pasted in place as she took names for inscriptions.

Troy glanced at Saffi, worry shadowing his eyes. When she mouthed, "Tell you later," he saluted with the book. "Catch you after I catch some fish, Aunt Saffi."

As the signing line spooled past, it didn't take long for Saffi to realize that, today, murder was the main draw. If fans weren't asking her point-blank what she knew about the competitor who had died on the bridge, they were talking about it among themselves. The ones who had met Jay yesterday afternoon and purchased one of his books already knew how full of crap his claim to have written the "Original" *Bedside Reader* had been. They quickly disavowed others of the notion that Saffi might have bumped him off to avoid a lawsuit.

"GoodVender was a total poser," said a plumpish young woman with bright blue hair. The people on either side of her agreed, but a fussy man wearing a Mr. Rogers sweater over a T-shirt and black jeans leaned toward Saffi.

"He was trying to destroy your career, wasn't he? Seems like a whale of a motive for murder." His high-pitched tenor cut through the chatter and heads turned his way.

Saffi froze, Sharpie poised above a signature, as the whole line went silent. It was a legit comment. After all, the first murderer she had helped put behind bars had been trying to protect his career.

"I call dibs on that motive for my next mystery!" a female voice broke the silence. Uneasy laughter rumbled along the line.

"It's all yours!" Saffi finished signing the book and returned it to the blue-haired fan with a smile, but her mind kept spinning. By now, the fact that Jay GoodVender had come to the convention to destroy Saffi would be pinging around the exhibit hall. His author poster, his book covers, his promise to "reveal the truth" about the origins of the *Bedside Reader* during the Saturday panel. If Saffi couldn't throw doubt into the trade show rumor mill, her reputation, and Poppy's, would be ground to powder.

Right now, the L & L team would top everyone's suspect list but who belonged on Saffi's list? Willow? Surely not. Poppy? *Please, God, no.* Saffi pushed away the flicker of doubt. After a red-eye flight followed by a day of convention and conflict, her editor had gone back to the inn and fallen asleep. But without someone to provide an alibi—and with her engraved pen found on the floor— she might as well have "GUILTY" stamped across her forehead.

If it wasn't someone connected to the *Bedside Reader*, then who? Her stalker had only been in Seaside for a few days, at most. Could he have driven someone gull-crap crazy that quickly? Someone whose temper exploded. Someone who grabbed a string of lights, wrapped them around Jay's throat, and squeezed until his neck turned purple.

"Saffi?" Willow brought Saffi's attention back to the table and the next fan waiting anxiously for her to sign.

"Sorry." Saffi pushed her sleuthing self to the side and bent to the task at hand.

The line remained steady for the rest of the hour. Saffi fielded questions, pooh-poohed suspicions, and reassured supporters, especially booksellers who dropped by to make sure this year's *Bedside Reader* would not be Saffi's final one, as Jay GoodVender had intimated on her blog. By the end of the hour, Saffi felt like she had run a gauntlet of readers, each of whom had taken a swing at her with a hardback the size of her *Reader. Ouch!*

Friday's lunch plan had included Poppy as well as the rest of the Lowry & Lowenstein crew. Without her editor, Saffi did not have the heart to follow through. She made her apologies to Willow and Reese, then asked Willow to check in with the New York office. "See if you can find out when a lawyer will show up. We need Poppy out of jail. Now!"

Saffi didn't realize how jittery she was until the memory of what she had seen this morning made her turn right where the boardwalk met Broadway to avoid crossing the bridge, instead of left toward the inn. She passed a wooden building so weathered a puff of breath would probably knock it off its pilings into the river. Two jagged red planks, one above the other, identified the place as the Bridge Tender bar. If she'd been the type to turn to whiskey to settle her nerves, she'd have headed inside, despite the early hour. Since she wasn't, she kept walking.

Broadway was Seaside's main tourist drag. She passed one souvenir shop after another as well as several ice cream parlors, a fudge shop, the Carousel Mall, and an arcade blasting the sound of alien invasions into the street. At the next corner, she spotted a sea-blue restaurant with a tiered tower meant to mimic a lighthouse. The menu board outside featured her favorite seaside lunch special —chowder, fresh-baked bread, and salad. This was the place.

A harried server stuck a pen behind her ear and ushered Saffi toward a booth on the back wall. Once she gave her order, Saffi realized eating solo was a mistake. With no one to talk to, clues started darting like flies in her head. She could walk and think, practice tai chi and think, doodle and think, but, for Saffi, thinking required her to do something, anything, besides just sit. She dug out her cellphone and opened the notes app.

The clue-flies landed on a fact: Jay GoodVender had done something to put his neck in a strangler's grasp. But what?

She tapped the app to start a numbered note. It looked a lot like a *Bedside Reader* listicle—one she would never *ever* publish.

How to Become a Murder Victim

1. Stalk someone until they're so terrified they strike first.
2. Threaten to destroy someone's career so they have to destroy you first.
3. Trigger someone's protective instincts.
4. Discover a secret someone wants to stay buried.
5. Be a first-class yellow-bellied weasel to everyone you meet.

Saffi imagined a police officer writing suspects' names beside each of those actions. "Saffi Graywood" would be written beside numbers one and two. If she had actually stolen GoodVender's original *Bedside Reader* idea, number four would apply as well, but that had happened in his warped head, not in the real world. And then there was number five. Given Jay's behavior, that could be anyone at the convention, or in the whole town, for that matter, Saffi included.

She started adding names beside each item in the list to keep track of who seemed most likely to have turned Jay GoodVender from obnoxious stalkery perp to murder victim.

She reluctantly typed Poppy's name beside number two alongside her own. Then she added Willow and Reese. Any Lowry &

Lowenstein employee might have felt threatened by Jay's vow to ruin Saffi. Despite the fact that her publisher was successful and well-established, her annual *Bedside Reader* had been their number one bestseller for nearly two decades. When book sales faltered, junior staff like Willow and Reese were usually the first to go.

Beside number three? Saffi took a deep breath before typing "Troy." He had bristled over Jay's treatment of Saffi and made an unfortunate comment about what he would do if he got his hands on her stalker. Last summer during a murder investigation, he had shown himself to be excessively protective of his half-sister and his niece. Now... his urge to protect might extend to Saffi as well. Coincidences happened, but Troy chasing after Jay as he cycled across the bridge? Then *strangling* him? That defied even Saffi's overactive imagination.

When her lunch special arrived, it was special indeed. The clam chowder was every bit as yummy as what Delilah served at Last Chance Café, creamy and packed with tiny potato cubes and tender clams. The bread was fresh-from-the-oven warm with a satisfying crunch to the crust. The salad was standard restaurant fare, but the poppy-seed dressing kicked it up a notch, as well as almost making her cry into her iceberg lettuce. Every poppy seed made her think of her editor.

Poppy! In jail. Her chic suit rumpled. Her hair unkempt. No cellphone. What kind of godawful food would they be trying to force on her? Saffi pictured a soggy bologna on white bread sandwich with limp lettuce and a razor-thin tomato slice. She could hardly choke down the thought, much less another bite. After wiping her mouth with her napkin, she caught the waitress's eye, paid her check, and headed into the chill of a winter afternoon by the sea.

If things had not gone sideways, she would be spending the afternoon in the exhibit hall browsing other booths for trivia books that might compete with her own. Why not? Saffi owed it to Poppy to not just sleuth, but soldier on. Do the things she had come here to do. Act... what did those vapid life coaches everyone quoted say?

Act "as if." She could do that... act *as if* Poppy would be released instead of facing charges. *As if* her career would continue to be nurtured by the best editor in the business. *As if* Jay GoodVender had not died because of his threats against Aunt Saffi and her *Bedside Reader*, despite the lunch list that pointed directly at the Lowry & Lowenstein team.

TWELVE

From the seafood restaurant, Saffi headed toward the statue of Lewis and Clark in the middle of the Broadway turnaround. In 1804, when the famous explorers set out to discover what lay west of the Missouri River, US President Thomas Jefferson fully expected them to encounter woolly mammoth herds, giant sloths, and—bizarrely—a native tribe that spoke Welsh. The president's suppositions had led to an article for *Bedside Reader*, #4 and they still made her grin like a kid.

The expedition hadn't found any of those things, of course, but the explorers *had* found exactly what they needed not far from where Saffi now stood: an endless salty sea. Expedition members had boiled seawater to extract salt for preserving meat, which kept them from starving to death on their return journey. Was research fun, or what?

The sky above Seaside's wide sandy beach bobbed with kites. They tugged against strings held by "kids" of all ages, from toddlers to elders. Saffi tracked the kites' long tails as they whirled in the wind, dipped toward the beach, then spiraled upward as their guiding strings went from loose to taut and back again. After a few minutes enjoying the show, she rubbed her hands together to warm them and glanced at her watch. *Back to the convention!*

Once the lunch hour ended and the afternoon convention sessions began, the exhibit hall crowd would thin. Saffi could check out the competition without, she hoped, the eyes of suspicious convention-goers tracking her every move the way she'd tracked the kites.

She headed north along the concrete promenade to 12th Avenue, the road her map app said would allow her to walk off her lunch and loop her back to the inn to freshen up. Once she reached 12th, she spotted Surrey cycles, just like the one in which Jay GoodVender's body had been found. After the cycles crossed the 12th Avenue Bridge, they turned left into a parking lot.

"The Sea King Bike Shop," Saffi read the sign. The shop's adorable logo showed a fish holding a trident and pedaling a bike.

As she crossed the bridge, Saffi slowed. How *had* Jay Good-Vender ended up strangled in a Surrey cycle? Fia had been in charge of the Jingle Tour cycles. Surely she would not have given one to the banned bookseller. If she hadn't, he would have needed to rent one himself, perhaps hoping to weasel his way into the Jingle Tour. If Saffi asked the right questions, she might find the answer in the bike shop.

A bell above the door jingled as she made her way inside. The frizzy-haired blonde in a blue vest behind the counter glanced up with a smile. "Looking for a bike?"

Best to tell the truth, Saffi decided, but hide her suspicions. "I'm in town for the booksellers' convention." She gave the woman behind the counter her most "I am not up to anything unsavory" smile. "I think an acquaintance rented a Surrey cycle here yesterday. Jay GoodVender?"

The woman's gaze sharpened, and her lips pursed. "If he rented a Surrey in Seaside, this would be the place, but GoodVender? The dead guy?" She pointed at her blond hair. "Don't let the color fool you. It's fake."

"Sorry." Saffi's smile slid toward contrition. "You got me. I'm after information, not a bike."

The woman barked out a laugh. "You've got smooth gears, lady.

Which is more than I can say for that GoodVender guy. A first-class jerkoff, that one."

Saffi held out a hand. "I'm Saffi Graywood."

"Enid Seamans-Atwell."

After they shook hands, the woman grinned. "Never met anyone at the top of Chief Boyd's list of most likely murder suspects."

Saffi stepped back in shock. "Me? If I'm at the top of his list, why did he arrest my editor?"

The woman did a "come closer" move with her pointer finger. "If I know the chief, and I do because he's my hubbie's best bud, he's hoping you'll do something rash. Dumb even." She shrugged. "But he hasn't read those readers of yours for years like I have."

"Oh." Saffi beamed. "Well... thank you?"

The woman nodded. "So, you want to know whether Jay rented a cycle here."

"Yes." She pressed her lips together, raised both brows, and waited.

"I'll tell you the same thing I told the chief. GoodVender came in here right before we closed and demanded a four-seater. I told him Larry had donated the whole kit and caboodle to the chamber of commerce for the Jingle Tour."

Saffi's eyes widened. "That's incredibly generous."

"No biggie." The proprietor waved away the compliment. "Larry's head of the Chamber and he loves doing the Santa thing during the Jingle Tour."

The Santa thing? Of course! Larry had been handing out promotional brochures and taffy last night.

"Besides," the woman went on, "it's good publicity. Once you find out how much fun those Surreys are, you can't resist renting one yourself."

Unless you'd seen a dead guy strangled with fairy lights in one. Saffi tried not to grimace.

"So Jay didn't rent a cycle from you?" she probed.

Enid rolled her eyes heavenward. "The guy went *ballistic.*

Ranting and raving and pacing the floor. Demanded to speak to the proprietor. Larry came out of the workshop and gentled him down. Has a way with folks, does my Larry. Told GoodVender he had a Surrey in the back with sticky gears if he wanted to wait." She quirked her finger and Saffi leaned closer. "Did more than wait, didn't he? Stormed into the workroom and yammered Larry's ear off while he worked. I charged him three times the usual rate for being such an entitled arse."

"He wanted it badly enough to pay that?"

"He did." The woman grinned.

Now, *that* was interesting.

"What time do you close?" Saffi asked.

Enid shrugged. "Depends. This time of year, it gets dark around five. When the sun goes down, we lock up."

That meant Jay had rented the cycle not long after his altercation with Saffi. By that point, he had been banned from the convention. What had he been up to?

Saffi's detour to the bike shop put her behind schedule, but what she'd learned had been worth it. GoodVender had rented a Surrey cycle. The triple price he paid meant he was up to no good. No one would pay that amount to tootle around town of an evening. He had been planning something. Most likely something meant to harm Saffi. If so, his plan had backfired, in a deadly way.

When Saffi opened the door to her suite, a cloud of steam surrounded her. The sound of a running shower and someone whistling a slightly sour version of a familiar tune turned her toward the bedroom. "Troy?"

The plastic shower curtain rustled, and a soaped-up head stuck out. "Back so soon?" Troy wiped foam from his eyes.

"Just freshening up before I do another round of the hall."

Troy retreated behind the curtain. "Then I can keep my whiskey date with Scott."

Saffi laughed. "You can. But drink one for me, would you?"

"Yes, ma'am!" He hollered, then went back to whistling.

Saffi recognized the "Drunken Sailor" sea shanty, despite Troy's tendency to be slightly off-key. She had last heard it sung by the piratical but vocally gifted Bill Kidd at the New Year's bonfire. She brushed her teeth then wiped steam from the mirror to touch up her minimalist makeup. A brush with the mascara wand, a puff of dusty rose on her cheeks, and she was done.

"Gotta go!" she called toward the shower.

Troy's head emerged again for a sloppy, wet, soapy kiss. Much as Saffi enjoyed it in the moment, she feared she would be tasting soap for the rest of the day. Before heading outside, she zipped her down coat over her keynote attire in anticipation of cooler weather after sundown.

Walking always pumped enough oxygen into Saffi's brain to turn stuck wheels. As she crossed the bridge, she let her mind flow elsewhere, not to the horror of what had happened to Jay, but to why it might have happened and who was most likely to have wrapped those fairy lights around his scrawny neck.

What about Jemma? Jay had fallen victim to her once, but knockdown by convention tote was a long way from murder. She had, however, made a point of saying that some men needed killing. Had she been justifying her own actions? Or letting Saffi know that if someone connected to her *Bedside Readers* offed the obnoxious man, well, he deserved it.

Poppy? Much as she wanted to cross her editor's name off the list, Saffi couldn't. At least, not without honestly considering the clues that pointed Poppy's way. Poppy had been livid from the moment she saw Jay's "Original *Bedside Reader*" booth. She had threatened to murder him. Her pen had been found in the Surrey cycle. She had plenty of motive, but no alibi.

The man singing in the shower? Despite his tendency to be over-protective and whistle off-tune, Troy was good to his bones. Besides, if he wanted to do Jay in, he would drown him. He'd told her that himself. Saffi wasn't sure why the memory felt like a huge relief, but it did.

Willow? Uber-efficient, stylish, always ready with a perfect mocha when Saffi needed it. Absolutely not. Saffi wouldn't allow it. And Reese? If he had made it to Seaside before midnight, he might have run Jay's Surrey cycle over in a fit of fatigue, but he had no reason to strangle a man he'd never met.

Saffi shrugged out of her coat as she reached the double doors into the convention center to let her badge fly free. The security guard in the gray uniform from Thursday afternoon waved her through without an ID check. The brouhaha at the Lowry & Lowenstein booth must have been enough to stamp her into his memory bank.

As she headed toward the hall, Saffi spotted Fia's dangling black braids approaching the exhibit hall door. *The North Coast Booksellers Association reps!* Just like Saffi's team, they had come into conflict with GoodVender. Eileen had been frantic when the guards in security hoodies tackled Jay on the boardwalk. Saffi had seen "potential lawsuit" in the woman's eyes as she had rushed from the banquet. George? The only thing remotely suspicious about George was his man bun. But Fia? After helping a line of tipsy convention attendees into cycles, Fia had hopped into a four-seater with someone wearing a black hoodie. Now that Saffi knew Jay had been freed shortly after his arrest, she wondered... had it really been one of the young security guards? Or had Fia joined Jay in his rented cycle? And if so... why?

One of the two young guards stood at the exhibit hall entrance, checking IDs. Saffi leaned sideways to get a better view of his interaction with Fia. No knowing looks. No snarky grins. No lingering eye contact. The guard simply took Fia's ID, glanced at her face, looked back at the ID, then returned the card to the young woman and nodded her into the hall. Either they didn't know each other, or they were Broadway-caliber actors. That left Zach—the guard who'd told her about Poppy's pen being found in the Surrey cycle —or Jay as Fia's companion for the Jingle Tour. Given the heated argument they'd had and the way Fia left the cycle mid-tour, the latter was a definite possibility.

Once past the guard, Saffi scanned the exhibit hall. She had planned to scout booths for competitive titles, like the hard-at-work author her editor expected her to be. That did not happen. The minute she entered the room, a mass of people entangled like a wormball in front of the Lowry & Lowenstein booth caught her eye. *What the heck?*

The minute she asked the question, she knew the answer: *Poppy was back!*

THIRTEEN

"Poppy!" Saffi shouted and smashed her way through the moving mass. She nearly knocked her editor off her feet in her excitement. Luckily, Reese had positioned himself at Poppy's back to keep the worms from circling behind her and braced her before she toppled.

"I can't believe you're here!" Saffi squealed. "I mean, Bob Lowry said he would get you out but... I just—" She wrapped her arms around Poppy before she remembered that her uber-chic editor was *not* a hugger.

For once, Poppy did not back away. In fact, she clutched Saffi as if she were the last life preserver on the *Titanic*. When she finally let go, they both straightened, sniffed back tears, and pasted professional smiles on their faces. Poppy tugged her ivory wrap Chanel jacket over her black slacks. Saffi wrestled her red scarf into place and checked to make sure hugs and static cling had not hunched her fox-print dress up her hips. Then she reached for Poppy's hand, gave it a squeeze and leaned forward. "Don't worry. I'm going to find the real murderer. I promise."

Poppy's eyes went hard. "When you do, I'd like to give that perp a piece of my mind. I feel cheated. I wanted to take down that lying bastard myself."

Saffi glanced at the crowd milling behind her, hoping no one else had heard Poppy's proclamation. When she turned back to Poppy, her editor's eyes were sparkling. "In the courts, Saffi. Legally." She chuckled. "I finally get to see that suspicious mind of yours at work. My name is on the top of your suspect list, isn't it?"

When Saffi couldn't meet her eyes, Poppy patted her shoulder. "Good. It should be." She turned Saffi toward the listening swarm. "Don't fret, folks. The one and *only* creator of *Aunt Saffi's Bedside Reader* is on the case. If anyone can solve this murder, Saffi can!"

Talk about over-promising! Poppy had always droned on and on about "under-promising" and "over-delivering."

"Give them more than what they expect, by even the smallest amount, and your readers will love you," Poppy had told her time and again. But this time, she was promising something Saffi might *not* be able to deliver.

As the thought crossed her mind, Chief Boyd strode past the booth, hat clutched against his armpit sweat. His gaze swept the scene, stopped for a moment as if searing Poppy's location into his brain, then took in the others gathered behind her: Willow, confident and composed; Reese, nervous and fidgety; Saffi, clutching her arms across her chest as if they might protect her from the suspicion in his pale blue eyes.

Did he really think Poppy murdered Jay? Or did he think Jay's green folder pointed in a different direction—to Aunt Saffi, the person who appeared to have the biggest motive for murder? Maybe the chief had shown up to see how Saffi and her editor interacted. Were they close? Or had Saffi planted the engraved pen on the Surrey cycle's floorboard to incriminate Poppy?

Poppy might have over-promised, but if the chief wanted to pin the crime on Saffi, she would have to deliver. For her editor, and herself. And if she didn't want to get stuck in Seaside for who knew how long, she would need to find the killer before the trade show ended Sunday afternoon.

Suddenly, perusing books did not seem like the best use of her time. Getting answers to questions would be. What had Jay been up to when he rented that Surrey cycle? Had anyone seen him join the tour? As the person in charge of the Jingle Tour, Fia seemed the most likely prospect to find a few answers.

Saffi found Fia at the booksellers association booth in the entry hall. Her box braids had begun to fray as if the frazzled fawn had nervously run a hand over her head one time too many. When she spotted Saffi heading toward her, Fia's brown cheeks reddened. If the young woman hadn't reacted to Saffi the same way when she met her yesterday morning, she would have thought Fia had something to hide.

"How are you handling all of this?" Saffi waved an arm as if taking in not only the convention center but the whole town.

Fia folded her hands over her belly—a protective move if Saffi had ever seen one—and looked down. Her eyelashes were as long, thick, and dark as any deer's and Saffi didn't detect any cosmetic enhancement. She looked like a natural beauty who had not yet grown confident enough to own her own power.

"Things seem to be getting back to normal," Fia said when she finally looked up. The glint in her eyes could have been a reflection from the wall of glass across the way or a glimpse of something jagged and sharp behind her demure behavior that Saffi had yet to deduce.

"They do. Especially now that Poppy is back in our booth where she belongs."

Fia's brows shot up in surprise. "They let her go? After she kil—" She bit her lip as if realizing just how much Saffi might resent her acceptance of Poppy's guilt.

Saffi was never one to pass up a chance to catch a suspect off-kilter. "You were on the Jingle Tour last night, weren't you?"

"I-I... the tour was for convention attendees. Not staff." Fia stumbled over what seemed to be a lie of omission.

"Don't worry. I won't rat you out to Eileen." Saffi waited, giving Fia time to admit she had jumped into a Surrey cycle with someone when she should have been working. Fia clasped and unclasped her hands but said nothing.

Saffi knocked on the table. "I saw you."

Silence.

"I was in the Surrey cycle behind you. You were riding with a guy in a black hoodie. One of the young security guards, perhaps?"

Fia blinked. Licked her lips. Thoughts chased across her dark eyes. "He, uhm, had his own rental. We didn't take one meant for attendees."

Notably, Fia hadn't said who "he" might be.

"I see." Saffi leaned forward. "The only reason I ask is..." She looked side to side as if checking for anyone who might have stopped to listen. "I wondered if you might have seen Jay Good-Vender out there. I think something he did last night got him killed. So, if you saw anything—like Jay harassing someone else the way he did me—that could be a clue that would help catch a killer."

Fia's dark eyes widened. "Jay was arrested during the banquet. You saw it yourself. How could he have been on the tour?"

Jay. Fia and Jay were on first-name terms? *Don't jump to conclusions, Saffi.* As the convention program assistant, Fia would have greeted all of the exhibitors and done what she could to keep them happy.

Saffi pulled her convention badge taut. "Chief Boyd told me Jay was released right away." *Right after he turned over that incriminating green folder.* The lanyard from which her badge hung dug into the back of her neck as she unconsciously wound it. Saffi let go before she could give herself a rope burn.

Fia shifted from foot to foot but said nothing. Clearly, she was hiding something. Whether it was an unsanctioned assignation with a cute security guard or a confab with a sleazy stalker who'd been kicked out of the convention, Saffi didn't know. But if she didn't press harder, she would never find out.

"Look, Fia. Jay rented a Surrey cycle from the bike shop. I talked to them earlier. Did you see him? Or not?"

Voices broke the bubble of quiet that surrounded them as doors opened and convention sessions ended. Attendees flooded into the corridor, chatting excitedly about new books, debut authors, and the latest upgrade of the most popular inventory management system.

Fia grabbed a stack of programs and moved from behind the table. "If you'll excuse me, I need to..." She waved the stack toward a group of attendees slowing to a stop in front of the booksellers association booth.

As Saffi walked away, she realized that Fia had not shared a smidge of information. She had deflected every question so deftly that someone less suspicious than Saffi would never have noticed. She was hiding something, but slacking off her job still seemed more likely than murder.

She should talk to Eileen next, try to get a better sense of the association president's management style. If Fia's hesitation stemmed from fear of the association's president, rather than something more sinister, Saffi wanted to know.

She snagged a convention schedule from the association booth and ran a finger down the sessions. Eileen would have just finished moderating a panel on bookstore author visits. Saffi hurried down the corridor to the room listed in the schedule, but Eileen and the other panelists were still at the front, swarmed by attendees. Clearly, this was neither the time nor the place, especially if Saffi didn't want to embarrass or alienate the woman who represented some of her best-selling outlets. Unlike previous cases, this one burrowed into the heart of her own world. If she did not handle it with discretion, she would be helping Jay GoodVender take her down from beyond the grave.

The last convention session ended as the afternoon waned toward evening. Bedraggled attendees hauling bags bulging with books broke into groups of two and three as they headed for the exits. Saffi had failed to find an appropriate time to talk to Eileen but hoped to touch base at the after-hours Mix and Mingle at the local independent bookstore, Beach Books.

After showing her badge and ID at the exhibit hall, Saffi swam against the stream to reach the Lowry & Lowenstein booth. She wanted to touch base with Poppy before she headed back to the inn, but her editor wasn't there.

"Poor Poppy." Willow's perfectly highlighted hair waterfalled around her face as she shook her head. "Spending all day in that awful jail! With nowhere to sit but a cot with a horrible soiled mattress infested with l-lice and b-bedbugs and all kinds of other vermin. Rats, probably. I can't even imagine." She hugged herself as if bugs might crawl on her at any moment.

Saffi stiffened. "Wait. She told you that? Lice and bedbugs and rats?"

Willow's blue eyes narrowed. "No. Of course not. But you know Poppy. She would never admit those things had come anywhere near her perfect self."

Funny, Saffi thought. Willow saw *Poppy* as the perfect one. What was it that made all women see themselves as "less than" others? Saffi sighed.

"How about a drink?" Saffi nudged Poppy's dispirited assistant. "I spotted the funkiest old bar you ever saw by the bridge. My treat."

Saffi thought Willow would beg off, opting for a long walk to stretch out the kinks of a day spent stuck inside. Instead, she perked up. "A drink is exactly what I need!"

Reese was dead on his feet after yesterday's drive from Portland, so they parted company with the intern outside the Bridge Tender. Saffi opened the heavy wooden door to a wood-paneled space that reverberated with noise. Locals bellied up to the bar and convention attendees crowded the tables tucking bookbags beneath their chairs. Willow commandeered a small table with a view of the river just as two women gathered their things to leave. As a frazzled busboy cleared, spritzed and wiped the table, Saffi draped her down coat over the chair, hoping it would keep the wooden chair's cracked leather seat cushion from nicking her fox-print dress or leggings.

As she eased into the chair, she caught sight of a woman with sea-kinked red hair and a fearless grin perched on a stool at the end of the bar. The woman caught Saffi's eye and saluted with a foamy nut-brown pint. "I see you found the OG place for a wind down."

"Jemma!" Saffi waved. "You made it out of the exhibit hall alive." She clenched her teeth when she realized how crass the comment sounded, but Jemma snorted.

"Barely. How are you two doing, considering?"

Instead of answering, Saffi glanced at Willow. She hoped the question in her eyes would convey her wish to have Jemma join them. When Willow's mouth pursed in a kittenish mew of displeasure, Saffi leaned close and whispered, "I have a few questions I would love to ask Jemma once she gets to the bottom of that beer."

Willow's eyes widened. "You want to sleuth? Count me in!"

A few minutes later, Jemma had clacked her convention tote across the floor and pulled up a chair to join them. When the server showed up, order pad in hand, Jemma greeted her like an old friend. "Hey, Debbie my girl. Treat these two like locals, would you? None of those super-sized tourist prices, OK?"

"Anything for you, Mama Jem."

"Wait!" Saffi slid back in her chair. "Is this your daughter?" She was a bit surprised, since Debbie looked native and Jemma most certainly did not. The minute she had the thought, she cringed. Some natives wore their lineage in their skin and hair. Others... not so much. Coastal Oregon had so many tribes Saffi couldn't keep them straight. In this area, if she had to speculate— and she probably shouldn't—Debbie was most likely Tillamook or Siletz.

Jemma grinned. "Ain't she a beauty?"

She was, even wearing a stained bar apron over a Bridge Tender T-shirt with her thick jet-black hair braided down her back. Debbie looked twenty but her slightly hardened air made Saffi wonder if she was older than she looked or just jaded from serving one too many drunks. When she rolled her eyes at Jemma, she looked more like a teen. "What's it gonna be, ladies?"

Willow cocked her head to look up at Debbie. "You wouldn't have Fifty Stone single malt, would you?"

"Nope. Got McCarthy's. That do ya?"

"I guess I won't know unless I try it. Bring it on." Willow had the kind of smile only money could buy, perfectly straight and whiter-than-tooth-enamel white. When she let it loose, it lit up the dingy bar like floodlights on a trawler.

Much as Saffi would have loved the instant heat of a shot of single malt, whiskey would put her under the table after two sips. She ordered a half-pint of raspberry cream ale and ignored the other women's derisive hoots. The trio sipped their drinks as book-ish-looking men and women flowed in and out of the bar like the tide in an estuary. Local workers getting their pints on before going home trickled in and out of the mix. The room filled, then emptied. Filled, then emptied.

As they talked, Saffi discovered that Debbie and Jemma weren't blood relatives. "She's my best friend's daughter. I'm her foster mom. But, really I'm the only mother she's ever known. I've raised her since she was knee-high to a seal's nose. After her mom..." Dismay washed across Jemma's face and her lips clamped tight.

Saffi reached for Jemma's weathered hand and gave it a squeeze. "I'm so sorry. I lost my husband just over three years ago. If I hadn't had my writing, I think it would have wrecked me."

Jemma rubbed the moisture from her eyes. "What took him?"

Saffi stared into the foamy dregs of her ale. "Sudden heart attack. It was..." Saffi took a deep breath. "Unexpected."

"I wish I'd lost Helen quick like that."

"Cancer?" Some cancers came with a long, slow, unbearably painful death.

Jemma clasped the glass handle of her pint so tightly her knuckles turned white. "No. She disappeared. *Poof!* Like she'd never existed. Helen was younger than Debbie is now. Just as beau-tiful, inside and out. Cop in charge of the case had a racist streak whiter than a skunk's stripe. Wrote her off as a runaway mom, not ready to raise a kid. I call shark shite on that one.

"Thing is, Helen was a foster kid herself. She lost her parents in a freak landslide on the 101. When she got pregnant, she got kicked out of the system. Dad and me took her in, stuck with her till the baby came." Jemma stopped talking long enough to drain her beer. "Helen was gobsmacked over that kid. She would *never* have left Debbie behind." Her pointer finger stabbed the air.

Saffi's gaze flitted to Willow. The younger woman's pupils had widened in shock and her lips trembled as she pressed them together. "Was she... taken?" Willow whispered.

"Could have been. Indigenous women going missing isn't exactly new, is it?"

"I don't—" Saffi hesitated, then shook her head. "I'm sorry, Jemma. I don't know as much as I should." She had written about all kinds of horrible happenings in history. Her books included plenty of articles meant to shock, to enlighten... but doing a deep dive into the exploitation of indigenous women and writing about it for a book meant mostly to entertain? Could she do that? Should she? No.

Jemma suddenly hefted herself out of her chair. "I need another pint. Can I get you anything?" She glanced from Saffi to Willow, but both shook their heads.

Saffi had tucked Jemma's memoir into her Lowry & Lowenstein convention tote. She resisted the urge to pull it out and thumb through while Jemma waited for her pint at the bar. *Mermaids at Midnight* was a whimsical, magical title but the life story within the book's pages was probably far darker than she could have imagined. Dark enough, Saffi realized, to make a woman think some men needed killing.

Mentally, she put Jemma's name beside Troy's as a protector. The fisherman's daughter carried deep anger, deep pain, as if the perpetrator who had taken her friend had never paid the price, but somebody needed to pay. The person who had strangled Jay Good-Vender had to have been strong enough to both overpower and strangle the man. Jemma's sinewy weathered hands when she returned to the table with another pint looked capable of doing the deed. But would she?

If Jay had threatened Debbie, Saffi had no doubt Jemma's protective instincts would have kicked in. But the way she had taken Jay down yesterday afternoon made Saffi think Jemma had no need to kill him. She had shown him to be a petty tyrant. Easily toppled. Unless, Saffi mused, he had done something that equated him with her friend's abductor in her mind. If that had happened, Jemma's anger and pain could very well have morphed into murder.

FOURTEEN

When she returned from drinks with Willow and Jemma, Saffi stretched out on the sofa in front of the living room fireplace with her sock-clad feet in Troy's lap. She wanted to relax, maybe take a quick nap, then grab a bite to eat before the Beach Books Mix and Mingle. But she also wanted to fill him in on the case. She started with that and by the time she finished, he had eased her feet off his lap and leaned forward.

"Saffi, Poppy's out of jail. The police are on top of this. You really don't need to—"

Saffi held up a hand. "Let me stop you right there. Poppy being freed doesn't have anything to do with whether the police think she did it or not. The publisher hired a lawyer. That's why she's been released.

"And if that's not reason enough, Chief Boyd has a file Good-Vender gave him. A file that makes it look like *I* have the biggest motive for killing Jay. I have even more of a vested interest in finding the killer than before." As she spoke, her chest began to ache and it wasn't just because her heart rate had kicked up. It was because the look in Troy's eyes said he wasn't buying her reasons.

Troy pushed the fingers of both hands through his slate-gray curls. "It's just... you keep getting caught up in murders. Charging around asking questions. Putting yourself in danger. It's like, wherever you go, murder follows." He shook his head.

Troy's dart hit a bullseye right over her heart. "You didn't mind me putting myself in danger when it helped Nicole." He knew very well that her sleuthing had kept his sister from being charged with murder last summer. Saffi had also thwarted the kidnapping of his niece and a plot to kill him and dump his body at sea. The more she thought about it, the more heat pounded through her veins.

"I know. I know." Troy took a deep breath as if giving himself time to collect his thoughts. "The thing is... I barely knew you then. Now, when we're here... together... I don't know. I feel like I should be protecting you!"

OK. She could understand that. She felt the same kind of urge to protect Poppy, and Willow, and even Reese from whoever was out there killing people. "Troy, I can understand why you might feel that way." She reached for his hand. "But I *really* don't need you to protect me."

Troy stood, stretched his arms toward the ceiling, rolled his shoulders and walked toward the flickering gas fireplace before turning to face her. "I know you don't. Before I met you, I had this idea that writers were namby-pamby artsy-fartsies."

Wow. Saffi pressed her fists into her thighs and narrowed her eyes. "I take it you mean weak? With our heads in the clouds?"

"Sorry. It's easy to stereotype when you don't really know people." His Montana-sapphire eyes sparked. "You're not weak at all, Saffi. You're one of the strongest women I've ever met. That's one of the things I appreciate about you. It's also why I think you'll understand when I tell you what's going on with Scott."

Scott? How did his pilot friend fit into what had begun to seem like a "will this relationship work" conversation? It didn't take long to find out. Apparently, Scott's visit with Amanda had soured.

"I really wanted to stay through the weekend, but the poor guy didn't get a wink of sleep last night. All five of Amanda's minions piled into bed with him. He was all but crying in his whiskey this afternoon. I don't think he'll last till Sunday afternoon." Troy paced in front of the fire, keyed up, anxious about the situation with his friend and wondering what he should do if Scott decided to fly home in the morning. "I mean, he invited me along to keep him company." He stopped pacing to scan the room. "If he leaves, what am I supposed to do all day? Cool my heels in the suite while you sign, schmooze, and sleuth?" He raised both brows.

"Got it." Saffi had hoped for a whole weekend together, but if Scott vamoosed in the morning, who was she to try to convince Troy to stay?

"Trust your gut." She let a wan smile cross her face. "That's what I always do."

At the moment, Saffi's gut was prodding a memory. Last summer, when she ran toward a body floating in the Elk Creek Estuary, Troy had run in the opposite direction. If he flew back to Last Chance Cove with Scott in the morning, he would be leaving her to deal with the repercussions of Jay's murder on her lonesome.

You just told him you didn't need protecting! Her inner snark pushed back.

Yes. She'd done that. So why did she suddenly feel as if the world had been pulled out from under her? And why did her gut warn her that, despite the very romantic holiday season she had just shared with Troy—she was essentially as alone as the day Levi died in that campground at the foot of Devil's Tower?

Streetlamps lit the way as Poppy led her crew along the sidewalk to the bookstore a few blocks down North Holladay. Despite Seaside being a tourist destination, most shops shuttered at six in the offseason. The only people on the street seemed to be conventioneers heading to the same place they were.

Glenn, her favorite cookie baker back in Last Chance Cove, had once said he saw her as part of Last Chance Cove's tribe of "outsiders." He hadn't meant non-locals. He had meant artists, writers, bakers selling cookies out of vans, and middle-aged baristas. People content to live outside the mainstream. She had agreed then, and she still did. But really... the tribe gushing over books and authors as they excitedly made their way to a mixer at a *bookshop*? Those folks had been her peeps for as long as she could remember. She felt at home among them, far more at home than she had felt when she parted company with Troy in front of the inn. She was off to the mixer. He was headed to movie night at Amanda's. His goal was to keep Scott from being piled on by the minions and, even more, to keep his friend from permanently alienating his sister.

She understood. She did. To Troy, a bookstore mixer would be the equivalent of scraping barnacles from the bottom of his boat. A necessary evil, but one he would do anything—including watching *Sing 2* with five people under the age of ten—to avoid.

"Aunt Saffi!" Footsteps hurrying up behind Saffi made her turn. "Oh, my gosh. It *is* you!" The blue-haired young woman who had called GoodVender a poser caught up and matched her steps to Saffi's.

"And it's *you*!" Saffi tilted her head toward the young woman. "Except, I'm sorry. I signed an ARC for you, but I don't remember your name."

The young woman pulled her badge away from her heaving chest and turned it so Saffi could read it. "Lyndie!" she huffed.

"Nice to meet you, Lyndie!" Saffi stopped for a second to zip her coat over the raspberry tunic and black leggings she'd changed into for the mixer. The breeze coming off the ocean was chillier than she'd thought when she first stepped outside. "I didn't get a chance to peruse the hall today. Did you spot any irresistible books?" Asking about new or favorite books was a sure icebreaker for bookish folks.

"Other than yours?" Lyndie grinned, then went on to describe book after book she planned to order for her bookshop, all, inexplicably, about animals.

Saffi's mouth fell open. "Wait. You own your own bookshop?"

To Saffi, Lyndie looked about as young as Jemma's foster daughter, Debbie.

Lyndie blushed. "It's just a hole in the wall right now. But we're hoping to expand."

"We?" Saffi glanced behind her as if she might spot an obvious match for the blue-haired girl. "You have a partner?"

Lyndie motioned someone forward.

"George!" Saffi recognized the third member of the North Coast Booksellers Association by his man bun and gray blazer, but tonight's turtleneck sweater was maroon instead of bone-white. "I had you pegged for one of those big Seattle indies like Elliott Bay."

Lyndie laughed. "Two years ago, you'd have been right."

George gave Saffi a shy grin and reached for Lyndie's hand. "Lyndie's from Portland. We met at the booksellers' convention when it came to Seattle a few years back. We both attended this *amazing* session Eileen offered about starting a niche bookstore. Turned out, we shared the same indie dream." When George nuzzled his nose into Lyndie's blue hair, Saffi realized the two were a lot more than business partners.

"Eileen helped us turn that dream into reality." Lyndie nudged a plump shoulder into George.

So, Eileen might not be the she-witch Fia's skittish behavior seemed to imply. If that was the case, why had Fia been so closed-lipped about the Jingle Tour?

"So, what's your niche?" Saffi kept the conversation going, hoping to learn more about Eileen, as well as their store.

"Animals!" the two shouted in unison.

They went on to describe their venture in far more detail than Saffi really wanted, given that her actual goal was to pump them for information. Their tiny bookstore, Tails and Tales, was not only pet-friendly—browsers could bring leashed, well-behaved pets inside—every book in the place was about animals. The store was housed in Portland's Alphabet district between a handicrafts emporium and a popular sushi spot.

"We're upstairs in one of the old Victorians," George said. "The space used to be the best tea house in town but it went belly-up during the pandemic. A shame, but the timing could not have been better for us. Portlanders love pets! And during the pandemic, everyone and his sister adopted a dog or cat from the pound."

"So did we." Lyndie grinned. "Roxy. She's a gorgeous Bengal kitty. Looks like a little leopard with a coat that's been dusted with gold. George does TikToks of Roxy pawing over her favorite books. She's become quite the little influencer."

When they reached Beach Books, Saffi realized she had fallen far behind her colleagues. "I loved hearing about Tails and Tales," she told the bookselling pair. "I hope we can talk again before the trade show is over." Before she went inside to find Poppy, she turned to George. "It sounds like Eileen helped mentor your store into being."

George squeezed Lyndie's hand and they both nodded. "Absolutely," he said.

"But, I, uh, kind of got the idea from Fia that Eileen is a real slave driver."

George's eyes widened. "Eileen Esterhaven?"

It was Saffi's turn to nod.

"A slave driver? No. Eileen is smart, a great problem solver, super organized and hard-working. She expects the same of Fia and me," George told her. "But Fia's flighty, so Eileen might be a bit tougher on her." He shrugged.

"George." Lyndie tugged her partner's hand. "If Fia's talking smack about Eileen, you should tell Saffi why."

Saffi cocked her head. "I'm listening."

George licked his lips. "OK. Look, Eileen blames Fia for Jay GoodVender being at this convention, and pretty much everything that followed."

Eileen blames Fia. The words reverberated in Saffi's head. "But... Eileen told me Fia fought for me to be the keynote speaker."

George nodded. "She did. And—I'm sorry, Saffi, but facts are facts—Jay came here for one reason. Because you were going to be here."

FIFTEEN

Determined not to feel guilty for something that was Jay GoodVender's fault, Saffi left the cool outside air for the oppressive heat of an overfilled bookstore. Booksellers, authors, fans, and publishing personnel twisted and turned in near unison, like a school of sardines trapped inside a fishbowl. The voices reverberating off the walls made Saffi want to cover her ears.

She barely got a glance of the frontmost tiered table as she was swept past, but she saw enough to know that it featured books from trade show authors and publishers. Copies of her most recent *Bedside Reader* sat on the top tier. *Nice!*

The store's center featured a five-sided sales counter with lots of space for special displays. Tonight, three of the counters had been cleared of books and impulse purchases. Hors d'oeuvres trays now took pride of place. Soon, every hand in the twisting, turning mass held a shrimp skewer, a brownie bite, or a glass filled with wine or sparkling soda.

Saffi spotted a few faces that had become familiar: besides George and Lyndie, she saw Jemma with Debbie at her side, Fia, Eileen, and... surprisingly, Chief Boyd. He was standing against the back wall pretending to page through *The Pacific Northwest Birdwatcher's Companion.* Clearly, he wasn't here to spot birds; he was here to keep an eye on suspects. Saffi determined to do her best to track who he was tracking, if he focused on anyone besides herself and Poppy.

Keeping track of anyone in the moving fishbowl turned out to be far more difficult than Saffi had imagined. After grabbing a shrimp skewer and a glass of what tasted like Grocery Outlet red, Saffi allowed herself to be swept from one side of the shop to the next. She tried to touch base with Poppy in the trivia section, but the school of fish swept her toward the mystery shelves. There, she had a brief conversation with a woman who owned a bookstore called Crime Pays.

"At least, it does for me." The woman grinned. Then she leaned close to Saffi, and whispered, "Just so you know, I've read enough mysteries to figure out that your editor didn't murder that guy. It's *never* the first person the police arrest."

Saffi could not argue with that. In books and on TV shows, a glaring spotlight usually pointed to a suspect right away. More often than not, that person was not the killer. The identity of the murderer stayed secret until the "big reveal" near the end. The sleuth rarely made the final connection until the killer had stuffed her into a car trunk or tied her to a chair or—as had happened to Saffi a few short months ago—locked her into a shed and set it afire.

In real life, "whodunit" seemed just as difficult to determine. In Saffi's two previous cases, her first clues had led toward the wrong person. The frustration she had felt sorting through clues that either went nowhere or led in the wrong direction had prompted her to start taking notes for a future *Bedside Reader* article that would feature stranger-than-fiction murders. The Pacific Northwest had some doozies. Her favorite, so far, was a self-published romance author who had written an online essay titled "How to Murder Your Husband." *All of us,* the writer had claimed, *are capable of murder... when pushed far enough.* She proved her own point when she shot and killed her husband of twenty-six years. What pushed her far enough? His 1.5-million-dollar life insurance policy.

Note to self: cancel life insurance policy.

While Saffi had been thinking, the Mix and Mingle tide washed her out of the mystery section and beached her at the feet of Chief Boyd. *Perfect timing!* The crime bookstore owner, Saffi mused, had given her a way to challenge the small-town chief's rush to arrest Poppy. At least, that's what she thought when she asked her first question.

"I was just talking to a mystery lover who pointed out that, in books, the person police arrest first is never the real villain. In your experience, is that true in police work as well?"

The chief clenched his lips together as he reshelved the birding book he had been clutching. "I won't know the answer to that question until this case closes."

It took Saffi a few blinks to get his meaning. "You've never investigated a murder!" She shook her skewer, unintentionally launching a shrimp at the chief. It smacked into his pristine white uniform shirt, bounced off, and landed on the toe of a boot that had just stepped into Saffi's peripheral vision. She glanced up: Eileen Esterhaven.

Eileen clapped. "Marvelous! Best performance of the evening." Then she reached down with a paper napkin and scooped up the shrimp. "Don't worry." She winked as she walked away. "I'll get rid of the evidence."

Saffi could feel just how red her face must be, but she blustered on anyway. "Is that why you arrested an incredibly talented, well-respected editor with no criminal history? Because you've never investigated a murder?"

"I did not say that." The chief pulled his shirt collar away from his reddening neck. "You did."

"So you *have* investigated a murder?" Saffi sipped her lackluster wine while she waited.

"Unfortunately, I have."

Saffi thought back through what she had asked and what the cryptic police chief had said. If he had investigated a murder but could not tell her if the person he had arrested had been guilty...?

"You investigated but never made an arrest."

"If you'll excuse me," the chief said. He stepped around Saffi and headed toward a door in the back corner with a restroom sign, either to avoid Saffi's questions or to clean the shrimp slime from his uniform shirt.

Once the chief stepped away, Eileen worked her way back to Saffi. "Did you get anything out of him?"

Saffi glanced past Eileen's shoulder. Fia stood a few feet behind the association president, head cocked as if trying to overhear what they were saying. There was little chance Fia would glean any information from anything Saffi said. The volume of conversation had not lessened. In fact, it had increased as people raised their voices louder and louder to talk over one another. Saffi squeezed her forehead, trying to ease away the beginnings of a headache. Then she met Eileen's eyes.

"The chief has investigated at least one murder, but this is the first time he has arrested a suspect."

Eileen crossed her arms and stared down at her boots as if thinking through the implications or making sure she had wiped away all evidence of Saffi's shrimp attack.

"That could be why he jumped to such a quick conclusion about Poppy," Saffi pointed out. "He wanted to nab someone right away. You know, to boost his reputation."

"Or..." Eileen mused, "he could have simply followed the clues and reached a logical conclusion. Only one person at this convention owns a pen inscribed *P. Morales.*"

Poppy's run-in with Eileen yesterday was probably coloring the association president's opinion of the editor. "But more than one person had access to that pen," Saffi said. "*And,* at the banquet, Poppy couldn't find it. That was *before* the murder."

Fia edged closer without Saffi noticing until she broke in with an opinion. "That could have been a ruse. Pretend to look for the pen. Make everyone at the table a witness to the fact that it's missing."

Eileen whirled on the young woman. "Fia! That is a totally inappropriate thing to say."

Fia threw up her hands. "How is it inappropriate? You just said Poppy's pen made her the most logical suspect. Didn't you?"

Eileen's face set into a scowl faster than quick-drying concrete. "Eavesdropping does not become you. Why don't you head out and take care of that little task I gave you?" By this point, Saffi would not have been surprised to see sparks flying out of Eileen's eyes. Fia fled, box braids jingling, before she got singed.

"I'm sorry. I don't know what has gotten into her." Eileen massaged her face as if to loosen the tightness in her chiseled jaw.

"What do you mean?" Eileen had given Saffi the perfect opportunity to engage in a discussion about her young colleague.

"She's usually very responsible, but she has dropped a lot of balls this time around." Now Eileen was manipulating the pressure points in her eyebrows with her fingertips. The association president seemed wound tight enough to snap.

"Mmm." Saffi hoped the hum would encourage Eileen to keep talking. It did.

"For one thing, she let Jay GoodVender's booth application slip by her. Somehow, she failed to notice that he had written 'The Original Bedside Reader' on the product description line. If I had been the one approving applications, he would never have set foot in the convention center."

"I wish you had been." Saffi took another tug of wine and tried not to grimace. For more than a year she had hoped Jay Good-Vender would go away. Stop stalking her. Allow her to RV from place to place without looking over her shoulder to see if he was following her. But she had *not* wanted the man dead. Just... far, far away from her life.

"Yes, well." Eileen sighed. "Lesson learned."

"So, Fia dropped other balls as well?" Saffi prodded.

"I see what you're doing." Eileen wagged a finger. "You're hoping to find someone who looks more suspicious than your editor. Someone acting out of character because she's, what? Trying to cover her tracks?"

"You caught me." Saffi looked toward the ceiling in contrition.

Eileen put a hand on Saffi's shoulder and squeezed. "I understand, but there's something you might want to consider."

"What's that?"

"Poppy Morales built her career on your success. Think about it, Saffi. Where would she be without *Bedside Reader*? A pen by itself doesn't amount to much. A pen plus a massive monetary motive? If I was Chief Boyd, I would have locked her up, too." The click of Eileen's boot heels on the wooden floor as she walked away sounded enough like certitude to poke the tiniest of holes in Saffi's belief in Poppy's innocence.

By the time the Mix and Mingle wound to a close, Saffi had talked to so many fans and booksellers, she sounded—and thanks to her headache, felt—like a bullfrog with a sinus infection. Poppy, Willow, Reese, and Saffi clutched their coats tight against the January night as they scurried back to the inn. Other than the swish-swoosh of the ocean and the giggly conversations of young convention-goers threading their way to the hotels lining either side of the river, it seemed as if the entire town had closed its shutters and bundled into bed.

A quick elevator ride took the Lowry & Lowenstein group to their respective floors—Reese to the second, Willow to the third, Poppy and Saffi to the fourth. Before they parted company, Poppy invited all of them to meet in the morning for breakfast before the exhibit hall opened. Willow had discovered a cute little coffee shop during her wanders and recommended it for their Saturday-morning meet-up.

When Saffi unlocked the door of her suite, she found the fireplace lit and the living room comfy-cozy warm. Troy's boots sat just inside the door and when she peeked into the bedroom, she saw him sprawled across the bed as if he'd fallen on his face and couldn't move. Though Saffi had never had kids of her own, she imagined that was what five of them on a movie night could do to a man.

Before joining Troy—if that was even possible given his sleeping position—she needed to decompress. She traded her raspberry tunic and black leggings for a pair of flannel pajamas, thick fuzzy socks, and the inn's equally thick white robe and cozy slippers. Bundled for the balcony, she slid open the glass door that led her out of the living room into the moist, fresh night air. Damp fingers tickled the back of her neck and shivered her shoulders. When they reached beneath the collar of her robe, she grasped it closed just beneath her chin.

She leaned against the balcony rail, trying to ignore the cold metal pressing into her midsection. The riverside looked far too tranquil to be flowing beneath a bridge on which a life had ended. Jay GoodVender, her stalker and nemesis, was dead. The police seemed to have collected a single piece of evidence: Poppy's engraved pen. There had to be more. On the first day of the convention, Jay had run afoul of a whole list of people. He had also, Saffi was certain, attacked the inn's housekeeper. Was Chief Boyd investigating the attack on Marisol? Or had Saffi's insistence that GoodVender had chloroformed the housekeeper given him a reason to close the case, now that Jay had been murdered?

The next time she saw Phyllis, Saffi would ask her if Marisol had identified Jay as her attacker. That proof should convince the chief that GoodVender had lied. The so-called "evidence" in his green folder showed his obsession—not Saffi's, or Poppy's, guilt.

The weariness in Saffi's bones made her feel as if days had passed, but she had woken this very morning to the blare of horns. She had rushed out to see what had happened in that Surrey cycle on the bridge. After that, the day had been a blur that started with her aborted keynote and ended with antagonizing the police chief.

As she gazed into the night, a light in the corner of her eye turned her toward Tillamook Head: the moon. The fat round globe emerged from a layer of thin, wispy clouds. A halo of bright white light encircled it, made—Saffi knew from researching atmospheric phenomena—of millions and millions of tiny ice crystals. It never ceased to amaze her that something too small to be seen by the naked eye, when multiplied, could create a picture too clear to ignore.

She wanted, no needed, the tiny bits of information she had spent the day gathering to form a picture of who had killed Jay GoodVender. So far, they revealed... absolutely nothing.

Beneath the moon's glow, a flash of movement turned her gaze to the opposite side of the river. A slight figure hurried along the boardwalk going from shadow to light to shadow as it passed beneath one streetlamp after another. To Saffi, the brisk, lithe gait looked like that of a young woman, but she couldn't be sure. She watched as the figure hurried up to the convention center, glanced over her shoulder, then pulled something out of her coat pocket. A few seconds later, the door opened and the figure disappeared inside. Someone with a key. A cleaner perhaps? Who else would go to the convention center at this time of night? Someone, Saffi suspected, who either wanted to find something... or make sure something would not be found.

SIXTEEN

Saffi grabbed the clothes she had shed earlier and dressed without making a sound. She left Troy splayed on the bed where she'd found him. *Poor Spudnut.* Saffi had conducted a weeklong writing workshop for middle and high schoolers at Vermont College almost every summer during Levi's tenure. Every evening, she came home to their petite Victorian and faceplanted on the bed exactly as Troy had done tonight. Kids, she had discovered, were energy vampires. They sank their fangs into adults and sucked out every calorie. That, Saffi had decided, was why they were so creative and the adults around them were too drained to put pen to paper.

The elevator arrived with a ding that reverberated down the empty corridor. Saffi hurried inside and pressed "L" for lobby. She expected the lift to go straight down, but it didn't. It stopped on the second floor and Reese stepped inside, staring down at his phone. When he looked up, his eyes went wide. "Uh... hi?"

"Burning the midnight oil?" Saffi teased.

Reese glanced back over his shoulder. "Please don't tell Poppy. Or Willow!" His eyes went wide. "Thing is, I met someone at the Mix and Mingle." His eyes went from slightly terrified at the thought of his colleagues finding out what he was doing to shimmering as if seeing a vision of loveliness in his mind's eye. "We're getting together for a drink at the Bridge Tender."

"Not to worry." Saffi winked. "Your secret's safe with me."

They crossed the Broadway Bridge together, both huddled into their coats and too lost in thought to converse. Just as they reached the bar, a raspy croak brought Saffi's attention to the post at the end of the bridge. *Raven. Again?* Saffi froze but Reese kept going. When the intern reached the weathered wooden door, he turned, grinned, and flipped her a wave. "Wish me luck!"

"Luck!" Saffi held up a hand, then, as Raven croaked louder, she folded her fingers so that only her pointer remained, asking him to hold on a sec. "Reese?"

Raven's obscure messages had never gotten any easier for Saffi to interpret. The bird could be warning her, leading her to a clue, telling her to pay attention, or... for all she knew... having a laugh at her expense. *Still.*

Reese turned back with the door halfway open. "Yeah?"

"When you got to the inn last night, did you see anything, uhm... suspicious?"

Reese chuckled. "Willow told me you were an amateur sleuth as well as a best-selling author. I thought she was pulling my leg."

Saffi felt a blush warm her cold cheeks, but forged ahead. "So, did you? See anything odd? Anything at all?"

Reese looked thoughtful. Music spilled out of the door he held open and wound its way across the bridge to Saffi: Bruce Springsteen's underground anthem "Born to Run." After a few seconds, Reese shrugged. "I remember being so tired I could barely stay awake. I missed the inn on the first pass and almost ran over an old dude coming out of the bar. And then, as I looped around the block to the parking lot behind the inn, I was pissed off."

"Why?" Saffi frowned.

"Those dingbat Surrey cycles were taking up most of the spaces. I had to drag my bag all the way from the back of the lot."

Right. The tour had ended there, probably because the inn was so close to the bike shop. "Did you see Jay GoodVender?"

Reese shook his head. "I wouldn't have known him if I had. Never met the man. Glad I never will."

Before Saffi could respond, a familiar dark-haired beauty stepped forward into the open door behind Reese. The young woman's unbraided hair fell in waves over her shoulders.

"In or out, handsome. You're letting January into the bar."

"Debbie!" The look on Reese's face told Saffi exactly who the intern had come here to meet.

Well, well. Lucky indeed. For a second, Saffi wondered if she should warn him what might happen if he messed with Mama Jem's foster daughter, but the door closed behind the couple before she could.

The raven on the bridge post croaked again and bobbed its head at Saffi. Maybe that post was the Seaside ravens' equivalent of the Bridge Tender, a neighborhood gathering spot, but for corvids on the make. Was the black bird simply hanging out on a Friday night hoping to find a mate? Was he keeping an eye on Reese? Or was he warning Saffi to turn around, go back to the warm inn and crawl into the comfort of Troy's arms?

She eyed the raven. "If you were *the* Raven, you would know me better than that."

She crossed the road, hit the boardwalk, and hurried toward the darkened hulk of the convention center. She should have been thinking about who she was walking toward—the mysterious person who had crept inside after dark—but the young couple's hookup at the bar made her think of Troy. Not about nestling in his arms. About what he had said earlier.

He was right about one thing: lately, murder seemed to follow wherever she went. It wasn't because she attracted trouble. It was because she paid attention. Tracking things down, figuring things out, and, yes, charging around asking questions... those things were integral to who she was as a writer, and as a person. They'd put her outside in the January chill, flickering between two states—shadow and light—as she passed beneath the streetlamps, just like the figure she had spotted earlier.

Maybe things with Troy had moved too fast, been too surfacy, too physical, for either of them to really get to know the other. Raw from losing Levi, and, admittedly, randy after three years without sex, she had practically swooned into those muscular arms. Who wouldn't?

Saffi thought back to an article she had written for the *Bedside Reader*, published two years after Levi's death: "The Widow's Guide to Dating." One of the tips she had shared struck her now: take things slow. When you come out of a long, intimate, loving relationship there are things you miss so much they throb like a toothache. Touch. Kisses. Holding hands. Resting your head on someone's shoulder. A warm body to snuggle up to when it's cold outside. Missing those things, the counselor she had interviewed told her, could turn into a ticking time bomb. A widow's first relationship could blow up in her face if she jumped into it with the first person who tripped her trigger.

Troy had definitely tripped hers. The last few months had been the slow burn of a fuse lit when they first met, but now... if his protective instincts expanded as their relationship grew, things might blow apart.

Saffi pulled herself back to the boardwalk. Her stride was shorter than the woman she'd seen earlier, with a bit more hip sway and the occasional sucking in of her gut as she gulped air to fuel her speed. But in a few short minutes, she would reach the convention center's front doors. Then what?

Planning, Saffi admitted, was not her forte. Much to Poppy's irritation she followed the "stumble upon" method of discovering great content. If the two murder cases she had solved so far were any indication, she relied upon the same tried-and-true but far more risky method as a sleuth. It was what it was, and if that was part of what seemed to be scaring Troy away? So be it.

Saffi slowed as the boardwalk opened onto the broad deck in front of the convention center and took stock of her surroundings. The sound of raised voices drew her attention to the street behind the center. It sounded like a couple of drunks on the way to the next bar. One of them was massacring Paul Simon's "Sound of Silence." The other one was telling him to shut his flapping trap. If they were smart, they would stumble home to sleep it off before the argument turned to a fist fight which turned into... a night on a cot inside Chief Boyd's jail. Perhaps right beside Saffi, if she got caught sneaking into the convention center after hours.

Saffi stepped closer to the door, hoping to get out of the street-lamp's illumination and into the shadow the building cast as the moon rose higher. As she reached for the door handle, realization hit her. She had barged over here expecting to walk straight into the building, as if the woman who had unlocked the door was one of those silly girls in a slasher movie without enough sense to lock it behind her. Saffi grasped the handle and pulled. Unbelievably, the door swung open.

Thank heaven for silly girls! She stepped into a lobby made eerily strange by the icy moonlight shining through the floor-to-ceiling windows.

Where to? Sight wouldn't help her now. Smell told her that someone with a heavy hand on the Lysol trigger had already spritzed and wiped the building's surfaces. Either she was on the trail of a cleaning lady or the cleaners had come and gone before the late-night intruder arrived. She held her breath to listen, hoping that her ears would clue her in to where the woman with the key had gone. At first, she heard nothing, but as silence descended, she picked up small sounds. A rustle. A shuffle. A quiet thump. A rip. The sounds were coming from inside the exhibit hall.

Saffi moved slowly, grateful for the commercial-grade carpet muffling her steps. She eased the door open and pressed her hand against it to soften the pressure as hydraulics shut it behind her. She stood for a few seconds, trying to pinpoint the direction from which the sound was coming. The far aisle, she decided, where Jemma—and the now-deceased Jay—had their booths.

Step by step, she crept down the center aisle. She passed the Lowry & Lowenstein booth and headed toward the river-facing windows. Once she reached the front of the hall, she slipped along the edges of the booths, trying to stay out of the moonlight. As she crept forward, the sounds got louder, clearer, and she heard a woman's voice, mumbling under her breath.

Saffi's shoe caught on a stanchion. When it toppled to the floor, the thud reverberated through the empty hall.

Up ahead, the rustling and murmuring went silent. Tension built like a storm holding its breath until the first sizzle of lightning. "I have a gun!"

Saffi might have expected the statement to boom like thunder. Instead, it bleated like a baby deer. *Fia!*

Saffi marched the rest of the way, making each footfall land as loud as she could. She reached the final aisle and swung into it. She curved her arms wide and hunched her back, hoping the pose would make her look big and scary, but fearing it probably made her look small and spooked, like a chimpanzee on the loose from a zoo.

Saffi had never heard a baby deer scream, which explained why the sound that came out of Fia's mouth almost made her pee her pants. "For God's sake, Fia. It's just me."

Fia blinked into the moonlight. "Saffi? What the hell? Oh my God. I have to sit down." The young woman turned this way and that among the mess of boxes, police tape, and other remnants of what had been Jay GoodVender's "Original *Bedside Reader*" booth. When she didn't spot a chair, Fia collapsed onto a box so low her knees touched her dangling braids.

Saffi found a folding stool tucked beneath the table. She tugged it out, unfolded it, and perched on top. Her bottom fluffed over the edges of the seat a bit, but Saffi wasn't going to let a few pounds stop her from grilling Fia. From what she could see, the young woman was breaking down a booth that had been taped off by the police.

"Explain." She crossed her arms and leaned forward expectantly.

"This was not *my* idea." Fia spread her arms wide to take in the deconstruction of Jay's booth. "Eileen wants this booth cleared out before morning. I was supposed to make sure Jay packed up yesterday, right after the exhibit hall closed, but I lost track of him."

Probably when he zipped out to rent himself a Surrey cycle.

"Did Chief Boyd give his permission for you to do this? I mean, you've torn down police tape."

"I'm not getting rid of anything." Fia fiddled with the cuffs on her box braids. "Eileen just wants it all moved to the storage room. She doesn't want book browsers to be reminded of a *murder* every time they walk past."

Saffi straightened. So this was the task Eileen had given Fia! The booksellers association president was wicked smart, but, Saffi wondered, was she cunning as well? It made sense that she would try to shield convention-goers from a murder investigation. But what if there was something in this booth the association president did not want the police to find? Eileen was too clever by half to dig through the booth herself. If Fia got caught boxing things up, the association president could plead ignorance.

Saffi glanced around the booth. Not much remained of Jay GoodVender's scheme to bring down her series. A table. An author poster. A few unopened boxes that probably contained books. Long ribbons of police tape. The small box on which Fia sat, looking more uncomfortable by the minute. And—just behind Fia —a large plastic organizer box with a handle. The Lowry & Lowenstein booth had one just like it, filled with miscellaneous exhibitor's supplies: packing tape, pens, sticky notes, a box cutter, pads of paper, business cards, and the official paperwork every exhibitor received when they checked in to set up their booth. Jay's box had a half-opened drawer that seemed to be filled with paperwork. Fia caught Saffi's eye and reached out to shut the drawer and latch the organizer's top closed.

Suspicious much? Saffi clapped her hands. "OK. If Eileen wants this junk out of here, let's do it."

The moonlight shone bright enough for Saffi to see Fia's mouth fall open in surprise.

"Really? You're gonna help?" The young woman sprang to her feet fast as a fawn.

"Fia." Saffi reached a hand toward the young woman. "Are you sure you didn't see Jay GoodVender on the Jingle Tour? I just... I have a gut feeling that whatever he was up to last night got him killed."

Fia shook her head so hard her box braids whipped out. "I'm sorry. I can't tell you any more than I already did."

Which was... diddly squat on a toothpick. *Great.*

"OK. Shall we get started?"

Fia grabbed the box in one hand and Jay's author poster in the other. "It's this way."

Saffi stood, then bent to pick up one of the book boxes. "Yikes. These are heavier than they look." She grimaced and rubbed the small of her back as if she'd strained it. "I think there's a box dolly in our booth. I'll see if I can find it, then follow you with a load." She was counting on the young woman's naïvety. After all, Fia had left the front door unlocked for any random slasher to follow her inside the dark, empty convention center.

"Sure." Fia clasped the author poster to her side. "Just take a left outside the exhibit hall. The storage rooms are at the end of the corridor on the right-hand side."

Saffi waited until Fia was halfway down the aisle before she snatched the organizer box and hurried away with it. She stuffed it under the table in the Lowry & Lowenstein booth, then grabbed the box dolly, trundled it back to Jay's booth, and easily hefted one book box after another onto its small metal platform. Once loaded, she grabbed the handle, kicked the wheels forward and pushed it down the aisle to the door. Looking through the organizer box could wait till morning. For now, the best way to keep Fia from suspecting what she was really up to was to help her complete the —seriously suspicious—job Eileen had given her.

SEVENTEEN

If yesterday had been a rush, Saturday morning was a whirlwind. A desperate Scott had filed a flight plan that would get him out of town before the minions woke up.

"They're terrifying," Troy informed Saffi, "but they have these big brown eyes. Scott just can't face their disappointment." Troy talked as he stuffed clothes and the *Bedside Reader* Saffi had signed into his gym bag.

Bailing. Saffi folded her arms, pressed her lips together, and kept her peace. If this was Troy's way of backing out of their budding relationship, she could wait until she returned to Last Chance Cove to talk it through.

Troy glanced up as he zipped his bag. "Scott found another fare to fly out of here with you, so no worries on that score. He'll be back for your scheduled pickup tomorrow afternoon."

Unless I'm stuck here, still under suspicion, abandoned and alone. Saffi bit back the whining and focused on logistics. "I would expect nothing less," she said. "Well, except a bit of a refund. He did charge me for a round trip with a single paid passenger." She let the words ring in the air before softening them with a smile. "I'm kidding, Troy."

His eyes sparked with the first hint of humor she'd seen this morning. "Ah. Right. So—" He opened his arms and she stepped into them. Their hug was tight, pulsing with suppressed emotion, but brief. He pressed a kiss on her brow before hefting his bag onto his shoulder. At the door, he turned back and met her eyes. His shone with feeling. "Promise me you'll be careful."

Saffi shrugged. "No promises given, none broken."

He blinked twice, taking in her double meaning. Then he bowed his head and swept the door closed.

Saffi prepared for her day as if that closing door did not reverberate through every cell of her body. She showered, applied makeup, wiped it off and started over, dressed, then stood on the balcony staring at the ocean. After what might have been five minutes, or an hour, she went back inside, pulled up her big girl pants—metaphorically, of course—and went on with her day.

She was due to meet Poppy and her editor's staffers at the coffee shop at seven thirty. After that, she would worm her way into the exhibit hall early enough to dig through Jay's organizer box before anyone else arrived. As she walked the windy block to the coffee shop, she decided to keep that bit of information to herself. If she was wrong, and Eileen had simply wanted to keep the convention free of murdery vibes, she did not want Poppy to go off half-cocked and blow the rest of the show to smithereens.

The coffee shop Willow had found was no kind of chic. In fact, it looked like a barista had inherited a thrift store, turned it into a coffeehouse but kept the décor. The front window featured a great blue heron standing on one leg on top of a spindly table, surrounded by straggly succulents in repurposed 32-ounce cans. It looked like a lawn ornament had wandered out of someone's yard, found the best view in the house, and permanently nabbed it.

Saffi expected a musty smell when she stepped inside. Instead, she inhaled coffee with an overlay of bacon. *Yum!* A mixed bag of locals sprawled on the faded sofas and under-stuffed chairs. Saffi was floored to see Chief Boyd holding court among them. She was not surprised to overhear questions about the murder or to see the chief shush his listeners with his hands as he spotted Saffi joining Poppy and Willow at the coffee counter.

"Willow!" Poppy's face had a look of absolute betrayal. "This is the place you were gushing about?"

"The coffee is the best in town. I promise!" Willow put her hands together. "And the breakfast is excellent. That's what matters, right Saffi?" Her eyes pleaded for Saffi to agree.

Saffi didn't need persuading. Willow was right. She had experienced way too many chic coffee shops with vapid drinks and tiny metal stools designed to discourage spending too much time in them. This place had "Welcome to my living room" written all over it. It also had locals who looked a lot like regulars. To Saffi, that was the highest recommendation of all.

"Where's Reese?" Saffi glanced over her shoulder.

"Late." Poppy spat out the word. "One time too many."

Willow's eyes shadowed. "I'm sure he'll be here soon."

Saffi put a hand on her editor's shoulder. "Give the youngster a break, would you? He hooked up with a beautiful young woman last night."

Willow sucked in a breath as if ready to either ream Reese out or plead his case, depending on Poppy's reaction. The editor's mouth pursed but her eyes looked amused rather than angry. "Well, good for him. But if he isn't at the booth when we get there, he's gonna learn a few things about work love-life balance."

As the three women perused the menu, the locals' convo lowered to a murmur with the occasional expletive that drew Saffi's attention to the living room vignette.

"Are you shitting me?" an old guy with a barrel belly bellowed before the rest of them could shush him.

Saffi quirked a brow then returned to the almost impossible task of choosing something from the menu. Every item looked more scrumptious than the last. She ordered the French Connection—an egg-and-cheese sandwich on a toasted croissant—with a Mexican mocha. Willow ordered a vegan version of the same sandwich with a cappuccino. Poppy ordered Bob's Red Mill oatmeal topped with craisins and sliced almonds.

"And black coffee." Poppy pointed to a chalkboard sign on the wall that read, *In a hurry? Help yourself and pay the honesty box.*

"Can you imagine a New York bistro trusting customers to pump and pay for their own refills?" Poppy hooted. "I mean, just the tips they'd lose would have the baristas fainting into their foam."

Saffi chuckled her agreement.

Poppy led the crew away from the counter and commandeered a table near the front window, as far from Chief Boyd and his locals as she could get.

Before Saffi could sit, Willow pointed to the back corner just beyond the locals area where seafoam-green walls had been transformed into a makeshift art exhibit.

"Look!" Willow grinned. "Aren't they fabulous?"

The rogue's gallery of portraits fell somewhere between naïve and surreal: whimsical, witty, and weird as well as colorful. A white-wigged glutton with a fake mole on his cheek brandished a fork. A smirking woman wearing cat-eye glasses gave the side-eye to a ruddy-faced man one portrait to her left. The wilting yellow carnations clutched in the man's meaty fist sent a quiver of nausea through Saffi, but Willow's blue eyes sparkled. "It's like something out of a Wes Anderson movie," she gushed.

The locals corner went silent. Saffi dared a glance. Six faces that could have starred in that slasher movie she'd been imagining last night glared back at her. Then the loudmouth with the belly leaned back in his faded floral-print chair and roared, "These are your murder suspects?" He shook his head and pointed a finger at Chief Boyd. "No wonder you never found Sonya's killer."

The chief's naturally pink skin went scarlet. He slapped his police cap on his head and stood, throwing his napkin onto the remains of his breakfast. "You mean, the way you found Helen?"

Helen, Saffi remembered, was Jemma's missing best friend. *But Sonya? Who was Sonya?* From the look on Chief's Boyd's face, she was his unsolved murder. After the chief stormed out of the coffee-house, the remaining locals chided the man with the barrel belly.

"Pops, give Boyd a break, would you?"

Saffi recognized the chief's defender by his round cheeks and sparse comb-over: Chief Boyd's best bud and the head of Seaside's chamber of commerce, Larry. She had seen many an adult "child" stare an aging parent into putting a sock in it. Were the grump and the good guy father and son? If so, that nut fell a *lo-o-ong* way from the tree.

The belligerent old man ran a hand across the white feathery hair ringing his scalp. "Yeah, well, Sonya was one of ours."

Heat rose up Saffi's neck. If she hadn't been a stranger in a strange town and a murder suspect to boot, she might have plowed into the fray. One of the locals—a string bean of a black woman with white braids woven around her head—did it for her.

"I've had enough of that 'us and them' bullpucky," the string bean said. "Sonya was one of us because she *lived* here. Not because her skin was the same color as yours."

An elderly Hispanic man sitting on the sofa jabbed his walking cane toward the curmudgeon in the comfy chair. "Stop blaming Eric for getting kicked off the force, Luke. You did that all by yourself."

As the pair stormed out of the café, Larry stood up from one of the flumpy armchairs and approached their table. "Sorry you had to see that. Seaside prides itself on being welcoming to everyone." Then he reached a hand toward Saffi. "Larry Atwell, Ms. Gray-wood, and a big fan."

"Larry." Saffi gripped his hand with the strong shake she reserved for men, and women who thought they could intimidate her. "You came by my book signing. Nice to see you again."

A big grin made Larry's cheeks look even puffier. "My wife and I own the Sea King Bike Shop."

"Oh! Right!" Saffi nodded. "I spoke to your wife yesterday. Enid, right?"

He glanced back at his father and a shadow crossed over his

face. "Ah. Yes. That GoodVender debacle." He shook his head. "Wish I'd never rented him that cycle. Maybe he'd still be..." Larry's voice faded away.

"Alive?" Poppy scoffed. "Doubtful. If anyone needed killing it was—"

Willow tugged Poppy's arm as if to remind her that she was still under a cloud of suspicion. Talking about killing Jay in front of the head of Seaside's chamber of commerce? Not helpful.

"If you have time to explore, I'd be happy to make recommendations." Larry handed business cards around the table. "But try not to kill anyone." He winked, then sketched a wave as he followed in Chief Boyd's wake.

EIGHTEEN

After breakfast, they left the coffeehouse, headed south on Holladay and turned right onto Broadway. When they passed Beach Books, Saffi thought about Chief Boyd. He had fled to the restroom during the Mix and Mingle to avoid her question about previous murder investigations. Now, she thought she understood why. The failure to find Sonya's killer was a sore spot that some members of the community—like the former police chief—kept raw through constant poking and prodding. No wonder Chief Boyd wanted to close the GoodVender case as quickly as possible. She empathized, but that didn't mean she would let him get away with pinning the murder on Poppy. *No.* She would double down and find the killer herself.

As the Lowry & Lowenstein trio reached the Broadway Bridge, Saffi noticed a line of people bending over the concrete rail. They seemed to be trying to get a better look at something below. A woman pointed. A man shouted. A few people covered their mouths with their hands.

"What now?" Poppy demanded, as if the hubbub was a personal affront.

The three of them pushed their way through the gawkers to reach the rail. Saffi gripped the rough concrete and leaned forward to see the river. She spotted a duckboat like the ones she had seen on her first day in Seaside. The boat seemed to be wedged against rocks reinforcing the bank beneath a deck jutting out of a two-story hotel. A single person lolled back in the boat, as if drunk or unconscious, or…

"Reese!" Poppy recognized her intern first. "Oh my God. What's wrong with the boy?"

"We have to get down there." Willow pushed away from the rail and sprinted down the center of the bridge, hair flying, perfect highlights flashing in the morning sunlight. Saffi jogged after her, curls bouncing, at a much slower pace. Poppy tried to keep up, but her orthopedic pumps were made for carpeted convention centers, not rough concrete. When they reached the post at the end of the bridge Saffi realized two things. One, Raven had perched on this very post last night, which meant its croaking calls had been a warning. Two, there was no way to get to Reese from where they stood.

One of the gawkers pointed in the other direction and shouted. "The duckboats!"

"Poppy, call 9-1-1!" Saffi yelped as she and Willow crossed the bridge to the boardwalk on the opposite side. They thudded along the wooden walkway, then clanged down a steep metal gangplank to a floating dock lined with duckboats bobbing in the river.

"I have the keys!" The gawker who had pointed them toward the duckboats ran up behind them and jingled a ring of keys. He ran to the end of the dock and unlocked the first duck. Saffi and Willow scrambled aboard and back-pedaled into the river. Then they reversed direction and pumped the pedals as if Reese's life depended on it. Saffi prayed that it did not.

"Maybe he tied one on," she huffed out between breaths, "and passed out."

Willow's gaze flickered toward Saffi then back to the river in front of them. From the way she chewed her lip, Saffi doubted Poppy's assistant believed that was what had happened. As they passed under the bridge, sirens wailed in the distance, but they reached the stranded duckboat before help arrived.

"Reese!" Willow jumped to her feet and the boat rocked as if a tidal wave had hit it.

"Whoa!" Saffi grabbed Willow's hand just before she pitched into the water. "You can't help Reese if you drown."

Somewhat reluctantly, Willow let Saffi pull her back into her seat.

"Saffi!" Poppy's familiar voice shrieked from the bridge. "Is Reese OK?"

A half-pedal took them side by side with Reese's duck. Saffi reached out a hand to his chest. Her own heart almost stopped when she felt it move. "He's alive!" She waved at Poppy, who let go of the bridge rail to turn, bend forward and breathe.

Seconds later, a fire engine's horn blasted the crowd on the bridge out of its way. Saffi reached for Willow's hand and gave it a squeeze. "Help is here."

It was. She could hear it. Doors slammed. Voices shouted. But it took several long, excruciating minutes for the firefighters to find a way to scramble beneath the hotel balcony and clamber down the rocks. Four of them worked together to hoist the unconscious intern from the duckboat.

Saffi glanced up at the bridge, hoping to catch sight of Poppy. Instead, she saw Jemma standing at the rail, face set in concrete, brows furrowed. When Saffi lifted a hand, Jemma stepped back and disappeared into the crowd. *Some men just need killing.* Jemma's words echoed in her memory. Did that include interns who dared to date her foster daughter? God, she hoped not.

Once the firefighters evacuated Reese to the waiting ambulance, Saffi and Willow pedaled their duck back to the dock. They thanked the person who had loaned them the boat profusely and filled him in on what they knew, which wasn't much. Reese was alive, possibly drugged, drunk, or concussed. A few minutes later, they reconvened with Poppy on the boardwalk.

"I'm going to the hospital," Poppy said, clutching her *Bedside Reader* tote to her chest like a life preserver.

"Let me do that for you." Willow composed her face into something closer to her usual professional demeanor. "You've barely been in the booth and store reps keep asking for you."

Poppy pressed her lips together as if thinking, then shook her head. "No. That young man is my responsibility, and Bob will expect me to keep on top of this personally. You two can handle the booth until I get back."

After they reassured Poppy that they would, she ordered an Uber and hurried off to the corner where the driver said he would meet her.

Saffi glanced at Willow. "Worst book convention ever?"

It was a question that had only one answer. Saffi and Willow walked the rest of the way to the convention center without another word. Once inside, Willow scurried off to the ladies' room and Saffi made a beeline for the booth. The first thing she did was dig Jay GoodVender's organizer box from beneath the table where she'd stashed it in the night. She took it to the chair in the corner of the booth, trying not to think about the first time she'd met Reese, sitting in this very chair scrolling on his phone as if he didn't have a care in the world.

Be OK. Be OK. The chant ran through Saffi's mind as she scrabbled through the box. Maybe something inside would explain why the booksellers' convention had become the convention from hell.

The top two trays held the exhibitor essentials she expected to find: pens, scissors, a box cutter, paper clips, sticky notes, business cards, and packing tape. The bottom tray held paperwork. Saffi slipped receipts and folded papers from the box one by one. She spotted a brochure from Seaside's chamber of commerce sticking out of a thin spiral-bound composition book Jay had titled *Silenced in Seaside. What was that about?* Under the notebook, she found check-in paperwork from the Necanicum Inn.

Saffi stiffened. Jay had been *staying* at the inn? Why hadn't

Phyllis told her that? The thought of him wandering the halls, maybe standing outside her door, wishing her nothing but ill, made her stomach turn. How easy it must have been for him to catch the housekeeper unawares with a chloroform-soaked cloth.

When the next thing she found in the drawer was a receipt from Ocean Blossoms for yellow carnations, Saffi crumpled the flower receipt in her fist. Seconds later, she rethought the urge to trash it and smoothed it out against her thigh. Combined with the check-in sheet from the inn, she now had tangible evidence that Jay GoodVender had been behind the bloody petals on her bed. If Marisol had identified his photo, she would have enough proof to crush GoodVender's credibility and convince Chief Boyd to file that green folder in his office trash can.

Saffi fumbled in her tote for her cellphone and found Phyllis's number among her recent messages. She picked up on the fourth ring.

"Hello?" The desk clerk's voice sounded wary.

Was that because she didn't recognize Saffi's number... or because she *did*?

"Phyllis! Saffi Graywood. Did you show that photo I shared with you to Marisol?"

Phyllis sucked in a breath. "I'm sorry, Ms. Graywood. Marisol was released from the hospital before I could get over there."

"Oh! Well, that's great news, isn't it? You didn't recognize the man in the photo, did you?"

"I-I don't think so."

Saffi snapped a photo of Jay's check-in sheet and messaged it to the desk clerk. "How about now?"

Phyllis gasped. "He was a *guest*?"

Saffi found the check-in date and time on the page. "Checked in on Wednesday at three p.m."

"New Year's Eve!" Phyllis breathed a sigh of relief. "I had the day off. Someone else would have checked him in."

The papers in Saffi's hand shook. "OK. Thanks, Phyllis."

She nudged the plastic organizer away with the toe of her boot and stood, glancing around the booth. The exhibit hall hummed with activity and conversation. Nearby vendors were busy straightening their booths for the day as well as filling displays with books and advertising materials. Willow had yet to return from the ladies' room, which seemed a little out of character. Maybe what had happened to Reese had shaken her more than Saffi realized.

Saffi checked her cellphone for the time. She still had twelve minutes until the hall opened to browsers.

Time enough to look for more clues! She splayed the papers loosely across the table and picked her way through them. She found receipts for gas, coffee, books, restaurants, printing... the same kinds of receipts she squirreled away in her own files. She knew exactly why Jay had kept them: he hoped to make enough money from book sales to deduct business expenses on his taxes. A knot formed in Saffi's belly. She did the exact same thing.

For the first time, she saw their commonality and a wave of compassion washed over her. Jay GoodVender had been a struggling writer, a man with a sharp mind filled with an eclectic mix of knowledge. He must have come to the convention where she debuted her *Bedside Reader* with high hopes. Somehow, in his eyes, her success had crushed his chances.

As Saffi picked listlessly through the rest of the papers on the table, a signature on the bottom right corner of one paper caught her eye, one that ended with "Booksellers Association." She eased the paper out of the stack. She barely had time to determine that it was a copy of the application form Jay had submitted for his booth before a voice sounded at her shoulder.

"What's that?"

Saffi jumped, crumpling the form in her hand. When she looked up, Willow leaned over the table, brow puzzled as she squinted at the papers Saffi had spread across it.

"I, uhm, nabbed that from Jay's booth." Saffi glanced over her shoulder at the open organizer.

"You what?" Willow yelped.

Saffi had not intended to share that she'd sleuthed her way into the convention center last night, but Willow would not take silence for an answer. Once she explained, Poppy's assistant started hastily snatching up receipts. "Do you have any idea how suspicious this makes you look? Makes *us* look?"

Willow took all of the papers Saffi had gathered—minus the application form she refused to let go of—and carefully layered them into the bottom drawer of the organizer. While her back was turned, Saffi folded the form, lifted the long edge of her asymmetrical emerald-green tunic, and tucked it into the left pocket of her black stretch jeans.

When Willow hefted the organizer, Saffi shook her head. "Fia emptied Jay's booth and put everything in storage." Willow's razor-straight shoulders slumped.

"So what am I supposed to do with it?"

Saffi pointed to the spot under the table where she'd stashed the organizer last night. Willow's eyes narrowed. "I can't get caught with this thing. My family does not do scandal. My parents would murder me." She punctured the last two words with a finger jab.

When Willow's lips started to tremble and she collapsed into the chair Saffi had just vacated, Saffi realized something. The young woman's poise and perfection were part of a carefully constructed facade, one Willow probably had to struggle to keep in place at all times. Saffi knew a little bit about protecting a name, although hers was a brand and not a family dynasty. Willow's dynasty included everything from a detergent, soap, and toothpaste empire to cosmetics and pet food companies. Saffi's brand was plankton in comparison to the blue whale of businesses attached to Willow's family name.

"Don't worry." Saffi reached for the organizer. "I got you."

"No." Willow held tight to the organizer. "I'll get rid of it."

Saffi shook her head. "We're not going to 'get rid of'"—she made air quotes—"evidence in a murder case."

Willows shoulders slumped and she held the organizer out to Saffi. "What will you do with it?"

"Put it back where I found it." Saffi grinned. She carried the organizer out of the booth, down the aisle, along the river-facing wall of windows, and into Jay GoodVender's empty booth. She looked both ways before putting it down. Since the hall had yet to open, the only people roaming the back aisle were vendors, including Jemma, who gave her a considering look, then sketched a wave and went back to stacking copies of *Mermaids at Midnight* on her table.

There. Eileen might want Jay's goods hidden away, but his booth was where they belonged. Too bad Saffi wouldn't be there to see Chief Boyd's face when he showed up to find the organizer and nothing else.

NINETEEN

After leaving the box in GoodVender's booth, Saffi slipped out a back door into the cloud-shrouded morning. She made her way to the wooden rail at the edge of the convention center's deck and stared into the mirrorlike river. A wild-haired woman wearing a halo of puffy clouds stared back at her. Her reflection wasn't clear enough to show worry lines on her forehead and chin, but she didn't need to see them to know they were getting deeper by the minute.

She had been hoping for a call from Poppy. Something, anything, to let her know if Reese was OK. She eased her cellphone from her sling bag and was about to make a call when it rang. She startled so violently the phone would have gone into the river if she hadn't slammed it against her belly.

Troy. Saffi pressed her lips together so hard she could feel her teeth. More than enough time had passed for Scott to land his Beechcraft and Troy to climb into the blue pickup truck he'd parked in the pilot's hangar. Saffi stared at the phone. If she answered, what would she say?

Things here have gone from bad to worse? We found Reese unconscious in a duckboat. Jemma—remember the memoir writer who plowed Jay off his feet? Well, she might be responsible for what happened to Reese. Fia, the convention program assistant, is keeping secrets. The current police chief has never solved a murder, the former chief is a racist. Poppy still didn't do it, and neither did I, so I'm going to keep digging until I find whatever someone has buried in the muck. How was your flight?

That little speech would go over like a poop-filled water balloon. Saffi let the call go to voicemail. A few seconds later the phone dinged to tell her a message had been left. She would listen... at a less stressful time. She opened her cellphone favorites and poked Poppy's name. Her editor picked up after one ring.

"Saffi! I'm so glad you called. Reese is awake. He's OK."

Saffi clutched her phone to her ear. "What happened? Has he told you?"

A long slow sigh passed through cyberspace. Saffi could almost feel Poppy's breath in her ear. "He has no idea. He was out in the duckboat with Debbie, who turns out to be Jemma's ward or some such. I guess they'd both had a few, then Debbie suggested a moonlight cruise. She jimmied the lock on a duckboat and off they went. Pedaled under the bridge and *whap!* He doesn't remember anything else until he woke up in a hospital bed. He has a whale of a goose egg without the vaguest idea how he got it."

Pedaled under the bridge...? The same bridge where Raven had croaked a warning. The bridge from which Jemma had watched her find Reese, then ducked away once Saffi caught her eye. "Poppy. Are the police there?"

Poppy sighed. "Yes. Chief Boyd is bludgeoning the poor kid with questions."

"Would you put him on the phone, please?"

After a few huffs and scoffs, Poppy obliged.

"Chief Boyd here." The police chief sounded more than a little annoyed.

"Chief? Saffi Graywood. I was thinking... if something was dropped from the bridge, it could have hit Reese as he pedaled out from under it."

"Possibly." Chief Boyd stopped with the one word.

Saffi rubbed her chin as she thought. Then she scratched her nose. Just before she said, "There's someone I think you should talk to..." She stopped herself. Did she really think Jemma would hurt Reese? Debbie was a grown woman. She had arranged to meet Reese and have a drink. They'd partied and then absconded with a duckboat for a bit of harmless fun. Besides, if Jemma had dropped a rock from the bridge, she could have brained Debbie just as easily as Reese. The look of love Jemma had given Debbie at the bar told Saffi she would never risk hurting the young woman.

"Do you have any more information to share, Ms. Graywood? Did you see something... suspicious?"

The sarcasm in his voice made Saffi clutch her phone harder. "Maybe you haven't noticed, Chief, but since we arrived in your fair town my group has been harassed, first at the conference by Jay GoodVender, and, since his murder, by the police. And now, one of us has been attacked. Instead of mocking me, you might try listening. Maybe chase down a few *leads*." Saffi paused to let her words sink in.

Chief Boyd cleared his throat. "I have an entire folder filled with leads, Ms. Graywood. They point straight to you, but, so far, you're walking free on our fair streets. Enjoy the rest of your stay, which... might be quite a bit longer than you had anticipated."

Saffi heard Poppy's gasp even though Chief Boyd held the phone.

Son of—! OK. Those are your cards on the table. Time to play a few of mine.

"Wait!" Saffi stopped the chief before he could hang up on her. "There's an organizer box in Jay GoodVender's booth with some paperwork you need to see. Proof that he was behind the bloody flower petals on the bed in my suite, and almost certainly Marisol's attacker. My guess? It will help you wrap up at least one case, although... I'm sorry to say you won't be able to arrest the perp."

.   .   .

By the time Saffi returned from the deck by the river, the Lowry & Lowenstein booth had a line of jabbering fans. She was scheduled to sign copies of previous years' *Bedside Readers* at the reduced trade show price of ten dollars. She settled into the chair at the table, plastered a smile on her face, and took the Sharpie that Willow thrust at her. Unlike her first signing session on Thursday, there was no hot mocha at her elbow. Saffi had never seen Willow so flustered. In fact, until today, she had been pretty sure Poppy's assistant was unflappable.

As she left the booth to write names on stickies, Willow nervously tucked her hair behind her ears. They were, Saffi noticed, adorably protruding rather than stereotypically "perfect." Saffi dug through her memory for a *Bedside Reader* article about physiognomy: the study of personality by decoding facial features. Protruding ears were associated with outgoing, curious, and intelligent people. That certainly sounded like the Willow she thought she knew. Of course, she also knew it took a lot more than the shape of one's ears, eyebrows, and lips to determine character.

Saffi had spent time with Willow at conventions before, but those were stress-free compared to this one. Oh, there were the usual headaches: late flights, boxes not arriving on time, hard concrete floors without the extra-cushy carpeting Poppy usually ordered for the Lowry & Lowenstein booth, overbearing fans with booming voices or bad breath. Willow handled all of those problems without a hair out of place. Of course, compared to a stalker, a murderer, and a concussed intern, those problems were nothing. No wonder Willow looked more frazzled than Saffi had ever seen her.

Somehow, they made it through the hour-long signing. By the time they were done, Poppy had returned to the booth. She updated them on Reese's condition. He was woozy and nauseous but whatever had whapped him on the head seemed to have done no permanent damage.

"I wanted to fly him home immediately, but the doctor said no. She wants to do a brain scan before she clears Reese to fly. Apparently, cabin pressure and lower oxygen levels can worsen a concussion. And if he has a hidden brain bleed…"

Something whammed to the floor behind her and Saffi whirled around. Willow bent to pick up a book she seemed to have dropped.

"Willow! Get a grip." Poppy blinked back what looked a lot like tears. "I absolutely forbid Reese to be anything but mildly concussed, just as the doctor has assured me."

Saffi dared to stand and give Poppy the second hug in a week that she actually returned. "He's going to be fine. Really." She glanced over her shoulder at Willow whose face was white-rose pale. "A few days of vacay in Seaside to let his noggin heal and it'll be blue skies all the way home."

I hope. Saffi had once flown with a sinus infection and been certain her head would explode all over the cabin during takeoff. Flying with a concussion, even a mild one, would be a miserable experience, even if it didn't activate a hidden brain bleed.

Poppy knocked a fist on the stack of books Willow kept trying to straighten, tugged her jacket over her lean hips and plastered a professional smile on her face. "Alright, ladies. Let's get down to business. Saffi! Get out there on the floor. You know what to do."

Saffi saluted. "Yes, ma'am. Spy and schmooze!"

"Willow!" Poppy's assistant automatically turned toward her boss's voice but her mind was clearly elsewhere. "Willow!" Poppy snapped her fingers in front of the young woman's face. "Let's get more books on this table. And those postcards the graphics department made for the spring release."

Saffi watched in horror as Willow tried, and failed, to put on a professional face. "I'm sorry, I can't… I just— This is *all* my fault!" she wailed. Then she shook her shimmering hair and fled from the booth.

"What the—?" Poppy put her hands on her hips.

Saffi went after her, what else could she do? Since they'd seen Reese in the duckboat from the top of the bridge, Willow had been acting totally out of character. Saffi had expected her to run for the restroom and, perhaps, have a good cry. She pushed her way into the closest women's room, but when she bent down to look along the stalls, she didn't spot a single pair of shoes. The second floor had another set of restrooms. Under the stalls she saw sneakers, Doc Martens, and a hideous pair of platform boots, but she didn't spot the black ballet flats Willow had been wearing.

This is all *my fault!* What had Willow meant by that declaration? Saffi's sleuthing antennae tingled but her receiver seemed to be on the fritz. She had no idea what Willow could be talking about.

If she couldn't figure out what was going on with Willow, the least she could do was the job Poppy had assigned her: spy and schmooze her way through the exhibit hall. The whole Jay Good-Vender fiasco had shoved her so far off-kilter she wasn't sure she'd ever be able to stand straight again. Especially when the Lowry & Lowenstein team—the rock of Aunt Saffi's success—seemed to be crumbling. Poppy accused of murder. Reese literally knocked out of commission. Willow falling apart in a way Saffi would have never thought possible. *I mean, tucking her hair behind her ears! Unbelievable!*

Saffi started with the middle aisle of the exhibit hall so she could stop by the Lowry & Lowenstein booth and update Poppy.

"I don't get it." Poppy put her hands on her hips. "Willow and Reese aren't even close. They avoid each other like the plague at the office."

Saffi shrugged. "Maybe she just reached her limit. As controlled as Willow is, she might have cracked like an overboiled egg with the pressure we've all been under."

"Yes, well." Poppy wet her mauve lipstick with her tongue. "Pressure and publishing go hand in glove. I fear I might have to make some changes when we get home."

Poor Willow. Despite the fact that she had outlasted Poppy's other assistants, her meltdown might have tanked her career.

Leaving Poppy to stew over her hiring choices, Saffi strolled through the exhibit hall. One thing she loved about small conventions was discovering regional publishers. Farther along the aisle from Lowry & Lowenstein, she found Sasquatch Books, a Seattle publisher best known for books about hiking, cooking, foraging, and exploring in the Pacific Northwest. She picked up *The Reset Workbook*. It recommended a reset if you were feeling out of sync. This whole convention could use a reset, Saffi decided, but a journal that promised to help you find your "inner magic" was probably not the key.

Down the next aisle, she passed Tundra Books, which featured children's titles, and Ooligan Press, a student-run publisher out of Portland State University. At the Dark Horse Comics booth, she spotted a book that made her question Poppy's insistence that the *Bedside Reader* brand would have protected her from Jay Good-Vender's knockoff. The comics series "Survival Street" seemed to be a dystopian take on *Sesame Street*. If America devolved into feudal states run by unscrupulous corporations, *What would Grover do?* According to the book's lurid cover, the loveable blue Muppet with the bright pink nose would pick up an automatic rifle and patrol the streets.

Clearly, none of the regional presses had anything meant to compete with *Aunt Saffi's Bedside Reader*.

On the river-view end of the next to last aisle, a tall blonde wearing a flower-power dress with knee-high white boots bounded out of the Midtown Books booth and thrust a brochure into Saffi's hand. "If you're looking for a publisher, you came to the right place."

A publisher was the last thing Saffi needed, but the young woman's aggressive approach reminded her of something Jay GoodVender had told her on the first day of the convention. "I've signed my series with a publisher." The Midtown Books booth was just around the corner from what had been Jay's booth.

Saffi opened the brochure. Midtown Books offered a type of hybrid publishing. The author bore the costs on the front end of the publishing process, from editing to cover art to printing. Midtown Books provided marketing and distribution. How many authors, she wondered, would earn enough from their books to make the deal profitable? Few, she imagined. *Jay's terrible karma had struck again.*

"Are you the publisher Jay told me about?" Saffi ventured. "He was so excited about the deal he made."

The mod girl noticed Saffi's badge for the first time. Her heavily mascaraed eyes widened, then she ripped the brochure from Saffi's grip so quickly she almost took off a finger.

"Hey!" Saffi sucked at her fingertips.

"I don't know any Jay," the girl said as she flounced back into the booth. She sat down in the booth's single chair, ready to ignore Saffi until she gave up and left. She picked up a vintage vinyl handbag, clicked open its top clasp, and took out a mirrored compact to check her teeth.

"Good idea." Saffi picked up one of the books Midtown had on display. "You do have a bit of..." Saffi tapped her own teeth with a fingernail.

The young woman glanced into her mirrored compact and rubbed red lipstick off her teeth.

Saffi paged through the book she had picked up. "This is high quality." She wasn't just flattering the young woman. The book had the look of a professionally published book. "I'm not looking for a publisher, but I met someone at the trade show who might want to have a chat with you."

"And who might that be?" The girl's eyes narrowed.

"Police Chief Boyd."

The young woman jumped to her feet, fists clenched. "Jay said you were a wench."

Saffi chuckled. "Oh, I am. If the deal you signed with Good-Vender doesn't die with him, you'll find yourself on the wrong side of a brand infringement lawsuit."

Saffi heard a gasp and a thud in the booth around the corner, the one that now held nothing but Jay GoodVender's organizer box, then a jingly clinking sound that faded so quickly she thought she might have imagined it. Why had she left the box in Jay's booth? She should have put it directly into Chief Boyd's hands. She would rectify the situation and, while she was at it, she would tell the chief about the Midtown Books connection to the murdered man. She wanted the chief to grill the young woman in the white go-go boots like the flopping fish she resembled after Saffi's lawsuit threat.

"Be seeing you!" Saffi waved, then headed for the booth around the corner. When she stepped inside, it was empty. The organizer was gone.

TWENTY

Besides Saffi, who knew the box was there? Jemma had seen her leave it earlier. Willow knew. And, Saffi realized, so did every book browser who had strolled along the aisle since she'd left it. Any one of them could have grabbed it, as could Fia or Eileen if they had seen it in the booth and wondered why it hadn't made it into the storage room.

Saffi patted the pocket of her jeans, relieved to hear the crinkle that meant the form she'd held onto was right where she'd put it. In retrospect, the application form did not seem very important. She should have kept the flower receipt and inn check-in sheet instead.

Let's just see, shall we? Saffi sat cross-legged on the floor and smoothed out the form on her thigh. As she'd seen before, it was Jay GoodVender's application for a booth in the exhibit hall. Saffi ran her finger along the standard gobbledygook of wherebys and whateverfors that vendor forms required. Then she flipped it over to check the signature at the bottom, and... froze.

Eileen Esterhaven, President, North Coast Booksellers Association. Saffi blinked, licked her lip, and read the signature again. Why had Eileen blamed Fia for Jay being at the convention when she had signed the form herself? Had she thrown Fia under the bus to protect her reputation? Or maybe... she had a more sinister reason. Saffi pictured Eileen's face when the security guards tackled GoodVender on the boardwalk. She had fled the banquet as if the ghosts of lawsuits future harried her steps.

Beyond the shock of Eileen's signature, the form also made her think of the green folder Jay had presented to Chief Boyd. The man had assembled a dossier of what he saw as evidence that Saffi had stolen his series idea. If he acted true to type, this form might not be the only "evidence" he'd held onto during the convention. Who knew what he might have squirreled away! Something—given that the organizer box had disappeared—that someone might not want Chief Boyd to get his hands on. But what? Grocery store and gas receipts? *Ridiculous.* The receipt for flowers, but Jay was the only person who would be incriminated if that one was found. What else? If only Willow had not gathered the papers before Saffi had a chance to finish examining them. Who knows what she would have found?

Footfalls thudded along the carpet, getting closer and closer.

"What in the name of Poseidon's trident are you doing down there?"

Saffi recognized the gruff voice. She glanced up to meet green eyes filled with either worry or wonder.

"Jemma. Hi!" Saffi shifted to her knees then tried to push herself to her feet. "Ouch!" Her right hip—the one that twanged like a sour guitar string when she sat for too long—refused to cooperate.

"You're up to something, Aunt Saffi." Jemma stretched out a hand and Saffi took it, allowing the much stronger woman to heft her to her feet. "Since you keep showing up at this booth, I'm pretty sure it's related to old GoodVender and that fairy-light noose around his good-for-nothing neck."

"Jemma, I..."

Jemma twisted her sea-kinked hair into a faded red mass on top of her head and stuck a ballpoint pen into its thickness to hold it in place. "How 'bout we trade this place for a bit of fresh air and cloudshine." Her roguish smile was both challenge and invitation.

"Cloudshine?" Saffi pursed her lips.

"Yup. We get a lot of that around here. Clouds, per usual, but with the sun lighting them up from the inside out."

Now *that* Saffi wanted to see. "Lead the way!"

Today's tapestry skirt swished around Jemma's leg warmers as her Birkenstocks marched them out a back door to the riverside. Sea-swept air and cloudshine were just beyond the door and Saffi sucked them in like the mood-altering forces they were. Gulls soared overhead and laughed as Saffi whirled with delight. That "ha, ha, ha" sound of theirs always made her wonder if they were laughing with her... or at her. Today? She didn't care.

"You have no idea how much I needed this." She grinned at Jemma like a kid set free on the last day of school.

"Oh, I had an inkling. Every time I look at that booth I feel a storm coming on. You know, the way the air feels charged and the world holds its breath until it's about to bust? That GoodVender guy had a dark aura on him if I ever saw one. Left the stink of it behind."

Saffi nodded. Jemma was right. "That he did."

Jemma placed a weathered hand on Saffi's forearm. "I don't blame you one bit, you know."

Saffi stiffened. "Wait. You don't think I...?"

Jemma raised one grizzled brow.

"No." Saffi shook her head. "No, no, to infinity no. It was *not* me. And it wasn't my editor either. You haven't said anything to Chief Boyd, have you?" She glanced over her shoulder as if the chief might be standing behind her with handcuffs. How many people at the convention suspected her the way Jemma did? Saffi clenched her fists. Jay GoodVender's vendetta lived on.

"Have I told the chief you probably rid yourself of Good-Vender before he could get rid of you? Nah. Course not." A salty sea breeze set loose Jemma's twisted hair and the ballpoint pen fell at her feet. She scooped it up but instead of re-coiling her hair, she rolled it between her fingers. "Chief Boyd's a good 'un, though. Not like that sea snake he replaced."

Saffi remembered the curmudgeon at breakfast. "Big-bellied racist named Luke?"

The way Jemma gripped the ballpoint pen told Saffi exactly how she felt about the old chief. The same way Saffi had felt about Jay when she tried to strangle Poppy's pen.

"Why did Luke get fired? If you don't mind sharing."

Jemma snorted. "Don't mind at all. Got caught shooting gulls from the prom with a speargun."

Saffi reeled back. "Are you kidding? That's insane."

"Him and some of his cronies thought it was a hoot. Luke always thought Boyd turned him in, but he didn't." Her grin went feral. "I did.

"So, Aunt Saffi, you OK with pub grub?"

Jemma's question threw Saffi for a loop. She'd been picturing cops shooting gulls like it was some kind of dystopian arcade game. Lunch was the last thing on her mind, and when she thought about the grub she'd seen on the pub's menu yesterday she couldn't muster a smile.

"Uhm." Saffi had never been good at hiding her feelings. "Sure?"

Jemma punched her shoulder. "Just messing with you. If you don't mind a bit of a hike, I've got fresh-picked crab and coleslaw at my place."

This time, Saffi tried harder to school her face. If Jemma had killed Jay or knocked out Reese, she should not traipse off to her place without anyone knowing where she'd gone.

Jemma leaned into her and whispered, "The only thing I plan to murder is a crab roll. Promise." A devilish smile deepened the leathery ruts in her weathered face.

Saffi decided to run with it. "Actually, I *could* kill a creamy coleslaw right now."

Why was it, Saffi wondered, that she ended up liking so many of her murder suspects? Or at the very least, getting to the end of a case with deep empathy for what had pushed them to such extremes? Perhaps it was because the clues had never led to someone who seemed truly evil. The other murders she had investigated had been crimes of passion or protection: "Good People Gone Bad." The idea for a *Bedside Reader* article popped into her mind, one well worth researching. If she continued to sleuth her way into the lives of murderers, she needed a deeper understanding of what made them tick—and suddenly turn. The urge to protect, for example, ran deep in humankind. The killer she had caught last Halloween certainly had it. Jemma had it, too. Much as Saffi wanted to trust the fisherman's daughter, she would walk into lunch at Jemma's warily, with eyes wide open for clues.

Instead of taking the boardwalk to Broadway, Jemma headed toward 12th Avenue. "Fewer tourists to avoid this way!" She grinned as she hit the sidewalk toward the promenade and picked up the pace. Saffi could hardly wait for another glimpse of the ocean. She had been cooped up inside the convention center for far too long. She missed her daily beach walks and early-morning tai chi by the sea. When they turned left at the promenade, the perpetual Pacific-borne breeze plastered Saffi's curls to the side of her face. The cold air coming off the sea pierced all the way to her eardrum. What she wouldn't give for a pair of ear bags right now. She'd left hers in the pocket of a jacket back in Last Chance Cove. She planted a hand over her right ear and kept it there as she hurried to catch up with Jemma.

A few blocks past the Broadway turnaround, they passed out of the commercial area and walked in the direction of Tillamook Head. Though she wanted to watch the sea shoosh toward the beach and sanderlings skitter across the sand, she needed to pay attention to where Jemma was taking her. She hoped for the best but needed to know which way to go if she had to make a run for it.

To her left, streets filled with gray-shingled houses dead-ended at the promenade. Thanks to their proximity to storms roaring off the Pacific, the asphalt-paved streets leading away from the prom were potholed, gravel-strewn, and overflowing with rain and seawater. Saffi was relieved to see a residential neighborhood holding back the tide of hotels and gift shops. Plenty of doors to knock on if she needed help.

The homes closest to the prom, Saffi noticed, looked newer, their pine-colored shingles not yet weathered to gray. They were taller and grander, with massive sea-facing windows. Part of her hated the fact that families living in Seaside for generations might have lost their ocean views. Another part of her eyed the houses for future writing retreats.

As they hurried past street after street, Tillamook Head loomed closer and closer. Soon, she had followed Jemma beyond the houses, beyond the paved promenade, and onto the side of a narrow road. The appropriately named Ocean Vista Drive soon gave way to Sunset Boulevard. Saffi's heart started to thud, whether from trepidation over venturing out of town or the memoir writer's speedy ambulation, she wasn't sure. Where *was* Jemma taking her? They had already walked at least a mile and, out here, only the gulls would hear her if she yelled for help.

TWENTY-ONE

As if sensing Saffi's tension, Jemma stopped and turned toward her with a smile sweet enough to gentle a horse—or maybe a seahorse, given their location. "Not to worry. We're almost there." She turned again to point toward a cove tucked against the headland. "That's Seaside Cove. Most tourists don't even know it's here. And that"—she nodded to the opposite side of the road—"is home."

On a small patch of land—half sand, half scrub-grass—separated from the sea by a raised road, a humped berm, and several hundred yards, Saffi spotted something totally unexpected: a horseshoe of vintage trailers. A carved and painted sign in front of the tiny park featured a mermaid with flowing locks. "The Mermaid's Purse," Saffi read the park's name aloud.

Mermaid's purses, Saffi knew from an article about whimsically named things in nature written for *Bedside Reader, #9,* were bladder-like casings in which some sharks and skates laid their eggs. They were usually found along the debris line among the seaweed and shells left behind by the ebbing tide. Mama sharks and skates laid the purses on the seabed floor. When the baby shark or skate hatched, it swam away, leaving the discarded casing to be swept ashore by the tide.

"I live in an RV, too." Saffi grinned. "But nothing like this. I think I'm in love."

Jemma chortled. "Thought you might like to see it, considering your whole 'Travels with Aunt Saffi' blog thing."

The tiny park had elements to drool over, such as an octagonal gazebo at its center. Baskets of hardy winter fuchsias hung from planter hooks on each of the gazebo's wooden roof supports. How they survived with wind whipping off the sea, Saffi did not know. Magic?

"Built the gazebo with a firepit in the center and a hole in the roof. Smoke just goes 'poof'!" Jemma made two fists then quickly opened her fingers as if releasing puffs of smoke.

"You mean, *built it* built it? As in with your own hands?"

Jemma grinned. "I can swing a hammer when I need to."

"Wow!" Saffi admired the gazebo with fresh eyes. She had screwed together a bookshelf or two with an Allen wrench, but building an outdoor haven that would stand against the coast's notorious storms? That took skill. She was growing more fond of Jemma by the minute—which, Saffi warned herself, could blind her to any murdery tendencies the memoir writer might have.

Paving stones formed pathways from the gazebo to the park's eight trailers. Each sat on a concrete pad large enough to provide patio space. Each patio had a pair of wooden beach chairs with a tiny table between them. The trailers were all decorated with fairy lights similar to those used on the Surrey cycles during the Jingle Tour. At night, the place must be beyond enchanting.

"Home sweet rolling home!" Jemma stopped and spread her arms wide with pride.

"I can't believe you get to *live* here!" Saffi's eyes went round with envy.

"I don't just live here. I inherited this plot of land and a run-down trailer from my dad. It was the only thing he managed to hold onto after his arthritis forced him off the trawlers and into retirement. I have no idea how he got the town to grant him an RV park permit. Always wondered if he had something on one of the muckety-mucks in town."

She really was a fisherman's daughter. Saffi needed to find time to read that memoir.

Jemma waved her forward and they wound around the gazebo onto the walkway that led to the center trailer.

"Did the town limit you to eight trailers?"

Jemma lifted her brows as if to say, "Do you really think they could?"

Saffi shook her head.

"No. I chose eight because of its power. It's an even number. Balanced between the spiritual and material realms. It brings harmony but also abundance."

Saffi trailed after Jemma, taking notes in her head for a future *Bedside Reader* article. Numerology in... town planning? Architecture? RV parks?

Jemma stopped, put her hands on her hips, her sea-green eyes bright with challenge. "Turn the number eight on its side and what do you get?"

Saffi's lips twisted as she tried to picture the numeral "8" lying sideways. Then she gasped. "Infinity!"

"Exactly. Eight offers infinite possibilities. It also symbolizes karmic cycles. What goes around, comes around."

From the look on Jemma's face, Saffi had a feeling that the karma she thought someone deserved had not yet come around.

"After Pops died, I spent a year restoring his old trailer. It reeked, let me tell you. It took me seven more years to find and restore the rest of the trailers here. Half are occupied year-round. Half are vacation rentals."

Saffi stared around the circle. She recognized most of the trailers as true classics, including a vintage pink-and-white Shasta Airflyte with iconic "wings" still on the rear corners, a bullet-shaped polished-aluminum Airstream Safari, and a two-door Terry Yellowstone that was twice the size of the one her friend Delilah lived in at Last Chance Cove RV Park. The path Jemma led her on ended at a Spartan Royal Mansion that was even longer than Saffi's Rambler Trek. She could barely contain her excitement. She'd seen pictures, but had never stepped inside such a rare and sought-after rig.

"You restored all of these?" Saffi's head swiveled right then left, then back to Jemma's RV park mansion.

Jemma nodded, then she lifted a silver coil chain from beneath her sweater, unhooked a keyring hanging from it, and unlocked the door, which, appropriately—for a fisherman's daughter—featured a porthole. Just outside the door, a nearly life-size wooden mermaid posed on a cross-section of driftwood. Before Jemma stepped into the Spartan, she cupped one of the mermaid's naked breasts. "For luck." She grinned, then waited to see if Saffi would accept the challenge.

The wood on the mermaid's right breast was darker than the rest of the sculpture, as if the oils in Jemma's hand had been absorbed over time. Saffi did her one better and cupped both of the mermaid's hard round breasts, one in each hand. "I could use a double dose of luck right now."

Jemma opened the rig's wood-framed screened door and waved Saffi inside. Thanks to the blond wooden paneling and abundance of windows, the space was both rich and light-filled.

Jemma's living room was stuffed with memorabilia. Cobalt-blue fishing floats, the glass kind that miraculously made it across the sea from Japan from time to time. Carved gulls balancing on spindly metal legs. Baskets filled with shells, dried-out sand dollars, and sea stars. And photos, lots and lots of photos. Saffi spotted a young Jemma with a sea-salted older man whose tangled red hair and glinting green eyes told her he had to be her father. As the Jemma in the photos aged, the fisherman disappeared and a growing Debbie took his place.

The place of honor in the middle of the shelving unit under the trailer's front windows featured a framed photo of two teenaged girls. Their gangly girl arms were wrapped over each other's shoulders and their grins stretched sky-wide as they held their day's catch high for the photographer. The hand-painted resin frame featured two mermaids, one swimming up the frame's right side, the other swimming down the left. A wooden plaque stood on a small easel beside the photo.

Saffi read the quote out loud. "They whispered to her, you cannot withstand the storm. She whispered back, I AM the storm."

"Helen." Jemma sighed. "She was the storm, all right. But it didn't save her."

Saffi reached a hand toward Jemma but instead of accepting comfort she shook herself and headed toward the far end of the trailer. "Kitchen's back here!" she called over her shoulder. Saffi followed, leaving behind the shadows that must chase Jemma every time she entered her RV.

"Sit!" Jemma ordered Saffi toward one of three chairs at a small, round, yellow-painted wooden table and started pulling containers out of the fridge.

Saffi obeyed, sliding her bottom onto a turquoise chair-cushion swimming with red-haired mermaids, bright yellow sea stars, and ripples of seaweed.

The kitchen had been updated, rather than restored, Jemma told her. Years of her father cooking for himself had trashed the original stove and fridge. "I chose retro appliances to preserve the vintage vibe."

The matching appliances had a pale turquoise tint Saffi loved. The color went well with Jemma's mermaid theme. "You really have an affinity for mermaids." She smiled.

"Well, duh." Jemma returned the smile, then after a moment's consideration, squinted. "You haven't read my memoir yet, have you?"

Heat rose into Saffi's cheeks. "No. I'm sorry. I've been caught up in the whole murder mystery thing."

"You're gonna have to read it to answer that question. Might help with some of the other questions you have, too."

Jemma's eyes turned storm-at-sea green and Saffi vowed to delve into the book this very evening.

As Saffi settled into her chair, someone rapped on the door.

"Mama Jem! You home?"

Before Jemma could respond, Debbie swept inside. "Have you heard anything about Reese? I can't get a word out of the hospital." Her voice changed to a prissy whine as she mimicked the receptionist. "If you're not a relative we can't release any information."

The table Saffi sat at was hidden behind a room divider that also served as a shelving unit.

"Debs." Jemma nodded in Saffi's direction and Saffi leaned beyond the divider to wave.

Debbie's lips clapped shut like a startled clam.

As Jemma's foster daughter wandered into the kitchen, Saffi patted the table, hoping the young woman would join her. "I'm happy to share what I know about Reese," she offered. "If you'll do the same."

Debbie glanced at Jemma, who shrugged. "Your story. Your funeral if she blabs."

"How about I go first?" Saffi smiled, hoping she looked trustworthy instead of as treacherous as she feared she might be if Debbie or Jemma had harmed Reese.

Debbie nodded, then pulled out the chair opposite Saffi. She sat gazing out the window at the sea while Saffi filled them in on Reese's condition, including the fact that he probably had nothing more than a mild concussion. As Saffi told them about the MRI the doctor insisted he have before flying, Jemma busied herself at the tiled kitchen counter. She opened containers, toasted three hoagie rolls, then ladled gobs of flaky white crabmeat into them. She topped each one with cheese and stuck them—one at a time—into the microwave for a quick meltdown.

A microwave, Saffi noted, was definitely not a vintage item, but like the other kitchen appliances, it had a retro design with lovely curved edges. Once the last sandwich emerged with brie oozing over the top, Jemma filled white ceramic ramekins with creamy coleslaw and brought the feast to the table. Saffi could barely talk for salivating.

"Thank you for sharing that." Debbie bowed her head over folded hands. "I was so afraid I'd..." The young woman sat up straight, and then moved her thick black braid from behind her neck to over her shoulder. As she talked, she nervously ran the braid's tip back and forth across her palm as if it was a paintbrush and her hand was the canvas. "We were just having a few drinks, you know? Then Reese spotted the duckboats through the window and suggested a moonlight river cruise. He wanted to take selfies to"—she made air quotes with her fingers—"'quack up' his buds back home. He even messaged one to his big sister." Her smile showed fondness rather than a proclivity to conk a date on the head. "Said he loved waking her up in the middle of the night.

"Anyway, we were so snockered we had a hard time pedaling straight. Went around in circles for a while." She glanced at Jemma, who rolled her green eyes heavenward. "When we came out from under the bridge, someone chucked something off and it hit him. He went out like someone had flipped his switch." Debbie pressed her lips together and took a long slow breath that pinched her nostrils together.

"Eat!" Jemma insisted. "We can't sit here yammering the day away. I still have books to sell."

Saffi didn't need more encouragement. She grabbed the crab roll, squeezed one end together and took a massive bite. "Oh, mmh-gahd!" she mumbled around the sweet, tender, cheesy crab melt.

Jemma chuckled. "You'll never guess how I came by that crab."

Saffi shook her head but kept chewing.

"That man of yours stored his crabs in the Necanicum's kitchen."

"Mmphf." Saffi waved a hand. She had forgotten all about Troy's crabs.

"Guess he flew out without telling anyone what to do with

them. So, Phyllis—she rents the Shasta from me—gave me a call, and *voilà!* Crab rolls for lunch."

Phyllis? Saffi almost bit her tongue. She chewed the bite of succulent crab and crusty bread she'd just taken, then swallowed.

Jemma gave her a studied look. "Fleeing the scene of the crime, was he?"

Saffi pressed her palms into her thighs. "More like rethinking dating a writer who thinks she's Enola Holmes."

Debbie's face went blank. "Who?"

"Sherlock's little sister." Saffi winked.

Jemma waved a hand. "I like that about you. You sniff along crime trails like an anteater snorting ants."

The image sent both Debbie and Saffi into fits of laughter and by the time they stopped, they'd formed a bond that felt so much like trust it pained Saffi to ask, but she had to. "Debbie? Reese wasn't found until morning. Did you—" She sucked in a deep breath. "Did you leave him there?"

Tears sparkled in the young woman's eyes. "I jacked the duck-boat. And it wasn't the first time. The owners are friends, but the last time I 'borrowed' a boat I forgot to lock it up at the dock. It floated all the way to the estuary on the outgoing tide and headed out to sea. They're pissed as heck at me right now. If they found out I'd done it again, they'd go to the chief."

Jemma set down the half-sandwich she'd been holding. "Deb's got a wee record. Kid stuff. But... around here? They throw the book at native kids."

"I thought you said Chief Boyd was a 'good 'un.'" Saffi lifted her brows in challenge.

"Yeah. Well." Jemma shrugged. "With everything going on right now, if the chief finds out Deb left that guy and ran, he'd put both of us under that magnifying glass of his." The two women exchanged a look that told Saffi they probably had more to hide than a simple duckboat hijack. "Time to get back." Jemma jerked Saffi's plate out from under her so fast she barely had time to grab the last bite of crab roll. A few minutes later, she had shuffled Saffi out the front door.

"I, uhm. Aren't you coming?" Saffi stood on the concrete patio and glanced right. Would the map she'd created in her head take her back to the convention center?

"Prom." Jemma waved toward the sound of the sea. "Broadway. Left at the Bridge Tender and Sam's your uncle."

TWENTY-TWO

The path was clear but the clues were not. Debbie had abandoned Reese in that duckboat. Unconscious, on the water, in a town he'd barely stepped into. Her concern for Reese seemed real enough. It also seemed tinged with something—remorse? Maybe Debbie blamed herself for what had happened to Reese, especially the part where she'd facilitated an illegal, drunken joyride on the river.

What else had she learned from her lunch with foster mother and daughter? For one thing, Helen's presence hung over their lives like a restless ghost. The shrine to Helen on Jemma's shelf showed that, for the memoir writer, the past was present every single day. That photo would stab her through the heart every morning when she woke and every night before she slept. It would keep the pain of Helen's disappearance fresh, allowing the decades-old wound to fester rather than heal.

The fisherman's daughter was strong, capable, protective, loving, and filled to bursting with rage. Enough rage to strangle a man? Certainly. But, as far as Saffi could tell, Jemma had absolutely no motive to turn that rage on Jay GoodVender. If she ever caught the person who'd torn Helen from her life—and Debbie's—that would be a different story.

And Debbie? Her childhood had been shadowed by her mother's disappearance, and Mama Jem's inability to let it go surely shaped Debbie's attitudes toward the community she grew up in. There had been no mention of a father in her life. Was he a local? If so, why didn't he seem to have a role in his daughter's life?

Could these family dynamics have anything at all to do with the murder she had committed herself to solving? Probably not, but if she wanted information about Helen's cold case, she knew just who to ask: Chief Boyd.

Her cellphone told her that the police station wasn't far from The Mermaid's Purse. A quick detour would not take too big a bite out of Poppy's plans for the rest of Saffi's day. There was, she remembered, a publishers' roundtable she was supposed to attend later, and an after-dinner chocolate martini and marshmallow schmooze at the Necanicum Inn's riverside firepit.

Instead of following Jemma's easy instructions, Saffi walked north until she hit Avenue U. From there, a brisk walk took her to South Holladay. She reached the police station in ten minutes. It took five more to convince the officer at the desk to tell the chief that she wanted to speak with him. She spent another ten minutes thumping her heels on the legs of the uncomfortable blue plastic chair the desk sergeant had directed her to. She waited... and waited... and waited. What had made her think the town's chief law enforcement officer would give her time in his busy day?

Just as she stood to retreat out the door, Chief Boyd strode into the lobby. The intensity in his pale blue eyes held her in place. "This way, please." He ushered her into the interior of the building and opened a door into a sparsely furnished office. The room smelled of stale coffee and stress with a hint of... what was that? Coconut prawns? The important police work that had kept her waiting was lunch?

The chief seated himself in a lumbar-support office chair behind a desk that had seen better decades. Then he waved Saffi into a padded metal chair that looked only slightly more comfortable than the one she had just vacated.

"How can I help you, Ms. Graywood?"

On the walk to the station, Saffi had thought about what she would share to soften the chief up so she could do a bit of probing into Jemma and Debbie. She started by spilling the beans on Fia's midnight booth move and the fact that, according to Fia, Eileen Esterhaven had instructed the young woman to clear the space.

Chief Boyd straightened. "You entered the convention center illegally? After hours?"

Saffi clutched her hands together and explained that she had seen someone go into the building and followed.

"Because you are *so* much better at investigating than the local po-po?"

Saffi unclenched her hands and sat on them to contain her nervous energy. "It seemed to me that time was of the essence."

He nodded, then pulled a notebook closer and jotted something down on a blank page. Then he looked up, his eyes shadowed as if a cloud had blocked the sun. "No matter the hour, we are always a simple phone call away."

"Of course." Saffi could not hold that intense blue gaze for more than a few seconds.

"And the nefarious Fia secreted Mr. GoodVender's items... where?"

"In one of the convention center's storage rooms."

Chief Boyd relaxed against the back of his chair and rolled it far enough away to rest his left ankle on his right knee. "Good."

"Good?" Saffi almost yelped.

The chief linked his fingers and stretched his arms above his head. "That's exactly where I told Ms. Esterhaven to move the items after she petitioned me to allow her to empty the booth. In the interest of the booksellers' convention, of course."

"But Fia said—" Saffi stopped herself. She remembered asking Fia if Eileen had police permission to pack up Jay's booth. She did not remember Fia answering the question. Instead, she had done her befuddled baby fawn thing, talking around the question to justify her actions. Eileen had told her to move Jay's "stuff." She was moving it. End of story. She had not implied that Eileen had something to hide, even though—Saffi pressed a hand against the folded paper in her pocket—she did.

"OK. Then can I assume that you or one of your officers picked up the organizer box I told you about from the booth?"

"The one with the flower receipt that would bust the case of the Necanicum Inn attacker wide open?"

Saffi got it. He was the cat, she was the mouse and batting her about was a game he liked to play. Now, she had no problem meeting and holding his gaze. This time, he dropped his eyes first.

"I sent an officer to the booth but she did not find an organizer box, incriminating or not."

Earlier, she had planned to share the form Eileen had signed with Chief Boyd. Now the amusement in his eyes prevented her from embarrassing herself any further than she already had. She had also lost her enthusiasm for putting Deb or Jemma under the scrutiny of those far too intelligent blue eyes.

"If there's nothing else..." He pushed his chair back and stood, ready to escort her out of the office.

Saffi got to her feet, but stood her ground. "Apparently, I have just enough experience helping law enforcement solve murder cases to irk someone, but not enough to know when I'm being helpful and when I'm getting in the way."

His amusement softened toward appreciation. "Solved a few murder cases, have you?"

Saffi nodded. "Two, in fact."

Chief Boyd scratched the gingery late-afternoon bristle on his chin. "That's two more than me."

She could hardly believe he'd admitted such a thing. "The most useful information I have right now is that, if you still think my editor killed Jay GoodVender, or if you see me as a suspect, you're throwing your net in the wrong part of the ocean."

Chief Boyd chuckled. "Your editor told me that if I wanted to understand you I should read one of your books."

"And did you?"

He twisted his lips into a grin. "I might have skimmed a page or two. I like the way you make a convincing case no matter the topic. And I like the way you turn a phrase even better." When he blushed to the tips of his ears, Saffi realized he'd noticed more about her than her way with words.

"Well, thank you." She licked her lips then immediately regretted what that probably looked like. "Ah, so... OK. I, uh, better get back to the convention center." She scurried out of his office like a mouse with its tail between its legs. She had gone there to learn more about Jemma and Debbie, and possibly about Helen's disappearance, but all she'd managed to learn was that Chief Boyd could discombobulate her like nobody's business. *Blast!*

Security at the convention center had gotten a bit lax since yesterday. The guards had checked the same people in and out so many times they probably recognized everyone on sight, Saffi included. This time, Zach stood at the entry door. The young security guard gave her a quick wave through, but she hesitated. Now seemed as good a time as any to ask him about whether he'd ridden with Fia on the Jingle Tour.

"Have you seen Fia this afternoon? I saw the two of you sharing a Surrey cycle the other evening." The blank look Zach gave her said a lot.

"I wouldn't be caught dead in one of those things." He snorted, as if appreciating his own gallows humor.

"Sorry, my mistake."

Just as Saffi entered the lobby, Fia hurried across, and Saffi stepped into her path to block her escape. "Do you have a sec? I'd like to show you something."

Fia sighed. "Fine. If you must, but the publishers' roundtable is about to start. Aren't you taking part?"

Saffi shook her head. "Poppy wants me there but she's the insider. This one's her show."

"Let's walk and talk." Fia headed down the corridor at a fast clip and Saffi double-timed to keep up. "What did you want to show me?" Fia turned toward Saffi.

Saffi patted the pocket of her jeans and pulled out the folded form. She unfolded it and held it out to Fia. The young bookseller took the form, glanced at both sides, then frowned. "How did you get this?"

Instead of answering the question, Saffi took a page from Fia's playbook. "Eileen told me you had approved Jay's application. That she would never have done so, and that all the mess that followed was your fault."

Fia braked so fast her clinking braids kept going while the rest of her stopped. She clenched her fists and turned on Saffi. "Eileen never said that."

"Didn't she?" Two could play at answering questions with questions.

"You're trying to turn me against her but that's not going to happen. If I keep this convention on track—and, so far, I have done so, despite one of our vendors getting himself *killed*—Eileen has promised me a management position in her Portland store." The minute the words left her mouth, Fia's brown eyes widened and she put a hand over her lips.

So. The truth was out. Fia had a career-building promotion at stake. And if she had something at stake... Saffi would have slapped her forehead if she hadn't been facing the young woman. Neither of the two young security guards had even *met* Fia, which meant she had *not* ridden in a Surrey cycle with either of them. Saffi thought back to the moment before the man in the black hoodie pedaled toward Fia. He had looked so much like Jay GoodVender she had thought about warning Fia. Saffi went for the kill while Fia's damning admission still hung in the air.

"You were on the Jingle Tour with Jay. Did you kill him?" She'd seen Fia leave the cycle and hurry into the Carousel Mall, but Jay could have waited for her to rejoin him.

Fia's cheeks bulged behind her hand and, for a second, Saffi thought the young woman would spew. Instead, she turned, fled down the hall and disappeared into Necanicum West, the room in which the publishers' roundtable would take place.

Why, Saffi asked herself, would a young woman so intent on climbing the ladder as a bookseller risk it all by killing someone? She could not come up with a single reason for Fia to resort to murder. She also could not imagine Fia wrapping those lights around Jay's neck and strangling him to death. She wasn't even sure the young woman would have the physical strength to overpower GoodVender.

What she *could* imagine was Fia following Eileen Esterhaven's instructions. If Eileen told Fia to ride with Jay on the Jingle Tour, she would do it. If Eileen asked her to smooth things over? To make sure GoodVender would not sue the booksellers association for the security guards' treatment? Fia would do that as well.

Eileen Esterhaven was shrewd. She had bribed Fia with a plum position to get her to straighten out the mess she had made when she let Jay into the convention. If things went prune-shaped, Eileen could disavow all knowledge of everything she asked Fia to do. Would she go so far as to set Fia up for a murder she intended to commit?

Saffi rubbed her temples. Trying to picture the polished Eileen Esterhaven as a strangler made her head hurt. Eileen had the moves of a practiced executive. Like Poppy she would rely on lawyers—or underlings—to get what she wanted or needed done. But Saffi knew her rationalizations were colored by the facts: Eileen's stores sold thousands and thousands of *Bedside Readers*. It would be career suicide to accuse the president of the booksellers association without evidence of any kind.

If there was evidence to be found, there were only two places she knew to look. In Jay's organizer—which someone had spirited away—and in the storage room where she and Fia had secured his boxes. She had to find a way into that storage room, but before she could, she had to show up at the publishers' roundtable, or risk a genuine Poppy Morales meltdown.

TWENTY-THREE

Saffi peeked into Necanicum West. Nearly every seat had already been filled with booksellers eager to hear publishing pros talk about their spring releases. Poppy waved Saffi to the front row where Willow had somehow managed to hold a seat for her. Her editor sat in front of the wall of windows behind a semicircle of convention tables loaded with books. Each roundtable participant had ten minutes to book-talk spring titles, after which they would take questions from the audience. Most roundtable speakers were from sales and marketing, though the group included a few editors, like Poppy, who represented their company's biggest titles.

As the panelists talked, Saffi's attention wandered. She spotted Fia plastered against the far wall like a newborn deer trying to blend into the foliage. Unfortunately, the wall was gray and Fia's pantsuit was blue-green. It looked gorgeous with her fawn-brown skin and long box-braided hair but showcased her beauty instead of allowing her to disappear into the background. Zach should be so lucky. *Not.*

If Fia had climbed into that Surrey cycle with Jay GoodVender, what had happened next? Had he laughed in her face? Told her that he planned to sue the North Coast Booksellers Association along with Aunt Saffi's pals at Lowry & Lowenstein? Had she cracked under the pressure from Eileen to fix things and wrapped those fairy lights around his neck?

Fia's reaction to Saffi's challenge told her the young woman would have been far more likely to flee than fight. That was, after all, her *modus operandi*. From their first encounter at the association's booth on Thursday afternoon to their most recent exchange outside this room, Fia had fled. Her other MO was to obfuscate. Saffi had no doubt Fia had been on the Jingle Tour with Jay and that the young woman knew things she wanted to remain hidden, things Saffi intended to get out of her, one way or another.

Sudden silence brought Saffi's attention back to the round-table. The book talks had ended. The moderator, who turned out to be George, asked the audience for questions, then pointed to someone who raised her hand.

"I get my *Bedside Reader* order two weeks before the on-sale date." A woman leaned forward in her padded folding chair. "The books just sit in the back room taking up space but not earning a dime."

"On-sale dates" referred to the exact day books ordered by a store could go on sale. For eagerly anticipated titles—the next book in the best-selling Chief Inspector Gamache mystery series by Louise Penny, for example—selling a book before its "on-sale" date could put a store in hot water.

To Saffi, this seemed as good a time as any to slip out for a quick search. "I'll be right back," she whispered to Willow.

She passed Larry from the chamber of commerce handing out brochures in the hallway. His friendly wave and greeting helped convince a convention center staffer to let her into the storage room.

"Anything for Aunt Saffi." Larry winked.

The staffer—a middle-aged man dressed in khakis, a green convention center polo shirt, and the kind of cheap black sneakers worn by underpaid service workers—led her to the storage room at the end of the corridor. After he unlocked the door, Saffi promised him a free signed copy if he came by the booth before the exhibit hall closed. "I should be there between four and five."

He thanked her profusely, then showed her how to make sure the door locked behind her when she was done. His dimpled smile and friendly wave made her feel guilty about misleading him, and she vowed to hurry so that her search would not get him into trouble.

The storage room had floor-to-ceiling metal shelving units. Cardboard storage boxes with lids lined most of the shelves, each with a white identification label on the front of the box. When Saffi and Fia had moved Jay's things in the middle of the night, they had simply found an empty shelf toward the back and stacked his boxes and other materials on it. The mess looked exactly as Saffi remembered, which begged the question, Had Eileen really been trying to hide something or had she told Chief Boyd the truth about why she wanted Jay's booth cleared?

Saffi had half hoped Fia or Eileen had discovered GoodVender's organizer box in the booth where she had left it. If either of them had, it had not been stored with the rest of his things. Since Fia had packed most of Jay's belongings into boxes before Saffi intruded, this would be her first—probably only—chance to look for clues in what he had left behind.

She found boxes filled with Jay's "Original *Bedside Readers*" and quickly closed each one with distaste. Another box had been hastily stuffed with marketing materials: postcards, flyers, printed newsletters—a bit of an oddity in the online age—and boxes of business cards. She found pens, fridge magnets, tumblers, and baseball caps bearing GoodVender's series title and a dorky duck logo that had probably been AI-generated. She had to say one thing for Jay: he had gone all in for this convention. Between the printed books, promotional products, booth fee, convention registration, and travel, food, and hotel costs... he had invested at least fifteen grand, probably more. Clearly, he had been convinced that the trade show would turn the trivia book world against Aunt Saffi and toward him.

"And all he got for his money was a string of fairy lights," Saffi murmured.

The last box Saffi opened held thin, spiral-bound composition books, like the one she had seen in the bottom drawer of Jay's organizer box. She lifted one off the top labeled *Danced to Death*. Inside, she found notes... the same kind of notes she took when writing *Bedside Reader* articles. Anecdotes—short, fact-filled stories—about individuals or couples who had danced until they died. His notes included dates, names, and places, as well as notations about other sources to consult for verification. For each anecdote, he had listed the source, the date of publication, and the author. His notes were as meticulous as hers. For the second time since she had started digging through Jay's leavings, she felt a grudging connection to a kindred spirit—one warped by envy and malice, but motivated to find the most interesting true stories and share them with readers. If he'd spent more time developing his own style instead of trying to copy hers, he might have given her a run for her money. Envy and anger as primary drivers rarely led to success.

Each composition book had a different title. Each one was crammed with notes. Saffi had investigated graphology, the science of analyzing personality by examining handwriting. She had been hoping to find a correlation between sociopathic tendencies and handwriting to hang a *Bedside Reader* article on. In the end, she abandoned the idea as too speculative. Graphologists had found certain similarities to be characteristic of sociopathic tendencies, but, by itself, handwriting was far from enough to enable a psychologist to produce a diagnosis. Still, Jay's writing exhibited characteristics she remembered. In some places, his letters were larger, darker, and indented as if he had applied heavy pressure with each stroke. Every page included random bolded words or words and phrases in all caps, sometimes circled or underlined with dark, thick strokes. Every time he dotted an "i" the tip of his pencil punctured the paper. His writing fell above the ruled lines in some places, below it in others and the slants of his letters were equally varied—sometimes to the left, sometimes to the right.

After flipping through a few of the composition books, Saffi stacked them all back into the box. She did not need handwriting to diagnose Jay GoodVender's sociopathic personality. He had shown exactly who he was with both words and actions since the day he stopped gushing like a fan and started vilifying, harassing, and stalking her.

Saffi leaned against the storage rack, staring at the light filtering through the frosted clerestory windows at the end of the room. Something nagged at her—the notebook he had filed in the organizer box labeled *Silenced in Seaside*. If that had been her storage box, she would have carried the composition book inside for one reason: she was collecting information for an article. Had Jay discovered a story in Seaside after he'd arrived? One that drove him to dig deep into... what? Something that had gotten him killed?

The tiny tourist town by the sea had its share of secrets, two of which she had already encountered: Helen, a missing native mom who had never been found, and Sonya, a murdered local whose killer had never been apprehended. Was there some connection between the two? Had GoodVender found that connection?

Saffi picked up the top composition book and flapped it against her thigh as she thought about the notes Jay might have scribbled across its pages. "Silenced in Seaside. Silenced in Seaside. Silenced in—"

A sudden change in air pressure made Saffi start to turn, but before she could, steps rushed forward and an arm went around her neck. Saffi dropped the notebook to the floor and grabbed at the arm. She tried, and failed, to wrench it away. She tried a backward head thrust, but the arm tightened its grip, cutting off her air supply. Saffi's head throbbed. Her heart rate spiraled upward. As dizziness swept over her, she kicked out her feet hoping to force her assailant to bear her weight. When that didn't work, she went limp, hoping her weight would take her to the floor. Her brain had one final thought as she crumpled into unconsciousness: *silenced in Seaside, indeed.*

TWENTY-FOUR

"Saffi! Saffi, wake up!" A hand shook her shoulder and she tried to brush it away. For some reason, she couldn't lift her hand. She felt as feeble as the fawn bending over her, bleating her name into her ear. "Saffi! Oh, God, please wake the freak up!" The hand shook her harder, and Saffi tried to move away. "If you don't wake up my career is over!" the fawn bleated.

Did fawns have careers? Or words, for that matter? Something was seriously wrong with her brain. Lack of oxygen? Or was she dead? Maybe fawns could talk in heaven.

"Step aside, ma'am," a gruff male voice ordered, and the fawn's voice retreated. "Saffi." A work-roughened hand took hers and gave it a squeeze. "It's me. Chief Boyd. Help is on the way."

"Look! Her eyes are open!" the fawn bleated.

"Good." Someone strong put their hands beneath her armpits, lifted her off the floor, then eased her into a sitting position. Something that felt like a cardboard box dug into her back. "Saffi!" Fingers snapped in her face. Something pink and blurred and frowny came closer and closer. She blinked her eyes, trying to focus the image.

"Silenced," she mumbled, and, perhaps, drooled a bit.

"Yes. I believe you were," said the face.

Saffi tried to shake her head, but it simply flopped forward, and the lights went out again.

The next time Saffi woke, bright lights seared into her eyeballs and her head began to pound. She lifted a hand to shield her eyes from the glare.

"Well, well. My partner in peril awakens at last."

A young man sat near her feet on what—given the bleached white sheets, flimsy woven blanket, and antiseptic smell—could only be a hospital bed. Brown hair, designer glasses, slightly bulbous nose. Saffi's brain put two and two together and came up with, "Reese?"

"At your service." He inclined his head.

"Are we sharing a room or something?" she croaked. When Saffi looked around, she saw blue curtains enclosing the bed.

"Nope, that little throat squeeze didn't rate a room. Although, you did get that jazzy oxygen mask." He tapped on the mask covering Saffi's face and nose. She hadn't even realized she was wearing it.

When she took a deep breath, she felt dizzy, nauseous, and her heart was thumping along like a three-legged racehorse. A racehorse someone had tried—and fortunately, failed—to silence. *Silenced... in Seaside!*

Saffi sat up so fast her head spun. "I need to talk to Chief Boyd!"

"Whoa, Nellie." Reese motioned her back onto the pillows. "He stepped out for a minute, but he'll be back."

"OK." Saffi pressed her palms against her belly and tried not to barf. "Is there a...?" She tugged off the oxygen mask.

Her face must have turned green because Reese produced a plastic basin much faster than she could regurgitate the remains of the crab roll she had eaten at Jemma's. "Sorry." She wiped goop from the corners of her mouth with her hand, then looked around for something to wipe the yuck off her hand.

"Here!" A hand held out a moist towelette.

"Chief! You were in heaven with me and the fawn." Her voice sounded like she'd swallowed gravel. She put a tentative hand to her throat, grimacing when her fingers hit sore spots.

The flabbergasted look the chief returned told Saffi she should probably stop talking. But, that was not Saffi's way. She immediately plowed into her search of the storage room, the box filled with composition books, and her theory that Jay had stumbled on a story here in Seaside that had gotten him killed. "So, you see... it had nothing at all to do with Poppy, or with me." By the time she finished talking, her throat was on fire and she could barely whisper.

Chief Boyd crinkled his nose. "What is that smell?"

Reese looked sheepish. Instead of taking Saffi's barf to a bathroom and flushing it, he had tucked the basin under her bed. "I'll just..." He slid off the bed, leaned down to snag it, then hurried into the corridor where he proceeded to sympathy-gag. When the intern came back into the room, he took a hasty leave. "I think I should call Poppy. Let her know you're awake."

Chief Boyd sat down on the rolling stool that was usually reserved for the ER doctor. He removed his policeman's hat, perched it on his knee, and ran a hand over his ginger buzz cut. "Did you take down the box and strew those journals all over the floor?" His eyes shone with challenge.

"What? No." Saffi shook her head and the room went spinning. "Whoa." She clutched the sheet until the room stilled and her belly settled. "I put them... back," she rasped out. "Had one in my hand when... attacked."

"So, someone choked you unconscious, went through the journals, then left you and the mess they'd made behind."

"'Xactly." Saffi continued to clutch the sheet to remind herself that headshaking was a bad idea.

"OK. So, your attacker took the, uhm, *Silenced in Seaside* composition book. The one you think might break open a local case. The one that got Jay killed."

"Yes." Saffi caught herself. "No!" She swallowed to lubricate her throat. "Organizer box."

"The composition book was in the missing organizer?" Chief Boyd took a black notepad and a pen out of his shirt pocket and scribbled a few notes. "Did you show the notebook to anyone else? Tell anyone else about it?"

Saffi licked her lips, wishing her mouth tasted of something besides sick. "No. I don't think so."

"Saffi." The chief leaned forward, twirling his hat between his hands. "Was the notebook in heaven? You know, with me, you, and the fawn?"

Great. He thought she had hallucinated the notebook. "When Fia found you, you were mumbling about being silenced in Seaside. Perhaps your brain—while trying to make sense of your experience—conjured that particularly pertinent journal."

Saffi leaned back on the pillow and squeezed her eyes shut. "You're making my head hurt."

"I'm sorry." The chief's voice went husky. "I don't want to cause you any pain. I just want to have the facts in hand as I track down your attacker."

Saffi forced her eyes open and met his. "Give me that!" She held out a hand for his notepad and pen. Reluctantly, he handed it over.

The composition book is real, she wrote. *It was in an organizer box in Jay's booth. When Fia took a load of boxes to the storage room, I took the organizer and hid it so that I could search it for clues. I saw the title on the journal but, at the time, I was looking for something else, so I didn't pay it any heed.*

When she handed back the pad, the chief read what she'd scribbled and nodded. "Ms. Graywood, are you alert enough to understand that you just confessed to taking evidence in a murder investigation? In writing." His mouth quirked sideways.

Saffi! Stop talking! Her fuzzy brain tried to warn her but she plowed ahead. "I didn't put myself in this hospital bed." She clutched her sore throat and glared.

"OK." Chief Boyd tightened his grip on his hat. "Did you show Jay's notebook to anyone else?"

Saffi thought back to her search of the organizer box. She had just found Jay's booth application form when Willow showed up and snatched up the papers. Willow might have seen the notebook, but Saffi hadn't shown it to her. She saw no reason to put a target on Willow's back. "No."

The chief flipped his notepad open to a blank page. Then he asked Saffi for a timeline of when she had taken the box, when she returned it to Jay's booth, and when it "disappeared" again. She did her best to recall exact times but had to admit that they were only guesses. He asked her for names of anyone she had seen in the area. This time she gave him a name: "Jemma Weathers."

The chief looked up, startled. "Jemma?"

Much as she liked the memoir writer, Jemma was a local. If Jay had been investigating Seaside cold cases, Jemma had a strong personal motive for wanting to know what he might have uncovered.

With a click of his pen, the chief was done. He stuffed his notepad into his pocket and stood, rolling the kinks from his shoulders. "Look. I really don't want to be known as the small-town police chief who let Aunt Saffi get killed on his watch. Could you stop with the sleuthing? Please?" He jammed his hat on his head and gave Saffi a pleading stare.

Saffi couldn't agree, but she also couldn't lie. Especially not when the chief had asked so politely. "I need a nap." She pressed her lips together, closed her eyes, and breathed slowly and evenly until the door swooshed closed behind him.

Though she still felt slightly woozy, the attending physician—a young doctor with a Punjabi accent—released her after two hours of observation. "Take it easy this evening," he instructed. "Put an ice pack on your neck if it feels sore. Take ibuprofen for pain relief, but avoid alcohol, at least for tonight."

Getting out of the emergency room was almost as painful as getting in. The bill shot her blood pressure sky-high, but when she presented her insurance card to the man behind the billing window, his frown turned to a relieved smile. "Oh, good. You have no idea how many patients come through here with absolutely no insurance. It's *so* stressful." He pressed his hands on either side of his face to emphasize his point.

Saffi lifted a brow. *Not half as stressful for you as for the person trying to heal while being dunned for money.*

Now, all Saffi wanted was an Uber, a shower, and to reconnect with the Lowry & Lowenstein team at the chocolate martini and marshmallow schmooze, which was, fortunately, at the firepit directly below her balcony.

The shower helped, and after a short nap on the sofa in front of the fire, she felt refreshed. Her mind had cleared and the oxygen she'd inhaled at the hospital had given her a bit of a happy high. The ER visit gave Saffi the perfect excuse to dress down... way down. She bundled up in thick flannel jammies and a hotel robe, pulled on woolly socks and stuffed her feet into sloggers. She wrapped a fluffy scarf around her neck for warmth, and to hide the bruises. Then she tucked one of the inn's extra blankets under her arm to take to the firepit. She would have to forgo the chocolate martinis, but she was ready to roast marshmallows with the best of them.

As Saffi passed by the check-in counter on her way to the gathering, she spotted Phyllis. The light from the computer screen made the desk clerk's face glow. She glanced up with an open, friendly smile but when she recognized Saffi, a guilty look replaced the smile. *What was that all about?* Despite the chief's warning about staying safe, she decided to stop for a chat.

"Hi, Phyllis!" She used the clerk's name, hoping the overture would seem friendly, but her newly acquired vocal croak sounded downright stalkery. "Sorry." She put a hand to her throat, hoping the scarf still hid her bruises.

Phyllis's eyes widened with concern. "Are you OK?"

"Bit of a sore throat." She waved away the pain, determined to push through it. "Your neighbor, Jemma, told me you shared the crab my friend left in the kitchen fridge with her."

Phyllis glanced over her shoulder as if checking for a supervisor. "Yes, well, he didn't leave any instructions so when he checked out..." Now the desk clerk looked guilty.

Saffi reached out a hand. "Perfect. I had forgotten all about them until Jemma invited me over for crab rolls. They were delish."

Phyllis's eyes brightened with relief. "Oh, I'm so glad you got to enjoy them, too."

Saffi put her hands on the counter and leaned in conspiratorially. "Much better than having crabs in the bathtub, let me tell you."

Phyllis wrinkled her nose and made scratching motions with her fingers. "Or in the bed." Her brown eyes widened as if she realized she'd broken the invisible barrier between hotel staff and guest. "Oops!" She immediately fell back into desk clerk mode, which turned out to be an even bigger mistake. "I hope you're enjoying your stay at the Necanicum Inn, Ms. Graywood." Her look went from mortified to terrified as she waited for Saffi to pounce.

Saffi offered an understanding smile. "It's a lovely inn. I hope to come back sometime, for play, I mean. Not for work. Or murder." Saffi pulled a face.

"Listen." It was Phyllis's turn to lean forward. "I'm really sorry about the flowers. On the phone, Mr. GoodVender sounded so... normal. I had no idea he was a stalk—" She stopped herself before she revealed just how much she now knew about Jay. The Seaside grapevine had been busy.

"No worries." Saffi waved away her concern. If Phyllis was in the mood to gossip, maybe she should ask *her* some questions about the cold case she'd hoped to discuss with Chief Boyd earlier. "Listen, Phyllis, Jemma told me a little about her friend, Helen. The woman who disappeared. I didn't want to probe a raw wound but it left me a bit... concerned... about whether law enforcement will be able to wrap the Surrey cycle murder up before it's time for me to fly home."

Phyllis wrung her hands together. "That case was bungled, but not by Chief Boyd. Luke Atwell was in charge and he could not see beyond his stupid prejudices. It was a happy day in Seaside when he got the boot."

Phyllis's face saddened. "They were inseparable, Jemma and Helen. Sonya, too." The memory brightened her face. "Called themselves the three mermaids. You know, like the three musketeers, but for girls. When Helen went missing, it fractured Jemma and Sonya's friendship beyond repair."

This was new information. Important information. Helen had gone missing. Sonya had been murdered. The two things had happened decades apart, but if Jay had found a connection, he could have stuck his nose into a case someone wanted left cold. She tried to remember if she'd seen any pictures in Jemma's living room with three teenaged girls, rather than two. No. If there had been any of those, the fisherman's daughter must have stored them away.

"Why did they fall out, Sonya and Jemma?" Saffi probed. "I would think losing Helen would bring the other two mermaids closer."

Phyllis's lips tightened into a thin, hard line. "Jemma thought Sonya knew something. No matter how many times Jemma begged, she wouldn't tell her what it was. Protecting that uncle of hers, if you ask me. Cops' families stick together tighter than ticks on a hound's hind end." After that pronouncement, Phyllis seemed to realize she had divulged too much, and to a near-total stranger. She excused herself and fled to a small office behind the check-in counter.

Saffi had heard enough to make an educated guess. Sonya—the woman whose murder Chief Boyd had not solved—was one of "theirs," not just because she was white, but because she was part of a police officer's family. The portly Luke's, perchance? Once she returned from the martini and marshmallow schmooze, a quick search online into Sonya's murder seemed like a purposeful—and, hopefully, safe—next move.

TWENTY-FIVE

Saffi huddled beneath the blanket she'd brought from her room and sipped the spicy hot chocolate the inn's staff had brought her. A dessert tray had been set up on a slatted wooden side table beside her Adirondack chair. "Chef put this together just for you." The server smiled.

She sampled a truffle—dark chocolate and Grand Marnier—and groaned her thanks. "Cognac with bitter orange... my favorite! How did he know?" She leaned forward. "Just don't tell my doc I'm imbibing."

The server laughed. "Your secret's safe with me."

As the most recent victim of "the creepiest convention ever," Saffi could have held court into the wee hours, but grilling Phyllis had wrecked what was left of her voice. Instead of talking, she sat back to watch, listen, and—hopefully—learn something useful to her investigation. Her eyes tracked Poppy as she paced through the milling crowd, talking, sipping from her martini glass, and glancing with hungry eyes at marshmallows browning on skewers over the fire. At any moment, Saffi expected her editor to snatch someone's perfectly toasted marshmallow and stuff her face with its sticky sugary goodness.

As the chocolate martinis flowed, the voices rising and falling around Saffi got louder and louder. Most of the booksellers were bandying theories about a criminal mastermind who had taken over the convention. One quipster proposed that the cod they'd eaten at the opening banquet had spread "mad booksellers' disease." A mystery writer called dibs on the killer convention plot, saying it would be perfect for her cozy crime series.

A group of young booksellers huddled around George and the blue-haired Lyndie on the opposite side of the fire. They seemed to be engaged in a not-so-hushed debate over whether a certain amateur sleuth should stop stirring up trouble, "Before someone else ends up dead." The crowd went silent just as George finished his sentence. Every eye turned to Saffi.

The hotel blanket wasn't thick enough to keep Saffi from shivering. First Troy, then Chief Boyd, and now a member of the booksellers association team thought she should stick to writing and stop putting herself—and others—in harm's way. *Well... too late for that!*

The Lowry & Lowenstein team was under assault from forces unknown. The only way to know who was coming after them was to keep finding and following clues. Jay GoodVender had left behind a paper trail. If anyone knew how to follow one of those, it was Aunt Saffi. And, come morning, when her head stopped pounding, she planned to do exactly that. She would figure out why Willow had become so solicitous toward Reese and why he seemed to be trying desperately to avoid her ministrations. She would confront Eileen about the application form now sitting on the coffee table in Saffi's suite. She would shake information about what had happened on the Jingle Tour out of the reluctant, overly ambitious Fia. And, most of all, she would track down Jay's organizer and read the scribblings in his *Silenced in Seaside* notebook.

And as soon as she could manage to slip out of the schmooze, she would read as much of Jemma's memoir as she could before falling asleep. There had to be clues in those pages.

George's awkward dig brought Poppy to Saffi's side with two skewers and a purloined bag of marshmallows. She moved a tote bag off the chair next to Saffi's and sat. "I can't remember the last time I roasted a marshmallow." She threaded two on one skewer and handed it to Saffi. Then she threaded two on the other skewer. "Oh!" She snapped her fingers. "It was when my girl scout troop went camping at Lake Como."

"Your scout troop went to Italy?" In her surprise, Saffi dipped her skewer toward the flames and one of her marshmallows caught fire. She blew the flame out, but the perfect brown skin she'd been working toward had become a crispy black mess.

Poppy threw back her head and laughed. "Lake Como... *Pennsylvania*!" she said once she'd caught her breath. "Here. Give me that. The more burn the better." Poppy swapped skewers with Saffi, then she pulled the crunchy melted marshmallow from the tip and smooshed it into her mouth. "Mmm... merfect!"

"So, you weren't one of those editorial interns whose rich parents supported her until she could afford a room share in Brooklyn?"

"The Bronx." Poppy licked marshmallow melt from her fingertips. Then she cocked her head toward Willow. "Like our young friend over there? No. I was an only kid with two working parents. Lived at home and took the green line to work till my pop-pop died and my grams invited me to share their rent-controlled apartment on the Upper East Side. When Grams passed, I inherited the lease. Been there ever since."

"I don't know what's going on with those two." Poppy nodded toward Willow, who seemed to be stalking Reese from one side of the fire to the other. "But I'm afraid that when I figure it out, I'm going to have to fire them both."

As Saffi watched the advance and retreat of their strange little dance, it hit her. Willow's reaction on the bridge had been instantaneous. Instinctual. She needed to get to Reese as quickly as possible. Then, when she and Saffi had pedaled to his duckboat, Willow had leapt to her feet and almost fallen into the river. Next, she had offered to go to the hospital for Poppy, ostensibly so the editor wouldn't miss out on any pressing questions from bookstore reps. But the real giveaway was her reaction to the possibility of Reese having a brain bleed. "It's *all* my fault!" Willow had wailed before dashing off to... well, Saffi never did figure out where Poppy's assistant had gone earlier.

"Poppy, did Reese get his internship through networking?"

"Yes. When I promoted Willow, I asked her if she knew anyone looking for an internship. She recommended Reese. They were in the same publishing program at Columbia."

Saffi watched Willow snatch a chocolate martini from Reese's hand and put it back on a passing waiter's tray. The intern pouted, and the relationship clicked into place.

Saffi leaned closer to Poppy to keep the crowd from overhearing. "Remember Debbie? Jemma's foster daughter? She told me that Reese had been taking selfies on the duckboat. He messaged one to his big sister to tick her off. Look at them. They're not acting like colleagues."

"That's it!" Poppy's head snapped up, her eyes went shark bright. "They're acting like siblings!"

"I think he's her younger brother," Saffi said. "Maybe a step-brother, since they don't share the same last name."

Poppy's dark eyes narrowed. "The little minx. She knows how much I hate nepo hirings. Families like hers thrive on them, believe me. I had to claw my way over more Willows than I can count to get where I am." Poppy snatched a marshmallow from the end of her skewer and shoved it into her mouth. After demolishing it, she licked the stickiness from her lips and fingertips. Her dark eyes tracked the siblings from one side of the fire to the other.

At some point, Willow must have felt the heat because she looked straight at her boss. Poppy pointed from Willow to Reese then shook a furious finger at her assistant. The devastated look on Willow's face said she understood exactly what Poppy was telling her.

Saffi sighed. Willow had made a terrible decision for a caring reason. Clearly, she loved her little brother, step or not. "She's the best assistant you've ever had. Do you have to let her go?"

Poppy leaned her toasting skewer against the firepit. "One

thing I've learned along the way, my dear. In publishing, and in life, you have to surround yourself with people you can trust in all kinds of situations." She turned toward Saffi. "The way I trust you, and you trust me. All the crap that has happened at this convention? You could have flown back to Last Chance Cove with Troy and left me to deal with it. Heck, maybe you should have, given what happened to you." Poppy reached for Saffi's hand and gave it a warm squeeze. "But you didn't."

Poppy was right. It had not even occurred to her to run away from the trouble her editor had found herself in. That's not what people did when they were truly invested in each other. Bringing up Troy reminded her of two things: she hadn't listened to the message he left on her cellphone, and when trouble came, he *had* flown away. Without her.

Saffi pleaded the lingering effects of a choke hold and took her throbbing throat up the elevator to her suite. She went into the bathroom and popped two ibuprofen, then returned to the living room. Without Troy in it, the suite seemed excessively large. It reeked of things that might have been—but not, thank God, of the fishy smell of crabs in the bathtub.

A bath, Saffi decided, was exactly what she needed. With bubbles. Lots and lots of bubbles. She dribbled bubble bath under the tap and ran the water hot enough to ease the kinks from her muscles. Then she peeled off her clothes and stepped in. She immediately hopped back out. "Too hot, too hot!"

She turned the cold tap on full strength and stood there with her arms around her naked body until the water cooled enough to dip in a tentative toe. *Perfect!* Body part by body part, she sank her exhausted body into the steaming water, past the hips, over the belly, leaving nothing but two mounds with tender pink nipples sticking out.

"Your loss, fisherman."

If the trip to Seaside turned out to be their relationship's swansong, she could pedal her own duckboat just fine, thank you very much.

Saffi sighed hard enough to send bubbles floating toward the ceiling. She wasn't kidding herself. She *could* go it alone. She'd done that for three full years before letting the man with the Montana-sapphire eyes into her life. She could go it alone again, but boy would she miss the things she knew she'd be missing.

Saffi soaked away the blues until her body glowed cherry red, then stepped out to dry off on one of the inn's extra-large, super-absorbent towels. She stacked the pillows from both sides of the queen bed in the middle and settled beneath the covers to read. First, the message Troy had left earlier... the one she'd ignored. Then, as much as she could of Jemma's memoir before sleep took her under. She probably wouldn't last long.

She yawned as she opened Troy's voice message, then turned up her phone's volume. She could barely hear his voice over what sounded like the Beechcraft's propeller. "Saffi!" Troy had yelled into the phone. "Scott thinks he saw Jay GoodVender that night at *buzz... buzz.*" Saffi pressed the phone against her ear as if that would soften the propeller's whirr. "He was with *buzz... buzz.* Call me when you get this! And stay away from—" The message went suddenly silent, as if Troy's phone had lost reception.

"Troy!" Saffi yelped as if he could hear her. But he couldn't. And whatever he'd been trying to tell her was lost above the clouds.

TWENTY-SIX

When Saffi tried Troy's number, it went straight to voicemail. He had to be home by now. Why wasn't he answering?

Maybe, she admonished herself, because she had not answered *his* call earlier. What had she been thinking? Not only had she refused the call, she had not listened to his message. Since she didn't hear the message, she didn't return his call. Troy must think she had decided to ghost him after he abandoned her to accompany Scott home. Either that, or...

Her heart thudded beneath the blanket she pulled reflexively up to her neck. Troy was fine. The plane had not gone down. Someone would have said something, at the convention, at the hospital... for that matter Chief Boyd would have taken off his hat and shared the news with a face as solemn as death itself. No. Troy made it home. She tried his number one more time. It went straight to voicemail again, so she left a message. "I'm really sorry I didn't call you back earlier. Things have been... crazy around here. Call me back when you get this. No matter the time."

Troy's message had taken her from half asleep to fully awake, her body tingling with nervous energy. She threw the covers off and walked to the sliding glass door. Down below, the Necanicum

River looked mirror-still, though the tide must be moving it slowly either to, or away from, the sea. Lights reflected in its clear surface: the moon—waning but still close to full, streetlamps on the board-walk, lights from hotel balconies. A bike with a headlamp pedaled along the boardwalk.

All she could think about was Troy. Despite how much her sleuthing unnerved him, he had called to share information that might help her solve Jay's murder. He'd also tried to warn her to stay away from someone. But who?

Was the person who had choked her Jay's killer? If so, the fact that Saffi was still alive indicated that the strangler did not want—or need—her dead. Like Saffi, her attacker had been searching for something in that storage room. The mess left behind told her that the *something* was Jay's notebook. She needed to find that orga-nizer. Who could have taken it? Jemma? Some random exhibit hall browser?

Her brain went around and around in circles until it tripped over a memory: she had heard a jingling clink as someone walked away from the booth. She had heard that sound before—the clink of the silver cuffs Fia wore in her box braids.

Exhaustion hit so hard Saffi stumbled back to bed. Following that clue—or any other—would have to wait until morning. She desperately needed sleep, but she also needed to read Jemma's memoir. She picked it up from the nightstand and broke the freshly printed book's spine to smooth it open. Then she turned to the dedication, one of the most telling parts of any memoir: *To the three mermaids. One missing. One murdered. Both silenced... in Seaside.*

Saffi emerged from sleep like a drowning swimmer gasping for oxygen and put a hand to her bruised throat. She had read until her eyes salted over and closed against her will. She was nowhere near the end of Jemma's book, but she had read enough to know that the book's conclusion had yet to be written, might never be written. Unless Jemma herself wrote it, perhaps in blood.

Jemma's memoir was not the standard birth-to-present recollection of life's big events. It was a series of independent stories, each of which related to a different part of her life. Some were written as straight nonfiction narrative. Some were written as poems. One, a tribute to her father, reminded Saffi of a sea shanty. Like many a self-published writer, Jemma's work was somewhat clunky, but also raw, visceral, aching with emotion and loss. Saffi found the hodge-podge of styles intriguing, although the chapter that put her to sleep drew far too heavily on Hans Christian Andersen's *The Little Mermaid* and Disney's animated mermaid movie for her taste.

Jemma's retelling followed three young mermaids who lived in an undersea kingdom ruled by Poseidon. The three mermaids chafed against the sea king's reign and broke his ridiculous rules about what girls could or could not do on a daily basis. Saffi recognized Helen in the mischievous mermaid with silky black hair and Jemma in the feisty mermaid whose messy red tangles caught on coral reefs as she chased after her friend. The third mermaid—Sonya, Saffi assumed—spent most of the story ratting the other two out to Poseidon.

Jemma's retelling had familiar elements: a mermaid who falls for a prince and leaves everything she knows behind. And some that were not so familiar: the feisty mermaid clearly had a crush on her dark-haired friend. The third mermaid tried to snag the prince for herself by dancing naked in the moonlight. And the prince wasn't human. He was the sea king's entitled son. Disney censors would have nixed this dude long before his big-screen debut. When the dark-haired mermaid found herself pregnant, sheltered by his royal dad, the not-so-princely prince abandoned her to her fate. Soon after, she had disappeared, never again to be seen by those who truly loved her.

Last night, as Saffi drifted toward sleep, she had tried to hold onto a wisp of understanding. If the story was an allegory, as she suspected, it might hold clues to why Helen had disappeared.

Once she nodded off, her brain had churned in a far more surreal direction. She had dreamed of being trapped in an undersea storage room by the Sea Witch—who looked exactly like Jay Good-Vender in drag. Not a dream, she decided. A nightmare!

Keynoting at the North Coast Booksellers convention was supposed to have been about promoting her books—especially her spring title. But from the moment she arrived, she had been swimming in stormy seas filled with sharks, barracudas, and stinging jellyfish. If she wanted to step back onto familiar shores, she needed to put aside her fears and get out of bed.

Only one thing could shake away the early-morning grogginess: a Mexi-mocha from the Seaside Coffeehouse. She would dress, sneak out of the inn, and sit alone at a tiny table with a window view until caffeine surged through her veins and cleansed her brain cells of Jay in drag... and mermaids.

She checked her cellphone for texts or missed calls, but Troy had still not responded. When she called his number, it went straight to voicemail once again. She tried to tamp down her worry. His cell could have gone dead. He was prone to leaving it too long without recharging. And maybe, now that he was back in the cove, he had taken on a fishing charter. That was his business, after all, and the weather had been clear for days now. She would picture him stringing bait on a fishing line for a squeamish tourist rather than indulging in doom-thinking: her brain's equivalent of scrolling through negative news on the net.

She kicked her way from beneath the covers, scrubbed, tweezed, and brushed herself into some semblance of normalcy. She dressed for warmth, comfort, and the closing brunch she was due to attend, in an ivory Merino wool tunic over thick chocolate-brown leggings. She threaded her favorite dressy earrings, poppy-seed pearls dangling from silver strands, through her piercings, then tucked her silver-streaked black curls behind her ears to show them off. Then she slipped her laptop into its case, slung her bag over her shoulder, and hurried toward coffee, followed by whatever new disaster the day would bring.

Outside the inn, the early-morning streets were quiet. A bank of fuchsia clouds painted the town in a soft pink glow. Gulls argued in the distance, doing their best to interrupt the morning's peace, but Saffi ignored them. She had heard that fight too many times before. As she crossed to the coffeehouse side of the street, a barn swallow tweeted its morning song and she looked up to see it dance along an electrical wire. Her joy in the moment was interrupted by the most common of all calls—the car horn—as a driver in a rush beeped her out of the street and onto the sidewalk.

"OK. OK." She waved the car on its way, then pushed open the coffeehouse door into a steamy, cinnamon- and coffee-scented paradise without a single customer. *Bliss!*

"First one in gets coffee on the house." The thirty-something woman behind the counter lifted a coffee pot in greeting. She could have been a model: short black hair with sassy space buns, short bangs curved close to her hairline, manicured brows, ginormous brown eyes, full red lips and ceramic-smooth skin. What was she doing working in a small-town coffee shop?

Saffi stopped her just before she poured. "I'm afraid I'm addicted to Mexi-mochas." The barista answered with a quirky smile and bright eyes that told Saffi she was not behind that counter under duress. Like Delilah, Saffi's best friend in Last Chance Cove, she was probably a master of coffee concoctions.

"Coming right up!" She put the pot on the burner and wiped her hands on a teal apron with a saying that made Saffi chuckle: *The beach is calling but I must... make coffee!* "Anything to eat with that?"

"Toasted bagel with honey." Saffi smiled. After the woman rang her up, she paid what she owed, then headed for the small table at the front window. Not the window with the great blue heron balancing on one leg. The window with a view of the Necanicum Inn one way and Beach Books the other. The coffeehouse didn't have the best view for a beach town, but the location blocks away from the prom gave Saffi the quiet she needed to allow her brain to kick back into gear.

She needed to sort through potential suspects, mostly to figure out what—if anything—she suspected each one of doing. She started with people associated with the booksellers convention. Every one of her convention suspects was up to *something*, but none seemed to have a strong motive for murdering Jay GoodVender. Willow had been hiding the fact that Reese was her brother and, probably, nothing else. Fia had covered for Eileen's bad decision, hoping to earn a promotion. She had possibly—no *probably*—taken the organizer box from Jay's booth, but it seemed silly to think she was after the *Silenced in Seaside* notebook.

Jemma and Debbie fell into a different category. They had ties to the convention *and* they were locals. That fact tugged double-hard on Saffi's suspicious nature. Past run-ins with the law had led Debbie to abandon Reese in a duckboat. That story went deeper, but, so far, Saffi had not been able to plumb those depths. Debbie also worked at the Bridge Tender and could have been there the night Jay was killed.

Jemma? Jemma's life story seemed to have started and ended with the disappearance of her best friend, Helen. She had fallen out with the third mermaid, Sonya. What had Phyllis said? Jemma thought Sonya knew something, but she kept it to herself, perhaps to protect former police chief Luke Atwell. Were the two really related? If so, Saffi needed to know. She also needed to know how and when Sonya had died. If Sonya's death and Helen's disappearance were too far separated in time, the possibility that they were connected was tenuous at best.

Jemma's *Little Mermaid* retelling had put another question in her mind. Was Debbie's father the "prince" who had stolen two of the "mermaids'" hearts? A quick search of the local newspaper's online archive might pull up articles about Helen's disappearance and Sonya's murder. Details might include the names of locals she could press for information. Saffi tentatively touched her bruised throat. She had to be more careful. Troy's garbled message had been clear about one thing: there was someone Saffi should stay away from. Until they talked, she had no way to know who.

Saffi opened her laptop and did a quick search for the name of the local newspaper. The *Seaside Signal*, she discovered, had provided local coverage since 1905. Saffi had to give the paper props. Not many small-town rags had survived news media's move online. To access the paper's archives, she had to subscribe, but the seven dollars the *Signal* charged for a month was a small price to pay for clues that might break this case apart.

Just as she called up an article about Sonya's murder, the barista set Saffi's mocha and bagel on the table. When she glanced up to smile her thanks, she saw curiosity in the young woman's eyes. "You're that *Bedside Reader* writer, aren't you?"

Saffi nodded. "Saffi Graywood. And you're...?"

"Hannah."

"This place is wonderful. Is it yours?" Experience told her that owners of small coffee shops kept their staff lean, or nonexistent, in the offseason.

"It is." The woman smiled. "It's my happy place. Even though I have to work my fanny off to keep it."

Instinct told Saffi to turn her screen toward the woman instead of closing her laptop. "Hannah... when we were in here yesterday, I overheard a bit of a brouhaha about a woman named Sonya whose murder has not been solved. I sometimes write about cold cases, so I thought I'd look it up."

Did that make her sound like a ghoul? Probably, but Saffi was willing to risk the coffee shop owner's judgment on the off-chance she knew something useful.

"Chief Boyd and—was his name Luke?" Saffi screwed up her face as if searching for the name rather than admitting it had been branded into her brain. "They seemed to be at odds with each other over the case." She slurped a choco-licious sip of spicy mocha from the side of the mug, trying not to get whipped cream on her nose. She failed, of course, and swiped away the evidence with the back of her hand.

"Luke Atwell." Hannah nodded. "He was police chief back in the day."

"Before Chief Boyd?"

Hannah put a hand on her hip as she thought. "One, no... two chiefs back from Boyd. They come and go kind of quick around here. Tourist towns can be hard to handle, you know? Lots of push and pull between the mayor's office, the chamber of commerce, and the cops."

"Over...?" Saffi crunched into her toasted bagel, licking honey from her lips as she waited.

Hannah gave the empty coffeehouse a glance, then pulled out a chair and sat down. "Town like this one, we got tourism and nothing else. The mayor wants the cops to stamp out crime. The chamber wants to pretend it never happens. Who wants to bring their kids to a place where people get mugged or knifed or strangled, right?"

That comment hit close to home. Saffi touched her throat as she glanced at the article on her screen. "So, does it help or hurt the town when crimes go unsolved?" She altered bites of bagel with sips of mocha.

Hannah quirked a manicured brow. "If you write about unsolved crimes, I'm guessing you already know the answer to that question."

Now that she was forced to think about it, Saffi realized that she *did* know. When an investigation stayed active, unsolved crimes continued to make headlines. When a case went cold and files were stored away in a cardboard box, the stories stopped. Unless a squeaky wheel started turning, the case would grow dusty and die a quiet death. *Silenced... in Seaside.*

Sonya's murder had happened under Chief Boyd's watch, as had Jay's. What pressure might he be under to close the new case quickly? A New Yorker who flounced into town and committed murder would have far less impact on the tourist trade than a homegrown killer who might strike again. Pointing the finger of blame at Poppy would slam the door on Jay's murder.

Before Saffi could ask the barista if Chief Boyd had a "move along, there's nothing to see here" attitude, the coffeehouse door opened. A group of conventioneers lugging book totes washed in with the cold humid air.

"Better get back at it!" Hannah stood with a smile. "Good luck with your cold case story."

With the coffeehouse owner taking food and drink orders in the background, Saffi turned to the article she had pulled up. Dated June 5th the previous year, the piece was cryptic at best. *Sonya Atwell Fowler, late of Seaside, Oregon, was found dead in her apartment on South Holladay after a break-in. Local authorities believe the deceased arrived home and interrupted a burglary in progress. Cries from the deceased's cat, Ursula, alerted neighbors who then contacted police for a welfare check. "Crimes like this are rare in Seaside," said police chief Eric Boyd. "But our location on Highway 101 does bring unsavory types through town now and then." Neighbors reported seeing a white Chevy Malibu with Washington plates cruising the area a few days before Sonya's body was found.*

Sonya *Atwell* Fowler was definitely related to Luke. And *Ursula?* Sonya had named her cat for the sea witch in Disney's version of *The Little Mermaid.* Saffi closed her laptop and tapped the cover. A car with Washington plates in the area wasn't a clue. It was a cop-out. A few minutes gazing out of the coffeehouse window showed her cars from California, Washington, Utah, British Columbia, Texas, and Georgia. After talking to the barista and reading the article, Saffi had a bit more sympathy for Chief Atwell's outburst about Chief Boyd dragging his feet on the case, but less than none for his absurd "one of us" comment.

Where did Jay GoodVender's murder fit into this puzzle? Now that she'd seen the dedication in *Mermaids at Midnight*, she realized that Jay could have stolen the title she saw on the cover of his composition book from Jemma's memoir. If that was the case, the composition book could be blank inside or have just a few notes.

That didn't really fit the fact that someone had choked Saffi out in order to dig through that box of notebooks. At the very least, her attacker *thought* Jay had been investigating a mystery. Was it a mystery the person wanted solved? Or one he or she wanted to remain unsolved? If the latter, that person was probably determined to do *whatever* it took to keep the truth from being exposed. Including strangling Jay GoodVender or attacking anyone else who got in his—or her—way.

TWENTY-SEVEN

Saffi chewed the last crusty, honey-sweet bite of bagel and washed it down with the spicy dregs of her mocha. Poppy would no doubt be wondering where her best-selling author had disappeared to. If she left now, she could get back to the inn in time to walk to the convention center with her editor.

As she ducked into the lobby of the Necanicum Inn, someone hailed her from the front desk. "If you're looking for your colleagues, they headed out about fifteen minutes ago." Saffi thanked the desk clerk and headed upstairs for her windbreaker before going back outside.

The early-morning chill had been replaced by a brisk onshore wind. The tug of an impending headache signaled a drop in barometric pressure and a shift away from the past few days' unseasonably clear weather. Saffi recognized the signs of rain, or perhaps a storm, rolling across the Pacific toward Seaside.

She hurried across the bridge, scanning the boardwalk for the Lowry & Lowenstein crew instead of watching where she was going. Someone burst from the Bridge Tender's front door and Saffi plowed right into them. She stumbled, but caught herself against the bridge's concrete railing.

"Debbie?"

The young woman's dark eyes caught Saffi's. For a second, she thought she saw a lingering flash of fear—or perhaps revulsion—in them, but Debbie blinked and it was gone. Had she imagined it?

"Sorry," Debbie pasted on a smile. "Don't tell Mama Jem I almost sent her favorite author off the bridge, OK?"

"OK...?" Saffi dragged out her agreement as if doubting whether or not she should tell Jemma about the encounter.

Debbie excused herself, hunched her shoulders, and hurried across the bridge. To Saffi's surprise, after a quick glance over her shoulder, she ducked into the lobby of the Necanicum Inn like someone looking for a place to hide.

Though she knew Poppy expected her at the booth, Saffi could not pass up the chance to see who or what had spooked the young woman. She pushed open the Bridge Tender door—half surprised to find it unlocked so early on a Sunday morning.

"Sorry!" A curly-haired young man with flashing blue eyes looked up from polishing spots off shot glasses. "We don't open till noon."

"Oh. Apologies." Saffi walked up to the bar and leaned against it. "The door was unlocked, so..."

"Ah. Deb must have forgotten to lock it behind her."

"Debbie? I just saw her jetting out of here. She seemed a bit... unsettled."

"Deb?" The young man stopped polishing and gave Saffi a studied look. "Came in early to do the table setups she was supposed to do last night." He shook his head causing a lanky curl to fall onto his forehead. "Used to be my best server, but the last few days something's been off."

Something's been off? Something to do with what had happened to Reese? Or with a certain someone who was strangled a few steps outside this very door? The bartender's statement hung in the air as a deep silence descended over the bar. So deep, Saffi caught the sound of a toilet flushing before bootsteps pounded down the wooden hallway. Former police chief Luke Atwell sauntered into the bar, cinching his leather belt over a pair of gray slacks.

"Oh. Uh. Sorry." He dipped his head toward Saffi. "Didn't know we had guests." Then he looked at the bartender and narrowed his eyes. "You haven't been serving before opening time again, now have you?"

From the hard time he was giving the bartender, Saffi wondered if the ex-top cop owned the rustic joint. She stepped back from the bar and lifted a hand. "Don't worry. I'm just another clueless tourist wandering in where she's not wanted. I'll be off."

"Let me get the door." As Atwell stepped closer, Saffi caught the oaky scent of aged whiskey on his breath. *Different rules for yourself, huh?*

One of these two, Saffi decided, had caused Debbie to bolt from the bar. But which one? The bartender could have reamed her out for being lax on the job, but maybe the intoxicated former chief had done something to make her flee. If so, he wouldn't be the first aging boss to use whiskey as an excuse to harass a young server.

The exhibit hall was a hive of activity when Saffi arrived. The last day of any convention was about final sweeps through the exhibits. Saffi wasn't immune to the lure of the freebies publishers gave out just before exhibits closed. If she hadn't run into Debbie, she would have gone through the hall like a starving gull. Instead, she headed straight for the L & L booth.

She found Willow and Reese buzzing like worker bees. Poppy was, of course, the queen. The young staff members jumped to every command as if their boss might abandon them to their fates at the edge of the Pacific instead of waiting until they returned to New York to fire them. Saffi grinned. Poppy was obviously relishing the experience.

Fortunately for Saffi, packing the booth was a staff job, not an author's, although she sometimes pitched in to help. Today, she had clues to follow and information to gather. She needed to know what Poppy's lawyers had told her about leaving this afternoon as they'd intended—or staying put. She wanted to talk to Reese about what had happened in that duckboat before he left town. If something had been thrown from the bridge as Debbie said, she needed to look harder at Jemma as a suspect.

When Poppy spotted Saffi lingering at the front of the booth, she waved her in. "We came by your room but you were already out and about. Sleuthing, I hope."

Poppy's opinion of Saffi's murder-solving habit changed, depending on how many pages she had delivered or had due. This time, with her own freedom at stake, Poppy had been nothing but supportive.

"Guilty as charged. But, mostly, I was just trying to sort things out in my head."

"Any juicy culprits on that list of yours?" Poppy tapped the side of her head to indicate where she thought Saffi kept her list. In the process, she mussed her pixie spikes enough to make the cut look even more flattering.

"A few."

Poppy pursed her lips and gave her a pointed stare. "The person who took my pen. That's who's responsible."

At the back of the booth, Willow and Reese had just started taking down the Lowry & Lowenstein banner. They turned as one to listen, as if hoping Saffi would reveal her list of suspects. Willow had been in possession of Poppy's pen at one point, but the most nefarious thing she'd done was recommend her stepbrother for an internship without divulging their relationship.

"I'm sorry, Poppy. As a clue, your pen's a dead end. Anyone could have walked off with it, but no one in their right mind is going to admit it. The police think it points to the killer."

Poppy put her hands on her hips and gave Saffi her best queen bee scowl. "Because it does! The pen is a *massive* problem. If you find out who took it, the police will have nothing they can use to hold me here. I want to go *home*, Saffi."

Great. Poppy wanted to edit her investigation the way she

edited her manuscripts. Point out problems but not offer solutions. The method made Saffi a better writer. Would it make her a better sleuth? As far as Saffi was concerned, the pen was a distraction. But Poppy was right. If she could prove someone had taken the pen, her editor could wing her way back to Manhattan where she belonged.

"Fine. I'll talk to everyone who was in the booth when it went missing. Starting with Reese."

Instead of talking to Reese at the booth, she asked him to follow her outside. "If I don't come back, send the coppers."

As they left the buzzing exhibit hall, she leaned toward Reese. "Don't worry. I don't think you took the pen, but I do need some answers." Her reassurance did nothing to remove the panic from the intern's eyes.

Outside the convention center, they stepped into a wind so fierce it blew Saffi's curls backward. "Whoa. What is going on?" She pressed her hands to her head.

Like most of his generation, Reese went straight to his cellphone for an answer. He opened a weather app, typed in "Seaside, Oregon" and widened his eyes at whatever he read. "There's a massive low-pressure system off the coast. The weather service is predicting a bomb cyclone to hit within the next twenty-four to forty-eight hours."

"A bomb cyclone?" Saffi had experienced one of the sudden explosive storms in Vermont, but on the West Coast?

"Heavy rainfall on the coast and *blizzard conditions* in mountain passes." Reese gaped. "If we don't get out of here this afternoon, we're gonna be stuck. I need to tell Poppy."

Reese started to turn away, but Saffi reached out a hand to stop him. "Wait. I didn't bring you out here to talk about the weather, although it does sound like things are about to get rough. I brought you out here to find out what happened with you and Debbie." What she didn't tell him was that she'd already heard Debbie's version and wanted to see if his matched.

Reese's eyes widened and his fingers whitened around his cell-phone. "What do you mean? Nothing happened."

Saffi cocked her head back. "Nothing? Didn't you get bashed on the head and end up unconscious?"

"Oh. Yeah, that. Well, OK. But nothing else happened."

Why was Reese looking at his sneakers?

"Reese!" Saffi used her sharpest voice, the one she used on young writing students who wanted to chat instead of write.

"OK. OK. I might have tried to kiss her and she might have pushed me away and I might have tried again. I was drunk, OK? So was she. I didn't mean to come on so strong and she didn't mean to hurt me."

Saffi straightened. "Debbie knocked you out? With what?"

"Uhm, we might have taken a couple of beers with us and she might have conked me with a bottle when I got a little handsy."

A little handsy? If Debbie had felt the need to fend him off with a beer bottle, Reese had gotten more than just a little handsy.

When Saffi had figured out Reese and Willow's relationship, she had felt sorry for the young intern. Being fired from an internship would not look good on his résumé. Now? Knowing that he had pressured Debbie so much that she had felt the need to defend herself? That altered her perception enough that she involuntarily took a step backward. She let her face show not only her disappointment, but her resolve. She would make sure Poppy knew exactly how Reese got that bump on the head. If she knew her editor, Poppy would make sure the nepo hire would never step foot in another publishing house.

TWENTY-EIGHT

Saffi sent Reese back to the booth while she tried to control her anger. She leaned into the railing above the river and watched the clouds reflected in its surface be chunked by the wind into a Monet-like impressionistic painting. The blues and greens beneath the loose lumpy whites grew angrier by the moment. The wind chop made her grab the railing and a splinter jabbed through her skin. She jerked her hand away, then wriggled the sliver from her palm and sucked at the tiny red droplet left behind.

As she stood there with the stiff breeze turning her windbreaker into a parachute, Saffi realized something. She didn't need to consider suspects on a list. She needed to consider timelines. She saw two of them, stretching out in front of her. One began and ended when Jay GoodVender met Saffi Graywood. It started at a long-ago East Coast Booksellers convention. It included his early fandom, his stalking, the confrontation at the Haunted Wood RV Park on Halloween, the bloody flower petals, the attack on Marisol, and Jay's death. If that was the murder timeline, Chief Boyd would be right to point the finger at Poppy or Saffi.

On the second timeline, both Poppy and Saffi were innocent, as were all of the convention attendees except, perhaps, one—Jemma Weathers. That timeline began long before Jay's arrival in

Seaside and had not ended with his death. Jay, with his devious mad-genius mind, could have blundered onto the second timeline. That timeline began with a prince and a mermaid, included Debbie's birth, Helen's disappearance, Luke Atwell's ineptitude, Jemma's grief, a notebook titled *Silenced in Seaside*, and Saffi being choked in a storage closet. It potentially included Sonya's murder as well. That timeline was still a live wire that might kill anyone who touched it.

Saffi looked up from the river and stared into the sky. The clouds grew angrier by the minute. Reese was an arse but he was also right. If they didn't get out of Seaside this afternoon, they would be stuck for the duration of the storm. She pulled her cellphone out of her sling bag and glanced at the time. The morning was getting away from her. She needed to go back inside and try to find Jemma before the hall closed. If anyone knew who might still face danger along Saffi's second timeline, it was the memoir writer.

It only took seconds to discover that she was too late. Jemma's booth had been emptied. No evidence remained of the fisherman's daughter's presence. If Jemma didn't attend the brunch, Saffi would have to track her down at The Mermaid's Purse, a dangerous proposition in far too many ways.

During Saffi's time outside, the exhibit hall aisles had filled with carts. She was always amazed at how quickly and efficiently exhibitors folded away displays and packed leftover marketing materials, books, and supplies for shipping. Most of the booths had organizer boxes similar to Jay's. Saffi watched several exhibitors heft their organizers into large boxes crammed with miscellaneous materials and froze.

There had been a large box stored with the remains of Jay's booth. It had been taped shut so she had paid it no attention. She expected to see Jay's organizer sitting on a shelf, and when she hadn't spotted it, she had started digging through the smaller boxes. What if...?

She double-timed it to the storage room and breathed a sigh of relief when she found the door open. Exhibitors moved in and out of the room, collecting stored goods and hefting them onto carts in the corridor. She glanced back down the corridor toward the North Coast Booksellers Association's booth. The trio she'd met on day one—Eileen, Fia, and George—were all there, answering questions and directing people this way and that. None of the three had time to notice Saffi striding into the storage room as if she had every right to be there.

Though many of the shelves had been at least partially emptied, those containing Jay's boxes were still filled. The big box she remembered sat—thank Raven—on the bottom shelf, taped shut with crisscrossed layers of silver duct tape.

Saffi looked around, hoping to spot someone wielding a utility knife. When she did, she hurried over and asked the bedraggled bookseller if she could borrow it, "For just a sec."

"Sure." The young man brushed sweaty bangs off his forehead. The knife went *click-click-click* as he closed it. Then he handed it over, and hefted a box. "It's all yours till I get back from the loading bay." He carried the box to one of the carts in the corridor, then gave Saffi a friendly little wave as he pulled the cart beyond the doorway and out of sight.

Saffi wiggled Jay's box off the bottom shelf, sliced through the layers of sticky silver tape, then clicked the blade back into the knife. She set the knife aside so she could use both hands to wrench the box open. She peered into its depths then slapped the sides of the box. "Yes!"

Though she had suspected the organizer might be packed inside, finding it felt like a miracle. It took some shoulder strength and a bit of back-and-forth squiggling to lift the heavy organizer from its slot among the remains of Jay's hopes, dreams, and fiendish plans. She widened her stance for the final tug.

While metaphorically patting herself on the back for her sleuthing skills, Saffi maneuvered the organizer out and onto the floor. Then... she heard a quick *click-click-click* behind her.

Really, Saffi? You've been reading mysteries your whole life, and you set a utility knife down on a shelf?

"Don't turn around." The gruff voice sounded as if it had been muffled by something thick. It could have been anyone—male or female. Saffi could not tell. "Take two steps forward and link your hands behind your back."

Saffi's blood pressure hit boil faster than an electric tea kettle. Where was everyone? There had been people traipsing in and out of here. How could the room be empty enough for someone to threaten her with a utility knife?

"Move!" the voice ordered.

Saffi moved. She stepped forward and put her hands behind her back to link her fingers together. She held her breath and listened as the organizer's top latch clicked open. After a few seconds scratching about among scissors and binder clips in the top of the organizer, a drawer slid open. It was amazing how much you could hear if you weren't breathing, Saffi mused. Papers rustled. The muffled voice cursed. The first drawer slammed so hard she heard the plastic crack.

Saffi took advantage of the searcher's distraction to take two more steps forward. If she could get out of reach...

Another drawer scraped open. More papers rustled. Saffi took two more steps. At that moment, she realized something: she had walked out of arm's reach of the utility knife. She screamed at the top of her lungs, then whirled around in time to glimpse a leg in dark blue—or possibly gray—slacks disappearing out the door.

Before she reached the door, she heard the crash of two bodies colliding. "Hey!" Saffi thought she recognized the voice of the helpful young man who had loaned her the utility knife. Then the shock of being plowed into turned to a yelp of pain. "Be careful with that thing!"

Saffi bolted out the door ready to go after the person in the gray pants, but she stopped when she saw the way the young man hugged his right arm against his belly. He grabbed at Saffi with his left hand as if to steady himself, and then collapsed at her feet. The arm he'd been holding against his belly flopped outward. That was when Saffi saw blood, flowing like red ink from where the attacker had slashed the young man's arm.

Saffi sucked in a breath and yelled, belly-deep, "Call 9-1-1!"

Footsteps raced down the corridor and Saffi looked up to see George leaning over her.

"Saffi! What happened?"

"I need... something. A scarf, a tie, anything I can wrap around this." She nodded to her hands which were pressed over the cut but could not completely stop the blood that flowed between her fingers.

George paled, put his hands on his knees, and leaned forward as if trying to keep himself from fainting.

"George!" Saffi shouted into his face. "Get something, now!"

He straightened, eyes blinking, but before he could begin to think again, Fia rushed forward. "Here!" She slid onto her knees beside Saffi, opened a commercial first aid kit and started tossing things onto the floor. "Where is it, where is it?"

"There!" Saffi pointed her nose toward a thick roll of gauze.

Fia quickly uncoiled the beginning of the roll, then nodded at Saffi. "Ready!"

Saffi lifted her hands and Fia started wrapping: around and around and around until she reached the end of the gauze roll. To Saffi, it looked as if a butterfly had cocooned itself around the young man's wrist.

"Out of the way!" Bootsteps thudded down the carpeted hallway and before Saffi could rise to her feet she was surrounded by legs—all of them wearing blue or gray slacks. Rescue squad members, security guards, uniformed police, and Chief Boyd, pushing his way through the crowd to reach the victim. So much, Saffi sighed, for identifying the slasher by his pants.

TWENTY-NINE

"So. We're looking for a person with a gruff voice wearing dark slacks?" Chief Boyd narrowed his eyes at the scant information Saffi had been able to share. She couldn't blame him. She'd been too scared of that utility knife to turn around until she was out of its reach. As for the pants—whether policeman-blue or security guard-gray—the slasher could not have chosen a better outfit for disappearing in the confusion.

In response to the chief's sarcasm, Poppy—who could move those orthopedic pumps faster than Saffi thought possible when her best-selling author was in danger—shook her finger in his face.

"What kind of town is this?" she demanded. "I've lived in New York City my whole life and I've never seen such rampant crime."

"Neither have I." Willow crossed her arms over her chest and Reese, who'd just come up behind her, crossed his in agreement.

"This particular crime wave seems to have coincided with your arrival," the chief retorted. "Maybe you should pack it up and take it with you." He strode away, leaving Poppy spluttering in his wake.

"That supercilious bastard!" Poppy's hands shook.

Saffi could not get a read on Chief Boyd. He seemed to vacillate between curt and kind, observant and accusing. Did it coincide with pressure, or lack thereof, from the mayor's office or the chamber of commerce? She knew one thing: the chief paid attention to hard evidence. The file folder Jay had given him, Poppy's pen, and... the organizer. He had listened closely and taken notes when she told him about the organizer box and the notebook she'd seen inside. But, as far as she could tell, the searcher—like Saffi—had failed to find it.

Saffi watched the chief stride down the corridor in his bleached white shirt and dark blue slacks. Blue slacks? The police chief? Surely not.

Although... if that composition book had information about Helen's disappearance or Sonya's murder, the chief would certainly want to get his hands on it.

"What are we going to do?" Willow's wail of despair broke through Saffi's thoughts. Poppy's confident assistant seemed to have crumpled once and for all.

"For God's sake, sis. Buck up." No longer pretending he and Willow were anything other than siblings, Reese had gone into sulky little brother mode.

Saffi stepped toward Poppy and whispered something in her ear. Poppy whirled toward Reese with eyes blazing.

"*We*," Poppy pointed to herself, Saffi, and Willow, "are going to walk toward the beachfront and get in line for brunch. Saffi needs food to pull her out of her shock." Then she gave Willow the once-over. "And so do you.

"You!" Poppy thrust a finger into Reese's chest. "Stack the cart and get everything to the loading zone. Once you're done with that, hit the road."

"But I—" Reese's face settled into a petulant pout.

"But nothing," Poppy said. "As of this moment, you are no longer in the employ of Lowry & Lowenstein."

Boom! Saffi's whispered revelation of what Reese had done led to instant karmic repercussions. *Go, Poppy!*

Reese folded his arms over his chest. "If that's the case, you can load your own cart."

Those words seemed to hit Willow like a bracing slap to the face. She pulled herself up to her full height, flipped her perfectly highlighted hair over one shoulder, put her hands on her hips and leaned toward her brother. "You will do whatever Ms. Morales tells you to do. You will do it quickly, efficiently, and with the politeness expected by our *father*. If you don't, I will make sure you're on the next plane back to Minneapolis where you can live out your days in the lap of *mediocrity* with your cheating, money-grubbing wench of a mother."

OK. Stepsibling it is!

Reese hightailed it to the exhibit hall so fast he outran the awkward silence that followed Willow's threat.

"Ms. Morales." Willow turned to Poppy with hands folded contritely just below her belly. "I have drafted my resignation and will have it on your desk tomorrow morning." Willow's lips trembled. "I want you to know that it has been a huge honor to work with you. You are everything that I hope to be in an editor... well, *hoped* to be." Willow's blue eyes filled and she blinked rapidly.

Poppy looked Willow in the eye. "Maybe your father can buy you a publishing company."

Willow clenched her teeth together, barely keeping back what Saffi feared was a tidal wave of emotion. Then she shrugged. "He could, but Father doesn't reward failure. Only success."

The considering look on Poppy's face made Saffi wonder if Willow might find a way back into her good graces. "The brunch awaits." Poppy waved a hand toward the entry doors. "Shall we?"

When they finally exited the convention center, Saffi looked back over her shoulder into the now-familiar space. Had there ever been such an ill-fated gathering of booksellers in the history of publishing?

No. Saffi's inner snark chuckled. *If there had been, you would already have written about it.*

The ambulance carrying the helpful young man from the storage room had left a few minutes earlier. Saffi took comfort in the fact that its siren was not wailing. That meant his injury was non-life-threatening. Relief soon gave way to guilt. If she had not decided to search the storage room one more time, the young bookseller would still be sealing up boxes and carting them to the loading dock.

Troy had warned her against playing sleuth. After he left, she had done exactly what he feared: charged around asking questions, putting herself—and others—in danger. Could she really blame him for fleeing back to Last Chance Cove at the first opportunity? Maybe not, but unless Scott really had crashed the plane, she could... and did... blame him for ghosting her after her heartfelt apology.

As Saffi's group walked beyond the protection of the hulking convention center, the wind hit full force. Dirt, scraps of paper, and leaf litter swirled up from the boardwalk, forcing them to shield their eyes against the debris. They hurried along behind a group of booksellers who seemed to be debating whether to attend the brunch or skip it in favor of getting on the road before the storm hit.

"Have you heard anything?" Poppy wormed her way into the conversation. "I thought the storm was due tomorrow at the earliest."

A woman clutching the knit strings of her red Peruvian cap to keep it from flying away turned toward them. "That's what the weather service is saying, but... when are those guys ever right?"

Despite the headwind, the jumble of conventioneers plowed their way to the promenade. Saffi and crew used the group as a windbreak until they reached the prom. When they turned the corner, they found a windswept Fia fighting off clinking box braids as she guided people into the hotel where the brunch would take place.

Poppy and Willow wanted to get inside as quickly as possible, but Saffi hung back, exhilarated by the storm. "Look at those waves!" She pointed toward the beach where breakers crested and spray flew like mermaids' tresses as waves smashed against the shore. The smell of salt permeated the air. Charged particles surged through Saffi's body making her feel more awake and alive than she had in days.

She remembered an online article she had read while researching the way storms made her feel: "The Strange Blissfulness of Storms." There was an actual science devoted to the phenomenon: *biometeorology*—the study of how weather and climate affects living organisms. The cyclone building offshore made Saffi feel like a cellphone that had been plugged into a USB port just in time to keep it from dying.

"God! What is it about you RV people?" Poppy shouted into the wind. "Don't you care that your hair looks like... like seaweed?" She held up an arm to protect her pixie cut but it was too late. The wind had already sculpted it into a jaunty sideways wave that made her look like a drunken sailor staggering across a ship's deck.

Saffi grinned and waved them inside. "Save me a seat!" She had an ulterior motive for hanging back. She hoped for one more word with Fia about what she might have seen during the slashing. When Saffi turned to face the wind, sand blasted her skin. *Great. The last thing I need right now is a microdermabrasion facial.* Poppy was right. This was nuts. *Enough.*

As she headed toward the hotel, a bulky figure pushed past, shoulders stooped against the incoming storm, windbreaker whapping against thighs clad in gray slacks. "'Scuse me," a voice muffled by a knitted scarf apologized.

"Hey!" When Saffi grabbed at the windbreaker, the figure whapped her hand away. "Wait!"

The bundled figure did not wait. Instead, he—or she—pushed past the line waiting to get inside the hotel. Irked-off booksellers closed ranks to keep anyone else, Saffi included, from cutting in. Since she couldn't chase the guy in the windbreaker, she sidled up to Fia.

"Rotten deal, being stuck out here in this mess. Eileen should give you a break after what we just went through." Was administering first aid together enough of a bond to get Fia to talk? Given her skittishness, Saffi doubted it, but she had to try.

"I'd rather she thought I didn't *need* a break." Fia gathered her braids in one hand to keep them from lashing her face.

Saffi edged closer, right into Fia's personal space. "Fia," she decided to go for the jugular, "I saw you with Jay on the Jingle Tour. I haven't ratted you out to Chief Boyd because I don't think you murdered the man."

"Of course I didn't!" Fia's dark brown eyes went wide. "Saffi! You can't tell him. He'll..."

They both knew what the chief would do. Saffi let that knowledge hang in the air until Fia relented. "Fine. I was with him. He wanted me to talk Eileen into letting him back into the convention."

The sound of chatter behind them made Fia stiffen. "Could you please go inside? I have traffic to direct."

"OK. But you're not getting off that easy this time. We either finish this talk after lunch, or I *will* tell the chief."

As she rejoined the moving mass, Saffi's thoughts went back to the person in the windbreaker. Was the slasher inside? Calmly eating brunch as if nothing had happened?

When Saffi made it into the corridor outside the room where the brunch was being held, she spotted the windbreaker hanging on a hook among a mishmash of outerwear. She stopped just inside the doorway to scan the dining room. Did anyone look winded enough to have just shoved through a crowd?

Everyone looks winded, Saffi! And wind-blown.

Fine! But only one person had left a windbreaker hanging in the hall. Saffi turned around and wriggled like a fish swimming upstream until she once more stood in the corridor lined with coat hooks. She found the windbreaker and ran her hands over its bulk. The jacket had generous zippered pockets on the outside and a smaller protected pocket on the inside. She found two crumpled receipts from the Seaside Coffeehouse, a sticky lint-covered breath mint, and a parking ticket in the inside pocket. She also found a couple of Seaside chamber of commerce brochures in one of the zippered pockets. That was no help. At this point, every convention attendee had a collection of those. She failed to find the two things that would incriminate the wearer: a composition book and a utility knife.

Thoroughly disappointed, Saffi pilfered the parking ticket. Clues in this case had been few and far between. Maybe Chief Boyd could use the ticket to trace the identity of the slasher. If, Saffi realized, he would condescend to do so.

As she made her way into the dining room, she spotted Chief Boyd at a table in the back corner. Her first instinct was to waltz over, slam down the ticket, and demand that he find out who had been driving the car that received it. But the chief was not alone. Eileen Esterhaven sat to his right. Jemma sat to his left, chatting as if they were old friends. And, as Saffi watched, the chamber of commerce head, Larry Atwell, eased into the seat across from the chief. He'd loaded his plate with sausages as well as two Belgian waffles piled high with whipped cream and Oregon's famous marionberries which were, basically, blackberries on steroids.

Too many ears and eyes. Not enough evidence.

Instead of handing the ticket to Chief Boyd, she joined the brunch line. The smell of food—bacon and sausage, grilled trout and beer-battered halibut, home fries and egg scramble with hollandaise—made her belly rumble. A morning filled with stress supercharged by the oncoming storm made her want to chow down on everything she saw. Knowing she would regret it, she took a small sampling from each heated container along the buffet line. With her plate filled to overflowing, she turned to scout out a seat.

She glanced at the chief's table once again. What had compelled Eileen to join him? Maybe, Saffi mused, the people sitting with Chief Boyd were there to grill him for information. After the slashing, Eileen would be worried that the booksellers association had another potential liability suit on its hands. If so, this convention could very well end her tenure as president.

As for Larry? As head of the chamber of commerce, Larry's role, so far, had been to keep the town's image from being tarnished. He'd been aided, Saffi suspected, by his best bud—Chief

Boyd—who had probably been funneling information to him since day one of the investigation. On that fatal Friday morning, she had not recognized the red-faced man in the too-tight suit who rushed out of the Sunrise Room just as she went inside to be grilled by the chief, but she certainly recognized Larry now.

What had Hannah, the coffeehouse owner, told her? *The mayor wants the cops to stamp out crime. The chamber wants to pretend it never happens.* So far, Chief Boyd and his officers were o for 4 this weekend. *One murder. Three assaults.* As the chief's considering gaze met hers, the problem was clear: he still thought outsiders—Saffi or Poppy in particular—were responsible. Though she wanted to share the parking ticket with him, now was definitely not the time.

As Saffi watched the table, Larry scraped back his chair and started to circulate. He went table to table, smiling, nodding, and schmoozing, as if hoping to smooth away the sting of a convention turned criminal.

"Saffi!" a familiar voice called from a table by the front window. It had a breathtaking view of the storm building over the Pacific. Even snug inside the hotel restaurant, Saffi could feel the atmospheric pressure dropping. She steadied her plate and wound through the tables to join Willow, Poppy, George, Lyndie, and—surprisingly—Fia.

The group had saved her a seat between Poppy and Fia. Poppy raised one perfectly tweezed brow at Saffi's plate. She slid it onto the table and stared down her editor.

"I'm stressed, OK?" Saffi stuck her fork into the egg scramble, making sure to scoop up hollandaise sauce with the bite.

"I can certainly understand why." Fia patted her mouth with her napkin. "I was so excited about this convention, especially after George and Eileen agreed to invite you to keynote."

Was that an accusation in the fawn's eyes?

"If I had known your actual *life* was as full of nutcases as your books I would have backed Eileen's young adult author. The wolves she writes about are way less vicious than the people coming after you."

Wow. The fawn had grown fangs. OK. Saffi could handle it. "Yes, well, lucky for me you think on your feet. Handling Jay on the Jingle Tour." Poppy gasped, and brows raised around the table. "Oh, yes." Saffi nodded. "GoodVender tried to weasel his way back into the convention but Fia set him straight, didn't you?"

Poppy clasped her hands together and leaned forward. She gave Fia the look she usually reserved for manuscripts destined for the "reject" pile. "You rode with Jay on the Jingle Tour?"

George choked on the bite he'd been chewing and Lyndie patted him on the back as his face reddened. "You OK, babe?" She tweaked his man bun affectionately. Lyndie had not been there to see her man freeze at the sight of blood. But, hey! It was a normal reaction, especially for those who didn't stumble over crime victims on a regular basis, as Saffi now seemed to do.

As attention turned to George, Fia leaned toward Saffi. "That's enough, OK?" She glanced at a large manila envelope sticking out of the tote beside her chair. "I'll meet you." She dug through the tote for a North Coast Booksellers Association business card, scribbled something on the back, then handed the card to Saffi. *Carousel Boba Shoppe, 2 p.m.* Saffi read the card and nodded.

A presence loomed over Saffi's shoulder and she looked up. Larry Atwell did a smile-around at everyone seated at the table. "I hope you will all visit again. Give our little town another chance to show its best self." When every face around the table froze in dismay, a crestfallen Larry took the hint and scurried away.

Fia left on his heels, putting distance between herself and the accusation in Poppy's eyes. Saffi tucked the card Fia had handed her into her sling bag along with the parking ticket. If the skittish fawn finally broke her silence, she might have a chance to solve Jay's murder... before the killer silenced anyone else.

THIRTY

The lobby of the Necanicum Inn churned with people angling for printouts of final charges at the front desk. The rush to decamp before the storm plowed through town and dumped snow in the passes was on. According to NOAA, the bomb cyclone—if indeed the atmospheric pressure dropped far and fast enough for that classification—would come ashore either overnight or in the morning, depending on how fast it churned.

Phyllis had been joined by two other desk clerks—one male, one female. All three had smiles stretched so tightly across their faces they looked one complaint short of turning into killer clowns. For Saffi, that image would forever call to mind the face of Jay GoodVender.

As she crossed the carpeted lobby, Saffi dodged a group of booksellers dragging luggage and book totes toward the double front doors and immediately collided with another group heading for the side door to the parking lot.

"Sorry!" She rubbed her knee and wondered why she was the only one to apologize. Just as she made it through the melee to push the elevator's "up" button, someone called her name.

"Ms. Graywood! Saffi!"

She turned toward the front desk to see Phyllis waving her

over. Saffi was not in the mood to run the luggage and book tote gauntlet again but when she lifted a finger to point upward and mouthed, "Gotta pack!" Phyllis's wave became more frantic. Saffi drew in a deep breath.

"Once more into the breach!" she whispered.

Phyllis waved the people in line aside to let Saffi through. Half of them managed "accidental" luggage shoves or hip checks as she threaded her way to the desk. What had happened to these being her people? The chill, the bookish, the intelligent owls blinking through round glasses? If this convention made her wary of book lovers, she would find a way to bring Jay GoodVender back from the dead and kill him again. *Not that she had killed him in the first place, of course.*

Saffi glanced around herself as if someone might have heard the unspoken thought.

"I have a message for you." Phyllis thrust a phone message slip into Saffi's hand and then went back to checking out customers, leaving Saffi to the merciless mercies of the jostling crowd. She took a deep breath to prepare herself and zipped the message inside her sling bag so she wouldn't drop it. If she bent down to pick something up right now they wouldn't find her trampled remains until summer. Keeping her head high and her elbows up, she worked her way through the crowd. It was easier than she had anticipated. Apparently, even the pushiest hotel guests were wary of an elbow to the chin.

"Saffi!" another voice called, this one from the back of the line. She spotted Lyndie's blue hair and waved.

"You and George headed out?" Saffi asked.

"Yes, thank the gods." Lyndie hiked her backpack higher on her shoulder to keep it from being knocked off in the shuffle. "Eileen gave George the go-ahead to leave so we can get back to our fur baby before the storm hits. Thunder makes Roxy yowl non-stop. Sounds like a lioness in heat. Our pet sitter will be totally freaked."

"Safe travels," Saffi said. "And good luck with your store. I'll stop by next time I'm in Portland." She would, too. A *Bedside Reader* page about unique bookstores—including their animal-centered one—had already been taking shape in her head.

Lyndie flung an arm around Saffi's neck and gave her a soft, squishy hug. "We would love that."

"Even George?" Saffi grinned.

Lyndie pulled a face. "No utility knives allowed. And don't pick up any new stalkers along the way."

"Right!" Saffi crossed her heart then saluted. "No more ticking off fans!!"

When Saffi made it safely back to her suite, she pulled the message out of her sling bag. She wasn't so much surprised as disappointed. *Storm coming on too fast. Not safe to fly until it passes. Apologies... Scott.*

Saffi tossed her bag on the kitchen counter and threw herself down on the living room sofa. Now what? She had hoped the message would be from Troy. He still had not returned her call and the "out on a fishing tour" excuse she'd made up for him no longer held water. Not with a massive storm offshore. Where was he? And why had he not returned her call?

As she settled into the sofa's comfortable arms, the food coma she'd been half expecting hit. Within minutes, she was drooling on her Merino sweater.

Saffi woke with a start to someone pounding on her door. "Saffi! Are you in there? Open up!"

Even half asleep, Saffi recognized Poppy's "you're about to blow a deadline" intonation.

"Coming," she mumbled as she rolled herself off the couch and used the coffee table to push to her feet.

Poppy and Willow stood outside her door with a luggage cart between them. Suitcases, bulging book totes, shopping bags, and handbags formed a wobbly pyramid that looked like it would topple at any second.

Saffi massaged the crick in her neck that had formed while she snoozed. "When did you have time to shop?"

Poppy, the queen of the Manhattan eye-roll, straightened her shoulders. "There is *always* time to shop. Besides, we're celebrating!" Her eyes sparkled.

"Celebrating?"

"That information you dropped at brunch about Fia and Jay jingling all the way? It was just what the lawyer needed to demand a 'get out of Seaside free card' from the police chief. We're going home!" Poppy grabbed Saffi's hands. "And it's all thanks to you."

Instead of dressing for a long drive, Poppy looked like she was about to prance into an editorial meeting at Lowry & Lowenstein. Beige skinny suit showing razor-sharp ankles above stylish black pumps. Tailored white blouse. Cobalt-blue scarf to perfectly set off her silver-white pixie. Since Saffi had last seen her, she had moussed her hair in place against the wind. God help her if they got caught in a blizzard and had to walk.

Willow had exchanged her trade show attire for casual wear: salt-wash-denim jeans and a baby-blue hoodie with *Seaside, Oregon* scripted above a colorful carousel.

"Oh no!" Saffi's memory sparked. "What time is it?"

Poppy glanced at her smartwatch. "Two o'clock. Why?"

"I have to go!" Saffi ran back into her suite, grabbed her sling bag from the kitchen counter, tugged a windbreaker off a hanger, and snagged her cellphone from the coffee table. She would message Fia once she got outside to let her know she was running late.

Saffi nudged Poppy and Willow backward so she could close the door. "Call me when you get to Portland, OK?"

"Saffi! Did you hear what I said? We're off the hook. You can stop sleuthing and go home!"

She waved at her astounded editor, then pulled open the door to the stairwell. With so many people trying to leave the inn, waiting for the elevator would take far too long.

By the time she reached the bottom, her heart rate had gone

from "I could do this all day" to "I feel like I am going to die." The lobby was still a seething sea of sharks so she went straight for the side door. Once outside, she slowed her pace enough to slow her heart rate back to the "I think I can, I think I can" range. Then she messaged Fia and set a brisk—but breathable—pace.

The Carousel Mall was just a few blocks past the Broadway Bridge, but as she crossed the span the massive black bird she'd begun to think of as the "dire raven" swooped down to land on its favorite post. It shuffled from one foot to the other, gave a low, guttural *crah-a-a-wk, crah-a-a-wk* then leapt to the road's surface. A car blew its horn and swerved when the massive bird didn't budge. Instead, it bent its large black beak toward the pavement, picked up a chubby bright-pink straw and used it to point toward the Carousel Mall.

If Saffi had not written about the intelligence of ravens for *Bedside Reader*, #1, she would have thought the gesture random. It wasn't. Ravens, Saffi knew, were among the smartest animals on earth. They used a variety of calls to communicate and even picked up twigs and other items to use when trying to get someone's attention. Though a group of them was called "an unkindness," when it came to their friends, ravens were more than kind. They stayed with injured friends and fed them until they had recovered. And if they had seen who or what had caused the injury, they remembered and passed down the warning to the next generation.

The raven had seen who had killed Jay. Saffi was sure of it. And the black bird remembered. Too bad it couldn't actually speak. Now *that* would be useful.

"I'm going. I'm going." She put on an extra kick of speed for the watching raven's benefit. It was best to stay in the good graces of a mediator between life and death.

Once she reached the mall, Saffi made her way into a broad hallway with shops on either side. She hurried past a store with souvenir hoodies like the one Willow had been wearing and headed for the carousel at the mall's center. The feeling of unease brought on by the raven's warning dissipated as she took in the whimsical shops and eateries encircling the carousel. The hattery featured top hats worthy of Dr. Seuss's infamous cat. The toy store window was stuffed with sock monkeys and rubber chickens. She spotted Carousel Boba, the bubble tea shop where Fia was supposed to meet her, and hurried inside. She expected to find the young bookseller seated at one of the tiny tables with a judgy look on her face and a bubble tea in one hand, but Fia was not there.

She pulled her cell out of her sling and glanced at the time. She was ten minutes late. Would Fia have left when she didn't show right on the dot of two? Surely not. Not if she had something important to share. Her text message to Fia had been delivered, but the young woman had not replied. Was the entire world ghosting her?

Saffi wove between café tables to reach the counter. After glancing at the menu, she ordered a rose black oat milk tea.

"Hot or cold?" The barista's peach-fuzz afternoon shadow said he was somewhere between puberty and his junior year in high school. "If you order a cold one, I can offer you a reusable straw for half price." He gestured toward a wooden box that held chubby stainless steel straws with angled tips for piercing the plastic covers on boba teas.

"I think I'll go for hot. Thank you." Saffi turned to watch for Fia as the young man steamed the oat milk for her tea.

"Happy New Year!" The teenage barista handed over the drink with a grin.

Saffi blinked. The events of the past few days had nearly wiped the year's turning from her mind. "Back at you." She saluted with her teacup.

She started toward a table by the window, then turned back. "Was there a young woman in here a few minutes ago? Brown skin. Box braids."

The barista's face lit up. "Yeah. Yeah. I remember her! Lavender Earl Grey with tapioca pearls."

"We were supposed to meet." Saffi frowned.

The barista shrugged. "Sat for a while over there." He pointed to a window table. "One of the regulars came in and by the time I finished his order, she was gone. Left her boba on the table with barely a sip out of it." He shook his head at the waste of it all.

Saffi took her tea to the table the barista had pointed out. Maybe Fia had slipped away to the restroom and would return shortly to give the barista a piece of her mind for tossing her bubble tea. As she sipped, two kids with grandparents in tow rushed toward the carousel.

"Here it is, Mimi!" A sixish girl snuggled inside a fuzzy white jacket with bunny ears tugged her grandmother toward the ride.

"Pa!" A boy half the girl's age gave his grandfather a gap-toothed grin. "I wanna wide the wabbit!"

An attendant wearing elf ears and a pointy green hat took their money. Then he opened the gate to let them clamber aboard the platform and find their favorite animal. The grandfather hefted the boy onto the rabbit and stood beside him with a hand on his back. "Hold onto his ears!" he instructed.

The girl chose a teal seahorse but she climbed on by herself while her athletic grandmother swung a leg over the stallion beside her.

The carousel's tinny mechanical organ began to play as the platform slowly started to turn. Lights glowed from beneath the canopy and sparkled in the mirrors on the central structure that housed the gears and other mechanics. Saffi looked away to check her phone. Fia still hadn't read her message. Had she left in a huff when Saffi didn't show?

As she sipped her tea, wondering if she should stay or go, the glee on the kids' faces caught her attention. Happiness... such a welcome sight after the stress of the booksellers convention. She relaxed into her chair as the carousel animals wound past, up and down, up and down. A black cat with a pink fish in its mouth. A pair of reindeer. A plump pink pig. A giraffe with a blue saddle. Which would she choose?

A sleigh wound toward her, the kind made for people who couldn't climb aboard one of the animals. *Right now, that would be me*. Saffi sighed. As the jaunty red sleigh came into full view, she spotted a figure slumped sideways. Dark ropes dangled over the side of the seat.

Saffi jolted upright. Not dark ropes—box braids.

"Fia?" Her teacup wobbled against the tabletop as she set it down. As the sleigh rounded the curve, the yellow glow of carousel lights bounced off something protruding from Fia's shoul-der... something metallic. Saffi's belly went queasy. The silver tube looked exactly like the metal bubble tea straws in the boba shop.

THIRTY-ONE

Dear God! To save time, Saffi pushed the SOS button on her cellphone. Help would come to her location without spending time calling 9-1-1. She rushed around the carousel to where the elf stood with his back against the wall, eyes closed.

"Stop the carousel!" Saffi shouted, but the elf's eyes did not open. Was something wrong with him, too? That's when Saffi noticed cords coming from under his elf ears. She gave one cord a tug and the elf shot to attention.

"Hey! Whatta ya think you're doing?" He scowled.

"Stop the carousel," Saffi demanded. "Now."

"Get in line, lady. It'll be your turn soon enough."

"I don't want a turn." She wanted to shake him but she did the next best thing. She yanked the elf hat off his head and ran with it toward the carousel. That got his attention and he chased after her. She raced around the turning platform until she was side by side with the sleigh.

"Look!" She pointed at Fia's slumped form.

"Holy shit." The elf gulped so hard his Adam's apple went up and down. Then he ran back to the control box and hit a button. The carousel music started to slow and stretch until it sounded like a wail. The platform slowed with the sound.

The little girl put her hands over her ears. "Mimi! That elf said a bad word."

"I wanna wide the wabbit!" the little boy whined.

By that time, the grandparents knew something was wrong, something they probably did not want their grandchildren to see. The minute the ride stopped, they hoisted them off the animals, hopped down from the platform, hurried them through the gate, and headed for the mall exit. Normally, Saffi would have stopped them. She was certain Chief Boyd would want them to stay. After all, they could have seen something. *But the kids!* Saffi watched the family flee without saying a word, then she followed the elf through the gate and onto the platform.

The two of them stood side by side in front of the sleigh, looking down at Fia's still form.

"Can you—can you check her?" The elf clenched his hands at his sides as if the thought of touching a body was more than he could bear.

As Saffi leaned forward, Fia's chest rose slowly and then fell. "She's alive!"

Another opportunistic attack. The person who stabbed Fia had grabbed the closest weapon. It reminded Saffi of what had happened in the storage room. She'd laid down the utility knife, and the attacker used it. But why here? Why Fia? She glanced down at the tote settled beside Fia's feet.

The manila envelope! She handed the elf's hat back to him and squeezed his shoulder. "I'll stay with her until the EMTs arrive."

She waved the elf toward the gate side of the carousel and he scurried away. The moment he left, Saffi rifled through Fia's tote. *Where is it? Where is it?* The manila envelope that Fia had glanced down at when she asked Saffi to meet her was neither in the tote nor beneath the seat on which the young woman's body slumped. The person who had stabbed Fia must have taken it.

Who could have known Fia would be here? Poppy, Willow, George, Lyndie... none of whom were on Saffi's suspect list.

Saffi's head started to pound. Despite the fact that she had done nothing to harm Fia, she felt more than just a little to blame for what had happened. A few interminable minutes later, sirens started to wail, growing louder as they got closer and closer. A few seconds after the noise stopped, the mall's front doors whacked open and footsteps pounded down the hallway.

"Here!" Saffi stepped forward and waved the emergency medical techs toward the carousel gate.

Before long, the EMTs had taken charge. When they shifted Fia to move her from the sleigh to a stretcher, she gasped. Her eyes fluttered open. She blinked, as if trying to remember where she was, what had happened.

Saffi leaned forward, hoping a familiar face would take away some of the fear in Fia's eyes. "You're OK. Help is here."

Fia licked her lips. "Saffi."

"I'm here." Saffi gave Fia what she hoped was a comforting smile.

"Jay... Jay had Poppy's pen... that-that night. He showed it to me. Gloated about taking it. I-I'm sorry. I should have told the police the truth. I just—"

Saffi squeezed Fia's hand. "I get it. If you'd told Boyd the truth, he would have arrested you instead of Poppy."

"Told me the truth about what?"

The EMT looked over Saffi's head and lifted a hand. "Chief!" She waved Chief Boyd over. "We need to get this young lady into surgery." She nodded at Saffi. "Why don't you talk to the chief while we take care of your friend."

Saffi's head sank toward her chest. She did not want to talk to the chief, especially because, this time, she was right here... at the scene of the crime... within moments of when Fia had been stabbed. If her interview with Chief Boyd didn't end in handcuffs, she would be very, very surprised.

The chief talked to the EMTs then glanced at Saffi with cut glass in his blue eyes. When one of the EMTs asked him a question and he turned away, Saffi took the opportunity to jet into Carousel

Boba. She wasn't exactly avoiding him; she had a question to ask the barista *before* the chief dragged her off to jail.

"What's going on out there?" The barista stood rubbernecking in the tea shop doorway but followed her inside, perhaps hoping to get the scoop.

Saffi had been holding herself together but his question made her muscles dissolve. When she grabbed the back of a chair and flumped into it, the barista ran to the table she had abandoned earlier and snagged her now-cold cup of rose black oat milk tea. "Here. Drink some of this. You look like you saw a ghost."

Saffi drank. The tea tasted bitter as death, the subtle rose flavor overwhelmed by the sour taste in her mouth. Still, she drank it, then nodded her thanks. "The young woman who came in earlier? The one I was supposed to meet?"

The teenage barista's eyebrows shot up. "She's OK, right?"

Saffi put her face in her hands. "No. She's not."

The barista scraped a chair toward her then turned it to face Saffi and straddled it. Stress had dilated his pupils until she could barely see the ring of blue around them.

Don't push him, Saffi. He's a kid.

She didn't want to push him, but her memory of something he'd said earlier had driven her back into the bubble tea shop. She took a deep breath. "You said that someone came in for tea just after you served Fia."

"That's right." He nodded, then he lifted his head. "Wait! You don't think—"

She did think. She thought Fia had seen someone who frightened her. Like the skittish deer Saffi knew her to be, she had left her drink behind and gotten on that carousel to hide, not to ride. She'd done that while the barista was waiting on someone he had called a "regular."

"I think," Saffi said, "that the police will want to know about the man you said came in here after you made my friend's tea. If you can describe him, that would help."

The teen snorted. "Of course I can describe him. I've known

him my whole life. But if you think he hurt that woman, you are way off base. Larry's cool. Owns the bike shop."

"Larry Atwell? Head of the chamber of commerce?"

At that moment, Chief Boyd strode into the bubble tea shop. He glanced from the barista to Saffi and back. "Greg. You OK?"

"Yeah. I'm good. I mean, considering. This whole thing is wacked."

"It is," the chief agreed.

"How about a coffee?" The chief took his hat off and held it between his hands. "Black. Make yourself something, too. It's on me." Then he turned to Saffi. "Something extra sweet for Ms. Graywood. She's had a shock. After that, I'm gonna have to shut you down until my team finishes going over this place."

When Greg asked her preference, Saffi requested a mocha. She didn't expect much, given the shop's specialty, but she could not face Chief Boyd's interrogation on a cup of tea.

THIRTY-TWO

Chief Boyd interviewed Greg first, sending Saffi to one of the café tables outside the shop with her mocha. She was down to the chocolatey dregs when the barista and the chief sauntered outside. The young man locked the door behind them. He had called his boss at the chief's insistence to get permission to close the shop until the police reopened the mall. Once the teen walked away, Chief Boyd sat down on the opposite side of the table.

"Let's start with your arrival at the tea shop." He clicked a pen and opened the small black notepad he had pulled from his shirt pocket.

"Sure." Saffi nodded. "But first, did Greg tell you about Larry Atwell?"

The squint of confusion on his face told her the teen had withheld that critical bit of information.

After she filled him in, the chief pressed his lips together so tightly they paled. "Larry was in the shop when Fia left. She saw him and got spooked. Larry grabbed a metal straw from the tea shop, and went after her."

"Exactly." Saffi pressed her hands on the tabletop.

"Congratulations. You've solved the case. I'll just be going then, shall I?" The chief half rose, pretending to leave, then sat back down. "Unless... someone who is known to have had possession of a pen with *P. Morales* engraved on it, the only piece of evidence tying anyone to Jay GoodVender's murder, just happened to be on scene for *this* attack as well."

Chief Boyd was as determined as ever to pin the string of crimes on an outsider. Why? Was he protecting the town from scandal? Or protecting his murdery best friend? Either way, Fia had just given her the information she needed to prove Poppy's premise. The person who took her pen was responsible for everything that followed, and that person was Jay GoodVender.

Saffi licked her lips and blinked. "About that pen."

Chief Boyd's face went blank as she shared Fia's confession and apology. "So, you can forget about using that pen as evidence against my editor, or me, for that matter."

The chief clicked his pen twice. "Since Fia is conveniently unable to corroborate your story, let's start with your arrival at the tea shop, shall we?"

"Fine." Saffi sat back in her chair, arms crossed over her chest. The only way out of this mess was to slog through the muck. "I was supposed to meet Fia at two. I think she had something she wanted to give me, but I didn't get to the boba shop until ten minutes past. She wasn't here, so I ordered tea and sat down to wait." As he took down her story, the chief flipped back a few pages, now and then, as if checking what she said against what Greg had told him.

"After that?"

"I watched the carousel. A couple of adorable kids came in to ride with their grandparents."

Chief Boyd's pen hand froze. He looked up, confusion in his eyes. "There were other people on the carousel when the woman was attacked?"

"No," she said softly, staring down at her clenched hands. "I think the attack happened *before* they arrived."

The chief sighed, then squeezed the bridge of his nose between his thumb and forefinger as if she was making his head pound the way hers had been doing since she found Fia. "I suppose, after you discovered that the young woman had been stabbed, you decided to just—what? Let them leave?"

"*Yes*," she hissed. "The kids were *little*. Like six and maybe three or four years old. If you had been here, would you have kept them? Let those little ones see something like—" Saffi could feel her cheeks turning chili-pepper red as her eyes filled with tears.

"They were witnesses, Ms. Graywood. Witnesses who—if you're telling the truth—could have verified that you didn't show up until *after* the carousel was in motion."

Oh, holy heck.

"A bit... convenient that you let them slip away." His blue gaze bored into hers as he waited for... what? For her to confess that she had driven that metal straw into Fia's back?

"Ask the elf. He'll tell you."

"There's an elf involved." The chief sat back in his chair and crossed an ankle over his knee. "Of course there is."

Saffi stood up, looked through the shop window to the carousel. The elf had gone back to leaning against the back wall, eyes closed, listening to his music. "That elf." The moment she pointed him out she realized something. The elf would not have seen Saffi arrive any more than he had seen Fia's attacker. All he could tell the chief was that Saffi had yanked an earbud out of his ear and forced him to shut down the carousel, then led him to Fia's unconscious form. There were no paddles sturdy enough to row Saffi out of the crap her kindness had landed her in.

"The item the victim brought for you? Did you find it when you dug through her tote?"

"What makes you think I dug through her tote?"

The chief flipped his notebook shut, slipped it into his shirt pocket and clipped his pen in place beside it. "I've met you, Ms. Graywood. You dig and dig until you find what you're looking for."

Saffi shook her head. "Not this time. The person who stabbed her must have taken it. I don't even know what it was."

His eyes clouded over with suspicion... or worry. "I've never met anyone like you. You attract violence the way dead fish attract seagulls. Either that, or you are a menace to society."

Attractive image. Thanks!

"Or..." Saffi put her hands flat on the table and leaned forward. "I've been asking people what they saw the night Jay GoodVender died, and searching for evidence that might tie someone besides my editor—who is innocent—to the crime."

"If that's the case, it's time to rethink your methods." The chief stood and Saffi did the same. "Two people were attacked in my town today, Ms. Graywood. Someone extremely dangerous is running scared, perhaps because someone who is an *author*, not a member of *law enforcement*, is poking her pen where it does not belong."

Saffi had a retort on her tongue but held it back when she realized what he was saying. "You don't think I did it?"

The chief settled his hat on his head. "I have a few more resources at my disposal than you do, Ms. Graywood. You have no history of violence, no criminal record. You do, however, have an unpaid ticket for parking an RV in a restricted zone in downtown San Diego."

Parking ticket! The attack on Fia had driven the ticket she'd found completely out of her mind. "I have something for you!" She unzipped her sling bag and pulled out the ticket, holding onto it as she explained how and why it had come into her possession. As she ran her thumb over the ticket, she noticed the date and time: Jan. 3. 1:03 a.m. Saffi gasped and thrust the ticket into the chief's hand. "Look at the—"

"You know," he interrupted. "I've been thinking of you as a writer who thinks her research skills qualify her to meddle in a murder investigation. Irritating, but harmless. Like a mosquito." The accusatory glint in his eyes forewarned her and Saffi stiffened. "Then I read something in a *Bedside Reader* one of my officers loaned me. A countdown of the world's deadliest animals."

Saffi groaned. "Just look. Please."

The chief pointed the ticket at her, reminding her of the way the raven had pointed toward the mall with the pink straw.

"People think sharks are the deadliest animals on earth but they don't come close, do they, Aunt Saffi?"

"No. They don't." She looked him in the eye. "It's those pesky mosquitos. But they don't actually kill people. They just spread diseases."

"Exactly. They don't *mean* to kill anyone. They're just hungry for blood."

Saffi threw up her hands in defeat. "OK. I get it. I'm a mosquito who spreads death. But, before someone else dies, could you please take a look at that ticket? Someone was in exactly the right place at the right time to have killed Jay GoodVender. And you—as you just pointedly reminded me—have the resources to find out who it was."

He looked. Then he took the notebook from his shirt pocket and slipped the ticket inside. "I would advise you to go back to your hotel and stay there." He slid the notebook into his pocket. "That storm offshore is a beast. The safest place for you will be curled up in front of a fireplace with a book. And don't answer the door to anyone you don't know and trust."

When the chief walked her outside, the wind shoved her hard against him and he instinctively put an arm around her waist to steady her. As he did so, his hat went flying into the street where it was promptly squashed by a passing car. "Well. That's a first. I'd better give you a ride." He had to fight to open the passenger-side door of his patrol car and then dig in his heels to keep it from slamming shut before she could pull her legs inside.

He dropped her off at the side door of the inn where the building and parking overhang would shield her from the wind. She thanked him for the ride, and for not arresting her... yet.

She carried his admonition to stay put with her, as well as his mosquito death-spreading analogy. Finding Fia and knowing that the young woman had planned to hand over something she had withheld earlier didn't make Saffi feel justified at all. It made her feel... guilty. There was no other word for it. She felt it in her heart and in her gut. Fia had been stabbed for whatever was in that manila envelope.

Only one thing made sense: she really had heard the clink of Fia's braids in the exhibit hall when Jay's organizer disappeared. Fia had taken it. In the top drawer she'd found the composition book titled *Silenced in Seaside*. Saffi had no idea why Fia would have removed the notebook. That did *not* make sense, but if the person who'd been on a rampage the entire weekend had it now, maybe the chain of violence would finally end.

The Necanicum Inn's lobby had calmed down since Saffi rushed out to meet Fia. Most of the convention attendees were now on their way home—speeding along windswept highways, doing their best to keep their cars on the road while trying to beat the storm to their destinations. Saffi slogged up the stairs to avoid facing fans or conventioneers in the elevator. Some had probably decided to ride out the storm rather than get stuck in an airport or risk an accident on the road. Her shoulders hunched against the memory of seeing Fia with that straw stuck in her shoulder. How had it come to this? She felt as if she carried the weight of a fawn on her shoulders.

Saffi wanted to get inside, lay down her burden, pull the comforter over her head and sleep until Chief Boyd found whoever had gone after Fia. Like Greg, the young barista, the chief had discounted Larry Atwell as the culprit. To Saffi, that seemed absurd. Illogical. If the attacker wasn't the only person who had been in the tea shop just before Fia left, who could it be? Larry had opportunity and access to the weapon.

But motive? What about motive, Saffi?

The man seemed to be expending all of his energy promoting the town. A crime spree made no sense. Chief Boyd had seen the same flaw in her theory. If he followed through on the parking ticket—God, she hoped he would—maybe he would find a link between Jay and Larry. But she was reaching, and she knew it.

At the top of the fourth flight of stairs, Saffi stopped to catch her breath and slow her heart rate. *Think, Saffi!* It took a few deep breaths before her oxygen-starved brain restarted. The two timelines she'd imagined stretched out in her mind. If the trail of violence *started* with Jay's murder, there was probably a connection to the booksellers convention. If a conventioneer had killed Jay, getting out of town was the best way to avoid being caught. Staying in town to attack Fia made no sense. It was far too risky.

Fia's attacker had to be a local. Besides Larry Atwell, her only local suspect was Jemma. She had butted heads with Jay on more than one occasion. There was a connection between the dedication in her memoir and the notebook Saffi had found in Jay's organizer: *Silenced in Seaside.* Jemma had been seated at Chief Boyd's table. If stealing the manila envelope in the young bookseller's bag was the attacker's motive, how could Jemma have known what was in it?

As Saffi thought, and breathed, and thought some more, the fourth-floor landing became stuffy with too much carbon dioxide from her expelled breaths. *Enough lurking in stairways!* She pushed open the door to the hallway and headed for her suite, but when she reached the door, she froze. A large manila envelope leaned against it. A white envelope with Saffi's name printed in red Sharpie had been taped to its side. Saffi yanked the smaller envelope from the large one and tore it open. Inside, she found a note printed on Necanicum Inn stationery. Saffi's lips moved as she read the elegant script: *Fia handed this to me after the brunch for safekeeping. She wanted you to have it if anything happened to her. I hope it helps you nail the bastard! Eileen.*

Saffi ran a hand down the envelope and felt the bumpy spine of a spiral-bound notebook. Did she hold *Silenced in Seaside*—the mysterious notebook behind two violent attacks—in her hands? She glanced down the corridor. She needed to get out of the exposed hallway. Now!

She fumbled her key card from her sling bag and slipped it into the card reader. She expected a green light followed by a click.

Instead, the light flashed red and the door remained locked. Saffi tried again... and again... and again. Her key card no longer worked.

THIRTY-THREE

For a minute, Saffi panicked. How was this possible? The key had worked fine every other time she'd tried it. *OK. Don't freak out. There's a logical explanation. Just go downstairs and find out what it is.* Saffi pressed the manila envelope to her chest, then changed her mind and stuffed it under her windbreaker and tunic, then tucked it beneath the band of her leggings. It grated against her skin and made her waddle like a duck, but Saffi didn't care.

She hurried to the elevator, pushed the button and waited. Her whole body twitched as she alternated between looking toward the stairwell and down the hall. Her ears strained for boots on concrete stairsteps or muffled footfalls. Every second felt like an eternity. She poked the button again and chewed her lower lip as she waited. "Come the freak on!" The elevator whooshed open just as she shouted and a harried housekeeper holding a stuffed laundry bag shrank against the back wall.

"Sorry." Saffi glanced at the woman's name tag. "Marisol!"

The housekeeper's eyes went wild with fear, like a trapped animal's. Saffi held up both hands.

"No. No. It's OK. I just wanted you to know I'm so sorry about what happened to you. That man..."

Marisol straightened. "You are suite 402?"

Saffi nodded.

"Phyllis showed me the photo you shared. That man wanted to go into your room. See the petals. I say, 'No. Is not allowed.' And he – he..."

As Marisol gulped air, Saffi gestured toward the elevator. "Can I—?" When Marisol nodded, Saffi stepped aboard and pressed the button with the star for "Lobby." The door shooshed closed and Saffi gave Marisol as much space as she could. Having a stranger come close after being chloroformed would not ease the house-keeper's discomfort. They reached the lobby without a word passing between them, but when their eyes met, Saffi could see the acknowledgment that they were both survivors. And... Jay Good-Vender had reaped what he sowed.

The encounter with Marisol had driven Saffi's reason for coming to the lobby from her mind. When she glanced up and spotted Phyllis, her synapses sparked. "My room card stopped working. Can you fix it?" She handed Phyllis the card.

The desk clerk tucked her ash-brown hair behind her ears, adjusted her stylish tortoiseshell and cream-green specs, then tapped on the computer keyboard. "Let's see. Room 402." She moved the mouse on the desktop to scroll down the screen. "Ah. Looks like you were supposed to check out this morning. The suite is reserved for another guest this evening." She clicked the mouse a few times. "I'm afraid it needs cleaning before they arrive, so if you could just remove your belongings?"

When she'd seen Poppy and Willow heading out with their luggage, she'd been half asleep. Checkout time had completely slipped her mind.

"Phyllis!" Saffi used her name to remind the desk clerk of all they'd been through together in the past few days. "I can't remove my things if my key card doesn't work, and where am I supposed to go once I do?"

"I'm really sorry." Phyllis did look truly apologetic. "Normally I could extend your stay, but with the storm coming in? Demand for rooms has exploded. Everyone wants to get off the roads before it hits, you know?"

Great! Now what? She stood there with the manila envelope chafing her belly, wondering what on earth she was supposed to do now.

"Mr. Wilkins?" Phyllis stuck her head into the office behind the desk. "Would you mind watching the desk while I help Ms. Graywood with her checkout?" A prim and proper East Indian man wearing a silk suit gone shiny with wear stepped forward. The gold badge pinned to his lapel read *MANAGER*, in all caps. "It would be my pleasure!" He offered Saffi an odd little bow as if he hadn't just stepped out of an inner office but into the present from a more courtly time... or place.

"Don't worry," Phyllis whispered as she led Saffi toward the elevator. "I waived the late checkout surcharge."

Late checkout charge? Could this horrible day get any worse?

As they rode up the elevator, Saffi shifted from foot to foot. "Will any of the other hotels have rooms available?"

Phyllis pushed her glasses up her nose and shrugged. "Some of the less... desirable ones might have rooms, but I have a better idea." She gave Saffi a grin that said she'd left "desk clerk mode" behind.

"You do? What?" At this point, Saffi would take any idea that sounded less than downright awful.

As it turned out, Phyllis's idea landed in the "questionable" column.

"The Mermaid's Purse! A couple had the Airstream reserved for tonight but they canceled because of the storm. The trailer's clean as a whistle and ready for occupancy. The couple paid for the 'romance' package, so there are truffles on the bed, champagne in the fridge, and a charcuterie board with smoked salmon and other goodies. Jemma just called to let me know."

At any other time Saffi would have jumped at the chance to rent one of Jemma's vintage trailers for a night, or even longer. But right now? First of all, the park was a beach, a berm, and a few hundred yards from Seaside Cove. The massive storm marching toward shore was due to hit either overnight or tomorrow morning. Second of all—and most worrying—Jemma was one of only two people who remained at the top of Saffi's suspect list. If something in the envelope now stabbing her in the left boob pointed to Jemma as a killer, would Saffi want to be camped two doors down?

"Did, uhm, Jemma tell you to offer it to me in particular?" She had to ask, just in case she was being lured by a luxury vintage trailer into a trap.

"No. The two of us have a deal. If she has an opening and the inn's booked solid, I send business her way. She cuts fifty bucks off my rent whenever she gets a booking that way."

"That's very generous of her," Saffi said. And it was. Jemma definitely had a generous spirit. Loving foster mom. Creative. And more handy with a hammer and nails than Saffi would ever be. Jemma could *not* be a murderer. Saffi would not allow it.

"I get off work in a half hour," Phyllis said as she unlocked the door to Saffi's suite with her master key card. "I'd be happy to drive you and your things over there. That is, if you're interested."

At this point, Saffi didn't exactly have other options. If she left it to the fates to help her find a room for the night, she might not be silenced in Seaside... but she could very well be homeless.

"Tell Jemma I'll take it. And, thanks, Phyllis."

Phyllis went downstairs to finish her shift while Saffi hastily packed her bags. For safety's sake, she put the manila envelope on the bottom of her suitcase and folded her clothes on top of it. She gathered up books and other items, including *Mermaids at Midnight*, and stuffed them into the *Bedside Reader* tote Poppy had given her on the first day of the convention. It seemed almost fated that she would end up reading what Fia had risked her life for in an Airstream at The Mermaid's Purse. Nice as the Necanicum Inn suite had been, she missed the cozy comfort of her Rambler Trek. Jemma's trailer by the sea might be exactly what she needed to stave off a complete emotional meltdown.

. . .

When they reached The Mermaid's Purse, Phyllis turned into a paved drive Saffi had failed to notice earlier, probably because it curved behind the trailers rather than in front. The drive ended in a small, paved parking lot. A genius design, really. Saffi had to give Jemma credit. The view from the trailers would be of the gazebo, the picnic area, and the sea rather than a hodgepodge of cars, trucks, and SUVs.

Phyllis hefted Saffi's book tote onto her shoulder. Saffi wrestled her suitcase from the backseat and bumped it along the paving-stone path from the lot to the Airstream.

"There's a storytelling session at the gazebo after dark. We'll have a fire, toast marshmallows, and drink Jemma's amazing hot grog—it's got, like, rum, sugar, and lime juice. She adds cinnamon, star anise, ginger and bitter orange and just lets it simmer till it is... well, you have to taste it to understand."

"Are you kidding me? Have I died and gone to mermaid heaven?"

"Mermaid haven, more like. But, yeah. This place is magic. Be careful, it gets under your skin."

Once Saffi's belongings were stacked out front, Phyllis waved goodbye and headed to her silver Shasta trailer to relax.

Saffi felt beneath the Airstream's first metal step for a magnetic key holder Jemma had left there, excitement building as she unlocked the trailer and stepped gingerly into the front room. Vintage RVs often got spectacular redos. This one featured a cushy loveseat covered in turquoise velvet beneath a window with yellow-and-white-striped curtains, an unfortunate reminder of the awnings on the Surrey cycles.

Saffi shook off the shiver of memory. Tonight, she planned to do all she could to keep the shadows at bay. The plump yellow pillows on either end of the loveseat helped. She didn't know why yellow always made her happy—it just did. End tables on either side of the loveseat offered surfaces for some of the goodies Jemma had provided: a basket filled with fruit, a charcuterie tray, and a bottle of champagne chilling in a metal ice bucket. Two glasses sat beside the bucket, along with a corkscrew—part of the romance package the couple that canceled would miss out on.

Saffi felt a twinge of regret that Troy was not here to enjoy the treats with her. Not least because—on the front end of the Airstream—Jemma had installed a full-size bed with a deep mattress to put sleepers level with the wraparound window in the trailer's nose. The yellow-and-white-striped curtains had been tied back to reveal a majestic view of Tillamook Head. Saffi put a hand to her chest. How would she ever convince herself to leave this place?

A cherrywood bed tray held a small box of truffles from a local chocolatery, a "Welcome to The Mermaid's Purse" postcard that featured the carved mermaid outside Jemma's door, and a sheet with information on how to connect to Wi-Fi. Saffi glanced around the room. There was no TV, for which she was grateful. Since she didn't have Troy to share the view, she would prop herself against the red and yellow pillows, snuggle beneath the turquoise duvet, and lose herself in a book.

A night in Jemma's Airstream wasn't camping. It was full-on glamping. Unfortunately, before she could sink into the luxury of it all, she had an envelope to open. Secrets to uncover, one of which —Saffi hoped—would shine a light on Fia's attacker.

THIRTY-FOUR

Saffi tugged her suitcase to the loveseat. She dug the manila envelope from beneath her folded clothes and hesitated. Before she tackled the notebook she believed to be inside, she needed something hot to drink.

The Airstream was designed for delight, not sweating over a stove. The tiny kitchenette had a granite counter with a two-burner induction stovetop on one end and a sink barely big enough to wash a plate on the other. An electric tea kettle similar to the one Saffi had in her RV sat on the counter beside a tea bag carousel. Saffi put water on to boil, selected a Tulsi rose cinnamon tea, and plopped it into a depression-era pink glass teacup.

While she waited for the water to boil, she took in the view through the kitchen window. The storm looming offshore had set the clouds ablaze. No way was she staying inside.

She pulled a hoodie over her sweater and grabbed the wool throw folded at the end of the bed. With the manila envelope tucked in one armpit and cup and saucer balanced in the other, she stepped down the trailer's metal stairs to the concrete patio. Once outside, she tucked herself into the beach chair and breathed in salted air to let the sea suffuse her body.

Sky and sea had been painted by the oncoming storm, but—for

the moment—the wind held its breath. Above the horizon line, the sky was cobalt blue all the way to the light-infused clouds. Below, the sea shone like polished silver. Sunset-orange and twilight-blue streaks made looking at the water almost bearable. As the ocean hurled itself shoreward, the waves became blue-black walls with whipped white caps that spit foam and hurled spray as they curled earthward to break against the shore.

Though it was hard to take her eyes off the spectacle, Saffi had a job to do. She took a sip of cinnamon-scented rose tea, then ripped up the glued flap of the envelope and tore it open along the top edge. The spiral-bound notebook she pulled from the envelope was the one she expected: *Silenced in Seaside*.

Was the killer she'd been searching for inside the pages? If so, she owed it to Fia to discover his identity.

From the first paragraph, Saffi knew the pages didn't contain Jay's research notes. The flowing cursive bore no resemblance to the jabs and underlinings she'd seen in his notebooks. No. This notebook belonged to Jemma. It was the memoir she had not dared publish, filled with teenaged angst and a young Jemma's guilt-ridden love—and sexual desire—for her best friend, Helen. She was Jemma's first crush and—in Jemma's mind—her soulmate. No wonder Jemma never got over Helen's loss.

After the tragedy of Helen's disappearance, the journal began to show signs of the mature woman Jemma had become. Strong. Determined. Capable. Caring—especially for Debbie—and pissed off beyond her ability to communicate her rage in words.

Though loneliness pervaded the text, Jemma had not been alone in her journey. She had allies, most notably her fisherman father. He had understood and supported her gradual awakening into a self-aware and accepting lesbian. Saffi found herself surprised by Jemma's father. Too many men of his generation used their masculinity as a bludgeon, especially those who lived in the "man against nature" world of fishermen. Jemma's father had been her shelter against the storm.

Jemma had also had a high-school bestie, none other than the ginger-haired Eric Boyd, who had been tough enough, even as a teen, to fend off the narrow-minded bullies at their high school. He, and, surprisingly, Larry Atwell had been stalwart friends of both Jemma and Helen in their teen years. It did not take long for Saffi to understand why Jemma had opted for allegory in writing her mermaid story. The gang that made up her friend group—minus the missing Helen and the murdered Sonya—were still living in Seaside. She had used the *Little Mermaid* retelling to protect herself, and her friends, against judgmental small-town minds... and potential lawsuits.

Jemma raged on the page when Helen revealed her pregnancy. She exploded when her friend refused to name her teenage lover. Consumed by jealousy, she severed their friendship. She watched from afar as Helen's belly grew and her friend was forced to leave school. Rumors swirled, but none of the boys Jemma suspected stepped forward. Eric and Larry retreated into a boys' club of two that no longer included Jemma.

As the sun sank lower, it became harder and harder to make out Jemma's tiny, cramped handwriting, but Saffi already knew why the notebook had caused so much misery. When combined with Jemma's memoir, the narrative pointed straight to the "bastard" who had betrayed Helen and, probably, murdered Jay GoodVender.

A figure loomed over her, blocking the rays of the dying sun. "I believe that belongs to me." Jemma held out a hand.

What could she say? *Sorry, I'm sleuthing?* Of course not. The notebook was Jemma's and it contained an absolutely heartrending recollection of the days after Helen went missing. Jemma had bled over those pages. Before she handed it over, Saffi glanced again at the final words: "For Helen, my soul's partner," Jemma had written. "What happened to her was my fault. For that, I will never forgive myself. Silenced, in Seaside."

. . .

Jemma took the notebook and marched back to her trailer without a word. Saffi stayed seated, pondering possible next steps. Jay GoodVender's next steps after reading Jemma's notebook had gotten him killed. His eagerness to exploit the story for his own gain had made him cocky, careless. She had to be careful. Careful enough to consider whether it might be time to step back, instead of forward. Poppy had been cleared. Chief Boyd had as much as told her she was no longer a suspect. Nailing the person responsible for Helen's disappearance, for Jay's murder, was the chief's job. Not hers. If she backed away, could he do it? Would he? With his oldest friends involved, even implicated at every turn?

Saffi saw her frustration reflected in the darkening clouds and scowling sea. The sun had become a puddle of fire between horizon and sky. Sea-blown wind whipped her curls around her head, whispering of storms to come and sending chills down the neck of her hoodie. It was time to go inside.

Before she could, Jemma strode past with a pitcher in her hand and a basket hanging from her arm. "You coming?"

Saffi had been so caught up in her thoughts, she had not even noticed that people had begun to wind toward the gazebo. A tall thin black woman with white braids was tending a fire in the gazebo's firepit, nurturing it to greater and greater heights. Saffi recognized her from the Seaside Coffeehouse, as well as the elderly Hispanic man warming his hands at the fire.

"Why not?" She bundled the wool throw around her shoulders and followed the crowd, finding a seat on the gazebo's built-in bench. Phyllis showed up with a guitar and slid onto the waterproof cushion beside her. A woman holding back short multicolored dreads with a wide silk headband took the place to Saffi's right. Her empathic smile and caring eyes made her look exactly like writing guru Anne Lamott. "You're not...?"

Before Saffi could finish the question, the woman gave a throaty laugh. "If I was a less honest woman, I could make a mint teaching writing workshops using her name, but... no. I'm Ruby Atwell."

The name gave Saffi a jolt. "Atwell. Like Larry? And Luke, the former police chief?" she ventured.

"Oh, God. I'll admit to my nephew but if you've met my brother I probably shouldn't claim him." Ruby reached out her thin veined hands and pressed Saffi's between them. They were warm and soft, a writer's hands, Saffi speculated. "Whatever he's said or done, I apologize. Some people think police work soured him into the old prune he's become." Ruby's short dreads bobbed like snakes as she shook her head. "But if you ask me," she leaned closer, "once a bully, always a bully."

A little sister's painful memories haunted Ruby's eyes, but Saffi knew that investigating crimes could harden someone. After only a few murder cases, she had begun to see people through a different lens—the lens of suspicion. But if the man who'd been kicked off the force for shooting gulls had bullied his sister, police work could not be blamed.

Saffi glanced around the growing circle of people. "So, tell me, Ruby. What's this all about?"

"Sacred space." Ruby gave her a sage look, then her face broke into a smile. "Fill it up with sea breezes and moonlight, pass around the grog, and we closet creatives get brave enough to spout poetry, share stories, and sing songs at the top of our lungs."

Ruby had no sooner said the words than Phyllis started strumming her guitar. Saffi immediately recognized a feminist favorite, "You Don't Own Me." When Ruby and Jemma started singing along with Phyllis's sweet soprano, Saffi pictured Diane Keaton, Goldie Hawn, and the ever-divine Bette Midler belting out the song at the end of *The First Wives Club*. She didn't let her rich alto loose among strangers very often, but, on this night, with the moon burnishing the sea and fairy lights dancing on a horseshoe of trailers, how could she keep from singing? For the first time since Jay GoodVender had shown his sneering face at the Lowry & Lowenstein booth, Saffi felt as if she could let go and simply enjoy being alive.

A few minutes after the song ended, headlights bobbed along

the road and a Mini Cooper pulled onto the sandy roadside in front of the park's sign. Jemma stood and waved both hands over her head in welcome. Three women jumped out of the car, two strolled toward the fire: Enid from Sea King Bikes and Hannah, coffeehouse owner and barista. The third—Debbie—raced toward the gazebo whooping and hollering.

The three women grabbed mugs and found places around the bench. Jemma brought around the grog jug. After a few minutes of greetings and murmured conversation, Jemma walked to the firepit. She threw something in the fire that turned the flames ocean blue.

"To the mother of life!" Everyone around the fireside popped to their feet—Saffi included—hoisted their grog mugs high to salute the mighty Pacific, and echoed Jemma's words.

Elements of the poems Saffi had heard, the stories told around the fire, and the songs they'd sung echoed in her head as she hugged everyone goodnight. The gathering had been an evening of enchantment, punctured by the gut punch of Debbie's lingering loss shared in a poem. Ruby shared a short story about a princess who narrowly escaped being fed to a dragon by her bullying brother. Victor, the elderly Hispanic man, turned out to have worked trawlers alongside Jemma's dad. When he warbled a John Prine song about whistling and fishing in heaven, everyone stomped their feet and clapped to the beat.

Saffi took the two steps up to her trailer feeling the effects of just enough grog to warm her from head to toe and relax every muscle. She had refused a second cup, much as she'd wanted one, to keep her mind clear enough to think about that next step. Go and stay safe... or stay and catch a killer. The truffles on the bed tray and *Mermaids at Midnight* would help her decide. She chose dark chocolate with a pink swirl that tasted of roses and Campari, plumped the bed pillows, snuggled beneath the duvet, and opened the book.

Saffi made her decision while reading the last chapter of *Mermaids at Midnight*. Jemma, Helen, and Sonya had a shared ritual—a precursor, perhaps, to the full moon storytelling session Saffi had just experienced. At midnight on each full moon—if weather, temperature, and their ability to sneak out of their homes allowed—the "three mermaids" met on the beach at Seaside Cove. They built a roaring driftwood bonfire. Then they stripped naked to frolic like mermaids in what must have been bone-chilling and nipple-hardening seawater. Sometimes they lasted seconds. Sometimes they managed a bit of a swim before running back to the fire and scrambling into their clothes. Saffi could not imagine being so free-spirited as a teen. No wonder Jemma became the woman she was now.

The midnight-moonlight ritual was a shared secret, sacred to all three until one fatal night. Unbeknown to the others, Sonya invited their two closest male friends to join the fun. The book ended with two testosterone-driven teenaged boys stealing the girls' clothes and a boob-jiggling chase around the beach to retrieve them. The chapter would have been funny, if not for one inescapable conclusion: if Saffi retreated now, the case would never be solved.

Jemma had not named the boys on the beach, but she had identified her male besties in her notebook: Eric and Larry. Saffi flipped back through *Mermaids at Midnight* until she found Jemma's Disneyesque mermaid story to check her memory. When the silky-haired mermaid became pregnant, the sea king's son had abandoned her like an empty shell on the beach.

Jay GoodVender had read Jemma's retelling and mocked it. Saffi had no idea how her stalker got his hands on Jemma's notebook. But, when he did, his razor-sharp, misogynistic mind would have followed the clues to a door he should never have opened.

THIRTY-FIVE

Wind gusts rocked the Airstream all night, but, come morning, the "bomb cyclone" had stalled somewhere beyond the horizon. That gave Saffi time enough to indulge in one of her favorite treats: a hot bath. Though the tiny tub was not quite big enough to stretch out in, for someone deprived of the luxury of a scented bath in her own RV, it was big enough.

Jemma had provided luscious lavender handmade soaps for her guests. The printed paper band around the unopened bath bar said it came from a sundries shop at the Carousel Mall. All the amenities in the Airstream, Saffi had begun to realize, advertised other local businesses. Knowing Jemma, she had cut a deal with each business to show off their wares in exchange for wholesale pricing.

Saffi filled the small tub halfway before testing it with a bare toe. *Just right!* She eased herself into the water and stretched her legs as much as she could.

If the day unfolded as Saffi expected, she would need to be in top form. Relaxed enough to set her plan in place. Confident enough to not chicken out. Before her bath, she had crafted an email meant to catch a criminal. Beneath the subject line *Silenced in Seaside*, she had written what she hoped was an irresistible teaser: *Aunt Saffi of* Bedside Reader *fame has discovered a connec-*

tion between a murder at a booksellers convention and a decades-old disappearance in the same town. She would, the email shared, go live on her blog, *Travels with Aunt Saffi,* at noon today on a secret beach filled with messages on painted stones. *This is one reveal you don't want to miss!* her email teased.

The teaser sounded like one she would send to newsletter subscribers, but she sent it to a single email address on a business card given to her early in the convention. Then she made a phone call.

Saffi had concocted her plan based on an assumption: if the person responsible for Helen's disappearance had killed Jay to protect his identity, he would show up to stop Aunt Saffi from posting that video.

Risky as fireworks in 120-degree weather? Yes. But conclusions based on speculation were not going to convict this particular killer. In a small town filled with friends, he could hide in plain sight, just as he'd done for decades. She needed him to give himself away, by showing up.

Saffi had discovered the perfect place to "film" the big reveal in the chamber of commerce brochure Larry Atwell had forced on her. Locals had dubbed it the Painted Beach. For years, its existence had been a well-guarded secret. Luckily, the secluded beach was quite close to The Mermaid's Purse and only a few blocks from a breakfast café Hannah had recommended last night.

"We don't really compete," Hannah had said when Saffi asked why she'd revealed its existence. "I get tourists *and* locals. She gets locals who want to *escape* the tourists."

Saffi managed to snag the last available table and went for the fried green tomato and egg muffin with—*Why mess with perfection?*—a Mexi-mocha. She wanted to be fed and caffeinated before the sea spray hit the cellphone camera.

If Troy was here, he would tell her the plan was far too risky. If things went wrong, she could be hurt, even killed. She was counting on the person she had phoned earlier to make sure that did not happen.

Saffi washed down the last bite of muffin and checked the time. She wanted to reach the Painted Beach and conceal her cellphone before even the most zealous bad guy could arrive.

Here we go! She wiped her mouth and crumpled her napkin onto her plate, paid the check and added a generous tip, then headed into the windswept morning, shrugging into her windbreaker as she strode toward the sea.

Saffi had never seen the ocean so pissed off. She tried not to take it personally. While she'd been enjoying breakfast, the storm had shaken itself out of its stall and resumed its advance toward Seaside. At the horizon, the ocean had turned a bilious blackish green. Waves lunged at the shore, slamming into the beach hard enough to plow furrows in the sand. Those furrows sent water closer and closer to the weathered platform where she had planned to set up her cellphone tripod to tempt the killer to reveal himself.

There was just one problem: a lone figure was already seated cross-legged on the platform, her fading red hair more sea-kinked than ever.

"Jemma! What are you doing here?"

The grin Jemma turned on Saffi was fearless, as if she drew energy—power—from the oncoming storm. "Right now, I'm wondering if you tricked me into coming out here so Mother Nature could settle the score."

"Score? What score?" Saffi picked her way down the gravel path between the painted rocks toward Jemma warily. She glanced left, then right in confusion, thinking she might spot the person she had tried to lure to the Painted Beach.

All she saw were painted stones: hundreds of them, on both sides of the gravel path. She saw yellow stones and pink stones, blue stones and rainbow stones. Stones decorated with the sun's rays and stones painted with half-moons and dancing stars. Spray from the roaring waves made the stones glisten, and the salty overspray dampened Saffi's curls and plastered black-and-silver strands to her cheeks. She shivered inside her windbreaker, but not just because her hair was soaked. Because Jemma was not supposed to be here.

She had sent her email to one address. Why was Jemma here? Had she gotten the whole thing wrong?

"Sorry." Saffi shook herself like a drenched dog, hoping to shake off a bit of water along with the chill. "How did I trick you?"

Jemma squinted up at her. "The note on my door. *Meet me at the Painted Beach. Noon. Saffi.*"

Note? What note?

The temperature steadily dropped as the cyclone's frigid breath blew toward the shore. Jemma had come prepared. She wore thick leggings under her tapestry skirt, rubber boots instead of Birks, and a yellow rain slicker over her sweater.

Saffi should have said "I didn't write that note" and "you should leave, it's not safe." But Jemma's presence made no sense. Had the person she emailed left the note for the memoir writer? Or were Jemma and the person she had emailed in this together? The fried green tomato in her belly gave an oily squeak.

Luring a suspect to reveal himself was one thing. Sticking around to see what happened when one suspect doubled into two was as crazy as... well, as crazy as vlogging on the beach in a bomb cyclone.

"I'm, uh, here to shoot a video for my blog." Someone had twisted her plot. She didn't know who or how or why, but if she wanted to expose a killer, she had to follow through. Saffi took out her cellphone and the folding tripod she'd shoved into the pocket of her windbreaker before walking to breakfast. She scrambled a few feet downslope, unfolded the tripod, attached the phone, positioned the contraption among the stones, and shoved all three legs into the sand. She tested the camera until she had just the right angle to film whatever happened next. Before returning to Jemma, she pressed the red circle to start recording.

Jemma watched skeptically, as if she thought Saffi was about to pull the kind of publicity stunt she might have expected from Jay

GoodVender. "Interesting choice of place. I mean, there's a lot of history here but it's not gonna interest your fans. It's local, and personal." Jemma poked a stone with the toe of her boot.

"Tell me more." If getting Jemma to talk helped her figure out what was happening, that's what Saffi would do.

"Take that stone over there." Jemma pointed at an oblong stone with a mermaid curled around its edge. "It showed up a few days after Helen went missing."

Saffi leaned down to read what the painter had written. "Returned to the sea's embrace." Saffi straightened. "Does this refer to Helen?"

Jemma chewed at a raw hangnail on her thumb, then shrugged. "I think Eric painted it. The only way he could make peace with Helen's disappearance was to believe she'd been swept out to sea. That one..." She pointed at another stone, a muddy green one with yellow writing that read, *Family Comes First*. "Larry painted that one. Sonya convinced him that Helen had run away. Abandoned Debbie."

When Jemma looked up, her green eyes were glazed with tears. Saffi sat down on the rough-hewn box beside Jemma. "Debbie wasn't abandoned," she said. "She had you. You took her in. Raised her."

"Of course I took her in." Jemma's eyes filmed over with tears. "She's the daughter of the woman I loved."

"Jemma." Saffi licked salt spray from her lips. The last thing she wanted to do was push Jemma away, but her notebook and memoir had raised so many questions that, in Saffi's questing mind, needed answers. "You must have been devastated when Helen told you she was pregnant. In your notebook, you said you regretted what you did next."

Jemma's mouth set in a line. "There you go. Fishing again. And with an audience, to boot." She flapped her hand at the cellphone.

Saffi rested her elbow on her knee and put her chin in her hand. "I can't seem to stop throwing out those lines."

Jemma played with one of the toggles on her rain jacket. "Have you ever loved someone so much you would do anything for them?"

Levi. The love of my life. Gone just over three years now. "Yes."

"If they'd decided to take a different path, one that led away from you, what would you have done?"

Saffi's chest squeezed so tight it was hard to breathe. "I would have begged, pleaded, cried my eyes out." *Starved myself to a size six? Stalked him and anyone he dared date after me? Committed murder?* Saffi pushed dark wet tendrils out of her eyes. "At some point, I suppose I would have realized that he didn't love me the way I loved him, and I would have let him go."

"I didn't let Helen go. I *pushed* her *away*. I abandoned my best friend when she needed me most." Jemma's jaw set in a hard line. "And before I came to my senses, she was gone." She clenched her weather-worn hands into fists and pounded her knees.

Saffi put a hand over one of Jemma's and gave it a squeeze. "I can't tell you how sorry I am, my friend. But I'm sure whatever happened to Helen was not your fault."

Jemma snorted. "So I'm your friend now? Instead of the person at the top of your suspects list?"

Yesterday, Jemma had definitely topped that list. Yesterday, Saffi could picture the strong-willed fisherman's daughter killing Jay in a fit of rage. Today... no. The clues added up to a local, but it wasn't Jemma Weathers.

"There's one thing I don't understand." Saffi wrestled the hood of her windbreaker over her damp curls and tied the strings that had been stinging her neck and face closed beneath her chin. "How did Jay end up with your notebook?"

"That arsewipe." Jemma spit on the ground by her left boot. "Stole it from right under my nose. I brought it to read a few of my first scribblings in the panel Jay and I were supposed to do. When I told him my plan, he asked if he could take a look. Said he had a thing for primary sources."

Primary sources, yes. Saffi had a thing for those as well. But *stealing* someone's personal journal. *The rotter!*

Jemma glowered. "He came over all friendly like, thumbing through my notebook. Buying my memoir. Had a bit of a chuckle when he saw I'd included allegory to, you know, protect the innocent and all that. Said nonfiction was much 'more valuable to the reading public than retellings of mermaid myths that had been distorted and destroyed by Disney.'" Jemma pinched her nose and did a pretty good impression of Jay's adenoidal voice.

Saffi shook her head. "Sounds like the sleazy stalker I knew." Who would miss a man like that? Anyone? Saffi felt a twinge of compassion but it didn't last. Jay's actions had caused too much pain for too many people.

"I told him to take his supercilious butt back to his own booth, and he did. But when I came back from a restroom break, my notebook was gone. I was sure the weasel had snatched it. Wanted to read the 'real' story. Maybe put it into one of those readers the way you and him like to do. Someone like Jay GoodVender, what would *he* care if real people got hurt?"

Jemma was right. Jay would not have cared who got hurt.

Would you? Saffi's inner snark always knew how to make her squirm. If she had the chance to chronicle the story of a woman who had gone missing under mysterious circumstances, what *would* she do?

She definitely would *not* steal someone's notebook. If the people involved in something like a mysterious disappearance were still alive, she would interview them and request permission to dig into the story. She would find other sources and interview them as well. She would talk to the police. Read news articles. And if the story seemed worth telling, she would write it and show it to her original source. If that source balked, she would can it.

Saffi glanced over her shoulder. What had happened to the person she'd emailed? Had the storm scared him off? Had he sent Jemma in his stead, to throw her off his scent? Saffi turned back to watch the waves pound the sand. From her perch on the weathered platform, the waves howling toward them looked big as mountains. The next series that crashed into the shore surged across the beach and halfway up the graveled path, soaking the painted rocks mere yards from Saffi's cellphone setup. Perhaps it would be wise to postpone her plan until the storm blew through.

As if sensing her unease, Jemma asked if she wanted to move her setup to the gazebo. Before Saffi could answer, gravel shifted behind them. Rocks rolled down the slanted path.

"Actually, this is the perfect place," a grizzled voice followed by a dark chuckle made both women whirl around. Saffi's chest constricted. She had expected to feel gratified if and when the killer actually showed up. She had *not* expected him to arrive with a freaking speargun in his hands.

THIRTY-SIX

Jemma shielded her eyes and looked up at the man looming over her. "What the hell are you doing with that thing? You're gonna hurt yourself."

Or someone else. Saffi braced herself to bolt to her feet and run. She couldn't run fast, but she could zigzag like a wildebeest with a lion on its tail.

"You can stop pretending, Jemma Weathers. I read that book of yours. Didn't have the cojones to go to the cops with your innuendo, did you? So you disguised them in that ridiculous fairy tale."

Jemma went so still Saffi feared her heart had stopped. "What are you... what are you saying?"

Last night, at about the third scrumptious truffle, Saffi's brain had matched the sea king's son in Jemma's retelling to Larry Atwell, head of Seaside's chamber of commerce and proud owner of Sea King Bike Shop. Saffi had concocted her plan to lure *Larry* to the beach. She had used the email address on the business card he'd given her at the Seaside Coffeehouse. But it wasn't Larry standing at the top of the path with a speargun. It was his father, Luke.

Luke rested the speargun on his arm between Saffi and Jemma, ready to lift and fire at any second. Saffi fumbled behind her for something she could use to defend herself. Her questing fingers found a stone of the right size with enough heft to do some damage if she managed to hit him with it rather than dropping it on her own foot. Aiming at his sneering face felt like exactly the right thing to do. *Picture it happening, and it will be so.* Her inner voice went full-on Yoda. Saffi was fine with that; she would take advice from the pint-sized Jedi master any time.

"I might not have figured out what you were up to if that Good-Vender creep hadn't made the connection," Luke blathered on. "Whizbang of a brain, that one. Came to rent a Surrey cycle from Larry just after he'd read your notebook. Took one look at the name of his shop and, *zing!* Thought my son would be just the person to help him figure out who was who and what was what for an article he wanted to write called 'How to Solve an Unsolved Mystery.' Course, Larry put me right on the case."

"Larry? Larry's a part of this?" Jemma rose halfway to her feet, her face as white as the foam on the waves barreling toward them. Her entire body shook. "Luke, where in hades is Helen? Did you drive her away?"

"Drive her away..." Luke's chuckle chilled Saffi to the bone. "It didn't take much to convince Sonya that Helen had done a runner. The town wags did the rest. Indian girl. Irresponsible. Not one of us."

Jemma bared her teeth. For a second, Saffi thought she would lunge for Luke and rip out his throat. Rage pulsed from every pore.

"She didn't go anywhere, Jemma. All that mermaid returning to the sea shite you wrote. You know exactly where Helen is." He gestured toward the cove with the tip of the speargun. "Met up right here to talk about child support for the kid. She'd been threatening to take Larry to court if I didn't pay, but, come on. He was a *minor* when he knocked her up. My boy didn't owe that girl a plug nickel."

Saffi could feel Jemma's body coil, sense how close she was to leaping for Luke's throat.

"Mr. Atwell," Saffi tried to reason with someone clearly

beyond the ability to reason, "you might not think much of Chief Boyd, but it won't take him long to figure out whodunit if you shoot us with that speargun."

"Oh, I'm not going to kill you. Those will do it for me. Same as they did that slutty friend of hers." He waved the speargun toward the mountainous foam-topped waves. "And you, Aunt Saffi, won't be the first social media maven to pick the perfect place to die. All we have to do is take a little walk toward the water."

Saffi resented being called a social media maven by a murderous misogynist, but she couldn't argue his point. She'd picked the place and, with a bomb cyclone bearing down on them, she could not have chosen a more deadly one.

"Arseoff, Luke. We're not going anywhere." Jemma stood tall, fists on hips, and planted her feet.

Before Luke could respond, tires slid off the pavement and into gravel. A car braked and a figure leapt out. "Mama Jem!"

Jemma's body stilled. Her cheeks went white-rose pale with fear. "No, no, no. Goddess, no," she murmured beneath her breath.

Luke turned his head and Jemma acted. She lunged for him. At the moment of impact, Luke's finger twitched on the trigger and an arrow jolted Jemma's body.

"Jemma!" Saffi shrieked. Now it was her turn to say no over and over again. Before Saffi's amygdala could kick in and tell her to flee, she jumped to her feet, rock in hand, and fought like their lives depended on it. She smashed the stone against Luke's cheekbone, felt the force of the blow through her hand, and watched Luke and Jemma go down together in a macabre embrace.

Screams erupted above her. Some seemed to be sirens. Others came from Debbie. They blended together in a wail that matched the force of the cyclone as it picked that moment to explode. Lightning speared from the sky and sliced into the heaving sea. Thunder burst in Saffi's ears and she hunched down, trying to make herself as small as possible. Rain slashed sideways. Sea and sky became one and the world turned gray white.

Debbie slipped and slid down the gravel path. She shoved Luke off of Jemma and hunched over her, protecting the one who had always protected her against the pummeling rain. Blood ran across the stones, diluted by rainwater. So much blood. Saffi swayed, but before she could fall, boots pounded gravel. Stones rolled. A strong hand steadied her, then reached down to pull Debbie off Jemma's slumped and bleeding body.

"My phone!" Saffi reached toward the path behind her. "It-it's evidence."

The voice swore, then let go. A few seconds later, hands shoved the tripod and camera into her midsection. "We've got to get off the beach!" a stern voice shouted into Saffi's ear.

The voice was right. Saffi could no longer make out what was shore and what was sea. Rain lashed her body. Saltwater ran from her hair, down her forehead, into her mouth and under her collar. She blinked away enough of it to recognize Chief Boyd tugging both her and Debbie up the gravel path.

"You're late," she spat.

More vehicles careened toward the cove, more voices followed, EMTs shouting as they made their way down the path with stretchers, ordering them to clear the way.

A few minutes later, the three of them sat in the squad car, water steaming off their clothes. Chief Boyd sat in the front staring toward the windshield. Debbie and Saffi sat in the back, craning their necks to see through the downpour. It was impossible, of course. The breath heaving from all three of them had fogged the glass beyond any hope of visibility.

Chief Boyd turned and looked Saffi in the eye. "This is what happens when amateurs try to play cop."

"Are you kidding me right now?" Saffi slammed her palms into the back of his seat. "I called you this morning. I *told* you what I was doing. All you had to do was show up. Where *were* you?"

The chief rubbed his hand across his ginger-stubbled chin. "I went to the bike shop, OK? Larry and I have been friends since middle school! You were luring him over here to entrap him. He was at the shop and I told him to stay put."

Saffi met his eyes in the rearview mirror. "You're forgetting something, Chief. Besides you, only one person knew I would be at the Painted Beach. Your dear friend, Larry."

"No." Chief Boyd shook his head. "Larry's not like that. Besides, I ran that ticket you gave me and it had nothing to do with Larry. His old man got ticketed for parking in front of the Bridge Tender that night. The city had posted 'no parking' signs between North Holladay and the turnaround to accommodate the Jingle Tour. Luke was so used to being able to park there, he probably didn't even notice."

"Uh-huh." Saffi was so angry her chin began to tremble. "Well, you might be interested to know who we left behind on the beach down there. That's *Luke Atwell*. The man who just shot Jemma with a speargun. Larry Atwell is the sea king's son."

Red blotches suffused the chief's face as he tried to hold in his emotions. "A fairy tale is not an indictment."

"Yeah, well, I'm pretty sure that email I sent will lead to one."

Debbie turned to Saffi and glared. "What is *happening*? I came over to check on Mama Jem and there you were, down on the beach in the middle of a *bomb* cyclone. Are you nuts?"

"Probably." Saffi unzipped her windbreaker and pulled out the tail of the sweatshirt she wore beneath it to dry off the face of her cellphone. Then she poked the camera app, found the video, and held it up so that both the chief and Debbie could see what she had recorded. "But thanks to my kind of crazy, I just recorded a confession to not one, but two murders."

While Chief Boyd drove Debbie to the hospital to be with Jemma, Saffi returned to the Airstream. Checkout time had come and gone but, unless Jemma blamed her for what Luke Atwell had done on that beach, she was pretty sure she could stay at least one more night. No one else would be nuts enough to book into The Mermaid's Purse tonight.

After peeling off her soaked clothes, Saffi dumped them in the tub to keep the rest of the trailer relatively dry. The storm still wailed outside and the trailer rocked with the blows. It had hit the shore going 90 mph. Seaside had lost power at about the same time the ambulances reached the beach.

Saffi used a plush yellow bath towel to rub herself dry, and then snuggled into one of the two thick white robes in the Airstream's tiny closet. Fear had long since burned off her breakfast calories, so she picked through the leftovers from the charcuterie tray she'd put into the fridge last night. She smoothed smoked salmon spread on crackers and spewed crumbs down the front of the robe when she took a bite. *Saffi Graywood, back in stride.*

Was she? These past four days had morphed from the excitement of keynoting a convention to the terror of almost being murdered on the beach. So much had happened she could barely put one foot in front of the other, much less eat without making a mess. She had, however, tracked down a killer who was currently under arrest at the local hospital, recovering from her painted rock smackdown. There was only so much a woman could accomplish in a single New Year's weekend, after all.

For the first time since she'd arrived in Seaside, she had nothing to do but relax, and the cozy bed with the view of Tillamook standing stalwart against the storm seemed perfect. She carried the savory tray to the bed, along with a bottled cranberry orange kombucha she found in the fridge, and set both on the built-in bedside table. Before climbing into bed, she chose a cozy mystery from a wall-mounted shelf. It featured a beach, a body, and a bookstore—one of her favorite combos—on the page, at least. In person, not so much. She huddled beneath the covers, propped pillows behind her head, and read a chapter and a half before her body shut her down for a reboot.

When a knock came on the trailer door, Saffi startled so hard she threw the book across the room. By some quirk of synchronicity it whapped against the door.

"Ms. Graywood! Open up, please!"

She recognized Chief Boyd's voice with trepidation. Why was he here? Had Larry convinced his old buddy that Saffi got the whole thing wrong? If Jemma was awake and talking, she would soon bury that feeble ploy, and Larry along with it if she had the chance.

The thought of Jemma made her scramble out of the covers and launch herself toward the door. "Is Jemma OK?" she yelped into the startled chief's face.

"Jemma?" He held onto the hood of his rain jacket with two fingers to keep it from blowing off his head. "Can I come in?"

Saffi cinched the belt of her robe tighter, trying not to think about exactly how naked she was beneath it, and stepped aside. "Sure. If you'll answer my question about Jemma."

"She's in surgery, but the doc said the prognosis looks good. With all those layers she was wearing, the bolt didn't penetrate too deep."

Too deep? Jemma's physical wound might heal but the emotional ones? Those were heart-deep. Reluctantly, Saffi stepped aside to let the chief step into the trailer.

"I, uh... Sorry." He motioned toward his dripping police jacket and wet sandy boots.

Saffi folded her arms over her robe-clad chest. "Have you come to arrest me for assault with a deadly rock?"

Chief Boyd crossed his hands over his belly as if to protect himself. "No. I came to thank you for..." He took a deep breath. "For pushing past every objection on my part to find a criminal I couldn't. He was close enough for me to smell the stench for decades. I don't know if I ignored the rot, or if it rubbed off on me and I couldn't smell it."

Saffi unfolded her arms and held out a hand. "Here. I'll put your coat in the tub till you're ready to leave. Boots off on the mat, please."

After depositing his dripping jacket in the tub on top of her clothes, Saffi decided she would rather face whatever he had to say wearing a few more clothes. "Give me a minute!" she called, then grabbed fresh leggings and a loose, green-and-blue flannel over-shirt. After struggling into them, she slipped back into the robe for warmth and retied the belt.

"Can I get you anything? Cup of tea? Kombucha?" Saffi offered the two things she knew she could provide.

"If you have some Earl Grey, I would be grateful. Thanks to that early-morning call of yours, I haven't had caffeine all day. My head is about to implode."

"Coming up!" Saffi filled the tea kettle then set up two cups with tea bags. She squirted sweetener from a honey bear she found in the cabinet into hers while asking the chief if he wanted the same.

"Please."

She carried the teas into the living room and set one on the end table beside Chief Boyd. She set the other on the truffle tray, offered him the last truffle—which he snatched like a starving hound—and scooted onto the bed, legs crossed.

"So... Jemma." She took a sip and waited. "Any more details?"

Chief Boyd finished chewing the truffle, licked his fingers clean, then looked hopefully toward the charcuterie tray Saffi had taken out earlier. "Help yourself." She nodded.

"She's gonna have a helluva war wound, but the shaft didn't damage anything vital." His mouth set in a grim angry line. "How do people do it?"

Saffi lifted her chin. "Do what?"

"Wear a disguise that completely hides their real selves."

"Some do." Saffi shrugged. "Some don't. Look at Jay GoodVender. He didn't even *try* to hide who he was. He took pleasure in making others squirm, like he was a fear vampire or something. And Luke? I met his sister last night and she told me he had always been a bully."

Chief Boyd stared into his Earl Grey as if answers—or excuses

—might lurk at the bottom of the cup. "Yeah, Luke could be a bully, but not Larry. He was always the good buddy type, you know? Everyone's friend. Generous to a fault."

Saffi set down her teacup so hard it rattled the saucer. "I get that he's your friend, but he left Helen to deal with a teen pregnancy all by herself."

The chief looked mortified. "So did Jemma!"

He could not have missed the shock in Saffi's eyes. "Jemma didn't impregnate anyone. Did she?"

The chief rubbed a hand over his face and looked everywhere except at Saffi. "Guys back then, we thought... a girl gets herself pregnant, she has to deal with it. Sounds like Stone Age stuff now, doesn't it?"

Saffi pressed her hands into her knees to keep from going Stone Age on Eric. "As for Jemma, when Helen disappeared, she and her dad took Debbie in and raised her into a fine young—"

Chief Boyd raised skeptical eyebrows and Saffi stopped herself.

"OK. Raised her into a strong-minded young woman with a penchant for illicit duckboat rides."

"And conking overzealous suitors with beer bottles," he added.

Saffi licked her lips. "Heard about that one, did you?"

Chief Boyd took a slow sip of tea. "She came in yesterday and confessed everything while Jemma waited in the hall, clutching her book tote and chewing her nails to the quick.

"Look"—his blue eyes hardened to glass—"I wish I could keep every young woman safe from men on the make. But I can't, and, it seems, I never could. So"—he shrugged—"if a girl has to defend herself, then it's on the rest of us as much as it is on her.

"She'll do a bit of community service—probably help clean up after this storm blows itself out." He gazed past Saffi to the window with a view of a cloud-shrouded Tillamook Head above and the surging cove below.

When another fist pounded on the Airstream's door, both Saffi and Chief Boyd jumped to their feet. He motioned for her to stay behind him and grasped the doorknob. Saffi wasn't sure why her heart was pounding. "That can't be Larry, can it?"

Chief Boyd shook his head, then yanked the door open. A man bundled against the storm practically fell into the living room. Once he righted himself, his startled Montana-sapphire eyes took in the police chief standing in his sock feet with Saffi huddled in a bathrobe behind him.

"Who the bloody heck is this guy?" Troy demanded.

THIRTY-SEVEN

Troy took in the trailer's romantic vibe and quirked a brow. "Threw me over for the local copper, eh?"

The police chief spluttered, then rushed out of the trailer, cheeks flaming.

"Why not? You ghosted me the minute you flew home!"

Troy pulled her into a hug. "I would never ghost you," he whispered into her damp curls.

After piling Troy's streaming rain jacket on top of Chief Boyd's —which the chief had forgotten when he fled—Saffi demanded an explanation for why he hadn't answered her calls and texts, and how he had ended up on her doorstep in the middle of a bomb cyclone. "But first... why don't you get out of those wet clothes and put this on." She handed him the "his" version of her snuggly robe.

They cozied up in bed beneath the warm duvet while Troy filled her in. When Scott shared the news that the Beechcraft couldn't fly, he had thrown the bag he had yet to unpack into his blue pickup and driven up the coast like a madman. He hadn't ghosted her. He had left his phone at home on the charger.

By morning, the bomb cyclone had left Seaside bruised and battered, but Saffi and Troy's relationship was back on track.

Saffi emerged from the covers long enough to call Poppy. The cyclone had dumped three feet of snow in the mountain passes as it blasted toward Portland. It reached the iconic City of Roses as a downgraded storm, but one still capable of blowing down trees and power lines, and dumping a deluge on city streets. Poppy, Willow, and Reese had made it to the airport hotel but were stranded there until air traffic controllers deemed it safe for the big cross-country birds to fly. They were as astounded as Troy had been to learn that Saffi had solved two murders, cleared Poppy's name, and put a former police chief behind bars.

An hour later, they had sucked every ounce of oxygen from the tiny trailer. Their brains were screaming for caffeine and their lungs needed fresh air. A brisk walk into town took them to Seaside Coffeehouse where Saffi discovered that, by virtue of solving a decades-old cold case, she had sleuthed her way into the locals' coffee klatch. Hannah steamed up a Mexi-mocha on the house and, shortly thereafter, Saffi found herself on the thrifted sofa squeezed between the string-bean woman—whose name was Terra—and Victor, the elderly man with the cane. Troy pulled up a dining chair to join the circle. The main topic of conversation: the bloated stinker of a whale carcass who had been rotting away in this very room for so long they'd all gotten used to his stink.

"If I had that Luke Atwell here right now, I would snatch every last hair off his head." Terra jabbed a finger at the overstuffed chair that Luke had once claimed as his own.

Victor snorted. "That wouldn't take long."

"Hear, hear!" Terra and Victor raised their coffee cups and clinked across Saffi.

Today, Luke's chair sat empty. No one wanted to mix skin cells with a man who had stooped low enough to kill the teen mother of his granddaughter—unacknowledged though both had been. In fact, Hannah stopped steaming morning coffees for long enough to announce that "Luke's chair" would be removed and replaced before the day was done.

"I'm thinking a bonfire at the cove beach would be an appropriate end." That drew a round of applause.

Someone new sat in the chair that had tacitly belonged to Larry: the pudgy security guard who had escorted Jay from the exhibit hall on the first day of the convention. "Dougie Carver," he stuck out a hand to Saffi. "Security guard."

"I recognize you." Saffi smiled. "And thanks again for taking care of GoodVender."

Dougie chuckled. "Happy to do it." He turned to Chief Boyd, who had somehow dared to show his sheepish face among friends. "You were right about that eye for detail. She's the first convention-goer ever to recognize me in civvies."

Once the group finished trashing Luke, they moved on to his son, the second member of the klatch who would no longer be welcome at the morning meetup. Larry Atwell's days with the chamber of commerce were done, the group predicted, and Jemma would probably take his place. Given how well she advertised fellow business owners in her vintage rentals, Saffi thought she would be perfect for the job. Larry might not have killed anyone, but he was up to his earlobes in aiding and abetting.

"Aiding, abetting, and abandoning," Hannah said as she dropped off a plate of warm scones that smelled of ginger and lemons. "I never knew Helen, but I know Debbie. How could Larry do that to her?"

Saffi picked up a scone, bit into its soft, sweet yumminess and made the mistake of trying to talk around the crumbs. Her tribute to Jemma, the best mermaid mama in the world, ended in a mumbled mess.

Victor cupped a hand around his ear. "Did she say someone murdered Debbie's mama? I thought we were done with all this murder garbage."

"Are we?" Saffi raised an eyebrow at Chief Boyd. "What about Sonya? Did Luke kill her too?"

The chief took a sip of black coffee and nodded. "I went back through the records. That white car with Washington plates? Luke was the one who reported seeing it. Maybe Sonya discovered something about Helen's disappearance. Maybe Luke let something slip." Eric shrugged. "I don't know. But the only reason I can think of for that report was... he killed his niece, made it look like a burglary, then tried to throw me off his scent."

As she sat there in the funky café with its kitschy great blue heron, mismatched furniture, and absurdist portraits on the wall, Saffi couldn't help comparing it to Last Chance Café back home. Both made a heckuva good mocha. Both had excellent baristas and quirky locals. Both Seaside and Last Chance Cove had glorious ocean coves with lush green mountains nearby. And both had people who—in a fit of anger, driven by greed, or trapped by a warped sense of supremacy—took the lives of innocent, and sometimes not so innocent, people. But only one of the two towns had the fishing tour guide with Montana-sapphire eyes.

Saffi glanced Troy's way. His urge to protect those he cared for and his legitimate fear that Saffi would keep plunging into other people's problems might cause their relationship to flounder but for now... it was staying afloat, even in stormy seas. As for the smile he shot her when he caught her devouring him with her eyes? That was a lighthouse beam guiding her to safe waters.

Saffi left the coffeehouse with fond goodbyes to all, promising to stop in whenever she came back to town. Refreshed and re-energized, she took Troy's hand. She pulled him past Beach Books and onto the Broadway Bridge. The Necanicum River rippled in the wind and surged toward the sea, its waters muddied and multiplied by heavy rainfall. No ravens haunted the bridge today, but Saffi stopped at the post from which the raven had issued its dire warnings.

For the first time, she bent down for a closer look at the bas relief figures she'd noticed while pedaling through town on the Jingle Tour. She saw three mermaids, arms raised toward the moon. At the bottom of the figures was a plaque engraved with three words: *Mermaids at Midnight*. The sculptor's name was engraved below the artwork's title: Jemma Weathers.

Saffi breathed in storm-fresh air and breathed out gratitude. Two mermaids' voices had been silenced in Seaside. But, thanks to Jemma, their joyful dance would never end.

If you've been on the road with Saffi and me from the beginning, *Silenced at the Book Show* is our third RV sleuthing ramble together. *Wow!* I can't thank you enough for keeping the wheels turning and the pages churning. If this is your first read in my Pacific Northwest Cozy Mystery series, welcome! I'm thrilled and honored that you've chosen to visit the Northwest coast's majestic and mysterious forests, headlands, beaches, RV parks, and picturesque coastal towns with Saffi and me. If you're ready to buckle in for more mystery, join other readers in hearing all about my new releases and bonus content by signing up for my newsletter!

www.stormpublishing.co/kim-griswell

I don't know about you, but word of mouth and book reviews have introduced me to SO MANY good books and great series. As a reader, I'm grateful for every reader who takes the time to gush over a good book. If you've fallen for the cove, the coast, and the characters, I hope you'll introduce other readers to Saffi and friends. Even a short review can make all the difference in encouraging a reader to discover my books. Thank you so much!

The first time I flew above the Pacific Northwest coast was in a nine-seater prop plane. My seat was so close to the pilot I could reach out and—almost—touch him. When he pulled out a paper map and unfolded it, my tension ratcheted up from "settling my bum in the seat" to "writing my obituary in my head." Like Saffi Graywood, I like to keep my wheels firmly rolling over terra firma.

Seaside, Oregon, is a real place, one that I've lived in and love. I've strolled across its bridges noodling story ideas, lost hats to its fierce ocean-salted breezes, walked miles back and forth along its iconic promenade, and pedaled a four-seater Surrey cycle along its narrow streets. I've taken many a whirl on its carousel but the worst crime I've seen take place there involved a dad with motion sickness who almost lost his cookies. Since, to me, a town isn't complete without a bookstore, I like to namedrop real bookstores in my mysteries. That includes Seaside's Beach Books which I visit whenever I'm in town.

Needless to say, I have twisted and turned the people, places, and events in *Silenced at the Book Show* in ways that may mystify and perhaps even perturb locals (sorry!). I invented the Necanicum Inn and plonked it down by the Broadway Bridge where no inn exists. If you visit, you might spot the lovely hotel I stayed in on the river. (Hint: it has awesome suites, but no bloody carnation petals on the bed.) Any mistakes or manipulations are my own, but I hope I captured the essence of one of my favorite Oregon towns.

In Seaside, ideas swirl in on the tides and churn in the air, but they germinate over cups of coffee. As always, I raise my Meximocha mug to the baristas of the world and to you, the amazing readers who support my writing, coffee, and wandering RV habits. Thank you for being part of this amazing journey. I hope you'll stay in touch—I have so many more stories and ideas to entertain you with!

Kim

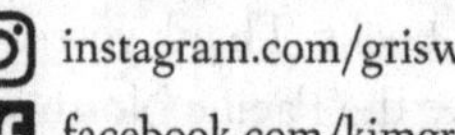

facebook.com/kimgriswellmysteries

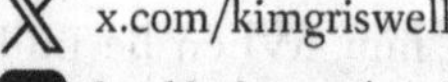

bookbub.com/profile/kim-griswell

ACKNOWLEDGMENTS

As a writer, I spend a lot of time in the company of characters who exist only in my head and on the page. That doesn't mean I create books alone. This book and the Pacific Northwest Cozy Mystery series that began with *Murder at Last Chance Cove* would never have happened without a long line of people who have supported my bookish way of life. *Silenced at the Book Show* goes behind the scenes at a booksellers convention. As an editor, I spent many a day behind tables at booksellers conventions across the US. The booksellers who attend these trade shows are among the biggest book lovers and promoters of books I've ever met. Thank you one and all!

Editors play a big role in this book as well. That's primarily because—sorry, tech bros—in my experience, editors are usually the smartest people in the room. They know something about just about everything! Special thanks to Gordon Javna who indoctrinated me into the totally ducky world of *Uncle John's Bathroom Reader* (yep... Saffi knocked it off—but only in my imagination), and a world of thanks to Kate Smith, the editor who fell for Aunt Saffi and took a chance on me. Without Kate, *Silenced at the Book Show* would never have happened. The enthusiasm and support of an accomplished editor is like fresh ocean air to a writer. Kate, you help my stories breathe more deeply in every book. Thank you!

To the talented, energizing, forward-thinking, and collaborative crew at Storm Publishing, it is a huge privilege to work with you. I know my work is safe under the Storm umbrella and I look forward to continuing our journey together. Special thanks to Editorial Operations Director Alexandra Begley for keeping the wheels turning smoothly, to Anne O'Brien for extra-careful copy edits, to Ann McKerrow and Elke Desanghere for marketing expertise, and to everyone at Storm who had a hand in introducing Saffi Graywood to readers. To Oliver Rhodes for conjuring the Storm, creating such a remarkable team, and being a publisher who actually connects with his writers—thank you!

To my husband Rob, the man who keeps our RV running, supplies me with lattes on demand (especially around deadlines), and appreciates the fact that a wife who sits at a keyboard all day is working and cannot be expected to cook. You are one of a kind... my kind!

Last but never least, to every cozy mystery fan who picked up this book and sleuthed along with Saffi... sharing my stories with readers is the reason I write. (That and it gives me the excuse to spend endless hours in coffee shops!) Thank you, with every beat of my over-caffeinated heart.

www.ingramcontent.com/pod-product-compliance
Lightning Source LLC
Chambersburg PA
CBHW011554190726
48287CB00010B/2884